A GATHERING OF TWINE

A TALE FROM THE SPIRALS OF DANU

MARTIN ADIL-SMITH

The Accipiter Corporation

Grateful acknowledgement is made to G & L Tate for permission to reprint the lyrics to "In Search" by Even The Lost.
Copyright © 1978 G & L Tate. All rights reserved. International copyright secured. Reprinted by permission.

Published 2013 by The Accipiter Corporation

10 Abbey Park Place, Dunfermline, Fife, UK, KY12 7NZ

ISBN: 978-0-9926964-0-5

Copyright © 2013 Martin Adil-Smith

www.spiralsofdanu.com

Join "The Spirals of Danu" at the following social networks
www.facebook.com/spiralsofdanu
www.twitter.com/spiralsofdanu

Dedicated to my wife, Jennifer.

... until our stars shine no more...

Also by Martin Adil-Smith

The Demons of Emily Eldritch (short story)

Forthcoming titles in The Spirals of Danu series:

The Beggar of Beliefs

The Shackles of a Name

CHAPTER 1

John 8:32
Then you will know the truth, and the truth will set you free

Thursday 15th September, 2033
A chain of events has been set in motion, Freeman reminded himself. *This is inevitable.* The sun rising that morning. The translated inscriptions. The body in his flat. All inevitable.

He glanced around the crowded carriage of the London Underground train. He did not like it. He could barely move and too many people were looking at him. When he met their gaze they turned away, but he would watch their reflections in the window and They would turn back to him when They thought he was not looking.

They. Them. The secret nightmare that crawled across the face of this world like an army of lepers, polluting and twisting wherever they went.

They had found him. Finally caught up with him... because he *knew*. He felt his skin begin to crawl, knowing what They would probably do to him. Of course, They never came alone. Always in threes – all the accounts told him They would come for him in threes. That meant there were two still out there. At least two. He was so close. Just a few more stops. He could feel his heart pounding as if it was about throw a rod, and greasy sweat clung to his back like so many fat leeches. He shivered again.

The carriage lurched and, for a moment, the lights seemed to sputter, as if whatever arcane technology was dying like a candle-flame in a draft. In that split-second, he swore that he saw Them. Their true selves revealed in the flickering half-shadows. Leering at him with those long faces, waxen and grinning, like a laughing Deaths-Head. All looking exactly like the body back

1

at his flat. He felt his stomach clench as one of the passenger-creatures began to move towards him and... the lights flickered back on.

A platform came into view, rushing by in a blur. The train stopped abruptly, forcing everyone forward under their own inertia. Several of those who he knew had been watching him fought their way off the train, and more passengers poured on.

Freeman thumbed the small pendant in his pocket. He could kill again. It was not murder. Not really. Killing changes you. It makes you realise that you can do it. It was like when his daughter had been arrested for taking drugs. That had changed their relationship. It had changed him. Sometimes it changes you for the better, and other times... the change brings a certain shadow with it. A watchful darkness.

Again Freeman looked over the passengers and wondered how many of them even had an inkling about the true reason for their existence. The lie at the heart of the world. They were all a part of it, whether they knew it or not. Each one of them, like the cogs of an infernal engine. Slaves to the snarling insatiable machine. Each playing their part in a secret show. Unknowing yet not unwilling. On they danced.

Oh yes. They were all part of it.

A chain of events has been set in motion.

Freeman stepped off the train onto the platform, which heaved with bodies like the unified pulse of maggots. He stood close to the wall for a moment, clutching his satchel and rucksack tightly. At seventy-six years old, he was no longer young enough to jostle his way in this throng. Best to let it ease off a bit. Again, he thumbed the pendant absently. It gave him a sense of comfort. If They came for him, he would be ready.

Freeman exited Mansion House Underground Station and began walking east along Cheapside, towards Gutter Lane. The sky was a light autumnal grey, reflecting his mood, and a heavy drizzle was in the air. The last vestiges of the stygian night were still fading and he was feeling his age. This weather was not helping his arthritis. Looking south, he saw the cloud darkening as a new front brought heavier rain to the polluted streets. It would not wash the stains away.

His heart was still pounding from the scare he had given himself. *Foolish old man!* Of course, They had found him. The resources They had... it was only a matter of time. It did not matter how careful he had been. He had tried to cover his tracks. Used go-betweens and patsies. Dead drops and...

They always come in threes...

He hurried on. He knew this place. He knew he should stop. Pay his respects as he always did whenever he went by... It had been what... three years? It didn't matter how many times he passed this spot, he could never get used to the absence of St Paul's Cathedral. It was like the loss of a most constant friend. Even after the initial period of mourning, you still look for them in familiar places. Freeman supposed that this was how New Yorkers must still feel, and that was what? Just over thirty years ago. He could still remember watching the television that September day. The numbness. The pillars of smoke and ash. How unreal it all felt. But not today. No time for remembrance. Head down. Walk on. Quickly. They were coming for him…

The sound of heavy building works startled him, reminding him of the sound of his flat door exploding inwards only a few hours earlier and the Thing that came towards him… He hurried on to his publisher's offices. Moira's Merit was one of the first tower blocks to rise out of the wreckage of London's worst terrorist atrocities. At nearly three-hundred storeys high, for a whole three months, it had been the world's tallest building. But the rebuilding works in Washington, Moscow, and Berlin soon eclipsed it. There was even talk that the rebuilding of Edinburgh City could see a skyscraper to rival all other capitals. Few people believed it, but at least hope was still alive in these desperate times.

Freeman marvelled at the sheer scale of this shard of darkened glass, remembered the film of Scott some fifty years before, and smiled at how life mimics art. Of course, that movie was now passé by modern standards, but the old man still held the old-style flicks in sentimental affection.

Such pretty lights.

The ground floor of Moira's Merit had the usual retail offerings: bitter coffee made with over-chlorinated water; sandwiches that tasted of nothing but wet cardboard. And of course the obligatory Net Station. Freeman paused to catch his breath and looked around him. No-one was following him.

He still did not see the attraction of the Net Stations. It was a young person's fad. For hours they sat in front of screens – rows upon rows of them – furiously clicking away at whatever the latest game was. Of course, they had not 'clicked' for years. Whole body sensors and Full Immersion Technology had seen the human form become the controller. Freeman marvelled at it and then shook his head.

Layers upon layers, always insulating us. Pretty lights blinding us.

Even at this time of the morning, the Station was full of slack-jawed youths, and there was a small but notable queue of punters outside, all itching to get their next fix. He could not blame them. It was not that things had become *really* bad, although they had.

It was that no-one could see how to make things better.

So why not? Plug in, log on and drop out of this world into some fictional realm where you could at least pretend to make a difference. And when you were paying by the minute to use a terminal… well, it was a convenient way to keep the kids off the streets, locked away in their own private domains, where they could not see what was going on around them. More accurately, they did not *want* to see what was going on around them.

He caught sight of a distorted reflection in the glass and his heart kicked up a gear. He turned sharply, seeing the figure on the other side of the square. The Second. The Second had found him. Despite the throng of commuters, It was coming straight towards him. It had followed him.

A chain of events has been set in motion.

He took a breath and plunged through the large revolving glass doors of the ground floor reception.

This was always inevitable.

Exiting the lift at the two-hundred-and-twenty-first floor, Freeman worked his jaw a little. The speed of those damn things always made his ears pop. He shivered – the air conditioning, as usual, had been set far too low, but Freeman was sure that his doctor would remind him it was just his poor circulation. Of course, it was years since he had been able to afford a checkup, but he could still hear the quack's voice.

Freeman's publisher, Danielle Kamal, was waiting for him in reception. He had never asked her age, but he guessed she was in her late twenties and still retained much of the youthful pertness of her earlier years. Freeman wondered if she had surgery or any of the myriad of cosmetic procedures that were now available – she seemed to barely age.

"Freeman! Great to see you," Danielle said offering her hand and the toothiest of plastic smiles. "I got your message. Come through to my office."

Freeman took the woman's hand with his own cold one and muttered a greeting, feeling her long fingers wrap around the back of his own. He shivered and pulled away a little too quickly. He knew that Danielle - it was never Danni - was a necessary evil in the world of publishing, but in his not inconsiderable experience he found that the level of diabolical intent was directly proportional to the toothiness of the grin. And Danielle Kamal was one of the toothiest people Freeman had ever met. But today was one of trading a certain evil against another.

"Here, let me have your coat. Please, take a seat."

Freeman sat down in Danielle's office. His heart-rate was returning to a more normal speed, and he tucked his flapping creased shirt into his grubby jeans. They would not try to get in here. There was security everywhere. It would be too high-profile.

As much as he disliked his publisher, he always enjoyed the views from her office. He had been at a book launch here many years ago, when it had belonged to another editor, and remembered how close he had felt to the stars as if he could reach up and pick them out of the sky.

The heavy clouds were descending on the city, like a lover's embrace, giving an effect of spires lost in some kind of magical smog, twisting and fading away, losing solidity, until they were just dreamlike forms without definite edges. As he took in the panorama, his eyes were drawn to a shimmer in the corner of the office. *A water cooler?*

Danielle followed the old writer's line of sight as she sat down behind her desk, and unbuttoned her black jacket. "Beautiful, isn't it? They installed it when I was made partner last month."

Freeman looked back at his publisher, almost disbelievingly. "Congratulations," he muttered.

"Would you like a glass?"

Freeman blanched. "Seriously?"

"Of course. Come on, you're one of our most valued contributors." Freeman knew that was a lie, but went with it. Hell, there was a glass of water on offer, and the stars alone knew how thirsty he was. "Now I will say, it's not fresh," continued Danielle, "but it is guaranteed to be not more than third recyke. Here," she finished, handing Freeman a glass.

"When do you make fresh?" Freeman asked laconically but knew it would be wasted on the young upstart. How many editors had this publishing house provided him? Fifteen? Twenty? They always moved on after a couple of years. Sometimes less.

"When I make Equity," she replied and then changed the subject. "I was surprised that you wanted to have a meeting. You've missed a few deadlines. Is your manuscript ready?"

"That's what I'm here about," muttered the old man.

Danielle leaned across the desk a little, hands clasped, with another award-winning plastic smile. "You've finished? We're all very excited. So have you got it?"

Freeman choked on his water. He did not remember when he had tasted water this pure. The supply at the flat was off the mains. That was ninth or tenth recyke at best. And that was when the supply was running.

"Ahhh... not quite. It's nearly there, but..."

Danielle's countenance darkened a degree. Imperceptible unless you were looking for it. Freeman was looking for it.

"I... I just need to finish the last few chapters... but I need to do it here."

She raised an eyebrow. "Here?"

"Yes. I can't do it at the flat."

"Why not?"

Freeman thought about telling her the truth. *I've killed... something and its body is in my flat, and now I'm being hunted. I need sanctuary!*

"The electricity... so unreliable." That sounded more plausible.

"Freeman, Freeman, Freeman," sighed Danielle, sitting back in her chair. "What am I going to do with you?"

"Just let me stay here. A few days. A week at most." Freeman said weakly. "I've got all the rough notes. I just need to put them..."

Danielle sat back and crossed her arms. "You're already three months over your last deadline. Now you want to live in our offices? Use our water to shower?" She sniffed, obviously able to tell that he had not washed that morning. Or probably yesterday either.

"Please. I wouldn't be asking if..."

"Look, I like your work." Freeman doubted Danielle read anything other than her monthly makeup invoice. "Your readers love your work. But it's been more than ten years since your last book. Sure those documentaries count for something, but we need to keep the momentum up. We need pace. If you want to stay here to finish your latest work, we'll have to come to some kind of... commercial arrangement. You understand?"

Freeman nodded. "We're on sixty-forty at the moment. I'll give you eighty percent. I'll sign whatever you want me to sign... right now. I just need to finish this."

Danielle agreed. "Ok. Let me put it to The Board." She pressed her Plex-Pad and sent the request. "In the meantime, why don't you give me what you've got so far? Help take off some of the heat the guys upstairs are giving me." Freeman knew well enough this was not a request. This was not the first deadline he had missed, and he knew how to play this game.

Making the customary faces of "Well... it really is a just a draft," and the obligatory huffings and puffings of "Only if you insist," Freeman produced a collection of papers from his battered satchel, and put them on Danielle's desk.

"Wow. Freeman. That's a lot of paper. You remember that you're only contracted for a hundred-thousand words, right?" She did not have to say more. Her expression was one of disbelief that the old man did not trust the Digital Information Service to safely deliver his manuscript. He was a creature of habit and he had always done it this way. No voice-interface-conversion for him. He prided himself on being old-school and insisted on typing his own work. On a screen.

Freeman shrugged. "That's about two-hundred thousand words there. There is probably another fifty, maybe sixty-thousand to come. But I've got the research and the outlines with me."

"Freeman, this is great. This is serialisation. This could be a three or four part-er." Danielle was getting excited.

"No," said Freeman firmly. "It is one book," and looking Danielle in the eye, "just one," he repeated. He *needed* to get the message out there. He had promised. He had to flush the truth out, wherever it was hiding.

"Ok. We can talk about that later. So what have we got? Proof of your theory? Proof of an advanced ancient civilisation? Alien technology? Tell me."

Freeman took a breath. "No. This book is part confession. I don't think that there ever was an advanced civilisation. At least not the way I thought."

Danielle's jaw hung slack. She closed her mouth. Opened it again. And then closed it once more. The effect was one of a stunned fish. "Freeman," she said. "You have a readership in the tens of millions. You can't just *change* your mind. You've built a whole career – what, fifty years? – on your theories. You can't just scrap them. I mean, look at what happened to Alford when he tried that. No-one read another book he wrote."

"I know," Freeman said calmly and with near icy resolve, "that's why this is my last book."

After this, it won't matter.

Danielle's mouth did not hang open this time and Freeman was disappointed. His publisher sat back into her chair with a sigh. "Ok. Ok." And then again. "Ok. I just need a minute to digest this." She paused again, and Freeman did not feel the need to break the silence.

"So this book is not about ancient technology or lost civilisations?" she said eventually.

"Not as such, no. There is evidence of a civilisation before ours, but..."

"So what it is about?"

It was Freeman's turn to pause. *Ah what the hell. She'll find out soon enough anyway.*

"Proof of a Creator."

Danielle blinked. And then she blinked again. "Proof of a Creator?"

"Yes. Incontrovertible proof," He took a breath, "and The Divine Plan." The translation of the last stele had told him all he needed to know. Confirmed what he already suspected.

George Tate had been right...

Freeman could see Danielle's cogs whirring. Either she was trying to come up with a marketing angle, or she was trying to find a way to completely disassociate herself from Freeman. None of the mainstream publishers did religion anymore.

Danielle cocked her head to one side. "Have you met our Creator? Is that where you were a few weeks ago when I couldn't get hold of you?"

"No," sighed Freeman. "I haven't met our Creator. If I had I very much doubt I would be here now. The reason you couldn't get hold of me is because I was screening you."

Danielle mocked an expression of hurt. "You've got me on the hook," she continued, "Proof of a Creator, and the revelation of The Divine Plan. Give me your pitch Freeman."

Freeman took a breath and looked his publisher in the eye. "Everything about you is a lie. Everything. Your life. Your home. Your family. Friends. Everything."

Danielle stared at him, genuinely offended. He had called the woman's character into question. That was probably a mistake, especially in these times.

He tried again. "Do you ever feel that there is something wrong with the universe? Like something is broken? Like there is a hole in the world? That this," he gestured to the office and the view of urban gigantism outside, "just wasn't meant to be?"

Danielle looked at him blankly, expecting the question to be rhetorical. She realised it was not. "You're talking about disaffection, right? The ever-growing divide between rich and poor? Social and political elites? Conspiracy theories about who gets what contracts?"

"No," Freeman said bluntly. "What I mean is that there is a Plan, but it doesn't involve you, me, or the rest of Mankind because it is bigger than that. It's not that we've been abandoned or forgotten. It's that we were never intended to be part of the Design. We are not even bit players. We wonder if we're being heard, but the truth is that the heavens don't care to listen."

His words hung in the air, like sandcastles on a shore, before the waves of more conversation would wash them away. And then Danielle did something unexpected. She laughed. Shrill and piercing.

"That's a great synopsis. I can see the jacket cover now. Civilisation forging its own path without the encumbrance of religious dogma. Admittedly, it's a little late in the day to be bringing that thinking in, but I'm sure we can put a new spin on it."

"I'm not joking. I know what The Plan is."

"I know you're not. I can see that. But come on. Your evidence is always called into question. You're a controversial writer. That's why your fans love you. Have you got any real proof this time?"

Freeman took a second. "Yes."

Danielle smiled. "Seriously?"

"Yes. From people who have seen the Creator... and survived. I don't mean the fairytale our books describe, but the real one."

Danielle smiled, indulging the old man. "Ok. Let's see it."

"Eye-witness accounts. Documented events. Proof of suppressed evidence. Forgotten religious writings. It's all in my manuscript. If you just see here in Chapter One..."

"Whoa whoa whoa," Danielle held her hand up to stop the old man. "Freeman. I am not going to sit here and go through a quarter-of-a-million words with you on a Thursday morning. Give me the whistle-stop tour. Start at the beginning."

"A whistle-stop tour?"

"Yeah. Compact it down for me."

Freeman could feel the anger rising up inside him. "The most powerful message Mankind will ever receive and you want the edited highlights?"

Danielle shrugged. "What can I say? I'm a simple gal. Short-attention-span. Give me something to believe in."

"Something to believe in. Ok. Ok, I can do that. You're a Muslim, right?" Freeman knew how to press a button.

Danielle raised a finger. "Hey. Hey now. You be careful."

"You know what this is?" Freeman said, ignoring Danielle's rising tone of protest, and threw a medallion onto the desk.

Danielle picked up it up and turned it over. Three concentric circles of pale blue enamel around a black pupil-like dot. "This? Of course. My mother keeps these. It's a Nazar. It wards off the Evil Eye. But this is very common. Maybe two or three dollars at Old Spitalfields. Please don't tell me you've bought this as an antique?"

"You haven't answered my question. You've told me its name, and what it does. But what *is* it?" There was an edge to Freeman's voice, and Danielle knew better than to say more and fall into the old man's trap.

Danielle shrugged again. "You got me."

"This, Danielle, is the All Seeing Eye. The eye that never sleeps. It wards off evil because it is the *most* evil, *most* formidable power there is. Imagine that you had nuclear weapons, and at any time you could fire them. Even though you know those same weapons could poison and kill you, your enemies know that it could do the same to them. That's what this eye is. And you know what else? It's not unique to Islam. The Christians call it The Eye of Providence. The ancient Greeks called it The Apotropaic – that which turns all else away. The Assyrians used it. So did the early tribes of Central America. This is a symbol of ultimate evil and power, and your mother hangs it in her house. Now, what about this?"

Freeman passed the pendant from his pocket to Danielle – he had to make sure. This one was made of black metal. Two concentric circles linked by nine zigzag lines.

"Another eye?" Danielle offered, picking it up and turning it over in her hand.

"Yes. That one is genuinely old, so please be careful. It's similar to the ones the Aztecs used and is known as the Black Sun. I think it represents both the womb and the tomb. Similar designs were worn by followers of the Goddess Itzpapalotl, the 'Obsidian Butterfly', the primal deity who devoured people to herald her coming."

"Eats her own people?" Danielle thought for a moment. "You're telling me that our Creator is evil, aren't you?"

"Good and evil are always subjective concepts. But from the perspective of Humanity, yes. The Creator is evil."

Danielle paused and looked at Freeman. "That's an interesting interpretation you have of the Koran and other world religions, but..." she said, handing the pendant back.

"Oh, the Koran. Yes, let's talk about the Koran," interrupted Freeman. "Do you speak Arabic?"

"Not as such, I..." Danielle could feel the argument beginning to slip from her. She had not even meant to get into a debate. She had already cancelled several meetings this morning to accommodate Freeman's sudden request to see her and as used to the old man's fringe thinking as she was, it was clear he had gone off the minaret.

"So you recite in English?" Freeman persisted.

Danielle gave up. "Sure."

"And like a good Muslim woman, five times a day?" The memory of this morning's chase was already fading. He was here – he had won.

Danielle did not bother answering and shrugged.

"Which Sura do you open with? The hundred-and-thirteenth or the hundred-and-fourteenth?"

Danielle struggled to remember. "Hundred-and-thirteenth." It sounded like an answer, but she knew it was really a question.

"Ah, one of my favourites. The Rising Dawn. Of course, some sects refer to it as Day Break. Literally, The Breaking of Day. As in to be broken. Never to be put back together. Please, can you recite?"

Danielle knew this was coming. She had learned this at school, practicing at every assembly. "Ah. Ok. I seek refuge with the Lord of the Daybreak.

From the evil of everything He has created,

And from the evil of the dark night when it penetrates,

And from the evil of the women who blow on the knots,

And from the evil of an envier when he envies."

Freeman clapped slowly and then leaned forward. "Beautiful. Danielle, have you ever thought about those words. I mean *really* thought about them and what they mean? Or even where they came from?"

Danielle shook her head. She knew she had lost. She might as well enjoy the ride.

"You know that Islam recognises its roots in Christianity and Judaism, right?"

"Sure."

"Did you also know that the Arabic language has its origins not only in Hebrew and Amharic but also in Akkadian, a language that can be traced back over five-thousand years?"

"I might have heard something like that once." Danielle wanted to be interested, but she had a lunch appointment at noon, and she could see that Freeman was on a roll.

"The Akkadians were some of the earliest traders. They had a whole network spread throughout what was Mesopotamia and Sumeria. Have you heard of the Valley of the Kings?"

"In Egypt? Sure. Where all the pharaohs are buried?"

"Yes. You know that even after more than a century and a half of excavation, they're still finding previously unknown tombs. Old tombs and I mean *really* old. Tombs that haven't been opened for thousands of years. Sometimes they find tombs still full of artefacts. Unlooted. About fifteen years ago, KV-One-Twenty-Two was opened. Current thinking is that is not pharaonic, but rather that of some unknown high priest. Here, take a look at this photo."

Freeman slid his Plex-Pad over. One of his few concessions to modern living was this A4-sized piece of plastic that could seemingly look up anything anywhere. Although Freeman knew that he did not use all of its features - most of which were a mystery to him - and that by present-day standards his model was almost an antique, the ability to research and reference had become invaluable.

"This was taken an hour or so after the tomb had been opened. See those hieroglyphs on the wall?" he continued.

"The eye?"

"Yes. That is The Eye of Horus. The ancient Egyptians invoked it as a sign of action. Not just protection, but also of wrath. Looks a lot like your Nazar, doesn't it? And like my Black Sun too."

"I think I've seen that before..."

"Yes. It gets used a lot. But it was originally ancient Egyptian. Now, there were also a large number of papyrus scrolls discovered in KV-One-Twenty-Two. Prayer scrolls. Written in ancient Akkadian. They were old. At least four-thousand years – maybe older. This is a translation of the one the mummified corpse was holding."

Freeman tapped one of the glowing icons on the Plex-Pad screen, and the image changed. "Please, read it out."

Danielle picked the pad up and scanned the first line, looked at Freeman, and then began. "Protect me from the Breaker of Days,

From the evil of everything She has created,

And from the evil of the dark night with which She penetrates,

And from the evil of She who unbinds the stars,

And from the evil of Her as she envies."

"Similar enough to your Sura, no? You see Danielle, Arabic is a beautiful language. But the written is wholly separate from, and a good deal more conservative than, the spoken dialects. Compound a few millennia, the odd political slant, and working its way from the Akkadian to the Egyptian to the Greek to the Roman, to..."

Danielle snapped. "I get the picture," she said, putting the Plex-Pad down. Then, more gently, "Freeman, if a Shia Enforcer ever heard what either of us has just said, he would declare us guilty of blasphemy, probably treason against the State too, and have us dragged down to Speakers Corner to be executed. I cannot print this," and with that Danielle pushed the Plex on her desk pointedly back to Freeman.

Freeman had been prepared for this. "It's not just Islam. Christianity and Judaism – just look at the Old Testament; an angry and vengeful god who smites Mankind whenever they obtain knowledge, and then commits global

11

genocide, only to come back later and blow up a few more towns who have once again broken from Him.

"The Hindus have Shiva – the principal Goddess within their Trinity. Her role is to destroy and inspire terror. In Greek mythology, the Creator so hates his children he imprisons them forever in hell. The Ohlone tell of a world before ours being destroyed to create this one, but that Mankind was so scared of the Creator that they ran into the sea and drowned themselves. Mandaeists believe that the Devil created the material world and those that do not worship Him will receive no food, shelter or sustenance.

"In just about every faith and religion, the creator is also the destroyer. Just stop and think about it; does that sound right to you? Does that sound like something that should be worshipped?"

Danielle was exasperated. "It doesn't matter what I think. No amount of religious interpretation will let this company publish that manuscript."

"It's not just religious interpretation. I've got evidence as well..."

Danielle sighed and rolled her eyes to the ceiling. "Look, Freeman. Unless your evidence is a signed confession by the Creator himself, none of that matters. You're saying that you know The Divine Plan. This means that you are saying that you know God's Mind. His Will. *You*. A dissenter and self-declared atheist – and that cost us more than a few readers, thank you very much – now knows God: something not even our holiest clerics would dare to say. It doesn't matter how good your evidence is. What matters is the reception you get. It matters what reception the book gets." She could not believe that she had cancelled her morning meetings for this.

Silence fell between them like a hungry guillotine.

"If you are worried about the reception, you should print it," Freeman said eventually.

"What? No, I shouldn't. And even if I could, I wouldn't. Can you imagine the public outrage? Not just in this country. Most of America. The whole of Africa. Asia. You're basically telling the world they are wrong. You'd be banned and have a fatwa on you before your first signing was..." her voice trailed off, and Freeman saw a light come on behind her eyes and smiled to himself.

"It would be one of the biggest scandals this century," he said to his publisher. "Heresy. Blasphemy. Challenging not only canon and rubric but also the basis of law. Could you imagine the column inches? The chat-shows deriding this so-called scientist. The burning of effigies. The condemnation by governments. The public marches and protests, all covered by twenty-four-hour news networks. An author in hiding. The search for the Dissenter. The investigative journalists. The exposés of a corrupt and wretched life. The story could run for years."

"... Bigger than Rushdie." Danielle said dreamily. She snapped back from her daydream. "But no. I can't."

"Why?"

"Because they would kill me too. I don't know about you Freeman, but I am very much attached to my head. No matter how wrong I think the world is."

"You could if you showed good faith," Freeman nearly whispered. He knew he had her.

Her eyebrow arched. "Good faith?"

"If you could show that you published in good faith, plus the usual publishers' disclaimer. And then later, just a little mea culpa and a token gesture of pulping however many copies are left unsold after, say... ten years?"

"I'd be an Equity Partner within twelve months," said Danielle wistfully.

"Your own Fresh Water."

"I've never had Fresh Water."

"Or had an Equity's salary."

"The money... wait. No. This good faith," she paused for a moment, thinking. "You need to convince me. I mean *really* convince me."

"That is a collection of eye-witness accounts," said Freeman said indicating towards the manuscript. "Some going back more than a hundred years. And let me tell you Danielle; there is some knock-out stuff in there. And I'm not talking crack-pots or stoners. I'm talking nuclear physicists; Justice Officers; Museum curators; Doctors: Respected, intelligent, rational people. And linking them all – and I mean every single one of them – are these... inscriptions. Most of them were found in the late seventies, in Dorset of all places. But the world these texts describe... these witnesses have actually seen it."

"If you really are that worried, and there is a public outcry at the first printing, you can say that the Justice has been through my early notes, and I had unscrupulously left out key statements. I had edited in a partisan way to promote my own agenda, and you're as shocked and saddened as everyone, and here is a second edition with all of the omitted passages."

It won't matter – the truth will be out there...

"Double money." Danielle was almost drooling.

"Maybe more if you phase the 'discovery' of the edited statements. Eight or nine editions good for you?"

Danielle could feel herself giving in. "These accounts. What are they?"

"On their own, each is little more than a tale of an unexplained encounter or event. Something that neither science nor The Clerics could explain. But each has a unifying aspect. The inscriptions I told you about and the man who discovered them – George Tate. He's been tracking this thing since I don't know when. At least since World War Two. But I also think that It has been tracking him. And maybe his family too. It's as if they're woven together – like strands. He believes that some people... some families are marked, and he calls them 'The Twine.' And wherever he goes and whatever he does, he leaves... I guess you could call it a wake. People get caught in it, and then they get... well, they either get themselves dead, disappeared... or recruited.

"His son and grandson have both vanished. Separately - and about ten years apart I might add - and they had got tangled up in whatever it is that Grandpa Tate is involved in. Stranger still, George Tate is still alive. He's a hundred-and-eight years old. Doctors can't explain it. He should have died thirty years ago.

"The first account is an investigation into George Tate by what was then The British Museum. Tate had been excavating a site in Dorset – Maiden Castle – in the seventies. He uncovered a vast basement and, on the lowest floor, he found huge stone reliefs – steles – on which were carved an ancient legend. What was discovered is not in dispute. It was George's interpretation of them that was to forever change his life and that of his family."

[Maiden Castle Stele 1-9]
[Text destroyed]

[Maiden Castle Stele 10-12]
It was the time before time when the hours were deep in violet, and there were none but the Oils of Namlu. By Her order The Goddess Danu parted *[translation contested; fought free of]* the Oils and rose, heavy and ripe with the weight of the cosmos.

By the Words of Power, Danu - The Great Outer Dreamer - parted her legs, and All That Ever Will Be came forth and hung as a bat above Namlu. As Her egg hatched, so Danu bathed in the tide of its river *[translation contested; Danu bathed in the dust of life]*.

Danu saw that her creation was as She intended, and with her mighty arms Danu drew down the breath of Namlu that all would know her word.

Plucking out her golden eye Danu created the sun.

From the dust of her shell, Danu formed the worlds.

Removing a lung, Danu created the sky and the clouds.

With her blood, Danu formed the oceans, rivers, and lakes.

With her nails, Danu created the land and the mountains.

There in the eternal strata of the tide, Danu fashioned the first womb *[translation contested; cave]*, blessed it with the Land of Sumer, and kept all safe from the Ire of the Canopies.

CHAPTER 2

John 1:1-5
In the beginning was the Word, and the Word was God.
All things were made by him,
In him was life, and the life was the Light of Men.
And the Light shineth in the Darkness;
And the Darkness comprehended the Light not.

My name is Sarah Slack. For most of my working life, I was a secretary and administrator at The British Museum, London. I had not long joined the BM when I was instructed to take the minutes at the disciplinary hearing of Professor Tate.

Tuesday 3rd April 1979
Walsh looked at Lawton and raised his silvery eyebrows as if to say *What are we supposed to do?*

Lawton ran a hand through his grey hair, looked back at the Chairman and shrugged in response. *Damned if I know.*

Both men turned to Thorne. "Don't look at me," he said adjusting his dark blazer. "I've got no idea."

It had been years since there had been a need to investigate a sitting professor in this manner. It had never been known for an employee not to show at their own hearing.

"Uh, Ms Sindent?" Walsh said to the young Head of Human Resources. "I think the panel could use some guidance."

Sindent looked like they felt – awkward. They all were. George Tate knew each and every one of them. They all knew him. Some of them had been his friends for at least twenty years if not more. And now this?

Sindent began. "Uh, Jerry... sorry, Mr Chairman. I believe that, from a procedural perspective, the hearing should go ahead, and we will treat Professor Tate as being in absentia."

Walsh shifted uncomfortably. "I'm not sure that would be entirely... fair," he said, looking to Lawton and Thorne who both nodded. Walsh turned back to Sindent. "Has anyone tried to telephone him?"

Sindent's response was curt. "Mr Chairman, Professor Tate does not have a telephone at his house yet..."

"Don't blame him either," muttered Thorne. "Damned infernal devices always intruding on our privacy."

Sindent continued, "... and it is Museum policy to continue a hearing in absentia."

Walsh turned to his colleagues. "Lance? Piers?" The two men shrugged. "Very well then. Uh, Ms Slack, could you please record that Professor Tate has not arrived and that the hearing will be held without him. Ah. Ok. Yes. So to read out the allegation?"

Sindent nodded.

"Very well. The allegation is that between March Nineteen-Seventy-Three and December Nineteen-Seventy-Eight, Professor Tate, whilst in the employ of The British Museum, did knowingly falsify his results from the excavation of Maiden Castle, Dorset. Further, Professor Tate plagiarised the work of a deceased naval colleague in order to obfuscate his deception."

Walsh looked at Sindent, who nodded again.

"Right. So George isn't here. Um... we enter Not Guilty on his behalf?"

Sindent continued nodding.

"Ms Slack if you could enter that into the minutes. Right. Yes. So, Ms Sindent. Over to you, I believe."

Lawton leaned in and whispered. "Jerry, are we really going to do this?"

Walsh looked back at him blankly. "What else can we do? There's been an allegation. You know the drill. It's not like it was before."

Lawton's voice came as a hiss. "But it's George."

Thorne leaned over. "His reputation or ours? The Museum's?"

Lawton sat back in silence.

They all knew what he meant. For too long the highest standards of research had been slipping. Each case on its own had been nothing. A misquote here. A slanted view there. But it had all been small steps over thirty-odd years, culminating in the Cowell case. Dr Cowell claimed that the nomadic tribes of Siberia had been using advanced metals for nearly a century. Under scrutiny, the metals were modern and made with present-day techniques. The Museum dealt with these matters in the way they always had. Cowell had the decency to quietly resign – and not force a charade like this one - and in return, he had got to keep his pension. The problem was that in Cowell's case, his 'misunderstanding' had not come to light until after a number of papers had been submitted to leading journals. By industry standards, the furore had been intense, although it had not made it through to the mainstream media. After that, The Museum instigated a zero-tolerance policy to any questionable research, be it unintended or otherwise.

"Sorry Ms Sindent. You may continue," said Walsh. *And please let this be quick and painless*, he thought.

"Thank you, Mr Chairman. I would like to bring Dr Lincoln in." Walsh nodded his approval. Sindent crossed the room and opened the door. "Mike? Come in please."

Mike Lincoln entered. Despite his relative youth, compared to that of the panel, his gaunt stature accentuated the fine lines around his eyes and his hair was beginning to lighten at the temples. In his nervousness, he seemed older than his years. He rubbed his fingers together, caught himself, and made a conscious effort to stop fidgeting.

"Dr Lincoln, when did you first meet Professor...?"

Lawton's sense of frustration rose again. "Oh for heaven's sake! There is no need to go into the tiniest of details! We all know the man! We know his track record!"

Walsh turned and looked at his colleague coldly.

Lawton met his gaze. "What? Jerry come on, this is just drawing out the inevitable. None of us wants to be here. None of us want to have to do this. Just ask Mike about that damned book and let's get this over and done with!"

Walsh agreed with him. But the procedure was the procedure. He looked to Sindent, who stared back impassively. *Fine!* He thought.

"Mike. Do you mind if we do this quickly and informally?"

"No Jerry... uh, Mr Chairman... uh..."

Walsh held up a hand in a bid to relax the man. He never stood on ceremony and did not see why anyone else should. "Mike. Whose idea was it to dig at Maiden Castle?"

"George's... Professor Tate. He had been looking at some unusual archaeological finds in the area for quite a few years and thought that the castle might have been a focal point or a hub. Like a regional capital."

"What unusual finds?" Walsh continued, making notes. Sindent sat down, clearly feeling redundant. Walsh did not care. He could not stand the blasted woman anyway. No one could. She was all sweetness with her pale complexion and shoulder length black hair, but her attitude... she could be poisonous whilst saying the nicest things. And the way she clicked her fingers.... urgh! Walsh just wanted this done and to be away from that wretched creature as quickly as possible.

Lincoln was still answering. "...and pottery mostly. A bit of jewellery too. It was the mix of styles and designs, though. There was very little consistency. It didn't match what we thought we knew."

Walsh looked up from his pad. "The dig began in seventy-three?"

Lincoln nodded and swallowed nervously. He could feel sweat prickling and beading on his back.

Walsh continued. "Finished last year?"

"Uh no. Well yes. The... the funding cycle was over, but there was more to excavate. George... Professor Tate was trying to secure more money when..."

"When he was suspended?" Walsh finished, and Lincoln nodded again. "The funding was a mix of the Museum and a grant from..." Walsh rifled through some papers. "Ah. Accipiter?" Turning to Lawton and then Thorne again, he said, "Rings a bell. One of ours?"

Thorne shrugged. "Never heard of it. Could be a side order. There are so many of them these days."

"Sounds like it," Lawton agreed. "What's the address... ah, Great Queen Street. Yup. Definitely one of ours."

"Mr Chairman?" Sindent had risen from her chair with an enquiring look.

Damn! Thought Walsh. He really didn't want to have to drag The Craft into this as well. "Yes, Ms Sindent?"

"Accipiter?"

"Yes. Uh... it's a charity. Run by former members of staff. Helps out with funding and whatnot if... if the paperwork gets jammed up and the boys need to crack on." Strictly speaking, it was not a lie. Probably. Most of the faculty were Masons.

Sindent sat back down.

Walsh looked to Lincoln. "Right. So you finished up last year. What had you found?"

Lincoln rubbed his sweating palms on his thighs. "Uh. Well, there were quite a few burial tombs. Some of them had a few interesting artifacts. Religious relics and some weaponry. Amulets and the like. But the biggest thing was the fogou..."

"The basement?"

"Yes. It was the biggest ever found. Not just in size but in ratio to the rest of the site. And it had levels. Three in total. Every other fogou... err, basement, we have seen has only one."

Walsh jotted the reply down. "And it was on the lowest level that the steles were discovered?"

Lincoln fidgeted again. "Yes. Most of them were well preserved. There was a little damage here and there. Water and damp mostly. Particularly on the first and last and..."

Walsh was not interested in the finer points of detail. "What was your opinion of them, Mike?"

Lincoln could not believe his view was being sought. "My opinion?"

"Yes. What did you make of them?"

"Well... They were incredible. Extraordinary. I don't think anyone has ever..."

18

Walsh began to make notes again. "Why?" he said without looking up.

"Why? I don't under..."

"Mike. Why were they extraordinary?"

"Well, they were so well preserved. And the script.... I'm not an expert on linguistics – I was focussing on the burial mounds outside – but from what George... Professor Tate showed me... the steles were inscribed in an archaic language that seemed to be some mix of ancient Germanic, forgotten Cornish, and an obscure Neolithic Irish dialect."

All three panel members stopped writing and looked at Lincoln.

Walsh knew a great deal about ancient scripts, but a blend like Lincoln had described was next to unheard of. Rosetta maybe. But nothing in England. "Mike?"

Lincoln smiled weakly. "I... I'm not an expert. But that's what it looked like. But...you know, you should ask some of the other guys. They are really hot on this stuff."

Lawton turned to Walsh and kept his voice low. "Have we got any preliminary reports on this?"

Walsh took his glasses off and pinched the bridge of his nose. "All in here," he said patting a bulging file. "It'll be in yours too."

Lawton's voice was nearly a whisper. "Have you read it?"

"Have you?" There was an awkward silence.

"So none of us has," Thorne interjected.

Walsh snapped. "Lance! This is George's work for chrissakes!"

Thorne held his hands up, sat back, and said nothing more. They had all trusted George implicitly. He just had that air about him.

"We know," said Lawton, putting one hand on Walsh's arm. "But this is important. We've long thought that there was more trade going on in the South West. This site could prove it."

Walsh exhaled. "Ok. Sorry," he said turning to Thorne, who nodded an acceptance. "Mike," he continued, "what do you know about the translation of the steles?"

"Uh... not much. George didn't discuss it with me that often. He hardly discussed it with anyone, to be honest. I was outside most of the time – on the burial site. Mr Tuther was leading the basement dig. And George shared a lot with Sam... Dr Cotrahens. He thought there was some cuneiform aspect to the inscriptions."

Walsh thought about what Lincoln had said – about not having read the file - and began flicking through some papers. "Uh, Mike? I've got Sam Cotrahens' details here. But who is this Tuther?"

Lincoln felt his stomach knot tighter. "I... I... Mr Tuther worked on the dig." The panel's faces remained blank. "He and George were already a team when I joined the Museum."

Walsh looked at his colleagues. "Do you know this fellow?"

Lawton shook his head. "Never heard of him."

"Nor me. I can't see his name in any of the reports," said Thorne who was similarly flicking through the overflowing file.

Walsh turned to the Head of HR. "Ms Sindent? If you please. Who is Mr Tuther?"

Sindent stood. "Mr Chairman, we have no record of Mr Tuther ever having been an employee of The Museum."

Walsh felt his irritation rising again. "Well, have you checked?"

Sindent reddened. "Yes, Mr Chairman. I checked when I received Mike's witness statement. No record at all," she said, trying to keep an even voice.

"Have you checked the contractors register?"

"Yes, Mr Chairman."

Walsh looked for help from his two colleagues. They just looked back at him and shook their heads. This case was becoming murkier.

Walsh turned back to Lincoln. "Mike? You're sure it was Tuther. Not anything else?"

"S... s... sure as I can be." Lincoln thought he was going to wet himself and wished he had gone to the toilet before he was called in.

Walsh looked through some of the papers on the desk in front of him. "Mike, when did you join us?"

"Err... fifty-eight."

"And George and this Tuther were already a team?"

Lincoln rubbed his sweating hands on his trousers. "Yes."

How does a complete stranger work for us for more than twenty years, and no-one asks any questions? Thought Walsh. He knew the answer of course. George had this... knack. You just trusted everything he said.

Walsh sighed. This was not looking good. "Right. Let's park the issue of this Tuther for the time being. Mike, did you have anything to do with the translation of these steles?"

"N... n... no. I just read over George's notes."

"And did he ever mention this other book. 'The Nine Trials of Greine'?"

"No."

"What about its author... oh what's his name. Latter. There we go. James Latter."

"Yes... once or twice."

The panel members all stopped writing again and looked at Lincoln.

Lincoln felt he should continue. "I think he served with him."

The panel continued staring at him.

"In the war... George was with him when he died... On the ship... When George caught a blighty one."

"Mike," said Walsh in a low voice, "I want you to think very carefully. What did George say about James Latter?"

"Uh... not much. We all swapped stories...you know... at night. George's boat got hit by the Germans. Torpedoed in the North Atlantic. Four or five died, I think. The rest got rescued, and the ship went down. George had shrapnel in his legs and he got brought home. They operated on him but he had to sit out the rest of the war. Latter was one of the dead. I think George knew him for maybe a few months..."

"When was this?"

"I... I don't know. Forty-two? Maybe forty-three?"

"And this was the same Latter who wrote this 'The Nine Trials of Greine'?"

"I... I... I don't know. It could be. Might be another James Latter. I... I really don't know."

"Right," Walsh sighed. "That's all from me. Lance? Piers?" The two men shook their head. "Ms Sindent?"

"Nothing from me Mr Chairman."

"Thanks for your help Mike." Walsh checked the clock. "Half-ten. Shall we break for tea? Mike, can you hang around in case we need to talk some more? We've got Sam next."

*

[Maiden Castle Stele 13-15]

Danu heard the lamentation of the land, which was lonely without a shepherd. Danu went to a cedar forest and there found a young strong tree. Calling the eagle from the sky, Danu bound the bird to the cedar by the mutual blessings *[translation contested; imprecations]* of Samūm. Next, she called the doe and likewise bound it to the tree. Finally, Danu called the salmon from the river and this too was bound to the tree.

As the sun began to set, the Mists of The Hand rose from the ground. When morning came the cedar tree was no longer there. The eagle was no longer there. Nor too the doe or the salmon. As the Mists of The Hand slipped back into the ground, Danu beheld the perfect form of a woman, and thus her daughter Riah, The First *[translation contested; The Transcended]*, came into being.

"I was of my Mother and Namlu. Yet here I am," said Riah. "Woe that I now feel *[translation contested; remember]* these stones beneath me."

"Stand fast Faithful One," replied Danu, "For in the struggle against the depths of the *[text incomplete]*, you will be by my side, when you behold a simple reminder." And Danu revealed that Riah beheld and knew and was willing.

So Riah was a shepherd to the land, nursing, and tending. And in the Seasons Of The Mother, she performed the Rite Of *[text incomplete]* by the gathering of the leaves and laying them out according to the ways of the two-hundred-and sixteen as directed by *[text incomplete]* nourished on high and on low.

*

"Dr Cotrahens? Please come in." Cotrahens followed Sindent in and sat down.

"Thanks for coming Sam," said Walsh. "We know you're busy. How is the Middle East treating you?"

"Ugarit is fantastic. Amazing finds." The short man was taking his blazer off and putting it on the back of the chair.

"Glad to hear it. Do you mind if we crack on?"

"By all means." Cotrahens sat and adjusted his tie.

"How long have you known George Tate?"

"George and I were at university together. He was a mature student and a couple of years above me. It was probably forty-nine or fifty. We renewed our friendship when I joined the Museum in fifty-five."

Walsh made a note. "And when did he make you aware of the Maiden Castle steles?"

"Probably seventy-four or seventy-five."

"What's your view?"

"They were extraordinary. The inscriptions weren't a single script. Some of it looked Roman, others looked Arabic. Sections looked as if they were some blend of Pictish pictograms and Sumerian cuneiform. Other parts looked Cornish. But it was all very basic. Almost as if the authors had travelled the world and surveyed the earliest civilisations."

Walsh frowned. "Authors?"

Cotrahens became animated. "Oh yes. There is little doubt that the texts were inscribed by numerous hands. There is even the possibility they were copies of earlier writings. But the texts themselves had been inscribed over several hundred years at least."

"What was your view of translating the steles?"

Cotrahens paused. "Difficult. Very difficult. There is no lexicon for it."

"Can it be translated?"

"Possibly... some of it. A few symbols and tracts of texts are similar to pieces that we do understand. As such we can make a best guess. But there are also portions that are so much older and are so far removed from anything that we could compare them to that to offer any translation as definitive would be nonsense. One of the many curiosities is that the older and newer sections are not sequential. They are jumbled. It is almost as if the older portions were written first and spaces deliberately left to be filled in later."

Walsh made a note. "Did you offer to translate the steles for George?"

"Yes. He shared copies of the inscriptions with me. To be honest he had already completed most of the newer parts. My service was more of a tweaking. Grammatical corrections mainly. We did it by correspondence mostly."

"What about the older sections?" Lawton asked.

"When George sent them to me, they had completely stumped him. I looked at them and thought there was something of the ancient Irish or Norse about them, but that was pure speculation. Neither of us really had any idea."

Walsh quickly looked through the file on the desk. "Did he tell you later that he had finished translating them?"

Cotrahens shook his head. "No."

"What about James Latter? Did George ever mention him?" Walsh asked. "No."

"Not even sharing war stories?"

Cotrahens folded his arms, feeling defensive. "I was too young to serve. Just. Don't think I have any right to intrude if I can't relate to it."

Walsh sensed the point was a sore one with Cotrahens and moved on. "What about this 'The Nine Trials of Greine'?"

Cotrahens shook his head again. "Never heard of it. George certainly didn't mention it."

"What about Mr Tuther?"

"Yes. I met him a couple of times. When I was home. In between digs."

The panel collectively raised their eyebrows.

"Sorry Sam. You've met this Tuther fellow?" Walsh asked.

"Yes. Twice I think. Maybe three times. But I often heard about him from various members of George's team. Why?"

Walsh looked to Sindent.

"Dr Cotrahens," said Sindent, "the Museum has no record of Mr Tuther. He's not mentioned in any of the field reports. He's not an employee of the Museum, and," she looked at Walsh pointedly, "he's not on the contractors list."

"That's impossible," snorted Cotrahens. "I've seen Celus here at the Museum. In the offices. He's been George's right-hand man since... well since I joined. A brooding Welshman. His name probably begins with a silent Y or L or something."

The panel looked at one another. They each had an uncomfortable feeling rising up inside of them.

Walsh continued. "Sam, what did this Tuther do for George?"

"Well, I understood that he led the basement dig, and he helped with the translation of the steles."

"What was he like?"

"Like I said, Welsh. Strong silent type. Not immensely popular with the boys. Kept to himself."

Walsh sensed there was more to Cotrahens' answer. "Not popular? Was there a problem?"

"You mean like a fight? No. Not that I ever heard of. Just a difficult Taff. Sullen. Withdrawn."

"When did you last see Tuther?"

"Oooo... it would have been last year. Maybe around December time. He and George had just come back from a holiday somewhere. Guinea? Guyana? Something like that."

Walsh frowned "He went without Irene?"

Cotrahens nodded "Oh yes. Boys' trip away. Irene stayed at home with the girl. The two of them often took jollies together."

"Do you know where Tuther is now?"

"He and George used to share a flat in Northolt. When George married Irene they moved over towards Slough. Might be that Tuther is still in the flat."

Walsh looked at Sindent. "Look into that please." Sindent nodded and made a note. Turning to his colleagues Walsh asked, "Gentlemen, anything further?"

Lawton shook his head but Thorne leaned forward. "Sam, you helped with some of the translation?"

"Yes."

"What was it that George found down there?"

"The inscriptions? It is difficult to be specific, but from what I could tell it was a sort of creation story. A bit Abrahamic, you know. The favouring of man. The loss of a paradise. Moral lessons stuff."

"Thanks, Sam. Do you mind hanging about in case we need you again?" Walsh said.

"No problem. I'll be in my office if that's alright?"

*

[Maiden Castle Stele 16]

Riah was lonely for she had no companion to share the land with and Danu saw her daughter pining for a mate. One morning Danu took a lock of her daughter's hair as she slept, and fastened one end to the sun, and the other to earth. As the sun rose, its rays were directed to the soil and out sprung a hot-blooded man, ripe and engorged.

"What new magic is this?" Riah asked her mother.

"This is Adammeh, for he is from the earth *[translation contested; of the clay]*. He is your companion and will give you many children," replied Danu.

"But Mother, all this companion does is give me children that I cannot tend the land or perform the Rite. How shall you be honoured? How shall we eat?"

With this, Danu took three more locks of Riah's hair and again fastened them to the sun and the soil. Out sprung three more men.

"These men shall provide. The first is Kuara, the fisherman. He will reap the waters for you. The second is Tibira, the farmer. He will tend the land for you. The third is Kiva, the mason. He will build you a home and fashion tools for you."

"And how shall I tend them, Mother?"

"You shall lay with them as you see fit daughter."

"But Mother, if these men provide children and food, and Adammeh only provides children, then he is of no use [translation contested; broken]."

Danu saw the wisdom of Her daughter's reason and so gathered around Adammeh, returning him to the earth saying, "What is shall be as once was, and so all must return from whence they came."

So it came to be that with the Men of the Earth, and Her daughter of the tree, that the clan of Tuatha was founded and spread across the Land of Sumer as mist [translation contested; smoke].

*

It was after lunch when the panel returned.

Walsh sat down and turned to the Head of HR. "Ms Sindent. What do you have for us?"

Sindent stood. "Mr Chairman, I have been back through our records and found Professor Tate's previous address. The telephone number is not listed, but we gave a salary reference to the landlord. I've spoken to him, and he was not aware that there had been a change in tenant. He said that Professor Tate was still paying the rent."

Walsh frowned. "When did he buy his place with Irene?"

"Our records have a change of address in sixty-nine."

Thorne leaned into his colleagues and spoke in a low voice. "Rent and a mortgage for ten years?"

"And a kid," said Lawton. "He had a daughter a few years back. She'll be a heartbreaker. You met her too – at that barbeque. What is her name...? Fiona, I think. I heard that Irene is expecting their second in a few months."

"Ms Sindent," said Walsh, "what salary banding is George on?"

Sindent rifled through her papers. "C-two."

The panel did not even bother to look at each other. There was no way a C-two could run a family, a mortgage and rent a flat.

"Uh, Ms Sindent, did George have any other declared interests? Consultancy perhaps?" It was a desperate attempt and Walsh knew it.

"No. Nothing declared in the register."

"Ok. Let's continue. Ms Sindent?"

"Yes, Mr Chairman. I would like to present the panel with a copy of Professor Tate's latest book. An initial run had been produced by the Museum Press."

"How many copies?"

"A little over twenty thousand."

The panel looked at her. Three thousand was generally considered to be a good first run.

Walsh was staggered. "Twenty thousand, Ms Sindent?"

"Yes."

"Two-zero?"

"Yes, Mr Chairman. Professor Tate's last book sold nearly forty-six-thousand. It may go to a third edition."

Lawton turned to his colleagues. "That's how he afforded the rent and mortgage. I'll wager that this Tuther fellow was retained directly by George too."

"What was his last book?" Thorne asked.

Lawton replied. "Can't remember. The man is a machine. He produces at least half a dozen papers a year. The National Geographic always picks at least one up."

Thorne thought for a moment. "Was it the Falkland Caves?"

"No, that was in the sixties," said Walsh. "Was it the one about the ancient Pictish cemetery at the new Edinburgh Airport? Ms Sindent?"

"'Neolithic Habitation In Ancient Carlisle', Mr Chairman."

"That's right. He found those worm fossils. Monstrous things. When was that published?"

Sindent was tiring of the panel and she was trying hard to keep a note of exasperation from creeping into her voice. "Seventy-three. Mr Chairman."

Walsh returned to his pad. "Any suggestion of plagiarism there?"

"No Mr Chairman."

"Any of his other works?"

"No. Mr Chairman," Sindent repeated.

Walsh looked about himself. His colleagues were both making similar notes. "Right. So we've got his new book. All pressed. And what? We have to pulp the lot?"

"Very likely Mr Chairman."

"How much will that cost the Museum Ms Sindent?"

"Nearly sixty-nine-thousand pounds. Mr Chairman."

The panel physically winced in unison.

"Ah. Ms Sindent? Is David aware of this?" Walsh said.

"Yes, Mr Chairman. I have informed The Director."

"Right. Of course." Walsh wished that Tate was here. There was bound to be some plausible explanation for all of this. He started to flick through the book in front of him, trying not to imagine how the conversation with The Head of The Museum would go.

"Ms Sindent, what are these passages highlighted in red?"

"They are the passages that are alleged to be copied from 'The Nine Trials of Greine' Mr Chairman."

"And do you have a copy for us Ms Sindent?"

Sindent approached the panel and put a book on their bench. Lawton picked it up and turned it over, inspecting the cover, before opening it and reading the copyright page.

In a rare moment of hope, Lawton thought he had found a flaw in the argument against Tate. "Uh. Ms Sindent? I understood from Mike that James Latter died in the war. This book is first printed in forty-six."

"Yes. There is a credit a few pages in. It is understood that Mr Latter wrote the book in the thirties, but was conscripted before it could be printed. His wife had it published after the war. We have been unable to contact her."

Lawton felt crushed. "Right. And this publishing house? Golden Cockerel Press. Have we had any statement from them?"

"No. They went out of business in sixty-one."

Walsh could see where Lawton was going. "Has anyone taken up their catalogue?"

"I don't believe so, no," Sindent replied.

Walsh frowned, looked to his two colleagues and then back to Sindent. "So no contact with the family and the publishing house is bust. Ms Sindent, who was it that made the allegation against George?"

"It was an anonymous letter, Mr Chairman." Seeing the expressions on the panel's faces, she quickly added, "But the Museum is obliged to take every accusation seriously, and we must investigate."

Walsh felt his stomach knot. He had the sensation of things moving out of sight, as though some hidden conductor was directing an orchestra, and he was just moving in time to the music. No, he did not like this at all.

"Err... Jerry?" Lawton interjected. "Have you seen this?" He had opened Latter's book and placed it side by side with Tate's.

Walsh looked at the two texts, and then back at Lawton, who remained stony-faced.

Thorne leaned over to read the two books. "Good Lord!" he exclaimed.

Walsh looked back to Thorne but said nothing.

"Jerry," Lawton continued, "it's not just one paragraph." He was flicking through both books at speed, marrying the passages that Sindent had highlighted. "It's near as dammit the whole bloody book! Word for word."

Walsh sat back, pressed his fingers together and arched his palms. The evidence was clear. He sighed and glanced at the clock. Half-three. "Well, then I believe that we are obliged to deliberate. Perhaps some tea?"

Sindent moved to say something, but Walsh shot her a look. They were going to consider their judgement and that was that.

*

[Maiden Castle Stele 17]
Riah founded Danu's temple of *[text incomplete]*, and there often sought her mother's counsel. One day Riah asked her mother "Do you watch over your people by day?"

"I do," replied Danu "For the sun is my eye *[translation contested; I see through all the stars]*, that I may keep you on the path I have prepared for you."

"Do you watch over us by night mother?"

Danu saw that Her daughter had indeed grown in reason, and so plucked out Her silver eye and created the moon, that She might watch Her children by night as well as by day.

And with Her third eye, Danu beheld all that She had made and saw that it was as She intended.

With Her *[text incomplete]* took Riah to *[text incomplete]* and Danu told her daughter of *[text incomplete]* and knew *[text incomplete]* never return without *[text incomplete]*. So Riah was taught the pleasures *[text incomplete]* forever turned *[text incomplete]* power over *[text incomplete]* that the Goddess Danu might *[text incomplete]* in time be born from *[text incomplete]* and return for *[text incomplete]*.

*

Walsh sipped his tea and eyed his two colleagues.

"Jerry," Lawton said dunking a digestive biscuit, "we've known each other a long time, but you can look at me like that all you want and I still won't know what you're thinking."

Thorne looked up from his cup. "He's wondering if we can get George off on a technicality."

Lawton looked back at Walsh and shrugged. "You're the Chair."

Walsh had a feeling of inevitability. All the evidence pointed in one direction. When he spoke, his voice had an edge to it. "It is a panel decision, Piers. Don't put this all on me."

"Very well then. Panel decision Jerry. This is what we've got. Does anyone doubt that George copied that infernal book?"

Neither man replied.

"No? Ok. Does anyone doubt that George at the very least wrote the majority of that supposed translation if not all of it?"

Thorne looked up again. "What about this Tuther chap?"

"What about him?" asked Lawton. "He's not a Museum employee, and it looks like he was retained by George. That makes him George's responsibility. And with George not showing up we have to draw our own conclusions."

Thorne shrugged. "I don't think we have any choice, Jerry."

Walsh looked to Lawton, who nodded. "We are all agreed then. Unanimous decision. Let's go back in."

*

[Maiden Castle Stele 18-20]

So the Land of Sumer turned, and Riah bore both daughters and sons. The First brought forth Fulla, Honos, Freia, Niord, and Ullar.

Freia brought forth Vana, Yam, and Gilfagin.

Yam and Gilfagin brought forth Asa-Oku, Tyr, and Briar.

Briar learned from Isden and was a mighty teacher. He brought forth Dallheim, Vidra, and Nanna.

Nanna and Vidra brought forth Lopt, Syng, and Farne.

Lopt and Nanna brought forth Order, Sorrow, and Horn.

Horn and Nanna brought forth Silfine, Rav, and Magda. And Nanna journeyed to her sister who dwelt within Shole

Silfine brought forth the warrior brothers Sera and Storn.

Sera and Partholan brought forth Agnoman of the Arimaspi, great grandfather of Fiacha, and a prince and ruler of Scythia

And all made offerings of thanks at the temple of Danu for their days were without number.

One day, Magda returned from the borders of Nod and said unto Riah, "O Matriarch, why must I lay with my brother?"

Riah replied "That he may give you children if he is worthy"

"Matriarch," continued Magda, "What if I lay with my sister?"

"You may do so if she is worthy, but you will have no children."

"And what if my brother lay with his brother?"

"He may do so if he finds one worthy, but he will have no children."

That night, Magda stole away and found the resting place of Adammeh. Cutting off his phallus, she pushed it into herself, and out poured all the broken beings of the world *[translation contested; Light of The Oils]* that whispered falsehoods into the hearts of men in the darkest hours where not even Danu could see. So the Adversary was made flesh and entered the world to gather the weak from the dark with the promise of light.

"What have you done, daughter of mine?" said Danu who had been watching from the moon.

"Lament!" cried Magda. "I craved the phallus and not the child. My sisters could not enter me, and my brothers would bring infants forth!"

"Who told you of Adammeh and where he rested?" asked Danu.

"I was there on the border of Nod, where I met the Ghazal who spoke in the voice of the cloud serpent, and they told me of such pleasures of the phallus that does not bring children."

"Foolish child," intoned Danu, "Now see what destruction your progeny has wrought. The forest and fields burn like lies. The lakes and rivers run with blood and tar, like untruths. Your people divide and the land is split from the sky. As horizons end, so the time of Sumer is over."

The Goddess called the Raven Men who, having banished the Sky Lords from the Holy Isle, carried the Tuatha up into the veil of the strata, and there across the jewelled waters that they might begin again. Danu bade three stars to turn that Sumer was spun from sight.

So the Land of Sumer was bound by the Goddess Danu that none should witness the Sundown Empire, and a mighty seal of Her sign was placed across it.

There on the Holy Isle, Danu gave instruction to the Tuatha that a Seeplin might be built to once again marry land and sky.

*

Walsh sat down and addressed the Head of HR. "Ms Sindent. The panel has reached a..."

A knock at the door cut Walsh off. Sindent looked to Walsh who nodded. Crossing the room, she opened the door, muttered a "thank you" and approached the panel.

"It's a letter. Addressed to the panel," she said and deposited an envelope in front of Walsh before returning to her seat.

Walsh looked to his two colleagues who sat in silence. "Ms Sindent? Are we allowed to open this? We were about to deliver our verdict."

"Yes, Mr Chairman. A verdict has not been entered, so you can consider any evidence or statement."

"Right. Good." Walsh started to open the letter. *Why can't this just be over?* Walsh read the single page, looked to his colleagues and showed them the letter. Both nodded and grunted.

Walsh looked to the Head of HR. "Ms Sindent. This is a letter from George. He has resigned. I believe that this hearing is now redundant."

Lawton and Thorne rose with Walsh and began packing their papers away.

*

Walsh and Sindent saw the two other panel members out of the room, and then turned to each other.

"It is probably better this way," muttered Walsh, arms crossed.

"Maybe. He'll get to keep his pension, although he'll probably have to pay our publishing costs. The pulping too I imagine," she said.

Walsh wanted to smile. Sindent was obviously frustrated, and that gave him immense satisfaction. "Judging by his previous sales, I don't think that will be a problem."

Sindent sighed. "No. It probably won't be." As Walsh turned to leave, she continued, "You know you never heard all of my evidence Jerry. There was more. The skeletons. The pendants. George's fixation with all those obscure religious texts. You know as well as I do what we found in his personal notes – he was obsessed with what he called 'The Gathering of Twine.' It was all in the file. You never let me present that."

Walsh stopped, turned, and looked Sindent in the eye. "No," he said quietly. "I didn't, did I?"

*

Danielle was silent for a moment. "What? That's it?" she said. "You can't leave it like that!"

Freeman smiled. "That was Mrs Slack's account. That's where her story ends."

30

"But did George really copy that book? What do those inscriptions really say? What about Celus? And the skeletons, and the pendants?"

"I said that was the end of her story, not the end of ours."

"Ok. So who was Celus Tuther?"

"Honestly? Even to this day, I'm still not sure. But I do know how George and Celus met."

CHAPTER 3

Anak 10:4-9
And God delivered His Word unto his all creation,
That the earth shall be thy alpha and thy omega,
That all the clay shall be nourished,
To be cherished and returned from everlasting to everlasting.
And the Darkness comprehended it not.

I am Dennis King, now retired from The Royal Air Force. I met George Tate in Falkland, in 1954, when I was a cadet with the Air Training Corps. We had mustered at RAF Leuchars and had then been driven across to witness the solar eclipse. I was seventeen.

Wednesday 30th June 1954

Warrant Officer Price was not a happy man. Even though the sky was overcast, and it was beginning to rain, it seemed that every soul and his dog had the same idea of climbing the East Lomond Pap to watch the solar eclipse. The road into the village of Falkland was bumper to bumper and despite it being only eleven-hundred-hours, he did not fancy the chances of finding a parking space let alone getting twenty cadets up the Pap within the next two hours. In frustration he fidgeted in his seat, trying to adjust his uniform.

"Mark," he said, without turning to Warrant Officer Cram. "Reckon we're going to make it?"

"Nope," replied Cram, arms folded and staring at the traffic in front of him. The minibus had been stationary for nearly fifteen minutes.

"Send Dennis?"

"Cadet King!"

A lanky youth ran up to the front of the minibus, nearly bumping his head on the roof along the way. "Sir!" King said to Cram.

"Want to earn a couple of merits for your sergeant stripe? Nip out and see what's going on," said Cram without looking at the boy.

King slid the door back and jogged past the queue of stationary vehicles. A few minutes later he jogged back again.

"Sir. Milk wagon has gone over. The horses have spooked and bolted. The crossroad at South Street is completely blocked and the police officer is asking if we can lend a hand."

"Boys!" Cram barked.

All twenty cadets piled off the minibus and followed King. Price and Cram sat in silence until their wards returned some time later, a police officer behind them. Price wound his window down.

"Thanks for the help gents," the officer said.

"No problem. What happened?"

"Don't really know. Dairy's horses bolted. Both of them. Turned the wagon over. Never had a problem with them before. They've got themselves caught in some barbed wire further up. Vet reckons he'll have to put them down."

Price did not reply.

"You're here for the eclipse?" the policeman continued.

"We are. Hoping to take this lot," Price thumbed back, indicating the cadets, "up East Lomond."

"You'll struggle for parking this side of the village. Here, I'll jump in and show you where you can park up. It's just at the other end of the High Street, but you can pick the footpath up through the Falkland Estate. It'll take you straight up the Pap."

Price nodded. "Get in."

As the officer walked around, Cram slid over in his seat and the officer got in. "Straight over, and keep going."

Ten minutes later the minibus pulled off the road and parked under the boughs of a mature spruce.

"That's it," said the officer pointing towards a narrow path leading through the lightly wooded forest. "Straight up there. You'll get to a fork. Keep left and then straight on till you get to the other side. That'll bring you to the base of the pap. No more than twenty minutes. Half hour at most."

"Thank you. Much obliged," Price said, shaking the officer's hand and then watched him head off along the road, back towards the village. Despite the coolness of the day, the smell of summer still hung in the air.

Price turned to Cram. "How do you want to do this?"

"Usual? You take the front. I'll kick the stragglers along."

"Ok. What time have you got?"

"Nearly noon. Say twenty minutes to the other side of these woods. Gives us nearly an hour to get up the Pap. Easy."

"Agreed." Price looked at the sky. The cloud was thickening and the drizzle was threatening to become rain. "Don't know how much we're going to see if it keeps up like this. It'll be a disappointment for the boys if they don't get to watch anything."

"My old man saw a full one in South Africa in forty-one," Cram replied. "Reckons that it doesn't matter how overcast it is – you'll know about it."

Price nodded. "Right. Let's get this lot going. King, you're with me. Everyone else – pace us."

The group started off. Price knew he could have made them march in formation, but as he kept being reminded, the Air Training Corps was supposed to cultivate enthusiasm. Best keep it informal for now. They would learn as they went along.

They had only been going a few minutes when Price caught a smell and stopped. As he turned he could still see the shape of the minibus at the end of the path.

"King. Smell that?"

King sniffed. "Yes, Sir. Kerosene?" A sharp tang hung in the air.

The other boys could smell it too and muttered amongst themselves.

"No. Not kerosene. But something like petrol or diesel. Cram?"

"Can't see anything," Cram replied from the back, looking into the forest for an overturned drum.

A few paces further on King found the source. "Here!" he said and knelt beside an oozing puddle of thick black liquid. The stench was surprisingly strong given how small the puddle was and the smell caught in the back of his throat. Price knelt next to him and the boys gathered round.

Price picked up a nearby stick and prodded the dark slime. "Looks like oil. There's something in it. Get another stick and help me fish it out."

King fetched a stick and helped lever out two unidentifiable lumps. Picking up some leaves from the ground, he started to wipe them down. "It's rabbits, Sir," he said to Price. "Two baby rabbits... urgh! They've been eaten... see the chunks taken out of them."

Price nodded grimly. "Looks more dissolved than eaten. If we see the Estate Keeper we'll let him know that someone is dumping in the woods. Let's keep going."

As they cleared the forest, they could see the East Lomond Pap directly in front of them and the path winding up it. The hill rose quickly from its rocky base, and more than once a tourist had commented on its teat-like appearance. There were already a few people scattered on its grassy sides and a few more on the craggy top, getting ready for the eclipse. Yet there was not as many as Price had feared - the incessant chatter of civilians always grated on him.

"Did you get any of that oil on you?" Price asked King. The smell hung in his nostrils, making him feel a little queasy.

"Just a little my fingers Sir," the boy replied. "I tried to get most of it off, but it has stained."

Price nodded. "The stuff stinks. If we see a burn, you wash it off."

"Yes, sir."

The party was about half way up the pap when Price stopped and looked out over the view of Fife. The patchwork of green fields that rolled towards the horizon was breathtaking – God's own country. With a sense of satisfaction, he noted that the cloud was breaking.

"This'll do," Price said to Cram, who just nodded. "Ok boys. Set yourselves up. Everyone got their glasses? Good. Jones? Where are yours? You've got a filter? Ok."

When it finally came, everyone fell silent. The first sign was the birds returning to their trees. Darkness began to creep across the land like a stain spreading from some spilt ink bottle, and the temperature fell. Even though everyone shivered, no-one stopped watching the sky to put a jumper or coat on. Through the breaks in the cloud, the shadow of the moon began to pass in front of the sun, like some divine curtain falling on a celestial stage. It was not going to be a full eclipse, but maybe eighty or ninety percent.

Price could feel a crick beginning to develop in his neck, but still he stood transfixed. They all did. For his wards, this was their first time seeing an eclipse. None of them had even been born when the last one occurred. When had that been? Twenty-seven? Twenty-eight? Something like that. That had been a total one. Price had been in the hospital at the time, having broken his leg in training. But the nurses had wheeled him out onto the patio to see it. Some of the other patients too. He remembered one nurse – he could see her face. What had been her name? Iris? Eileen? It was just there, at the edge of remembering, but he could not quite bring it to the surface of his memory. Never mind. She was pretty and he had been soft on her. She knew it and stood none of his nonsense. Price had been young and had not had the confidence to ask her out. He half smiled at how his youthful self had become tongue-tied whenever she stopped at his bed. She had an amazing smell. Light, like soft flower petals and sweet lemonade. What had her name been? It was quite infuriating. He remembered that her face was completely unlined, soft and pale, almost as if it were lit by an inner glow. Like it was carved from marble, or alabaster, and then polished to a perfect finish. She had been quite exotic. One of the chaps said that she was from out Persia way, but she did not look...

A single scream pierced Price's reverie, savagely jolting him back to reality. The hairs went up on the back of his neck. He knew that scream. Absolute terror. Instinctively his hand went for his service revolver.

What in the blazes? He jerked his head to the left, just as the girl screamed again. Everybody's attention had been dragged from the mystic play that was being enacted in the sky above, and they had all turned to look at the girl.

She was pointing to a figure, not more than two hundred yards from them. Stooped over, It was covered in the thick black substance Price had seen earlier, Its black hair matted to Its scalp. Its eyes bright with fear, It looked directly at Price, Its jaw slack and panting hard.

The man to Price's immediate left bolted across his line of sight. He had been with the girl who screamed, hadn't he?

"No!"

A shot rang out.

"What the bloody hell are you doing?!" shouted Cram, his service revolver still clutched in his hand as the man tried to wrestle it from his grasp. His revolver fired again. "It's a gorilla! It's wild!"

"It's a man!" the stranger shouted back.

For a second Price was torn. Already It – whatever It was – was running off. He had seen enough news reels at the picture houses to know that It was not a gorilla.

"Mark!" Price barked. Cram froze. His body knew an order when it heard it. "You stay with the boys." Price drew his own revolver and started jogging after It. If It was a man, then he clearly needed help. If It was an animal... well then it needed putting down looking like that. Price was not taking any chances.

Price heard feet running after him, and at the bottom of the pap he turned. King was right behind him.

"What are you doing?" Price demanded.

The boy was already panting. "Back up. Sir."

Price tried to suppress a smile. This lad would make a great officer one day.

A moment later the stranger arrived next to them, at the base of the hill.

"I don't know who you are," said Price, "but that was a damn foolish thing you did back there. You could have been hurt. Or worse."

"Tate. George Tate," said the figure, who was panting too. "And if it wasn't for me, your chum would be up on a murder charge. That was a man we saw. Not some animal to be put down."

Price did not reply. Cram was a difficult so-and-so at the best of times and him going off half-cocked had got him into trouble more than once before. In truth, Price did not know what that thing was.

"Well we'd best get after him," Tate continued. "Fellow looks to be in a heck of a state."

"He's over there," King said, pointing to a figure retreating across the field. Price turned his head and narrowed his eyes. It was moving fast, and it was already five hundred yards away.

"Come on," Tate said. "We're going to lose him."

The three of them set off west across the field. For a few minutes, they jogged in silence, always keeping the figure just in sight. Price could see that he was gaining ground, but the other two were tiring and beginning to fall behind.

"It's heading to West Lomond," panted King.

"There's a footpath just over there," said Tate indicating a little way north. "It'll be easier going than this field."

Price grunted and made to where Tate had pointed.

"Doesn't hang about your man, does he?" said Tate to King, but the boy was already moving off.

The two men and the boy continued jogging. They could all tell they were gaining on the creature. Maybe three hundred yards now. Price could feel his heart working hard, hammering at his chest. Sweat was beading on his brow and his back felt sticky despite the cool afforded by the brief night. The eclipse was well over and the sun continued to threaten to break through the blanket of cloud cover.

And then the figure in front of them was gone.

"Wha...?" Price panted.

King arrived at his side a few seconds later. Gulping lung-fulls of air the boy pointed towards the trees on the right-hand side. "In...there...Sir!"

Tate jogged past both of them without a word.

Civilians! thought Price. Fifty yards on the path forked. One spur seemed to be arcing around the base of West Lomond, whilst the other went into the woods. Tate was standing looking unsure which way to go.

It was Price's turn to jog past the man without a word. Following the smear of black ooze the three ran on into the woods. Although they could not hear their quarry, Price noticed they could smell It. That same stench of oily-kerosene hung in the air and his stomach involuntary turned over. For a moment he thought he was going to be sick and his mouth filled with the bitter saliva that told him vomit was on its way. It had been a while since he had been pushed this hard and he was starting to feel it.

King, on the other hand, Price noted, seem to have found a second wind. Pacing himself better than when he started, he was nearly thirty yards ahead as they broke through the edge of the forest.

The figure was there, less than a hundred yards ahead of them, and disappeared behind a rocky outcrop. King went to move off, but Price held the boy's sleeve. Wordlessly, he pointed to King to keep on the path and follow the route the thing had taken, and he would go round the other side of the outcrop, flanking the creature.

Tate was still fifty yards behind and Price could hear the man's wheezing. Price and King set off. Tate stopped and saw where Price was going and for a moment thought about following him, before changing his mind and going after King.

Price and King cleared the outcrop at the same time and stood looking at the other, each with an expression of *Well It didn't come past me*. There was no sign of the creature.

Tate was a few seconds behind and looked equally baffled. Surveying the hill that sloped away from the wood, there was no sign of whatever creature had chanced upon them during the eclipse. For a few moments, they looked at each other, not knowing what to do.

"Well It must be somewhere," said Price, exasperated. They had run a mile and a half, maybe two. He was not going to give up now.

Tate rested on his haunches, breathing hard, and looked at the ground. "He certainly came this way. Look. That stuff he was covered in… it's in the grass here." Tate rubbed the substance between his thumb and forefinger and smelt it. "Oil?" he asked Price.

"None that I recognise," Price responded.

"Could it be some sort of fuel?" Tate persisted, and then noting Price's uniform he continued. "Have any of your mob put up a kite today? Something experimental? Maybe one of them has come down."

Price could see the man's logic. A test plane comes down and the pilot survives but is covered in fuel. He had heard about these new athodyd models being tested, but that was out over Israel. No. The creature was naked. He had seen that much.

"Look, there's some more." King was searching around the base of the rocky outcrop. "It's quite thick here sir," he continued, pulling the long grass back.

Tate and Price joined him, following the trail of thick goo, and pulling the grass up away from the base of the giant stones. All at once a large clump came away in King's hands and the boy nearly toppled backwards. A small hole in the side of the rock, which had previously been covered in undergrowth, yawned at them. It was no more than two feet in diameter and did not seem big enough to have allowed the creature in.

"Well, I never…" began Tate as he peered in.

"He can't have gone down there," Price interrupted.

"I think he did Sir," King responded. He ran his finger around the inside of the hole and held it up to show Price. It was covered in the thick black substance.

"What do you think?" Tate asked, turning to Price, smiling. "Reckon we can all get in there?"

Price knew the civilian was daring him.

"I wouldn't if I were you," said a voice behind them. All three turned to see a wiry dark haired man, cresting the rise in the field, a length of rope around one shoulder, a shotgun braced on the other.

"Are you the Estate Keeper?" Tate asked.

A shadow crossed the man's thin face. "Yes," he said.

Well that was a lie, thought Price, noting that the safety was off on the shotgun. Things had taken a turn that he did not much care for.

"What's your name?" Price asked authoritatively.

"Tuther. Celus Tuther. Who might you chaps be?"

"Warrant Officer Price. This is Cadet King. We were up on the East Lomond watching the eclipse, when this Thing..."

"It was a man. Definitely a man," interrupted Tate. "He was naked and covered in oil or something. The poor devil looked out of his mind. He took off and we followed him. Looks like that he went down this hole. Can you help us?"

Tuther looked like he was going to say something, but thought better of it. Everyone seemed to have paused for a moment, and then Price spoke.

"You're not the Estate Keeper are you?" he said.

Tuther looked at Price but did not say anything.

"Thought not. Tuther really your name?"

"Yes," Tuther replied, bitter that he had aroused suspicion so quickly.

"So you found your tongue. What do you know about this man... creature thing?"

Tuther looked at Price coldly but did not reply.

Tate sensed the tension between the two men. "Look here Tuther. We need to help this poor soul. What do you know?"

Tuther turned his piercing gaze to Tate but was again silent. Price noticed that something rippled across his face. What was that? A suppressed expression? Recognition?

Tuther was beginning to tense. He really did not want to have to shoot the three of them.

Price's resolve hardened. He had not been in favour of going down that hole, but it was obvious that this Tuther was hiding something. "Look, if you're not going to help, we'll just..." Price made as if to wriggle into the hole.

"No!" Tuther shouted, lurching forward and startling Tate and King.

Price backed out and stood up. "Now why the blazes not?" He was very close to Tuther now. No more than six inches. He eyed the shotgun – looked like a slide action. Probably a Winchester. Maybe an M97. He had seen a few Americans use them in the war. Sure he could probably wrest it from Tuther but the muzzle sweep might see a discharge and hit Tate. Worse, the boy.

Tuther was silent. His jaw seemed to work as if he was going to say something. "Because there are probably more of them down there," he said finally.

It was Price's turn to narrow his eyes. "More of what down there?"

Tuther knew that he could not stop now that he had started. He sighed. "Those... things. They started appearing a week or so ago. Running around and then disappearing. I tracked one back to this hole, hence..." he hoisted the rope and then the shotgun.

Price eyed Tuther. Clearly, this man knew more than he was letting on. "What are they? What are those things?"

For a moment Tuther said nothing. "A threat," he said eventually.

Price was not letting the matter go. "What sort of threat? Military?" He knew well enough that the Germans had dropped all sorts over this area during the war, and the locals were still clearing up. Why not some sort of rabid creature that infected the local herds? Maybe it had got into the water and started to affect the local population. Whoever Tuther really was, he had come prepared. Price could see the outline of a pistol on the inside of the man's tweed jacket and what looked like the body of a torch. Various tool heads poked out of his rucksack, and he knew that few people travelled around that kitted up. Price suspected that Tuther was at the very least associated with the Intelligence Service, if not directly employed.

"Something like a military risk," Tuther conceded.

Price half smiled to himself. He had been around long enough to know when someone was having him on. Tuther was good, but not that good. A truth and a lie. But which was which? Whoever this Tuther was, his accent was not local. And he was good at not answering questions directly. What was he? Special Ops? All sorts of covert divisions had sprung up in the last few years. Some to watch the Ruskies, some the Yanks.

Price motioned to Tuther to move away from the other two. Turning his back on Tate and the boy he half whispered, "What department are you?"

Tuther looked at him and said nothing. Price waited. "You know I can't answer that," Tuther muttered back eventually.

Price nodded. "Very good." If Tuther had quoted a department, made up or not, Price would have known him to be a liar – those sort of fellows admitted to nothing. Price continued, "Looks like you need our help. I've got my service revolver. I'll bet that you're packing more than just that shotgun, and the boy isn't a bad aim. We're stuck with the civilian unless you want to send him off blabbering about a covert military operation. We'll need to keep him with us and give him a proper debrief when we get back."

Tuther looked to Tate for a moment and then back to Price. "Fine," he said eventually. Turning to King, he said, "Do you know how to use one of these?" fishing a revolver from his pack.

King looked to Price, who nodded. "Yes sir," the boy replied.

Tuther offered the revolver, butt first to the boy. "There's five in the chamber. Hammer on the empty. You will need to make them count." He turned to Tate. "Where did you serve?"

Tate was not sure what to say. Clearly, the balance of authority had shifted from Price to this man, but with Price's approval. "Seaman. ONS 5," Tate said eventually. "Took a blighty one in forty-three."

Tuther looked at him hard, his jaw working silently again, and Price was worried that he was going to hit the man. "What ship?" Tuther growled, never taking his eyes from Tate.

Price could see that Tate was beginning to look uncomfortable and pale. "SS Selvistan," Tate replied.

"I had friends on the Selvistan. Good friends. How many did you lose when she went down?" Tuther said.

Tate knew he was being tested. "We lost three when the Germans sunk us."

"Name them."

"What?"

"Name them," Tuther repeated, his eyes fixed on Tate.

Price could see that Tuther was getting ready to swing his shotgun from his shoulder. Perhaps there was more to this civilian after all. It was more than a bit strange that he was the only one to follow them from the pap. And he had been the one to put off Cram's shot. Could it be that this man knew about whatever infection had gripped that poor soul? There were always stories circling of rogue German agents who even now were subverting operations in a bid to weaken Great Britain and resurrect the Third Reich. There was even talk of Mosley returning from Ireland and who knew what passions that would inflame.

Tate stiffened. He could see Price was now staring at him too. The boy was far round on his left, out of his line of sight, but he would bet that his finger was tightening on the trigger of that revolver.

"Bill Kell, Harry Wright, and Jim Latter," Tate said. "It was a bad day for all of us. We lost the Dolius and West Makadet early in the afternoon. That night the Selvistan, Gharinda, and the Bonde all went down. Want to ease up now?"

Tuther did not relax. "Where were you hit?"

Tate went along with the game. "Port. Just after seventeen-thirty hours. We were hit first in the Number Five and then a few seconds later in the Number Four. She went down in two minutes. The Tay picked us up."

"What hit you?"

"I told you, the German..."

"What hit you?" Tuther said again.

Tate paused. "Two torpedoes." His mouth was dry. This Tuther, if that really was his name, was more than a little unhinged.

"You saw them?"

"What?"

"Did you see torpedoes hit the Selvistan?"

"Wha... no... no, I was below, in the Number Six." Tate was rattled now.

"So how did you know it was torpedoes?"

Tate took a breath. "The First Officer was on the bridge at the time. He sounded the alarm, and he said..."

"Oh, and you trusted Mr Head did you?"

Tate was silent. Clearly, this man knew an awful lot about the Selvistan. "Yes," he said eventually. "I trusted Mr Head."

Tuther continued to stare at Tate.

A minute passed.

Then another.

Tuther harrumphed, startling Tate who nearly pissed himself. He was sure that Tuther was going to draw on him.

"Right," Tuther said turning to Price and King, "you two mark this out. One hundred yard intervals," and threw the rope to them. "You," he continued in a lower voice, turning back to Tate, "were in the Number Six, were you?"

"Yes. That's right," Tate replied, still not relaxing. He did not like Tuther being this close.

"Where was Latter?" Tuther was now just inches from Tate's face.

"In the Number Four," Tate said quietly, casting his eyes to the ground.

"You look at me!" Tuther kept his voice low, but his teeth were clenched and there was violence in his voice. "How did you get to the life boat?"

"Through the Number Four, and..."

"What did you see?"

"What?"

"What did you see? Where was Jim Latter?"

Tate looked straight into Tuther's eyes. "The hatches, the beams... all the ballast had been blown clean off. High into the air. When they came back down... well Jim caught one. At least one. I took a rivet straight through my shin." Tate hiked up his trouser, showing an ugly scar that covered most of his right shin. Even after eleven years, it still looked angry and time had done little to diminish its savagery.

"Through and through," Tate continued, "Damn near lost the thing. Jim... I was carried right past him. Straight past him. I didn't even ask the lads to check if he was still alive. His skull was completely smashed in. I'd wager both his legs were broken as well... the number of beams on top of them. None of us stopped. We just made for the rafts. Happy now Mr Tuther? Is that what you wanted to hear? How all the rats leave a sinking ship?"

"Easy boy," Tuther drawled. Tate blanched. Tuther could not be more than five years older than him. Where did he get off being so patronizing... "When this," Tuther continued, nodding to the hole in the rocky outcrop, "is done, you and I will finish our chat. Latter was a good friend of mine, and I..."

It was Tate's turn to interrupt. "I don't know what you have against me Mr Tuther, but if you are going to shoot me, I'll thank you for getting it over and done with now."

"Shoot you, Mr Tate?" Tate didn't remember Price introducing him. Tuther was smirking. "Shoot you? Mr Tate, if I was going to shoot you I would have done so already and you would not have even seen me. What I need to know from you is all about the last days of my friend Jim Latter, from when you left Liverpool, until the day the Selvistan went down. But right now, we need to accomplish this mission. Then you and I will have a drink and a very, very, long talk."

Tate still felt uneasy. "And exactly what is this so-called mission?"

Tuther stepped back and addressed all the three of them, his voice assumed one of command. "Gentlemen, this is the Bunnet Stane. You will note that this is sandstone rather than the quartz-dolerite which makes up the surrounding area. It is soft, which is why our quarry probably burrowed in here. We've been tracking this... thing and believe that this is its nest. It has killed local cattle and we need to put a stop to it before it does anything worse."

That's twice he said "we", thought Tate. *Either he's playing a part very well, or...*

Tuther continued. "Gentlemen, this thing will resemble something human. Honestly, we do not know quite what it is... but Intelligence suggests that the Soviets might be involved..."

Price visibly stiffened at the mention of the Communists. Tate gave Tuther his due – he certainly knew how to push a man's button.

"...We know they took most of the German scientists involved with the Übermensch Projects back to Russia after the war and it is possible that this is some sort of prototype – a trans-human if you will. Whatever this thing is, we are not to take it alive. We kill it and then bring in my people who will collect it. Understood?"

The three men said nothing but nodded grimly.

"Good. We shoot to kill." Tuther reached into his rucksack and pressed the butt of another revolver into Tate's hand. "You'd better have this Mr Tate."

Tate was stunned. One minute he was almost being accused of lying, and now... this? Tate turned the weapon over in his hand, feeling its weight.

"Don't even think about it Mr Tate," Tuther muttered his back to the man and then continued addressing the group. "This hole is the mouth of a tunnel. Best guess is that it will carry on for a couple of hundred yards," Tuther squinted towards the Western Pap, "and probably come out in a chamber under that hill. I'll go first. King, you'll be next. Then you Tate. Officer Price, you're to bring up the rear. Secure the end of that rope to... to that tree. I'll take the other end with me. I've only got one torch, so stay close to me. Right, form up and check your weapons."

Tuther approached Price and pressed a small hard object into his palm. "If it goes bad, you blow the tunnel," Tuther whispered. "That way, it can't get out."

Price looked down at the grenade, said nothing, but nodded grimly to Tuther.

"Ready?" Tuther said, turning to the other two. "Good. Here we go."

Tuther got onto his belly and began to wriggle into the tunnel entrance. King followed, then Tate and Price brought up the rear.

The hole was the mouth of some kind of burrow and Tate fancied it had a slight downward incline to it. The walls were perfectly smooth, almost as if they had been worked or bored.

No animal did this, Tate thought.

There was only just enough room to lift his head and Tate had to rely on wriggling along on his belly. In places, the walls were smeared with thick dark goo, and Tate thought he could smell ammonia... and maybe something else, but he was not sure. It was warmer than he expected and just seeing the light from Tuther's torch bobbing intermittently in front of him did nothing to alleviate his growing sense of claustrophobia. Despite the slowly increasing temperature, all four of them felt the momentary chill of a cooling breeze.

It's ventilated, Tate thought. *There's more than one entrance into this thing.*

Scraping and scrabbling along, the four men made their way further down the tunnel. The light from the entrance only penetrated to about twenty feet, and they quickly found themselves swallowed by the darkness.

King's ears popped and he worked his jaw to clear the pressure.

Tate felt a slight kink in the direction of the tunnel. Left quite a bit, then a little to the right. He could not see Tuther's torchlight, but could still feel the rope moving underneath his hand. King had opened up a little lead in front of him, and Price was right behind him.

"Keep up!" hissed Price.

Tate grunted an acknowledgement. He could feel the tunnel narrowing. No longer could he scramble with his elbows out, but had to keep them tucked right into his chest.

If this was some freak natural formation, then it could very well come to a dead end. And then they would have to try and wriggle out in reverse.

What if the Officer has a heart attack? Came the voice in Tate's head. *He's not the youngest, and remember Ben? Ben had a heart attack and died at forty. The Officer is at least forty-five. If he died right now, you'd all be stuck in here.*

Tate did his best to ignore his internal monologue. But he knew it was right.

Suddenly something trickled down his face.

Tate instantly shivered, shrieked, and started pawing at his cheek. In his panic, his chest heaved and on reflex he tried to gulp fresh air. Instead, he inhaled the dry flakes of sandstone and started to cough, banging his head hard on the roof of the tunnel, which in turn sent him face first into the floor.

"What is it?" Price said.

"What's going on?" said a voice further ahead. Tuther probably.

"You alright?" That was King.

Tate's heart was beating wildly in his chest.

Maybe you'll be the one to have the heart attack.

Tate had managed to roll onto his back and was still pawing at the side of his face. Nausea rose quickly within him.

Bang-bang-bang his heart pounded, like an over-enthusiastic drummer. It felt like an engine that was going to blow a gasket at any moment. He could hear the blood pounding in his ears and he had coughed his throat raw. His eyes were beginning to stream and he could feel the roof of the tunnel just inches from his nose. Tate wanted to scream again.

"What is it man? Speak!" Price again.

Tate made a deliberate attempt to control his breathing. His heart was still making a break for freedom, but after a minute or two, he felt better. The others were still calling to him. He instinctively looked to his hand, to see if it had caught anything. In the dark, he could see nothing.

He felt something between his fingers. Something moist. What was that? Sweat? No. It was too thick for that. Like paste. He brought his fingers to his nose and immediately gagged. Excrement. He knew he had smelt it earlier, behind the ammonia. The walls were lined with it and it was wrapped into the goo.

"I'm ok," Tate eventually croaked. "Just some of this... stuff."

"We have to press on." That sounded like Tuther.

Tate nodded his agreement and then, realising that no-one could see him, he said, "Ok. Keep going."

Tate rolled onto his front, and could hear scrabbling at the front as Tuther made his way forward. More scraping – that was King moving. Now his turn. Tate forced himself forward. His arms and legs ached and could feel a lump developing on the back of his head where he had hit it on the tunnel ceiling. And the smell of faeces hung in his nose, turning his stomach.

I must be covered in it, he thought. *We all must. God knows what diseases these things are carrying.*

He caught himself, realising that he had bought into Tuther's explanation of some sub-human. Tate did not believe that. It was just not possible. He had seen it, with his own eyes. It was bedraggled, and clearly traumatised, but it was definitely a man. And the notion of Russian involvement... well maybe. The German's eugenics programme was notorious. If the Russians had cracked some sort of advanced growth or selective chromosome recombination...

"Hold up!" Tuther's voice broke his train of thought. "There's a small drop at the end here, into some sort of chamber."

Tate felt that they had come a lot further than a couple of hundred yards. Maybe five. Possibly as much as seven. He wriggled forward, seeing Tuther's torchlight illuminating the dark, and then felt hands underneath his arms pulling him forward. His feet touched solid ground and a few seconds later he heard Price being pulled free. Tate hurriedly brushed himself down, trying his best to remove as much of the muck and debris that covered him. In the darkness, he could see nothing.

"What have we got Mr Tuther?" came Price's disembodied voice. They all paused for a moment, taking in the echo of the officer's voice.

Tuther swung the torch beam out ahead of him, picking out a rough floor. The men held their breath. Wherever they were, it was immense. The torch beam did not hit a rear wall, but rather swung across the three hundred yard width of the chamber. Tuther brought his beam up and high above them an equally rough ceiling could just be picked out, vaulting into the gloom.

Tate heard Price click the safety off his revolver.

This was not a naturally formed chamber and they all knew it. Tate took his own revolver out and similarly took the safety off. No one creature could have made this. It would have taken hundreds of hands... possibly thousands. Tate felt his stomach knot tighter and it was not down to the smell of excrement.

Thousands of hands.

"We'll keep to the wall," said Tuther, and they all heard him slide his shotgun, priming it.

No-one is taking any chances, thought Tate.

The men shuffled to the wall and began to advance in step with Tuther's torchlight. Tate realised that their leader must have unhooked himself from his rope when they entered the cavern - it would not have extended this far.

Edging deeper into the chamber, Tate was surprised to feel a pronounced unevenness to the wall. Like indentations. *What was that? A straight line? A diagonal there? And that? A circle?*

"Tuther! Hold up!" he called out.

The light stopped its advance. "What is it?"

"Uh... could you take a few steps out and sweep your light across the wall."

"What? Why?"

"I think I can feel... something."

Tuther audibly sighed but stepped out. His torch swung across the face of the wall and the chamber reverberated as all four gasped in unison.

*

[Maiden Castle Stele 21-22]

46

Fiacha of The Tuatha, son of Sera, and father of Greine knelt before Danu and prayed for forgiveness for Magda.

"That which harms those who pray *[translation contested; sustains]* to me shall be *[text incomplete]*. Know that Magda dwells with me, and all her line bears the Stain Of *[text incomplete]* until the debt is paid and *[text incomplete]* restored to *[text incomplete]*," said the Goddess Danu.

"So mote it be," said Fiacha. "We, The Tuatha, take the Sign of Danu, that we shall serve until once more the waves shall slip away and *[text incomplete]*."

Thus Danu instructed Fiacha to construct The First Seeplin, and it was so; four columns, each nine paces apart, and four rods and three-tenths in height. Each column was one ell and four-fifths in diameter, hollowed to a depth of two rods and nine-tenths, and one shaftment and one-fifth in diameter. Each column was divided into thirds and therein inscribed onto the first was the birth of All That Ever Was. On the second was inscribed the coming of Danu and the end of *[text incomplete — high-resolution imaging suggests "waves" or "waters"]*. There on the third the revenge of *[translation contested; on]* Namlu. On the fourth *[text incomplete]*.

Into the hollow of the columns was placed the teachings of Isden that all the knowledge of the Great Teacher would pour upon the faithful. So the First Seeplin was constructed between the Mounts of *[text incomplete]* that but once a year the longest light would bless the deepest part and the waters would know.

In the first part, the Tuatha would gather with their offering of soil. In the second, the cleansed warriors and priests with their offerings of cattle. The final third was reserved for the most purified of the Conductors, with the offering of water, oil, and light.

Within this last third of the Seeplin were two more columns – one to the north and one to the south - built as the others and inscribed with The Ceremony of Marriage. Between these, the two the Well of Kidesh was sunk at a width of four shaftments and nine-tenths, to the water table, that Danu would manifest herself and be nourished.

So Fiacha finished the First Seeplin and the Earth and Sky were united in Sacred Marriage. Thus the Raven Men were called forth to carry the sun across the skies of Fiacha's kingdom, for as below so above.

Pleased, Danu bade Fiacha, "This land is married well to its sky. Yet there are others who are suffering the darkness of parting *[translation contested; light]*. Send forth your only son, Greine, to distant skies that they too might be married."

"So mote it be," said Fiacha.

"So mote it be," said Greine, who had studied his father well. "I take the Sign of Danu upon my skin that my mind too be like parchment with only the words of our Goddess."

"Until the dawn breaks me," finished Danu, "I remain."

On the night of longest light, Danu received into herself all of Greine and there in the Well of Kidesh was Greine blessed. By Greine's leadership, the Tuatha constructed a mighty boat, and, taking one-third of the able men, set sail for the next land. The Ghazal saw Greine leaving the Holy Isle and called up a storm wherein dwelt the Abgallu – The Mighty of The Deep.

Greine beheld the Abgallu and perceived the fear of his clansmen. Striding to the prow of the boat, Greine declared to the creature; "I am Greine of the Tuatha, son of Fiacha, and I bear the Sign of Danu. In the name of the Goddess, you will let us pass."

Seeing the Sign of Danu, the Abgallu quaked in fear and parted the clouds that Greine might pass. As an offering to assuage Danu's anger, the Abgallu searched the depths and presented Greine with the Four Lost Treasures:

The Stone of Fal – lost from the City of Falias, it would glow when it was touched by a righteous king

The Spear of Lug – stolen from the Kingdom of Esras, no battle was ever sustained against a faithful king who held it.

The Dagger of Nuadu – taken from the Court of Uscias, the sun would never set whilst it was unsheathed by a virtuous king.

The Horn of Dagda – lost during the Battle for Semias, all were honest friends when poured by a true king's hand.

So Greine was prepared for all that would come *[translation contested; befall]*.

*

"Gods..." gasped Price. He had never seen anything like it before, not even in Egypt, and he had a jolly good poke around The Pyramids during The War. King turned towards Tuther's torch. "The Russians did this?"

The wall was covered with inscriptions and carvings. Lines of text disappeared high towards the ceiling and extended along the width of the wall.

Tate guessed the opposite wall would be similar. "I very much doubt the Communists could be responsible," he said, filling Tuther's silence. "These are old. Very old. See that one; looks like a back to front R? And the one next to it, like half an arrow? That's Norse. Then these few here... and again here; round like cups and rings? That's almost certainly Pictish. Like those at Kilmartin, on the West Coast. Ah.... those, higher up. That could be Cornish. Those next to them – they look Pictish too, but it's an older script than these ones here and..."

In the pitch dark, Tate was suddenly aware of his voice and could feel the eyes of the other three staring at him. He gave a nervous laugh and turned towards Tuther's torch.

"What did you say you did for a living Mr Tate?" That was Price, and there was suspicion in his voice.

"I'm a curator at the British Museum... in the Department of Prehistory and Europe." The silence of the other three continued. "I specialise in Neolithic, Bronze Age, and Iron Age research," he said, acutely aware of how this looked. The only civilian amongst them just happened to know about ancient European scripts and had, by chance, followed them into a monstrous cave that was adorned with his specialty.

"Bit of a coincidence?" Tate said. He heard the weakness in his own voice and could feel the eyes of Tuther and Price narrowing on his single illuminated spot. For the briefest moment, Tate felt like a piece in a chess game, as though his movements were guided by another.

"I don't believe in coincidences, Mr Tate," Tuther growled.

Neither did Tate. There were not even half a dozen men in the country today who would recognise this. A score or less in Europe.

"What does it say?" King said.

"What?"

"The writing," came the voice of Tuther. The torch beam jerked back to carvings in the wall. "What does it say?"

Tate laughed properly this time. "My dear fellow, I have no idea. I can recognise some of the scripts, but that is like recognising French or Spanish as being a Roman script. Reading it is a totally different thing. I've only just got my doctorate. This is something for the experts. And even then it will take them years. Trying to raise the funding alone will..."

"Try Mr Tate. Try reading it." Price this time.

The sound of Tuther playing with his shotgun slide echoed around the chamber. For a moment no-one said anything.

"Right. Ok," began Tate. He could, of course, have made a translation up. Price and King would not have been any the wiser, but something told him that Tuther would know, or at least suspect. "Well, this is Norse. This Pictish.... uh. Well, this looks like an Irish dialect. I don't recognise all the symbols, but let's see... uh, this looks like something about building a boat. Many ancient myths speak of this, a variant of the Noah story if you will.

"Let's see. Sailing a sea. Something about a monster. Then being rewarded with four objects. A spear, a dagger – although that maybe sword- and a horn. I'm not sure about the fourth object. A stone. A pendant maybe. Perhaps a rock. It's not really clear. It's not entirely dissimilar to the Argonautica stories. And then the next section... I'm sorry I have no idea what this is. I don't recognise the script at all."

"How did they make it?" Price said.

"Who?"

"Those... things. The creature."

"Mr Price, it is nearly incomprehensible that the poor man we saw could have made these. These... these have to be thousands of years old. I... I'd say that our man probably found this cavern... or whatever it is, and has just been using it as his home. It is just a dark warm place for him to..."

A scrabbling scratching sound cut Tate off, and the single torch beam swung around wildly in front of them, trying to locate its source.

"What was that?" King said. His rapid shallow breathing matched the others. He sank to one knee, swept the barrel of his revolver about, keeping within the torch beam.

"Have you got anything?" asked Price.

"Nothing," came Tuther's voice.

"It was close. It sounded like... like a crab scuttling," Price continued.

Tuther was silent, his torch beam still swinging slowly across the width of the chamber.

There is something in here with us, thought King, *and it's more than just that creature.*

The light of the torch only picked out thick dust hanging in the air.

"Wait!" King said, making them all jump.

"What?" Price again.

"The dust."

"What about it?"

"My mum is always making me dust my room. She says it's all skin and hair and stuff."

"So?"

"It could just be flakes from the sandstone," said Tate, sensing where King's train of thought would lead.

"The boy is right," said Tuther. "All this dust. Either there are a lot more of them in here. Or our friend has been in here a very long time."

The four men were silent again, the torch beam still swung the across the cavern, desperately seeking the source of the noise.

"Or both," said Tate eventually.

"What?" Tuther turned to face Tate.

"Maybe there are a lot more of them *and* they've been down here a long time."

Tuther did not reply, mulling over whether to continue on or not.

"We should press on," said Price.

"Is that wise?" Tate asked. "We could be hopelessly outnumbered..."

"Or it could just be one of them," Price said, cutting Tate off. "We need to know what we are up against and, if necessary, how many additional bodies we need. What do you say Mr Tuther?"

Tuther said nothing, still considering the options. "Let's move on," he muttered eventually.

"Ah... Mr Tuther?" Tate said. "Could I just have a few more minutes with this wall? There is something else..."

The torchlight swung back towards Tate, glaring straight into his eyes.

"What is it, Mr Tate?"

"Well... just here. Could you just point that... yes just here." The torchlight illuminated a section of the sandstone wall, not far from the base.

"Do you see that?"

"No," Price said.

"See what?" King now.

There was a tense sigh from Tuther. "Yes."

Tate was running his fingers along an extended stretch of the wall. The torch light followed him. Twenty foot. Then thirty.

"That's far enough Mr Tate," came the voice of Tuther. "Come back please."

"Do you see it?" Tate was panting a little.

"Not really," said King. "What is it?"

"I'm not really sure. It looks like a fossil... of a giant worm. But I've never heard of anything like this. See here – this patch of perfect vertical lines. That's clitellum – it's like an egg sack. It's at least two foot high. I mean, I've heard of some marine worms four inches high, but this... I mean it could be at least five hundred foot long."

"So?" asked Price

"So?" Tate responded. "So? Mr Price this cavern or vault or whatever it is must be construed as possibly the most incredible treasure trove. Set aside that the world has never seen inscriptions like this before, but for creatures like this to have existed would have required oxygen levels on the planet to be higher than we have ever imagined."

"Mr Tate?" King said, stepping forward. "That... clitellum? The egg sack... How many does a worm have? Usually, I mean."

"One I think. Invertebrate biology isn't really my area."

"Well there is another one just above it... no, just to the right."

The torch light slowly made its way to where King was pointing.

"And there is another one. And there. And...."

As their eyes grew accustomed to the dark, and they knew what to look for, they began to pick out tens, then hundreds of the fossilised sacks, across the length and breadth of the cavern. The men were silent for some time, craning their neck to find more and more and more, eventually losing count.

"This is all very well," said Tuther eventually, "but we need to get on."

The four set off again. Tate still ran his hand along the wall, feeling all the inscriptions as he walked on. *There must be thousands of lines*, he thought. *Maybe tens of thousands. A million even. All written over the fossils.*

And they'll lavish all the awards you can imagine on you... if you make it out the voice said, rising unbidden within him. The feeling of dread was stealing over him, its grip getting tighter and tighter and tighter in the darkness. *George – are you sure about this?* Now it was panicky. *You really need to get out of here.*

But knew he could not. There were the inscriptions and he was not going to hand that glory to anyone else. If he turned back he knew what the others would think. *Tate bailed on another fight.* He knew that was what his doctors thought when he was brought back from the Selvistan.

Another rich kid malingering his way out of the war.

It did not matter whether it was true or not. It was what they thought that mattered and Tate knew they did not think much of him.

He could feel that the wall under his hand was no longer straight. It was beginning to curve, and... The scuttling came again. High above them this time. Tuther swung the torch straight up.

Nothing.

The ceiling of their cave stared back them unblinking. No one said anything. They did not need to. They had all heard it. The air grew warmer, carrying a sickly sweet smell and still more ammonia. For a moment King thought he was going to be sick. His stomach had been in knots since Tate's little episode in the tunnel and now that he knew, really *knew*, that there was more of them down here... well Tuther was here to kill them. And that would mean using their guns. But what did those things have? Teeth and claws most likely. And a lot of them too.

What if Tate was wrong? King thought. What if the creatures were responsible for the inscriptions? What if this was some Communists experiment or game? There were always stories circulating about the latest round of weapons the Russians were developing. Rifles that could fire hooks and rip your skeleton right out before you could even scream. Nets that were laced with acid and would melt the skin from your bones. What if these things had those weapons? What if they had turned on their Soviet masters? What if...

Tuther stopped abruptly, and King went straight into him. Tuther half turned and, in the semi-gloom of the torchlight, King could see the look on his face. *Watch it, Boy.*

The cavern curved sharply and, in the dark, Tate could see a lilac glow ahead, but could not make out the source. Tuther switched the torch off, handed it to Price and muttered, "Stay here."

The three of them watched in the murk of the cavern as Tuther got onto his stomach, and crawled across the floor to the opposite wall, his shotgun slung across his back.

From his vantage point, Tuther could see the remainder of the cavern. For what seemed an age, he sat on his haunches, taking in the sight in front of him. A sudden movement above distracted him, and he looked up.

Price saw Tuther flinch and instantly turned the torch on, the powerful beam cutting into the darkness.

Nothing.

Tuther pointed further over and Price swept the torch beam across the arc of the cavern ceiling.

Still nothing.

Both men knew that for certain now that something was tracking them. Or some *things*. Tuther guessed that the boy probably knew too. As for Tate, who could say? Surely he must realise that whatever element of surprise that they had was slipping from them.

Tate watched the torch beam sweep above him and was not surprised that it picked nothing out. He badly wanted to join Tuther on the other side, but Price had kept him in check. King had an unsettling sense that there was much more to this than any of them realised. They had tracked a single creature into a lair that was older than they could imagine and very possibly housed hundreds if not thousands of those things waited in the darkness for them.

King suddenly felt like a fly in a web that had just realised that the darkness falling before it was not a shadow but a clutter of...

Spiders!

Price had said that the scuttling sounded like crabs, but it was actually more like spiders. King and some of the other cadets had gone to Edinburgh the year before on the pretence of climbing Arthurs Seat but had gone to the Playhouse Cinema instead. The film they had seen was "Mesa of Lost Women", and there had been the expectation of at least seeing some thigh. They had been sorely disappointed, but the giant spiders in that film sounded very much like the scuttling they had heard here. King did not know much about spiders, or even if they could live underground, but he did not want to find out any more than he already knew.

Tuther's eyes followed the torch beam back to Price's side of the cavern.

It looked all clear, but now Tuther could see that the strange inscriptions on the walls extended all the way to the ceiling, seemingly meeting in the middle. It was impossible to tell where one side ended and the other began. Tuther stood up and walked to the centre of the floor. "Come on," he said nodding to Price and the others.

The three of them stood up and gingerly made their way to Tuther. Their eyes had adjusted just enough to the sickly half light that they did not need the torch.

Tate stopped, looking at the source of the glow, his mouth open. "What is that?" It was more of a hoarse whisper, and he was not sure he had been heard.

"A nest," Tuther replied. "Or maybe a queen. I'm not sure. I do know that it does not belong here."

A hundred or so yards in front of them a giant oblong sac hung suspended from the cave roof by a weave of thin sinews. The light was brighter towards the centre, shading from purple at the outer edges to a pale lilac in the middle. As the four men approached the sac, the smell of ammonia became almost overpowering.

"It's like a cocoon," said Tate. The ground immediately around it was covered with detritus, and Tate thought it looked like the sac had been shedding its skin in layers as if it were an onion.

"Err... sir?" King said.

Price did not reply but turned to face his young ward. His gun was in his hand and King realised that his own finger has been steadily tightening on the trigger of his own revolver. His mouth was dry and his heart was galloping. He flicked the safety back on.

"Sir, over there," King continued, nodding towards the back of the cave. Price followed his line of sight. The rear wall around the sac was lined with holes, similar in size to the one that had brought them down into this pit. Price counted a dozen of them.

Tuther nodded his approval to Price, who backed towards the wall, never taking his eyes off the glowing sac. Kneeling down, Price looked through the hole. Then, crab-walking to the next, he repeated the action, and again and again and again, until he had completed the semi-circle around the back of the sac.

"What have we got?" Tuther whispered.

"Twelve tunnels. Similar width to what we came down, but shorter. Maybe three foot. Each one goes into another cave. As far as I could see, each chamber has a couple of hundred of these," he nodded to the sac, "but their light is yellowish."

"A couple of hundred?" King whispered, too loudly.

Price looked to him. "At least." He looked back to Tuther. "How many more of these have you got?" he continued, showing the grenade.

Tuther looked back to the sack. "Four," he said eventually.

That's not going to be enough. Price thought. *We'd need at least two of these to take this chamber out. Maybe one to each of the others, but that's assuming that they don't have separate exit tunnels or whatever it is we came down.*

Tate took a step forward, pointing towards the suspended egg-sac. Later on, Tuther and King would agree that he was glassy-eyed and slack-jawed.

"Riah?" Tate said, and turned around to face the others, meeting Tuther's fist. As he fell back, hitting the floor, he fancied that he saw shapes moving on the ceiling, and then a black tide washed over him and all was darkness.

*

[Maiden Castle Stele 23-25]

It was there in the Land of Demnoni that Greine met Celus of the Coraniad.

"This land welcomes those who would watch over it," said Celus. "You may dwell within if you can defeat the Giant Ysbadden who had slain the family Custennin."

"So mote it be," replied Greine, "For *[text incomplete]*" and gathered himself to the domain of the Giant Ysbadden.

On his journey, Greine met three beggar women. "See!" they cried, "We are harried by these two oxen and this boar."

Greine chased the three animals away, and the women cast off their rags to reveal themselves as the Sisters Brigid – experts in fighting and warfare. So was Greine rewarded for showing generosity in aiding the women, and mercy in not killing the animals. The Sisters taught Greine the Way of The Willow, and Greine approached the Giant Ysbadden prepared well.

With his new fighting skills, Greine was victorious over Ysbadden and returned to Celus with the eyes of the giant as proof of his victory. In gratitude, Celus taught Greine the skill of being able to hear any sound the wind carried and took him to the Peak of Wynedesora.

Greine beheld the vastness before him and lamented. "Woe, for such is the expanse of all I behold. How may I serve my Goddess and marry so many lands to their skies?"

"Harken," said Danu unto her servants. "For time is time as time is. Those that believe in me time after time shall rest silent in heart."

So it was that Greine and Celus were blessed by the Goddess Danu. Their skin knew no thinning, their limbs no weakening, and their eyes no dimming.

*

Tate awoke to a throbbing jaw. He was sitting on the floor of the humid cave, his back to the wall, and was now some distance from the sac. His wrist and ankles were bound with his own shoe laces, and he could no longer feel the weight of the revolver on the inside of his jacket.

He looked up, and into the barrel of Tuther's shotgun. Price and King were on the far side of the sac working around the other tunnel entrances.

"Easy way? Or hard way?" Tuther asked, cocking the hammer on his shotgun noisily.

Tate was wide-eyed with terror. "What in the blazes?" He tried to move his feet to scramble away from this madman, but they were securely tied.

Tuther sighed and swung the butt of the shotgun round sharply, connecting with Tate's ribs. Tate tried to cry out, but Tuther jammed the barrel deep into his mouth. He started to gag and tried again to cry out. He could just make out the shape of Price, and looked at him imploringly.

Price turned his back and carried on with what he was doing.

"There is more of the hard way Mr Tate. Plenty more. Now, I'll be honest with you, I'm not going to let you live. But tell me what I want to know, and I'll make it quick. Play with me, and I'll feed you to your Mother over there. Understand?"

Tuther slowly withdrew the barrel from Tate's mouth. "Now, when does she hatch?"

Tate looked up at Tuther bewildered.

"When does the Riah spawn come?" Tuther tried again.

"Riah?" Then seeing that Tuther was about to swing the butt into him again, "That's what's written on the wall... behind that... thing." Tate was already curling up, trying to make himself as small as possible.

Tuther stopped, narrowing his eyes at Tate.

"It was behind that cocoon," Tate continued, seeing he had Tuther off guard. "It was the same script as some of the writing on the wall. I swear to you, and I don't know what Riah is."

Tuther paused. Then, still pointing the shotgun at Tate, he stepped back. Whispering to Price, he handed the shotgun over and made his way around the back of the sac. A few moments later he came back, and silently took the weapon back from Price who returned to his work with King.

Tuther approached Tate. "That could say anything." There was uncertainty in his voice.

"Why would I lie?" Tate was almost pleading.

"Yes, Mr Tate. Why would you lie?"

The question hung in the hot fetid air, but Tate made no attempt to answer.

"Those other tunnels. They have writing over them too. Can you read those?" Tuther said eventually.

"I... I..."

"Let's find out." Tuther took Tate by the scruff of the neck and lifted him easily to his feet. Tate was surprised at the strength of the wiry man and made no effort to resist.

Tate shuffled forward, acutely aware of the barrel being pressed into the base of his spine. At the first hole, he examined the script.

"Kara?" he said. "Or maybe Quara?"

Tuther said nothing but indicated him to move on to the next one.

"I don't know this one. It is in a different script."

Tuther did not move but just stood looking at Tate, barely blinking.

Tate moved of his own accord to the next tunnel. "I can't read this one either." Without looking behind him to where Tuther was, he shuffled on to the next tunnel. "Or this one." He moved again. "No, not this one either."

Again and again and again this repeated until they stood at the final tunnel entrance. Price and King had moved back around to the front of the sac.

"This... it's not the same script as the first one. This is much more modern. It's like a form of Proto-Fenya. But I think I can... it's like Gee-on..."

Tuther kicked him sharply in the small of his back, sending Tate sprawling to the floor.

Tuther's whisper was fierce. "What do you know of Jion? Do you know where he is?" He took a step towards Tate, raising his gun.

"I... I... don't..." Tate held his bound hands up to his face and began to curl up, sensing the impending kill shot.

Price approached. "The last one is the only empty chamber," he said quietly to Tuther.

Tuther looked at Price, and then back to Tate.

He approached the prone man, gun held high so that the butt was braced against his shoulder, the barrel coming up against Tate's face.

"Mr Tate. Mr Tate, look at me... there you go. Now, Mr Tate, I'm going to ask you about this cavern, and you're going to tell me you know nothing. But Mr Tate, I have a very good nose for liars. And I don't like them. It's liars that helped sink the Selvistan and kill my friend Jim. So, Mr Tate, you need to convince me, *really* convince me, that you don't know anything."

"I... I... I swear I only read what was on the walls. I have no idea who these characters are, or what it means. I swear by the Holy Mary I know..."

Tuther frowned and then seemed to consider the prone man before him. "Mr Tate, you can read the inscriptions on the walls?"

Tate nodded his head furiously. "Yes... yes. Well. Some of them..."

Tuther knelt next to Tate and looked the man in the eye. When it came, his voice was low. "Do they say anything about The Third Twine?"

Tate looked back at his tormentor, baffled. "The what?"

"Do they say how The Twine are gathered?" Tuther said, his insistence becoming increasingly fervent.

"I... I... don't..." Tate stuttered in fear and confusion.

For a moment, Tuther was silent. "Nevermind," he said eventually. Lowering his gun, he pulled a knife from his back pocket and deftly cut the bindings on Tate's ankles, and then those on his wrists.

Tate scrambled, still on the floor, until his back hit the wall. Breathing heavily, he looked at Tuther who was nonchalantly putting his knife away.

Tuther came close to Tate. "Mr Tate, let me be very clear. This is a nest. Something unnatural is growing here, and I mean to put an end to that. That wall is sandstone. A good blast will bring it down, maybe the other chambers too." Nodding towards Price and King, he continued, "We've pooled all of our gunpowder, plus my few explosives. I've got enough of a fuse to give us a few minutes to get out of here..."

"Why don't you just get reinforcements?" cried Tate. A few minutes were not going to be enough to get out, and he knew it. Maybe to get back to the mouth of the tunnel that brought them in, but not to get outside.

"Mr Tate. That... thing over there. There is something growing inside of it. Same for all those other chambers. That creature you saw on the hill? I think that was a premature birth, but it survived. That means that there is a good chance that these are all near enough to term. If we came back, even in a few hours, this lot may have already hatched. And I cannot take that chance."

Tate wanted to argue with him. To tell him what the loss of these inscriptions would mean to the world. That he had no way of really knowing what was in those sacs. That they might not be hatched by the time they came back. But he knew it was futile, and the dull ache in his ribs reminded him well enough to hold his tongue.

Instead, he just nodded.

The scuttling sound came again and from more than one place this time.

"We need to get going," Price said, eyeing the cavern roof.

Tuther started to lay out the fuse, and the other three began to retreat to the rear of the cave. Tate tried to guess how far they had come. A few hundred yards in that tunnel. Maybe the same again in the cavern. Tuther had given Price the torch, and Tate could see it bobbing ahead of him as they quickly traced their way back.

A deep moan pierced the silence of the cavern, reverberating around the chamber until it was filled with the ominous howl. All four men froze, and turned towards the giant purple sack. The cry came again, sharper this time, like a primitive animal in labour, but with the depth and resonance of a stag. The sac jerked sharply to the left and, for a split second, Tate saw the outline of a monstrous humanoid form pressed against the thick muscular walls of the makeshift womb.

Tuther cut the length of fuse, lit what was on the ground, and broke into a run, barrelling past Tate.

"Come on man!"

Tate turned and followed Tuther, his legs working like pistons. They arrived almost simultaneously at the tunnel entrance. Price met them there.

"Where's the boy?" Tate asked.

"I've sent him up. You're next. Go!"

Tate scrambled in. He could feel the rope underneath him. Pulling with his hands and scrambling with his feet he made his way up. Just ahead he could see King. A loud, wet slopping splash from the cavern below made him stop. *It's out!* He thought. *The waters have broken.*

"Move it!" It was Tuther. Right behind him. Price must be bringing up the rear.

Quickly scrabbling Tate began his ascent with a renewed urgency. His breathing became laboured and his arms ached. Sweat began to bead on his brow and his neck, and he still could not catch his breath in the warm dust filled air. Tate felt the tunnel twist slightly as it had done before. His ears popped and felt the air becoming cooler. Behind him, he heard a soft *wumph*. And then another. As if by reflex, he felt another jolt of adrenaline enter his system.

The charges are blowing!

And then an almighty explosion. Hot air began to rush up from beneath, and he scrambled as hard as he could as he felt the tunnel shake around him. Tate fell out of the tunnel entrance, coughing and choking. But there was no daylight, just the cool night air around him.

He heard a scrabbling behind him, and could just make out the shape of Tuther. Still nursing his ribs, Tate gingerly bent down to help the man up.

"Pull me out!" Tuther moaned. "My legs are caught."

The shape of King joined Tate as they pulled on Tuther.

"Caught on what?" said Tate, as they brought out the dusty form of their enigmatic leader.

Tuther was silent for a moment, his laboured breathing the only sound to be heard.

"Tunnel... collapsed."

King and Tate looked at each other helplessly.

It was Tate who spoke first. "How far behind you was Mr Price?"

Tuther shrugged and shook his head, still gasping for breath. "Didn't hear him...in the tunnel."

In the gloom, the silhouettes of Tate and King looked at Tuther in silence. Only their heaving wracking breath filled the night air and each knew the officer's fate.

"What now?" Tate asked eventually.

Tuther looked up, dust and dirt and muck streaking his face. "Now Mr Tate, we are going get this young man home. And then you and I need to have a drink."

As the three men set off down the hill, back towards the village, the sound of their own footsteps masked the quiet padding that came out of the forest.

A black-clad gaunt figure stepped forward from the shelter of the trees, dragging with him the lifeless body of the creature they had all seen earlier. Laying it down on the ground, he shouldered a rifle and took careful aim at the retreating figures.

Another stepped out of the dark and gently put his hand on the barrel, forcing it down. A third joined them. To a casual observer, the three were nearly identical. Triplets possibly. Tall, thin, with shoulder-length black hair, and hawkish features. Their impossibly pale complexion suggested a certain other-worldliness that sages had written about in antiquity.

The hairs on the back of King's neck prickled and he half turned.

"I would keep walking if I were you Mr King," said Tuther.

"But I thought I saw a man... maybe men. At the edge of the forest."

"I know you did son. But believe me when I say that this is not the time for that fight and they are most certainly not men."

*

"That's it?" asked Danielle incredulously.

Freeman shrugged. "The files were only recently declassified. Dennis King arrived at what was then RAF Leuchars nearly four days after he disappeared, without Tuther or Tate. He told his story. All of it. A search party went out for Price, but there was no sign of him. Neither the burrow nor the caverns were ever found. King was formally reprimanded and Price was declared absent without leave. He was never seen or heard from again."

"But what about the creature on the hill? All of those cadets must have provided statements."

"Oh, they did. For all the good they were. Some said it was a tramp. Others that it was a monkey or a gorilla. One boy actually swore that it was a werewolf, brought out by the eclipse."

Danielle could tell that the old man was holding something back. "Do you have any idea what it was?"

It amused Freeman that he was so transparent to his publisher. "I do. I think that whatever that beast was… it was the same thing that King saw as they left that cave."

"The three men?"

Freeman nodded. "I think that grotto, or whatever you want to call it, was some sort of hatchery, and the figures that King saw were its guardians. The steles that Tate translated refer to The Raven Men that serve the Goddess."

Danielle smiled. "That's a heck of a leap. I'm not buying that on the basis of this one story and besides, there is no evidence."

Freeman shrugged. "Fair enough. But later will come more accounts that will corroborate what I'm telling you. And you are wrong about there being no evidence. Traces of the gooey substance were recovered, but tests were inconclusive. The scientific techniques of the time were primitive compared to today. All they revealed was that it was some mix of amniotic fluid and unidentified oil."

Danielle could almost see another clue. "Did they keep any samples? Perhaps it could be retested…"

"Some were kept at the time. But over the decades they have been lost."

"So I was right - there is no evidence, only this cadet's testimony to what happened. We don't know if it was even Tuther and Tate there. He could have made it all up."

"I interviewed him myself. That cadet went on to be one of the most highly decorated Air Commodores in RAF history. And we know from Tate's bank statements that he was in Falkland at the time. The man was obsessive about his personal administration."

Danielle's eyes narrowed. "How did you get his bank statements?"

"The investigation by the British Museum was not the first time that Tate's credibility was called into question. He was questioned in seventy-five on suspicion of wasting police time, and as part of that they did a trawl of his life. When his son, and then his grandson, disappeared, it was all raked over again."

Danielle started forward. "Wasting police time? By doing what?"

CHAPTER 4

Wodiah 3:8-12
God saw the bounty of His Kingdom
And decreed that the Ravens shall bring Him all Thought and Memory,
So it was that the Ravens rode the heavens on the Skyworms of olde,
That they may shepherd the beasts of clay.

My name is Harold Gordon. In 1975 I was a pathologist for Dorset County Hospital and assisted the local police with the investigation of three alleged skeletons discovered at Maiden Castle.

Monday 8th September 1975

Tate and Lincoln stamped their feet in the cold of the autumn morning. The first frost had come, but it was more than the unseasonable cold that chilled them. Tucking their hands underneath their armpits, their breath hung in the air like miniature steam trains that had taken a bizarre wrong turn into this strange field in Dorset. Neither man said anything. They knew that they had done everything by the book, but this investigation was taking far longer than they had expected.

Dawn's early light was bravely trying to burn off the blanket of low cloud, and the two men eyed the police portacabin that sat at the side of the field. They should be able to hear the familiar sounds of their colleagues excavating the Maiden Castle site. But all activity in the field was frozen, like a glacier waiting for the inevitable sunrise.

Occasional noises could be heard from the Scenes of Crime tent, as though this temporary structure was mocking the impotence of history; that all ruins must fall to dust no matter how grand, whilst the new looked on. The grassy slopes that would have once formed the foundation of the castle remained silent, as if this modern science was not worthy of retort.

A figure in an all-in-one plastic white suit emerged from the tent, carrying a bag that bore the word "evidence". Tate and Lincoln had seen many of these come out and each one was like a razor blade being run against their heart. Who knew what valuable archaeology each bag contained? Or where it was being stored? *If* it was being stored.

Lincoln turned his back on the sight, feeling sick.

They had both been interviewed separately. All the staff had. Several times. The same questions over and over and over again. Who had access to the site? Had they seen anyone acting suspiciously?

The door to the police portacabin swung open, like a bad prop in a Hammer film, and the imposing figure of Sergeant Coombes emerged followed by Doctor Gordon. They had met the pathologist the previous day, but he had not said anything to them.

"Mr Lincoln. Mr Tate. Come in please." The men followed the Sergeant into the portacabin, and the pathologist joined them.

This would be the first time they were interviewed together. Tate thought that the police had stopped doing this many years ago, but did not say anything. It was warmer in the cabin, and both men were thankful for it, although it was the dry heat that came from overused electrical heaters. Lincoln instantly felt thirsty but the Sergeant did not offer any refreshment.

"Mr Lincoln," the Sergeant said, sitting down, "tell me again your version of events."

This would be what? His sixth? Maybe seventh time? Lincoln sighed. "I was excavating what we thought were the outer walls of burial tombs in the grounds of the castle. I uncovered a fragment of bone that looked like a human jaw. I sent Lana Collins to fetch George here, whilst I secured the area. George arrived. He agreed with me that it looked human, and went to call you."

The Officer's tone was blunt and direct. "Did you leave the area?"

"Not until your colleagues arrived. I had one of my team – Pete Homer – tape off the area where I was working."

"Was the ground disturbed?"

"Yes."

"How do you know that?"

Lincoln looked up from the table and straight into Coombes' eyes. "Because I was the one excavating it. I was the one doing the disturbing." His frustration was beginning to show.

Tate put his hand on Lincoln's arm. "I apologise for my colleague Sergeant..."

"Apologise for what?" exploded Lincoln. "We've been here three days now. We found skeletons around a burial ground. We called you," he said looking at the Sergeant. "Why are we still here?"

Coombes remained impassive. "And you Mr Tate. You surveyed the site prior to the excavation beginning?"

"Yes. We began works in the early part of last year. I surveyed the site six years before that as part of the dig request. I have telephoned London to ask them to send the files and photographs to you."

"Why so long between the dig request and works beginning?" Coombes asked, feigning disinterest as he made notes.

"That's a standard length of time to get permission and then funding."

"And is funding an issue?"

Tate looked at Lincoln. This was new. "Funding is always an issue Sergeant. There are any number of projects competing for a finite pot. Not all get backed."

"And what helps a project get backed?"

"How do you mean?"

"What helps get one dig selected whilst another is rejected?"

"Well, it is any number of things really. Perceived likelihood of success – something being found. Public interest. Profile of those involved. The possible number of papers that might be written..."

"So it's competitive?"

"Yes, I guess you could say that," said Tate.

"Look," said Lincoln leaning forward. "Can you tell us what this is all about?"

Coombes looked to Gordon and shrugged.

"Gentlemen," Gordon began, "you did not find human remains."

Lincoln frowned. "Are you sure? I'm not an expert, but I thought it looked human."

"Very sure."

"So what was it?" Tate asked, a little too quickly for Coombes' liking.

"We were hoping you would tell us."

"We don't know," Tate replied.

Coombes and Gordon exchanged glances again. "Gentlemen, is there anything you want to tell us?"

"How do you mean?" Tate said.

"Maybe a little joke that has gone too far? A little publicity stunt perhaps?"

It was Tate and Lincoln's turn to exchange glances. "Err... I... We... don't know what you're talking about," Tate replied.

Gordon slid a photograph over to Lincoln. It showed a recently dug square about four feet deep, at the bottom of which were three skeletons, one seemingly to be laying on top of the other, the third to the side.

Lincoln, still frowning, said, "They look human."

"Uh huh," Gordon replied, arms crossed.

"But they're not?" Tate asked, examining the photo.

"No Professor, they are not."

"What are they? Neanderthal? Look a bit tall for Neanderthal."

Gordon sighed. "They're fakes."

Tate and Lincoln looked up from the photo, startled.

"What?" Tate exclaimed.

"I've had them back to my lab, and these are not real. They're a hoax."

Lincoln could feel the colour draining from his face. He remembered Piltdown; that story had broken just as he had started university. The scandal had been toxic. So many people associated with that whole affair had never worked again. He felt sick.

Coombes noted that Tate seemed more composed.

"How do you mean they're a hoax?" the professor asked.

Gordon sighed again. "Do you really mean to pursue this line?"

"Doctor, I assure you that I have nothing to do with this whatsoever, and I would be jolly surprised if any of my team did. Now, how do you know these bones aren't real?"

Gordon leaned forward, drawing a sketch on a piece of paper for Tate. "Our first indications were the limbs themselves – overly long you see. I thought it was a case of Marfan's Syndrome. Then there are the shoulder blades, which were not just longer but also thicker than we would normally expect, by about thirty percent. We thought we were dealing with members of the same family with some congenital disfiguration. However, when we began to examine them more closely, we realised that this was more than disfigurement. When bones grow in infants and young adults, they inevitably reach a piece of cartilage known as the Epiphyseal Plate, where they stop. Once puberty is completed, the cartilage is replaced by bone, leaving a fuse line. These bones you found have no fuse points. They did not grow. They were made." Gordon looked for a reaction from Tate, but there was none. "Don't misunderstand me, Professor, these are very good fakes. There are excellent approximations of canaliculi and cortical bone. When we cut the bones open, we would have expected to see a honeycombed centre where the marrow had been. These bones had a network of vessels that were perfectly cylindrical, all the way through. The way the calcium was layered is all wrong. In this case, it has just been applied in a single coating. Unless you've discovered a new evolutionary branch..."

"What if we have?" Tate interrupted.

Gordon thought for a moment. "Is that likely Professor?"

"You tell me."

Gordon sat back. "No," he said.

"What about DNA extraction?"

"What?"

"Could DNA extraction prove these were living men?"

"Now, Professor. I don't know what journals you've been reading, but DNA extraction is a new and highly experimental technology. There is no facility in the UK, and to my knowledge only one in Europe that could run such a test; in Belgium, I think. In my opinion, this is not the skeleton of any living..."

Coombes interrupted. "Professor Tate, you said 'living men'. How do you know these are men?" The skeletons were approximations of three males, but Tate's assumption had set off his Copper's Nose.

Tate felt an invisible noose tighten around his neck. "Slip of the tongue," he said. "Call it a chauvinistic euphemism."

Gordon was inclined to give him the benefit of the doubt. "I don't know what else to tell you, Professor. The calcium deposits do not come apart in the way you would expect to see. The concentration of iron and magnesium is thousands of times higher than in a human. I even tried some radio dating. There are no carbon fourteen traces, so I cannot accurately date them. And then, of course, there are the teeth – there is simply no wear on them. Despite the humanoid appearance, these are not real skeletons."

For a moment there was an awkward silence.

"So what now?" Lincoln asked. "Can we resume the dig?"

Coombes narrowed his eyes at the younger man. "You know Doctor, a sceptical person would say that the impossibly well-preserved skeletons of a disfigured family had been forged and buried here to raise the profile of a dig which had found very little and that was about to run into financial trouble."

The awkward silence returned, bringing its friend Tension with it.

Tate eventually spoke. "I can assure you, Sergeant, that there has been no deliberate attempt to deceive on our part. We have no idea how those skeletons got there, who put them there, or why. We are as shocked as you are. We called you in good faith."

Coombes did not like Professor Tate. He was far too smooth, always saying the right things, at the right time, but with a complete lack of sincerity.

"Professor, do you know what the punishment is for wasting police time?"

Tate shook his head.

"Six months. And a fine. For each individual involved."

Tate just nodded, looking at the table.

Coombes could see the neither of the two men were going to offer up any more. "Pair of you. Get out."

Lincoln and Tate got up, neither of them meeting Coombes' stare, and left.

"What do you think?" Coombes said, turning to Gordon.

"Difficult to say. If funding is as competitive as those two make it out to be, maybe a rival set them up. The forgery is very good. To the naked eye, it may not have been discernible. They did follow protocol, and maybe they just called you in ignorance. Then again, we know how these London types view the regions. Like we've all got twelve toes. Maybe they thought they could get away with it."

Coombes breathed out hard through his nose. "Got anything to link them directly to it?"

Gordon shook his head. "I don't even know how they made it. Best guess is they applied some calcium type paste over a mould. But it would have had to have been machined afterwards, and I cannot find a single groove or nick. Even under the microscope. These processes are seldom that perfect. Maybe in a Japanese or German plant, but here? I don't know of any. I cannot even accurately date how long they've been there for. There's been no water penetration, but with bone, it is always difficult to say."

Coombes folded his arms and thought.

*

[Maiden Castle Stele 26-30]

The Lord of Dives, Master of Shole, was displeased that Greine knew the secrets of seasons everlasting.

Entering from the sky, The Lord of Dives said to Greine "The Breath of Namlu shall not dwell within the shell of flesh forever. The time of Man shall be no more than seasons of six score."

"Reviler! Usurper!" railed Greine. "We are of Danu and shall be commanded by Her Word, and Her Word alone."

"The Children of Trees may be, but The Brood of Clay shall not. Lest I take all you know that you should wander alone, you will submit to Shole at the end of your time."

Danu consoled her offspring and spoke unto Greine the Secrets of the Light. With grim resolve, Greine accepted Heaven's Visor from his Goddess that he might find the secret path to Shole and confront the Lord of Dives. Danu knew that Greine could not defeat the Lord of Dives, but gave him a Seed of Namlu. When cast into the waters of Shole, Danu's arm would sprout forth and bind the Lord of Dives.

The entrance to Shole was cut off from the mainland by the Waters of Nun. The only ferry was *[text incomplete]* by Shedu – the Ghazal who had recanted and knelt before Danu. Shedu divested Greine of all metallic substances but allowed him to keep The Horn of Dagda which was not metal.

Greine beheld the mighty doors of Shole, locked and barred to the living. *[text incomplete]*

"Then the doors are open to you," said Cassandra.

Greine journeyed down through the seven levels of Shole. At the first level, he saw the souls of the recently departed, waiting for judgement.

At the second level, Greine saw the Mists of The Hand, where unbelievers floundered without direction for all eternity. Greine prayed to Danu whose voice guided him through the mists.

At the third level, he saw all tyrants and false prophets of the world.

At the fourth level, Greine saw all the Shayatin and Ghazal who had turned from Danu to make the cosmos their own.

At the fifth level, he saw all those who had falsely proclaimed themselves Danu's heir.

At the sixth level, Greine saw the prison of abominations, sinners, and those of false witness.

At the seventh level, Greine challenged Jehoel, champion of The Lord of Dives and with the Words of Power defeated him. The Lord of Dives confronted Greine and beat him back. Greine threw the Seed of Namlu into the Waters of Shole, and there grew the Arm of Danu which bound The Lord of Dives and does still, turning as Shole still turns.

*

Tuther saw the two men leaving the cabin and nodded his head to bring them over.

"Well?" he said.

"Bloody skeletons are a fake!" exclaimed Lincoln.

Tuther looked to Tate, a solitary eyebrow raised questioningly.

Tate nodded but made no reply.

"What do you mean?" Tuther said, turning back to Lincoln.

"The pathologist says they aren't human. That they've been made somehow. George, I tell you if this gets out it's early baths for all of us. All of us!"

"Alright Mike, it'll be ok. No one has done anything wrong," Tate said soothingly.

"What happens now?" Tuther asked.

Tate shrugged and nodded towards the portacabin. "I think that there is still a case to answer. The pathologist said the remains displayed signs of Marfan's..."

"Hasn't Irene got Marfan's?" Lincoln interrupted a realisation dawning on him. It seemed more than a coincidence that the head of the digs wife and these 'fake' skeletons had the same congenital defect. Lincoln remembered meeting her at department barbeque – she had given him the chills. And the daughter too... what was her name? Fiona, that was it. She had Marfan's too. Those long spindly fingers. They reminded him of some aberrant spider. Both mother and daughter had a habit of clicking their joints when they were bored or unhappy.

"Yes," Tate said slowly, looking at Lincoln hard. "But hers is a minor case. Anyway, the Sergeant is deciding whether to charge us with wasting police time."

At that moment the door to the cabin opened, and Gordon stepped out.

Tate waved to him. "Tea?" he called.

Gordon started to make his way over. "Please."

"Mike," Tate said under his breath. "Run and get some tea would you?"

"What the bloody hell are you doing George?" Lincoln whispered back fiercely.

"Keep your enemies closer, my Commanding Officer used to say," he whispered, and then to Gordon, "How do you take it?"

"Milk and two please."

Tate looked to Lincoln whose eyes blazed back at him for a moment before he turned and stomped off to the canteen tent.

"Funny old business," Tate said. "Never seen anything like it. You?"

Gordon knew the man was fishing. "Is this a fake too?" he asked, avoiding Tate's question, and tossing a metal circlet at him.

Tate caught it and turned it over in his hand. Tuther examined it as well.

"Found it with the skeletons?" Tate asked.

Gordon just nodded.

The circlet was actually two concentric circles, with nine zigzagging lines connecting the outer to the inner. There was a ragged end of what was once a leather string.

"I don't recognise it as European," said Tuther.

"Me neither," said Tate. "You should keep hold of this," he continued, handing the pendant back to Gordon. "The Sergeant will want it treated as evidence."

Gordon accepted it back. "Gentlemen, what game are you playing here?"

Tate shook his head. "I assure you, Doctor, there is no game."

"Professor, you have just handed me back what could be a very important archaeological find with no attempt at protest or to keep it."

"Doctor, the protocols are very clear. Even if we expect to find a body, we must always inform the authorities. When they decide that the matter is archaeological then we continue. But until then, it is your site, and we are absolutely forbidden from interfering, lobbying, or bringing any kind of pressure to bear. Absolutely forbidden."

"That is very... honest of you Professor."

"Doctor, my team is experienced with these sort of digs. But we all know chaps who have been less... scrupulous, who have been in a hurry, cut corners and come unstuck. In our experience, it is never worth it."

"So what were you expecting to find here?"

"Outside? Well, Mike was working the burial tombs, so yes, we were hoping for bodies. But Maiden Castle has an odd history. From some of the artefacts we found, we thought there might be a royal or religious significance, although there is no mention of it in any records. To be honest, three complete skeletons is a good find – better than good, it's excellent. But to be so rudely interred, and with no jewellery or finery... well, either the burial tombs are not where we thought they were, or the site is not as significant as we had hoped. Either way, it is a bit of blow."

Gordon listened to the man. He seemed sincere. But there was something about him. He knew the Sergeant felt it too but had not said anything yet. It was as though the Professor knew a great secret that he refused to impart.

"So the skeletons are fake?" said Tuther after a pause. "Have you ever come across anything like this before?"

Gordon looked at the man. He had taken an instant dislike to him when he had first met him, and that feeling had not gone away. He was fishing as well.

"Once. Sort of. My father knew the Ashley-Coopers. They have an estate maybe an hour or so from here. Out near Wimborne. I used to play with the boys when I was a child. Both named Tony. Never got used to it. Of course, the War put all those friendships on hold. After the War, I saw the eldest once. He'd been in an Auxiliary Unit – and something extra special to boot. Lovely chap, but after a couple of drinks he would sing like a canary. He claimed to have been in Berlin at the fall. The Nazis were into all sorts at the end. Anyway, Tony brought back the skeleton of some worm-beast. At first, I thought it was the damnedest thing. It was perfectly circular, with a double row of teeth that looked more like razors. The jaw had no hinge and was about two, maybe two and half feet across. He also had a couple of vertebrae from what I would guess had been a spinal column, but it was incomplete.

"Tony said that he had found it after the Allies had moved in, as he was coming back through Wewelsburg. He claimed that some SS sect had started worshipping sky-worms if you can believe that. Of course, when he eventually showed it to me, I recognised it for what it was – a well-made sculpture. It wasn't bone at all, although it had been made to look like bone, with a bit of iron solution and chromic acid. It would have fooled the layman."

Tate and Tuther were silent for a moment.

"What happened to this Tony?" Tate asked eventually.

"Oh, he died. In forty-seven I think. Heart failure."

"We all die of heart failure Doctor. What caused it?" Tate persisted.

Gordon took a breath. "Heroin. When he got back, his nerves were shot. I think he saw some of the concentration camps. He could barely sleep, and... well, you can imagine the rest."

Tate nodded respectfully.

"Does his family still have it?" Tuther said, uncharacteristically brightly.

"What?"

"The sculpture of the skull that he brought back. Do they still have it?"

"I have no idea. It was thirty years..."

"Could you take us there? Maybe it's similar to what Mike found."

"Celus, I really..." Tate interjected quietly.

Gordon looked at the two men hard. Their relationship was not the normal sort he saw. Tate was clearly in charge of the site... but Tuther, although obviously younger, always came across as his equal. There was a depth to his eyes which unsettled Gordon, but at the same time made him feel as if there was a dark tale to be told. The man looked haunted.

This little episode clearly had further to run and he was curious as to where it would lead.

"Well, I suppose it couldn't hurt," mused Gordon. "The family is away in Belfast at the moment, but the housekeeper might be in. She'll remember me." His interest had been piqued. There was little chance of the jaws in any way being linked with the skeletons that had been found, but this case was so unusual that he wanted to spend some proper time with these men. See if they could slip up.

"My car is parked over there," Gordon continued. "Just let me tell the Sergeant where we are going, and we can be off."

*

[Maiden Castle Stele 31-33]

The Adversary saw the triumph of Greine over Jehoel, and His soul was as black as red with jealousy.

"No more shall the Tribes of Tuatha be blessed by the Word," and with this, the Adversary stroked the Heavens with His hammer until the stars rung as oceans and tongues.

And all was silent for none could behold The Word of Danu.

"Lament!" cried Greine, "for no longer can we be guided! See how what was once one is now twelve, and they turn from the path."

"Be not frail," replied Celus, "For Our Goddess moves amongst us still."

And Greine and Celus beheld the Portents of Danu, and they foretold that the Goddess would send a mighty dragon that the land would be purified of all the Fallen and non-believers.

So it was at the behest of the Portents, and with the help of the Coraniad, Greine, and his army built a fogou. The followers of Danu observed well, and as foretold, ninety-two days passed, and the ground rumbled and broke as with the beat of mighty wings above. Greine and the Coraniad retreated into the fogou, and there the huddled clan could feel the heat of a thousand suns against the walls and ceiling. Almost as quickly came the sound as of the landing of mighty feet and an ocean covered the fogou. So was all darkness as dust, and grave as violet. After thirty-two days and thirty-two nights the waters receded and Greine and the Coraniad emerged to find all non-believers had been smashed into pieces of iron.

*

St Giles House loomed over the three men, like a demanding elder patriarch, its numerous chimney stacks casting long shadows.

"Some money here," muttered Tuther.

"It's been in the family since the seventeenth century," said Gordon. "About fourteen hundred acres in all. Most of it farmed."

As they got out of the car, the main door swung open. A small but upright grey haired lady greeted them on the steps.

"Mrs Torinelli? I'm not sure if you remember me. My name is…"

"Little Harry Gordon!" Mrs Torinelli exclaimed in a thick Italian accent. "Let me look at you."

"Well, not so little any more Mrs Torinelli," said Gordon, blushing slightly.

Tate and Tuther stood slightly back, waiting to be introduced.

"My! You have grown. And a doctor I hear! Your mama would be so proud! And you have brought friends I see."

"Ah yes, this is Professor Tate and Mr Tuther."

They each shook Mrs Torinelli's hand, nodding and saying "How do you do?"

"Ah, but Lord Ashley is not here. He is away in Belfast."

"Yes. Mrs Torinelli, my friends are archaeologists, working at Maiden Castle... over Dorchester way. We were wondering if we could see Tony's room. He had a skeleton we'd like to look at."

"The jaw? It is an evil thing!" Mrs Torinelli spat on the ground. "Drove the Major mad!" she exclaimed, crossing herself.

"Yes. But could my friends have a quick look at it?"

Mrs Torinelli harrumphed loudly, turned and entered the grand old house, bidding them to follow.

"How old is she?" muttered Tuther, admiring the feisty housekeeper.

"No one knows," replied Gordon, crossing the threshold. "I was here as a boy in the late twenties, and she was part of the furniture then. She's got to be eighty, maybe more."

The small group congregated at the bottom of a large and imposing staircase.

"You remember where the Major's room is?" said Mrs Torinelli.

"Third on the right?"

Mrs Torinelli nodded. "I get you tea. I not go in there." The old lady retreated to the back of the house, where Tate assumed the kitchens were.

"Well," said Tuther to Gordon, "after you."

The three men climbed the staircase and presently found themselves inside the late Anthony Ashley-Cooper's bedroom. Tate noted it was almost a caricature of his expectations. A large double bed faced an equally grand fireplace, and the room was mostly wood panelled. Floor-to-ceiling windows looked westwards and Tate fancied he could just make out the outline of both Yeovil and Dorchester.

Mahogany wardrobes flanked the internal wall, and a small writing desk was positioned in the window bay. A chest of drawers was next to the wardrobe and above it shelves with an array of leather bound books. The room was spotless, with no indication that its occupant had been deceased for nearly thirty years.

Gordon cast his eye about. "It must be here," he muttered.

"Maybe the family got rid of it," Tate offered.

"No. Tony was fascinated by the thing. Lady Constance would never have let it be thrown away. I thought there was an ottoman in this room..."

A dragging noise at the end of room announced that Tuther had found a chest under the bed and was pulling it out.

"Celus!" said Tate, clearly exasperated. "Want to take a little bit more care? That thing's an antique. Probably the carpets too."

Tuther looked impassively at Tate and then opened the chest.

"Have you got it?" Gordon asked.

"Uh-huh," grunted Tuther, and with obvious exertion heaved out a giant jaw onto the bed. A few seconds later three more flattish stones came out. Tate assumed that these were the vertebrae that Gordon had mentioned.

Tate and Gordon bent over the bed, and as they did so, the sound of footsteps coming up the stairs could be heard.

"Ugh, you found it!" said Mrs Torinelli from the doorway. "Here," she indicated to Tuther, "you take this," and handed him a tray of cups, saucers, and a pot of tea. "I'll be in the kitchen if you need me." The Housekeeper moved off quickly.

"Well," said Tuther smiling, "she didn't want to hang about." He put the tray down on top of the chest of drawers and started pouring the tea. "So? What have we got Georgey boy?"

Tate stared hard at Tuther.

"Sorry. Professor," said Tuther in exaggerated tones.

Tate went back to examining the jaw with Gordon. The jaw was complete, almost perfectly circular with no hinge, and Tate surmised that the razor sharp teeth must have been to shred food before it passed into the gullet.

"They feel warm," Tate said eventually.

"Maybe there's a hot water pipe running under the bed, to the bathroom," said Gordon, nodding towards a narrow door that led to the ensuite.

"Maybe. Let's see. There is good detail for a forgery. Plenty of nicks along the tooth line. What did Lord Ashley say it was?"

"A worm's jaw," replied Gordon who had put his glasses on and was examining the jaw closely.

"Biggest worm I've ever seen," Tuther muttered. Tate shot the younger man a look but Tuther was rifling through some papers from the chest.

"Celus!"

"What?"

"Have some respect," Tate barked, clearly exasperated by his strange companion's behaviour.

Tuther said nothing but went back to shuffling through the papers, albeit more quietly.

"What do you think?" said Tate, turning back to the pathologist.

"Well setting aside the impossible size of such a beast, I still say it's fake. It's certainly not bone, but I'm not sure what kind of rock this was sculpted from. And I cannot see any obvious signs of the stone being worked. The teeth show wear like you say, but..."

A loud crack made them both jump. Tuther stood up and put the poker back in its rest by the fireplace.

"Celus! What the...?"

Tuther bent down, and picked up the two halves of the smashed vertebra from the floor, and examined them.

Without saying anything, he crossed the floor to where Gordon was and showed him the smashed ends of the vertebra.

"Well I never..." Gordon took both halves from Tuther to look at them closer.

The smashed vertebra revealed a network of perfect cylinders running inside, exactly the like the bones found at Maiden Castle. These felt warm too and Gordon turned them over in his hand. Little flakes of dust and debris rose up from the inside, and Gordon took a small torch from his pocket to look inside with greater detail.

"Incredible," said Gordon eventually, and then coughed a little as the flakes irritated him. Despite the cool day, the room felt warm, and he took his jacket off. "The makeup of these.... whatever they are is very similar to those skeletons at your dig. Do you think...?" Something seemed to click into place. "Germans?" he asked.

"I'm... not sure," said Tate doubtfully. Tuther said nothing.

Gordon continued to turn the vertebrae stones over in his hands. He was starting to feel quite unwell. His heart was beginning to race, and nausea rose up inside him.

"I... I... just need to sit..." he began, and then a wave of grey overtook him.

"He's going," he heard a far off voice say. Tuther maybe.

He felt something take his shoulders, and then his weight. His ears popped and it he felt like he was in a dream.

"Is he one of us?" someone else began, but the sound of his own heartbeat in his ears drowned everything else out.

*

[Maiden Castle Stele 34-36]

By Portents and Designs, Danu sent Greine and Celus to the east where they met the blind brothers Gofannon and Amathon, whose hands were bound by a rope to a giant eagle and followed wherever it led, as punishment for speaking out against Lord Shemel, who had taken their lands.

As Greine approached, the eagle changed into a Ghazal and they fought before Greine killed it. Restoring their sight by blues, Danu revealed that Gofannon and Amathon were her sons, once lost of the Tuatha and now found.

Gofannon was a mighty smith and forged the Plate of Danu from the shattered iron pieces left after the Great Flood. Through the Plate, Danu was once again able to speak directly to Greine. Danu blessed Greine's lands and the four surrounding kingdoms, that all may speak in the same tongue and rally to Greine's cause of building the Second Seeplin.

Amathon was a skilled mason, and so built the mightiest castle with the greatest towers on top of Greine's fogou and fashioned the Stone of Fal into a throne.

Danu gifted the castle to Greine and permitted him to use all the rooms for his court, with the exception of the Tallest Tower. The top of this tower was Danu's temple, and from time-to-time was home *[translation contested; host]* to Her presence. Permanently shrouded in cloud, Greine and Celus were forbidden from entering the temple but once a year, and even then only after many washings and purifications.

Occasionally, the presence of Danu in her temple could be seen from outside the tower, as though the Fires of Heaven were pouring forth.

Danu regularly visited Greine, in the form of a horse drinking in a river, to instruct him on the construction of the next Seeplin.

*

Gordon opened his eyes. What had happened?

He had been talking to Tate, and then he had started to feel hot... and then a bit ill... and now?

He started to his feet and looked about him. He was no longer in St Giles House. He saw a number of small rises in the land around him and fancied that he recognised them as being those on the Ashley Cooper Estate. But there was no sign of the building, the driveway or indeed his car, let alone the strange companions he had journeyed here with.

Behind him, he heard a clicking sound. Three figures ran past him. He went to call to them but stopped himself. He had taken them for men, but there was something wrong. Their gait was almost mechanical. Each stride was exactly the same as the previous. No stumble, or adjustment, just a solid sprint. Each was dressed in drab attire, with a black cloak or shawl draped over their shoulders. Their hair, jet black, reached their shoulders, and their skin was as pale as alabaster.

For a moment Gordon thought they were triplets. However as one turned, barking something to the two others, he realised that despite their hawkish features they were not quite identical. Brothers maybe?

"The Goddess blast you!" the one in front snarled. "Run you dogs! The Third Twine's army is right behind us!"

And then Gordon saw their eyes. Their irises that were not just black, but totally pitch as if they were pits that had never felt the sun's caress, and their faces smooth as glass, as if they had never smiled a single day in all their lives.

The three figures carried on running towards the west. Although it could only have been late morning, Gordon saw the sky was beginning to turn lilac, and then deepen to a more ominous purple.

Following the direction of the retreating figures, Gordon crested a rise and found himself at a line of trees. He was sure that there had been a dry stone wall here. Stepping out from the shade, he saw the land fall away from him, heading towards the coast. Even though the sky was free of cloud, the horizon was a sickening purple, like a new bruise, and he felt his stomach clench.

He saw lightning flash and fork. Where was it? Over the sea? On the coast? Gordon was not sure that he should be able to see that far, and yet he did. A distant peal of thunder came, deep and rumbling, like a mighty leviathan stirring from an eon of rest.

The lightning came again followed by more thunder. And then again. And again.

Whatever was going on, it was building up. Another flash. And another. And another.

The forks were nearly continuous now, overlapping each other, sometimes joining to form super bolts that left the air sizzling with ozone. And still more. Three bolts filled the sky simultaneously.

Gordon could just make out three dots of the men he had seen, all still running at full pelt. The purple sky had advanced from the horizon, now rumbling over his head, and away to the east. It was all around him, boiling like a cauldron.

Five bolts. Six. A seventh crackled into life like a possessed live wire. An eighth arched epileptically the length of the horizon. Gordon lost count how many were filling the sky at any one time. The peals of thunder were running into each other, becoming a single constant tone.

And then, above the cacophony of nature's savagery came a noise that he would never forget. Like some demon bovine giving birth, a deep wet tearing sound came from the south. From the sea.

The crackle of lightning intensified, and Gordon involuntarily shrank back.

The tearing boom came again and this time, the wind joined with it, rising in pitch, threatening to drown out the now constant roll of thunder. Something caught his eye, slightly to his right. He half turned, and in that moment another matrix of lightning bolts erupted, casting an impossible profile on the skyline.

The lightning blazed again, like heavenly fire, and Gordon saw it clearly. There, looking down from his elevated position, he saw the shape of a castle in the far distance. The stockade fence was clearly silhouetted, and behind that the rising walls of a primitive castle. At one end he could see a tower under construction like some incongruous stub, and the keep looked bulky and substantial.

But... his mind was reaching. He knew that area. He had played there as a boy. There was nothing there, only the grassy mounds surrounding a long dry moat. There had been no castle for... at least a millennium. Maybe more.

Another boom drew his attention back to the coastline, and the wind increased again. Behind him, Gordon could hear the trees beginning to creak against the unrelenting onslaught. Pieces of grit were being kicked up from the ground, and he had to narrow his eyes which were already watering.

Sensing that he should probably be clear of the trees, he continued forward a little way. The sky over the coast was now a complex weave of lightning bolts, and if he could have heard the thunder over the shriek of the wind, he would have known that its pitch had changed, becoming deeper and more menacing.

The boom came again, stronger now and drowning all else out. And something moved in the sky above the coast. Something colossal and monstrous and that should not be. There it was again. An impossible shape, arcing and swinging across the purple boiling clouds.

Gordon gasped and the gale instantly filled his lungs, forcing the breath from him, leaving him winded. What was that he had seen? It could not be.

He saw it again. Clearly this time. There was no mistaking it.

A fleeting glimpse of something resembling a single vast alien arm swung across the sky. Tens of miles... no, hundreds of miles across. It seemed to be descending from the very heavens. Bulging muscle rippled in the clouds.

Gordon could do nothing but stare, slack-jawed and terrified, as the impossible behemoth swayed liked some drunken apocryphal juggernaut across the skyline.

And what was that? There was something else there. His eyes were streaming and he could barely make it out. Things. Things were falling off the abomination. From his vantage point, they looked like matchsticks. Tiny slender pieces, of insignificant size, compared to the nightmare that was tearing itself from the sky, like the Antichrist cannibalising its own mother as it was laboured and delivered. And the pieces were falling. Thousands of them falling over and over and over. Falling into the sea and onto the land.

If they look like matchsticks from here, reasoned Gordon, *they must be... hundreds of feet long.*

His mind snapped back to the stone jaws of the Ashley-Cooper statue. And he knew. In that moment of terrible enlightenment, he knew the jaw was real. No mere approximations of a mad sculptor. No terrifying ravings of a deranged artist or falling fascist regime. It was real.

Gordon recalled reading a book once, by an American author. His mind grasped for his name but missed. He remembered the use of the word *cyclopean* and had not understood the sense of proportion it was trying to convey.

He understood now.

Then, like a dying bull, the tentacled monstrosity slammed into the ocean.

For a moment, Gordon did not comprehend what he had just seen. The creature – whatever it was – was obscured by a grey haze.

And then his mind caught up with his vision and screamed. A second later his mouth got the message but his lungs were too sore to oblige. Instead, he whimpered, and that too was snatched and stolen by the hurricane around him.

The ground began to heave. Slowly at first, but the oscillations quickly grew in intensity and frequency, as if some elemental housewife were shaking a carpet. The trees behind him surrendered noisily, throwing themselves into the dirt, prostrate in supplication. Gordon knelt to the ground to maintain his balance and watched helplessly as the grey haze moved towards the shoreline, thickening, and darkening like a drunken temper made flesh.

Its height began to build rapidly, and by the time it entered the shallows, Gordon had given up guessing how high the tidal wave was. Miles probably. Such considerations were irrelevant.

As the apocalypse hit the shore, Gordon noticed the white foam, high at the top.

It is travelling slower at the bottom, he mused. *It's going to break over you, Harry.*

Gordon watched as the castle was enveloped, like an actor on stage stepping behind a curtain. The ground continued to buck, and he found that he had to lay flat. He turned over to watch the last of the sky, as the wave came crashing down, erasing all in its path.

And then he closed his eyes and bade black sleep welcome.

*

Gordon's chest heaved and his lungs gasped. Something was on top of him... no, s*omeone* was on top of him.

He started to struggle, arms thrashing wildly. The figure cleared him, and he realised that there was more than one.

Gordon sat up choking and spluttering. Tears ran down his face.

"Wha...?" he began.

"It's ok Doctor," Tate said soothingly, his hand reaching for Gordon's shoulder. "You're ok."

"You gave us quite a turn there," said Tuther from behind Tate.

Gordon looked about himself, bewildered.

"Wha...?" he began again.

"You fainted," said Tate. The window behind him was open now, letting a cool freshening breeze in. "We were just getting you onto the bed when you came around."

Gordon was confused. "How long was I...?"

"A couple of seconds... a minute at the most."

He felt like he had been gone hours, but already Gordon's experience was fading, like a bad dream. Yet he knew he had seen something. The purple sky.

The tentacle. God, the worms. And the wave. The memory was distant, but it was there.

Gordon had an uneasy feeling. It was more than a dream. He knew what he had seen. And heard. You do not hear the wind like that in a dream.

"Did I hit my head?" Gordon asked, groggily.

Tate shook his head. "No. We were close enough to catch you. Do you have a headache?"

Gordon nodded.

"Fetch some water Celus."

Tuther left the room, and Tate heard the sound of his footsteps on the staircase as he tried to find Mrs Torinelli. He came back with the elderly housekeeper a few minutes later, and Tate took her to one side to explain recent events to her.

Tuther sat next to Gordon on the side of the bed, his back to Tate.

"Doesn't matter how many times you see it, it still shakes you," he said quietly.

Gordon looked at Tuther with a deep loathing but made no reply.

"You'll try to write it off," Tuther muttered, looking out of the window. "A dream. A flight of fancy. The illusions of an overworked mind in a stressful situation."

"What do you know of it?" Gordon asked weakly, his throat still dry.

Tuther shrugged. "Blake once said that if the doors of Man's perception were cleansed, everything would appear as it is, infinite and majestic. Man sees through these narrow chinks that he has built into his cavern. I think Blake knew that Time was an artificial construct." Tuther paused, and then looked straight at Gordon. "And if one was to truly open their perceptions, you could experience past, present and future simultaneously."

Gordon looked hard at the man, still trying to control his breathing, trying to comprehend what Tuther was saying.

"What was it?" Gordon whispered back, not looking at Tuther any longer, but out into the late morning. "Past or future?"

"Doesn't matter," shrugged Tuther, looking to the coast. "It's already happened."

"It matters to me Mr Tuther. And a good deal of other folk too I shouldn't wonder." Gordon's voice had a steely resolve.

"I know it does Doctor. I know it does." Tuther got up and joined the conference with Tate and Mrs Torinelli.

*

It would be a good hour before Gordon felt safe enough to drive and the journey back to Maiden Castle was conducted in total silence. They were greeted by a bad tempered Sergeant Coombes who demanded to know where they had been.

Tate let Gordon explain the events of the morning, the similarity between the Ashley Cooper relic and what had been uncovered by the dig. He offered no explanation, just the facts, and Coombes knew that the chances of conviction were slim, especially now that his team had reported nothing abnormal in Tate's financial affairs.

*

Gordon watched the last of the police vans leave the grounds of Maiden Castle. Already the sounds of activity were beginning, and a steady stream of young men and women came past him with their trowels and sieves, like latter-day prospectors.

He still felt uneasy. The remnants of his vision clung to him like a greasy shadow. He turned, and saw Tate and Tuther watching him. Having loaded his kit bag into his car, he approached the two of them.

He tossed Tate the amulet they had examined earlier that day.

"Gentlemen," he said, shaking their hand in turn, "I trust that you'll understand that I hope never to see either of you again."

Not waiting for a reply, he turned around smartly, got into his car, and drove away from Maiden Castle as quickly as possible.

*

"What do you think it was?" Danielle asked. "Did Tate and Tuther poison him somehow? To induce the vision?"

Freeman smiled. "Not Tate. Tuther, maybe. You see, Doctor Gordon kept the broken vertebra from St Giles House. When I tracked him down, he was more than happy to give it to me - told me the thing was cursed. He had barely slept a full night in the fifty years since meeting Tuther and Tate."

"You have it?" Danielle was astonished. "Can I see it?"

"It is safe," the old man said sagely. "I had it tested. It is infused with lysergic acid."

Danielle looked flummoxed. "I should know what that is, shouldn't I?"

Freeman nodded. "The UN legalised it not six months ago."

"LSD?"

Freeman smiled. "LSD is the man made product. Lysergic acid is the raw material. Like a poppy is to heroin."

Danielle's mind was racing. "It was Tuther who broke open the vertebrae... he knew what the dust contained?"

Freeman shrugged an affirmation.

"But why?"

"Who knows? Maybe he had put those skeletons in the ground, and was scared that the Doctor was getting too close to the truth, and caused his little trip."

"But he would have had to have known about the Ashley-Cooper statue before..."

Freeman smiled again but said nothing.

Danielle's eyes widened. "Did he? How?"

"Danielle, I need you to understand that there is no record of Mr Tuther. Ever. He might have been in the War, but not by that name. I've been up and down and left to right through every census, every parish entry, and every military database that has ever been kept. Celus Tuther has never existed."

"An alias?"

"Maybe. Men matching his description pop up throughout history, and usually not in very pleasant circumstances. I can place him in Wewelsburg at the beginning of the nineteenth century, and then later when the British Army were slaughtered in Afghanistan in eighteen forty-two. A lord closely resembling him fought Baron Stanley on behalf of Richard The Third... and lost most of his forces in that conflict. But is it always him? Who can say?"

"You never found him? During your research?"

Freeman was silent. *Find him? No. But he found me...*

Danielle sat back and then leaned forward again as another thought came to her. "There is a part of your story that doesn't make sense. In the cavern with Price. King said the air was thick with dust. And there were worm fossils down there. Why didn't they all trip out like the good Doctor?"

Freeman continued to smile. "Maybe they did. Huge foetal sacks hanging from the ceiling? Ancient inscriptions? A secret cavern that could never be found again? Sounds pretty trippy to me."

Danielle was getting confused. "You doubt your own argument?"

"I didn't say that. It is just one interpretation. Maybe the fossils need to be broken to release the dust. Maybe the dust King saw was all the dander from whatever herd of hellish beasts was being grown down there."

Danielle nodded. She could see that. "So what of Doctor Gordon?"

"He led a very full, satisfying life, albeit with an inescapable sense of foreboding - his words. I interviewed him five years or so ago. He died about six months later at the age of one hundred and ten."

Danielle whistled, and then stopped. "How old is George Tate?"

"Today, a hundred and eight."

Danielle mulled this over. "That's two very old men. In this day and age, most men get to what? Early seventies?"

"Sixty-four," Freeman interjected.

"Really?" Danielle raised his eyebrows. "So we have two of your characters, involved in who knows what, living a very, very long time indeed."

Freeman nodded. "Three. Dennis King is still alive."

"Coincidence?"

"No such thing." It was Freeman's turn to lean forward. He reached for his Plex-Pad and pressed another of the screen icons. Nothing happened. He pressed it again. "Damned thing." He pressed it much more firmly this time, and the screen changed, showing the image of a small vial. A chemical structure and formula was given on the side.

"And what is that?"

"Ergot oil. The active ingredient is lysergic acid."

Danielle looked blankly. "What does it do?"

"Bluntly, it blows your mind. It opens up the door to all the realities of the universe and sets your consciousness free to realise that time and space are merely constructs of our perceptions. It also kills you very painfully."

Danielle still looked blank.

Freeman sighed. He was going to have to spell it out for the girl. "Danielle, I think that George Tate unlocked some ancient religious text, and with Celus Tuther, or whoever he is, found a recipe to take this safely," he pointed to the picture of the vial, "and when he did he saw a version of Doctor Gordon's vision. A side effect is incredible longevity."

"The Doctors vision? With the Apocalyptic Tentacle of Doom? That's real?"

"These things are subjective. Look at some of the work that went on with the particle smashers. They showed the myriad of layers that make up the universe, and our interpretation of reality really is just a narrow band on that spectrum."

Danielle was trying to grasp the concept. "So if what we experience is only a small part of reality, then where is the rest of it? And why aren't other people experiencing it? Why aren't more people coming forward…?"

Freeman laughed. "Where would you put someone who told you about the layers of reality?"

Danielle paused. "The nuthouse?"

"Delicately put. Unfortunately, George took several attempts to get his recipe for Ergot right. His mistakes poisoned him, although he didn't know it at the time. As he compounded his errors time and again, he became frailer and his mind began to deteriorate. He was admitted as a day patient to a nursing home at the age of seventy-seven, and then as a permanent resident two years later."

Danielle could not see where this was leading. "And what? He spread his end-of-the-world-visions around a nursing home?"

Freeman smiled. "In a manner of speaking, yes."

CHAPTER 5

Daniel 2:44-45
And in the days of those kings
The God of Heaven shall bring His kingdom to Earth,
That it shall never fall but reign from alpha to omega.
It shall break in pieces all other kingdoms and bring them to an end.

And you will know when you see a city was cut from a mountain by no human hand,
That it broke in pieces the iron, the bronze, the clay, the silver, and the gold.
A great God has made known only to worthy men what shall be after this.

My name is Doctor Andy Cullum. In 2006 I was a General Practitioner and consultant Gerontologist, based permanently at the Paternoster Nursing Home, North West London.

Sunday 3rd December 2006
"Turn it down! TURN! IT! DOWN!" Kandian roared. The old man was sitting in his window bay, his paint brush an occasional flurry only broken by his insistence that his neighbour turn that accursed music down.

Nurse Dawkins sighed, and looked to the porter, Simon, who shrugged.

It was the same every night. They could almost time it. As the sun began to set, their charge, Eric Kandian – a once talented artist of no particular renown – would begin to rant and rage, demanding that his neighbours' music be turned down.

Of course, there was no music. There had never been. He had been this way since he was admitted eighteen months ago, but he had grown markedly worse in the last few weeks, and it seemed that each episode was beginning earlier and earlier in the day.

His daughter, Amy, came dutifully every night to sit with him and speak about the events of the day. Lately, the visits were becoming shorter, as if she sensed her father moving further and further from her, as his disease increasingly isolated the functional parts of his mind.

There was a knock at the door and Nurse Buckland came in, accompanied by Doctor Cullum.

"Time for your tablets Eric," Buckland said.

Kandian harrumphed loudly.

Cullum nodded Dawkins over. "How's he been today?" he asked, looking at Buckland trying to give Kandian his nightly medication.

"Not great," she replied. "He had a good night's sleep. Maybe five or six hours. He was quite bright this morning and had most of his breakfast. We took him for his bath around ten and he was good as gold. He became quite agitated towards the end of lunch and started throwing a few bits around. That's why Simon's here."

Simon nodded in acknowledgment of his role.

"We tried to get him painting, and he seemed to calm down for a bit, but... well you can see for yourself. It looks like he's building up for a full episode."

"Cognitive function?"

"Pretty disjointed. Not as bad as he was at the beginning of the week. He only asked for his mother once today, and then he had a bit of a cry after that. Occasionally he'll talk to me as if I'm his wife, reminiscing about a holiday or friends. But then he forgets."

Cullum's nose twitched, and he looked about.

"Sorry," said Dawkins. "His pad leaked during his afternoon nap. We've not had time to change the bedding."

"Has his daughter been yet?" Amy Kandian had a reputation for wanting everything to be just so for her father, and there were no exceptions.

"No. She'll be here around six-ish. Half-hour or so. Do you want to speak to her?"

Cullum thought for a moment. "No. I was thinking about adjusting his prescription, but I think we'll let the last lot settle down. Maybe give it a few more weeks. Make sure that bed gets changed before she arrives."

He turned, and watched Buckland hand Kandian his tablets. This was better than a couple of nights ago. That had been a major operation. Cullum wanted to spend a bit of time with Kandian, see if some behavioural therapy might help the man. He had only been recently transferred to his list from Dr Roberts, who had apparently left without giving any notice. The staff room had been awash with gossip of an affair with a nurse, who had also left at the same time, and that the two had eloped. But when the police visited and started asking questions it became apparent that something more serious had happened. The management were tight-lipped about it, as usual.

However, time was against Cullum tonight, and he wanted to try and have a proper conversation with his next patient. He left with Buckland in tow.

Cullum knocked at the next door. A little childish laugh was all the response he got, and after a moment Nurse Arnold opened the door.

No orderly was necessary for Professor Tate. The man was largely harmless, or at least had been for the last two years. Tate sat in the bay window, gazing out across the lawn, towards the road. Arthritis had balled his hands into little more than claws, and his spine curved alarmingly forward. But for all the discomfort the man must have been in, Cullum had always known him to be in a relatively good mood. He had his moments - a bit of confusion, occasional frustration - but on the whole, one of his more well-disposed patients.

"How has he been?" Cullum asked Arnold, whilst Buckland went over to hand Tate his nightly prescription.

"Fine today. His usual self. He had a patch around four-ish. Uh... did the late shift make you aware of what happened last night?"

Cullum shook his head. "No. What happened?"

"He hit his son. I don't mean a lunge. A proper right hook. I've never seen him move so fast."

Cullum frowned. This was unusual. "When was this? Last night?"

Arnold nodded. "About half-seven. Maybe eight. Just before shift change."

"What happened exactly?"

"I spoke to Mr Tate Junior..."

Cullum flicked through some paperwork. "Devon?"

"That's him. I was trying to convince him to go to the hospital. George here hit him so hard. I was worried that he had fractured his cheek but he refused."

"Did you find out what set him off?"

"Not really. I was outside when it happened - you know giving them some privacy - but the door was open, in case they needed me. The son – Devon – said something about selling George's house, and he seemed ok with that. Then he said that he had found some old boxes. Manuscripts and research, and that he had tried to donate it to George's old employer – The British Museum – but they had refused it. Well, George seemed to lose it. I mean in an instant. No build up. He told his son to burn it all, and when he protested, well that was when George hit him. I was in the doorway by that time. I had heard George change. But he moved so fast that I couldn't stop him."

Cullum nodded. "And he's been alright today?"

"Yes, quite lucid actually."

Cullum nodded again. "Do you think he'll be ok to talk to?"

"I should think so. Do you want me to call Simon just in case?"

Cullum shook his head. "I don't think that'll be necessary." The recent Patient Aggression Management course was still fresh in his mind. And besides, George Tate was a slight man. Agile maybe and perhaps his son had been complacent. It certainly sounded that he had done something to provoke the old man. He would try and catch him later to find out what it was all about.

Cullum approached Professor Tate. "George?"

Tate turned to look at Cullum, his brow furrowing.

"Hello, George. Do you remember me?"

Tate's furrows increased and shook his head. "You look like someone I used to know. Doctor type. Um... what was his name? Callum? No. Cullum, that was it. Colossal wanker of a man. Doubt he could even get it up!" Tate leaned forward and whispered loudly, "I think he was... you know... a gay. Walked like a mincer. Always wore those poncey pink shirts. Like yours."

Cullum looked hard at Tate. *So much for the lucidity.*

Tate's lined face creased into a broad smile, eyes twinkling. "Of course I know it's you! I'm just having you on. Grab a chair and have a sit-down, Andrew."

Cullum relaxed. Even though it was only ever his grandfather that had called him Andrew, he was man enough to admit Tate had caught him out. Again. The old man had a history of little jokes and was a favourite with the nurses.

Arnold stifled a giggle, and Buckland left quickly, suppressing a laugh. Cullum's salmon shirts were a running joke in the staff room. *No doubt this will come up later,* Cullum thought, drawing a chair up to where Tate sat.

"How have you been today?"

"Oh, you know. Mustn't grumble. Usual aches."

"Nurse Arnold said you're still not using the day room."

"Of course I'm not," huffed Tate indignantly. "They're all mad! I'm just forgetful."

Cullum made a note.

"That said," Tate continued, "if you were to bring back a few of those student nurses, I might be persuaded..." The old man smiled broadly again, eyes twinkling. "No offence Lisa!" he called over his shoulder.

"You know I'll always be your gal," Nurse Arnold chuckled back.

"Did you get out in the garden?" Cullum asked.

"A little. Legs aren't what they used to be."

Cullum noted the savage scar on Tate's shin. The skin was dry and flaking in places.

"How did you get that?"

Tate's demeanour changed and a coldness entered. "You know perfectly well Andrew."

"Just checking..."

"What? What are you just checking?" The characteristic twinkle had been replaced by hardness that made Cullum uneasy.

"George. You have ergotism. Sometimes you are gone for days. Sometimes it takes you a while to come back."

Tate looked out the window. "I know," he said quietly. "I'm here today."

"You were gone last week. For most of it."

Tate said nothing.

"Where did you go?"

Tate's lips started to curl into a rueful smile. "I don't know. It's far away, but right here at the same time. I suppose that is just a forgetful old man not making much sense."

"What can you tell me about your condition George?"

Tate knew he was being tested again. "What do you want me to say, Andrew? I did it to myself. You know that."

"Tell me again."

Tate tried not to be frustrated. "I took a heroic quantity of drugs in the eighties and nineties and now I'm paying the price. Can't write. Barely stand. Mind shot to buggery. Shit myself so the nice nurses will touch me down there..."

The twinkle was back.

"How much for a quickie Lisa?"

"More than you can afford!"

"See! And I thought this was private healthcare. Sort it out Andrew!"

Cullum smiled. He knew the old man was playing, but he also knew he had an uncanny knack of deflecting questions.

"George, I have your latest test results back. It's not good news..."

"Excellent! Does that mean I get to request a final supper? Can I have Nurse Arnold for dessert?"

"George." Cullum was being serious now.

Tate saw it and settled down. "Sorry Doctor," he mumbled.

"George, the vasoconstriction around your war-wound has been resisting treatment for quite a few months. I'm worried that gangrene might set in. I want to schedule you for surgery to..."

"NO!" Tate spat.

Cullum flinched. Tate never spoke like that.

"Andrew, I don't mind being your guinea pig. I know that what I've got is unique, and you want to prod and poke me and give me all sorts of pills. And that's fine. But Andrew, if you want to start hacking bits off me," Tate raised a gnarled finger towards Cullum, "you can take a long walk! A very long walk! By the stars, you people..."

"George," Cullum tried to soothe the old man. "If we don't remove your leg and gangrene sets in, it will kill you."

Tate laughed, braying maniacally. "Andrew, Andrew, Andrew. You can be a real wonder sometimes. Look at me. I'm eighty-one. My daughter never comes to see me. My ex-wife won't return my letters. My son is so liberal he's basically a commie. I've watched just about all my friends die, and now I'm paying good money to sit around all day and be patronised by boys like you. You keep promising an end, but it never happens. The liver failure was supposed to get me last year. The cock-rot the year before. Still not happened, has it? If Death is the best you've got Andrew my son, then bring him in! Let's liven the place up a bit. Lord knows it could do with it!"

Cullum let Tate finish and kept quiet as the old man turned to look back out of the window. Silence hung between the two men for a few minutes.

"*Hznuggah*," muttered Tate.

"What?"

"What?"

"You just said something."

Tate shrugged. "Just drifted."

Cullum looked at the old man. Of course, he was right. According to everything they knew about the human body, Tate should have died years ago. But here he was, still ticking over. He had even outlived a couple of his doctors. And that definitely was not supposed to happen.

"Ok. What do you want to do?" Cullum asked.

"*Yhzhera*,"

"George?"

Tate turned to his doctor, rheumy-eyed, and frowned, his lines appearing as furrows in a field. "Andrew?"

"Are you all right George?"

Tate's mind seemed to stumble, and he chewed his bottom lip. "Been here a while? You shouldn't sneak up on an old man."

"No George. I was just passing," Cullum smiled gently. "Thought I'd say hello."

"Hmm..." Tate returned to gazing out the window.

Cullum looked over to Arnold, who just nodded, and mouthed *It's ok*. She was more familiar with Tate's episodes and did not seem unduly concerned.

Tate was chuntering under his breath again, and Cullum strained to catch the words.

"*Da da Danu ha, da sa hznuggah, da da Danu ha, yhzhera, yhzhera...*"

The drone began to repeat, but Cullum fancied that Tate's eyes had brightened, and were fixed on a point far away.

Tate stopped suddenly, and turning to Cullum he asked, "What time is it?"

"A little after five-thirty."

"Hmmm... my nephew is late."

There was a knock at the door. "That'll be him. Celus get yourself in here!"

Tuther stepped through. "Alright, Unc?"

"No, I'm bloody well not. This quack keeps threatening with imminent death, and Lisa still won't give it up!"

"The world is going to hell Unc," Tuther made for Tate, smiling at Arnold and Cullum.

"You'd know you upstart!" Tate retorted, and then to Cullum, "Investment banker. Milked Argentina in o-one and o-two."

"Yeah, yeah. Who do you think pays for this place?" Tuther sat down, close to Tate.

"Well, could you see your way to paying for Lisa? I just want to do it once more before I go." Tate was beaming and his eyes sparkled.

"I'd snap you in two George," Arnold said, and then to Tuther, "I'll give you a bit of time. I'll leave the door open – bit of a to-do last night. I'll just be outside if you need anything."

Cullum followed Arnold out. "Is he always like that?" he said to the nurse, once they were in the corridor.

"How do you mean?"

"You know. In and out like that?"

"Oh yes. Always been like it. Even when he was an outpatient. I think of it like driving in the mountains and trying to get radio reception. He sort of fades in and out. One minute clear as you like. Next, static..."

"FOR GODS SAKE TURN IT DOWN!" the sound of an easel crashing in the adjacent room cut Arnold off. Cullum saw the red emergency light winking at the nurses' station.

Urgent Assistance.

Two orderlies had already barrelled past Cullum before he had even spun on his heel. He met Dawkins in the doorway. She was clutching at a nasty gash on the side of her head and it was evident that Kandian had done more than knock his easel over.

Cullum passed Dawkins on to Arnold who led her towards the nurses' station. Another orderly was charging up the corridor and an older nurse was following him.

Cullum entered Kandian's room. Simon and the two other orderlies were circling in on Kandian who was brandishing the end of his brush at them. His eyes bulged and there was spittle on his chin. His robe had become undone, revealing dark hair protruding from over-worn dark grey pyjamas.

"Alright boys," Cullum said to the two orderlies. If the man became violent then they would have to restrain him, and that was when things got broken. And he did not want to have to explain *that* to Amy Kandian.

The two orderlies retreated to the doorway. The older nurse said something to them and they stepped out of sight, although they were clearly still lurking in the corridor. Simon stayed where he was, watching Kandian.

"Now Eric," said Cullum. "You appear to have caused quite a mess here. Can you..."

"WHAT IS WRONG WITH YOU? CAN'T YOU HEAR IT!" screamed Kandian, pointing jerkily to the dividing wall between his room and Tate's. "ALL THE TIME! JUST TURN IT DOWN!" he screamed at the wall.

"Ah... Eric? Eric!" Cullum could see that Kandian was probably at his most agitated. "What can you hear?"

Kandian looked at him incredulously. "Are you joking with me? Are you really joking with me?" Kandian started towards Cullum and Simon stepped forward.

"Yeah?" Kandian said to Simon. "I'll have you too big boy. Pair of you! I know your game! But I won't! I won't tell! And I won't tell him!" He spun, screaming the last sentence at the wall. Spittle was flying from the man's mouth, and Cullum noticed a throbbing vein in the man's temple. He knew he did not have long to defuse the situation.

It had been quite a while since Kandian had been this bad, but Cullum knew it had been building for a long time. Maybe one of the more secure rooms would be best for tonight at least.

Cullum sat down in an effort to take some tension out of the atmosphere. "What won't you tell me, Eric?"

"Do you think I'm stupid?" he sneered.

He's ill, not an idiot.

"Maybe if you tell me, I'll turn the music down."

Are you sure you want to play into his psychosis?

"You can't break me! YOU CAN NEVER BREAK ME!"

This isn't working Andy. Cullum tried a different tack. "The music really bothers you?"

"How can it not bother you? How can you just sit there like it is nothing? Did they give you ear plugs? Did they did they did they?" Kandian started to circle Cullum, to get a look at his ear.

Cullum turned his head so the profile was facing Kandian. "No ear plugs. But if the music really bothers you, what about we move you to another room? Where it's quieter?"

Old Patricia McDermott had passed away late yesterday. It would not take much to get her room prepared. It would have been cleaned already. Perhaps just the bed to be made.

Kandian's whole persona changed. "No! No no no! Oh god, please. Don't move me. I'm sorry. I'm so sorry."

Cullum saw a dark stain radiating from the old man's crotch. Kandian had wet himself.

"I... I... I... please. No. I'm sorry about that nurse. I didn't mean to hurt her. I'll be quiet. I'll be good. Please don't send me away. I'll be so so so good. Please."

The smell of ammonia began to fill the air.

Kandian was imploring childishly now. "I... I'll clean up. Yes. I'll tidy everything. I'll do my double chores. Double chores. Yes? Yours too? Yes. I'm sorry. Please. No. Don't send me away."

Kandian sat on the edge of the bed and began to gently weep. The fight had left him completely.

The old familiar feeling of pity stirred in the pit of Cullum's stomach. "Hey now," he said gently, moving across to sit on the bed next to Kandian. "What's all this? There's no need..."

"I must see The Lights, Doctor. I need to see them."

Cullum frowned. "Which lights Eric?"

Huge sobs wracked the old man, and he just nodded towards the upturned painting in the bay window. Cullum, leant forward to pick it up.

"*Plllleeease* be careful. Oh please please please!" Kandian was starting to panic again.

"It's ok, I'm just making sure it's not damaged."

Cullum picked up the canvas, turned it over, and shivered. He knew that Kandian's therapist had been encouraging him to paint more. He was often at his most coherent when he was engaged in an activity, but this... this unnerved Cullum.

The style reminded him of something of an elderly Turner if Lovecraft had read to him. The immense cityscape seemed to pass beyond the boundaries of the canvas. Colossal towers arched from domed and spired buildings towards a vast canopy of stars above. At the forefront was some sort of dock where giant greasy waves seemed to lurch hungrily at the quayside.

There were no people, but in the background, behind the grotesquely twisted buildings, were the nearly invisible outlines of monstrous half forms in loathsome contortions that loomed over the city, almost blending in with the shadow of the night that appeared to be falling.

Whilst, not an expert, Cullum felt that there was an almost excessive attention to detail. A number of the buildings, hewn from a sickly blue and red stone, seemed to be clad in metal and were inscribed with an unidentifiable text. The pale green light seemed to fall limply through some of the impossibly elongated doorways, as though it had lost the will to shine properly. A light pall of smoke or mist hung in some quarters, whilst in others, some sort of creeper was threatening to encase the buildings.

Something inside Cullum was repulsed by this depiction of bloated wealth and hubris that had fallen into dereliction. But there was something else too... almost as if he recognised the setting. Something nagged at the back of his mind as if trying to place the city and answer a forgotten question.

"It's... ah... it's very good Eric."

"Thankyou!" Kandian replied in an excited gush, chewing on his own fingernails in a quasi-frenzy.

"What...er... what do you call it?"

"It's the Lights!" he said triumphantly. "The Lights of New York!"

Cullum had been to New York. The painting he held did not represent it in any way he recognised. He nodded his head. "I see. And when did you go to New York?"

Kandian's face contorted into disbelief. "I've never been. But I can see it from here." He pointed towards the window.

Cullum looked in the direction he was pointing. The sun was setting, and beyond the well-manicured lawns of the Paternoster grounds, he could see the thin line of trees, then Milton Road. On the other side of the street, the abandoned council flats sat squat, like unimpressed housewives of a certain age and weight. They were due to be demolished soon.

"You mean the flats? This is your interpretation of the flats?"

Kandian laughed falsely and loudly. "Ha ha. That's good. Ha ha!" Then seeing Cullum's question was genuine. "You know. It's where we all live. If She'd..."

Cullum tried to follow the tenses and failed. "You live here?" he said pointing to the painting.

Kandian nodded.

"This is the nursing home?"

Kandian looked confused. "I thought this was a nursing home," he said looking about himself as if he had only just realised where he was.

"It is."

"I thought so."

"So where is this?" Cullum pointed to the painting again.

Kandian's brow furrowed. "I told you. New York."

"And we live there.... here?"

Kandian nodded fervently. "We always did. But then we didn't for a bit. And then we always did again. That's where Dr Roberts lives now."

Cullum could sense that Kandian's disassociation was rushing back in like a tidal bore, but he had mentioned Chris. Cullum tried to get Kandian to focus.

"Eric, do you know where Dr Roberts is?"

Kandian nodded enthusiastically, still chewing on the ends of his fingers.

"Can you tell me? Or show me where he is?"

Kandian pointed to one of the smaller towers in his painting.

Cullum sighed inwardly.

"He is there," Kandian said, "He has always been there."

"Except when he was here," said Cullum. "When he treated you."

"Nope. He was there then too. And now. It's where he always will be."

Cullum tried a new tack. "Where do I live Eric?"

Kandian looked intensely at his painting, eyes searching maniacally. "Hmmm... nope. Not on this one."

The old man got up and crossed the floor with such swiftness that Cullum half flinched and Simon took a single step forward as if to close the distance between them, but seeing that Kandian was just reaching for his other paintings he relaxed.

Kandian began to rifle through a set of frames that leaned against the wall. Cullum had not noticed these before and began to appreciate how prolific Kandian had become in the last few months.

"Hmm... nope... nope... nope... hmm, this one!" Kandian said triumphantly, taking a frame out, and presented it to Cullum. "You live here," and jabbed his finger to a domed building.

The painting was not dissimilar to the one Kandian had been working on and appeared to show the same cityscape albeit from an alternate vantage point. The light that was cast on the buildings was a sickly red, giving the impression the whole thing had just been vomited up. Cullum noticed that there was no water in the foreground of this version, but rather the twisted foundations seemed to rest on a single great rotting leaf. A thick disfigured stem could just be seen connecting to the deformed foliage before disappearing off the end of the frame. Again, half-formed monstrosities lurked on the deep horizon, and Cullum fancied they were looking straight at him.

"I live here?" Cullum asked.

"Yup yup yup. You were born over here," Kandian pointed to an adjacent tower, "but when you married Mandy you moved here."

Cullum felt his blood turn icy. He had only just started dating Amanda Impsi, a district nurse who occasionally worked a bank shift at Paternoster House. He had not even mentioned it to any of the staff yet.

"Eric. How did you know about Mandy?"

Kandian looked confused. "Because you live together. Until the end."

"Until the end... of what?"

"Oh, everything everything everything."

Cullum felt a growing sense of unease. It was clear that Kandian's cognitive function was impaired, but could such lucidity and insight really be a by-product of a diseased mind? Maybe he had taken a phone call from Amanda and Kandian had overheard.

"You both looked after your mother very well," Kandian rambled on. "You think that no-one knows, but we all do. It was a good thing you did. A good thing, yes. Yes. Yes. You had to let her go."

If Cullum's blood was icy before, it was frozen now. "What do you mean Eric?" he said evenly.

"When she was ill. You helped her on her way. She walked with... you know."

Cullum had not discussed his mother's cancer with anyone, not even with Amanda. It was advanced, and the effect of the morphine was beginning to diminish. The previous weekend, she had asked him to give her something. Something stronger. Cullum knew what she had meant. He had refused. But she had asked again during the week. It would have been easy.

What do you say to a man who knows that you've killed your own mother before you do?

Cullum changed the subject. His attention was drawn to the top right corner of the painting. There seemed to be three bright stars and behind them a small spiral of a much dimmer constellation.

"What are these? The bright ones?" Cullum asked.

Kandian frowned again. "You know."

Cullum shook his head.

"You silly. Everyone knows. Three stars turn, She will come."

"Who?"

Kandian's entire countenance visibly darkened, and he looked around furtively. "You're not supposed to say," he said quietly.

"Who?" Cullum asked again.

"Don't say her name! The Third Twine says we should never say..." Kandian rose from the bed where he sat, the childish quality in his voice was gone, replaced by the raving desperation of only a few minutes ago.

"Ok, ok, ok. I'm sorry..." Cullum tried to calm Kandian.

"YOU MUST NEVER NEVER NEVER SAY HER NAME!"

"Ok, I won't say her name. I'm sorry. Here, what can you tell me about the other stars? The dimmer ones."

Kandian shrugged. "They say they aren't there. But we know they are." His temper had abated as quickly as it had come as if he had forgotten he was angry at all.

"Who says they aren't there?"

"The Raven Men. They say we are just playing games."

"Who are the Raven Men, Eric?"

Kandian shrugged again. "Just the Raven Men. They say the faithful never sleep, but still, they don't see. They tell us they do. But we know. And we still see them," he tapped at the dim constellation.

"We?"

"Yes."

"Who is the 'we'?"

"All of us. You and me and Mandy and Dr Roberts and all of us."

"Do you mean everyone at the nursing home?"

"No."

"Everyone in the world?"

Kandian nodded. "Everyone everyone everyone."

Cullum paused. He heard heavy footsteps from the adjoining room. *George's nephew must be leaving. He didn't stay long.*

"How long has everyone lived there?" he asked gently.

"Always. It's our home."

"Where are you now?" Cullum could feel that he was pushing Kandian's delusion to its limit. If he could let him find the flaw in it, then he might pull out of it himself.

"This place?"

"Yes. The nursing home."

"Oh, this should not be," Kandian answered quite cheerfully.

"But it is. This home is real."

"Yes. But only for now. When it is not now, then it will not be."

Cullum felt he was engaging in a battle of wits with a Zen Master, and he was losing.

"When will it not be now?" he asked.

Kandian laughed. "Always. It's never now."

Cullum knew he had lost. One last try. "Eric, can you see New York now?"

Kandian gazed out of the window, peering intently beyond the line of trees. "No," he said eventually. "The curtain is drawn."

"The curtain?"

Kandian just shook his head and offered no explanation.

Cullum gave up. "Well, I like your paintings, Eric. I like them very much. Will you paint some more for me?" he said, standing from his chair.

"Yes. But can you turn the music down?"

This again.

"I tell you what Eric, I'll go next door with Nurse Arnold, and see if I can turn the music down, and you paint some more for me. Ok?"

Kandian nodded.

As he got up, Cullum thought he heard something. Like a distant chanting, and then it was gone. He strained to catch it again, but nothing.

Cullum crossed the room. Standing in the doorway, so that Kandian could see him, he said very clearly, "Nurse Arnold, could you please ask..."

Kandian screamed.

Cullum knew that scream. It was not the scream of the demented or the insane. It was the piercing shriek of absolute terror. The shrill cry that goes through absolutely every soul without question and says *Do not turn, do not look. RUN! Just RUN!*

In the split-second that followed, Cullum was dimly aware of a roar, as if a prehistoric beast had awoken, startled and ravenous. He half turned, and fancied he saw a faint purple light through the window.

And then his world went utterly black.

*

[Maiden Castle Stele 37]

Danu sent Greine to rescue her daughter Kore, first child of Riah, who had been imprisoned for giving out apples to the peasantry, and setting them free from the evil Lord Shemel. Greine freed Kore and the peasants but was chased by Lord Shemel on a steed of thunder when he discovered that Kore had stolen his magic rod. The peasants were turned into rivers by Danu, and Greine and Kore escaped by sailing away leaving Lord Shemel to drown.

Danu gave Shemel's steed of thunder to Gofannon that he might provide a mate with it and so produce a herd of war horses for Greine's army.

*

Cullum coughed, and opened his eyes. He was lying on the floor. His brain was trying to process information, but his ears were ringing, and he could feel liquid dripping across his face and onto his lips. He instinctively tasted it. Blood.

It was stiflingly hot, and he was already covered with a thick sheen of sweat.

He tried to raise himself, but he was pinned. He moved his arm a little, sweeping aside some dust. He recognised the carpet. He was still in Paternoster House. For a moment his mind mused at how different things looked from this perspective.

His eyes fluttered up, and he could just make out a form in front of him slumped against a pile of rubble. Nurse Lisa Arnold. She was not moving, and judging by the amount of blood pooling around her, she probably never would again.

Cullum tried to turn his head to face the other way, but could not. He was held firmly down by something on top of him. Something very big and very heavy. And that something was slowly crushing the breath from him.

Despite his predicament and the carnage around him, Cullum felt a sense of serenity. There seemed to be some unspeakably twisted irony to the situation, and his dry sense of humour appreciated the cosmic joke. A man renowned for his penchant for control was now utterly helpless as events moved on without considering him.

How long had he been here? Perhaps an hour? Maybe more. He struggled to catch his breath. Nothing felt broken. Plenty of bruises. Maybe one or two cuts. Probable concussion. He waggled his fingers, and then his toes. Everything worked there.

Cullum tried to assess the situation. Clearly, something had happened. With all the dust, maybe part of the building had collapsed. He tried to recall the events before his had blacked out. He was talking to Kandian. Then he went into the corridor. And then... Something hovered on the edge of his memory. What? A sound? A voice? Maybe it would come back to him later.

Cullum returned to his idea of building collapse. Why? Paternoster House was purpose-built, albeit with a Jacobean style frontage to match the nearby manorial house. A structural defect was unlikely. So then what? An explosion maybe? But from where? His mind instantly went to the gas store, where they stored the oxygen cylinders and other gasses. For as long as he could remember he had told the management that the room needed to be temperature controlled. Or moved to an outside store. They had fobbed him off. Budget pressures and the like.

So there had been an explosion, and he was trapped. Probably under some ceiling tiles, and maybe some beams or rubble for good measure. His options were limited. He could barely move, and there was nothing to hand that he could prop against the dead weight on his back.

After nine-eleven there had been numerous documentaries about building collapse and miraculous tales of survival from within a zone known as a Triangle of Life. An area where beams and struts had fallen in such a way as to create a small space that someone could survive in. Cullum presumed that judging by the pressure on his back, he was not in one.

Whichever way he looked at it, he wanted to laugh. He was completely helpless. There was nothing he could do. No tools he could reach. No-one nearby that he could signal to. All he could do was lay there. And he found that he really needed the toilet.

He tried to call out, to cry for help. Only a low rasp came out.

Best save your energy, Andy.

Cullum tried to take a breath to call out again and felt a catching. Possibly a broken rib. Maybe serious.

He was amused by the things that were now running through his mind. He had broken that rib as a teenager when his youthful exuberance had seen him take up kickboxing with his younger brother. Tom had not lasted long. He never did. He was the feckless sort who drifted from one thing to another without really giving it a proper try. How many times had he tried university? Four? Five?

Cullum, on the other hand, had enjoyed the martial arts. There was always the odd knock or scrape, but one time, when sparring, a side kick had caught him flush on his lowest rib. He had felt it break, and the air evaporated from him. It was not bad, but his mother had hugged him like she was never going to let him go. That was his first serious injury as a child, and it probably took her some time to get used to the idea.

His father, by contrast, had seemed almost proud of the injury. Fighting was a Man's sport. And when you fought someone got hurt. Next time it would not be his son. Because his son would learn, and fight back harder. Like a Man.

Cullum half smiled to himself, at the memory of his father. A local John Wayne. *Shuddup and drink your milk pilgrim.* His father had often done that impression at breakfast. His two sons had always laughed along like it was the best joke ever.

He winced as the rib began to dig in.

Even now the rib was nobbly where it had broken. Amanda had caressed it on their first night together, and he had told her the story. She had been horrified that such violence was allowed in these classes. She did not understand. Few people ever did. It was a way of life. The discipline. The sweat. The camaraderie. Cullum was not a man with many friends. Plenty of associates. But few friends. And of those friends, he had met the majority at that kickboxing club.

His bladder reminded him that the need to urinate was becoming increasingly urgent.

He still tried to train at the club. But with work and now with Amanda, it was getting harder and harder to get down there. It had been at least a month since he had last been. His instructor was relaxed about it. He had been teaching for over thirty years, and he was used to seeing the cycles in his students' lives. Sometimes they came back to the club. Sometimes they did not. But they would always be part of the family.

Cullum had tried to get Amanda interested, and she had come along once and watched him training. But training is not a spectator sport, and he was unsurprised that she had decided not to take it further.

He tried to breathe again and felt himself wheezing.

The memory of his mother's hug came rushing back in an instant. Cullum remembered the old photos - how impossibly young they had all looked. His mother without a grey hair. Him without a line or a wrinkle. It was another time. Another life. When his father had still been alive.

Cullum remembered when his father had become ill, and when they knew it was terminal. The Old Man had laughed it off. *The wheel still turns, son. What starts ends.*

He had never known his father to be philosophical, but those words often returned to him. *The wheel still turns.* He supposed it was true. That we are ultimately heading back to wherever it was we had come from, whatever that might be.

Even though they knew it was coming, his mother had cried when the end came for his father. He cried too, but he knew he could cry. He did not know his mother could cry. That seemed silly now, but Cullum reflected briefly on how he had viewed his parents as demi-gods. Of course, the roles were reversed now. The Cancer was eating away at his mother, much the same way it had his father. The consultant had been honest with him. Brutally honest. His mother was happy to let go. She wanted to see her husband again. It was just the length of time it was taking.

At this rate, he would beat her to it.

He wheezed again. It hurt more this time. Whatever it was that was on his back was slowly pressing him insistently into the floor, like a rolling pin flattening some particularly lumpy pastry. He did not know where the break on the rib was, but he could guess, and if he was unlucky it would puncture his lung. He would survive for a while on the other, but if he kept on being crushed into the carpet... well best not to dwell on these things.

He hated the thought of someone having to tell his mother that he was dead. *Please don't let it be Tom.*

It had been years since he had spoken to his brother. Despite the similarity of their appearance, their personalities were near polar opposites. He had left home as soon as A Levels were over. University. Then training. Rented a place with friends. Then bought. He saw his parents often enough, but he never moved back.

Tom on the other hand... well, he never seemed to get going. He had done great at A Levels, better than his older brother, but then he had stalled. He tried a semester at university but that had not worked out. So he moved back home. Various retail jobs had wound up with him on a management training scheme, but he quit that before he could finish. More retail jobs, then a call centre. Still living at home. Then a decision to be a teacher. He had quit that half way through. Somehow he had then reached a decision to run a bar. That folded within a year. Back to the call centre. And now what? To be a DJ? Still at home. And through all of this, even though he and his mother had worried about him, Tom had seemed oblivious. His mother's enduring support had probably not helped, but that is what his mother did – encouraged regardless.

His bladder felt like it was bursting.

Cullum probably would have let his younger brother drift along, but when Tom started trying to force him to prescribe heavy drugs, Cullum guessed that perhaps all was not as great as his brother claimed. Shortly after that, Tom confessed his debt problems. They were sizeable.

Cullum did not tell his mother. He knew what the worry would do to her. Cullum had tried to strike a deal with Tom; he would clear his debts if his brother would knuckle down to something. He even offered to rent a flat for him, so he could move out. Get some independence. That conversation had not gone well, and the vitriolic recriminations that ended what had started as a reasonable discussion had been the last time they had talked.

Cullum wheezed again and this time, he felt the rib bite physically deeper. He tried to relax. Maybe help would come. Maybe not. Best to give them a sporting chance.

Tom had tried to make contact. A year or so after the argument he had emailed him. But it was more of the same. "I've been doing this and that and little of such." Cullum just did not have the energy to deal with him.

He kept tabs on Tom via the myriad of social networking sites, albeit as anonymously as possible. His mother always gave him positive news about his brother, but he knew that, at best, that was gloss, and more often than not she had been fed out-and-out lies.

Cullum had seen it before with his patients. Families rally around ne'er-do-wells who had been admitted for whatever it was they had done too much of this time. They always believed that this was a turning point. This was just the scare they needed. It seldom was. It tended to be nothing more than a slow spiral into oblivion and those personalities were like black holes – stand too close, and you got sucked down with them.

He had seen it once. A boy, not even eighteen, came in with his uncle. The uncle had overdosed, and the nephew had called the ambulance. What had emerged was a history of cocaine abuse, a long stint in prison, and when he had come out, the Uncle's sister – the boy's mother - had taken him in. Even though she had two young sons, she had promised her husband that her brother was clean and would get his life back on track. He just needed a place to stay for a year or two.

The husband knew otherwise, but what could he say to his wife? The uncle had taken a cleaning job and, for a while, it looked like he was going to stay sober. It did not last. Before the twelve months were out, he was back on the smack, and when his sister had refused to give him money, he put in as many windows of their house as he could before the police had arrived. She had not wanted to press charges, but the husband would not let him back in. Cullum could not blame him. And so the Uncle drifted from sofa to sofa until he found himself in a squat. Somehow he had got hold of his eldest nephew's mobile number and begged to meet him, probably in the hope of getting some cash. What had happened in-between was hazy, but it seemed the Uncle was unable to cope, and when the nephew found him he was unconscious. He never came round.

Best intentions and all that. But always get as far away as possible from black-hole personalities. Cullum had to cut Tom loose.

Cullum wheezed again. The bite was deeper this time. A lot deeper. *Nearly time Andy.*

He sighed, and let his bladder go. He felt the warm liquid spreading over his trousers, and seep into the carpet. Too quickly it started to go cold.

Cullum wondered if his vocation had made him cynical. He loved the idea of a wife and kids. He had seen how happy it had made his friends. But he had also seen the flipside with his patients. Shifts within A&E were a mandatory part of the training, and that was where he had seen the worst. Car accidents where the baby seat had not been strapped in properly. Cabinets full of bleach that had not been locked. Stabbings at a school. Who takes a knife to school?

It did not matter how old the child was. The mother's howl was always the same. It came from a deep place. The core of her being. The father grim-faced desperately trying to physically hold his wife or girlfriend together as she fell apart from the inside.

Cullum hoped his mother would pass away before the news of his death reached her.

Wheeze...gurgle.

Cullum felt the bite sinking in. He knew it was probably only a quarter-inch or so, but it felt like it had gone all the way through him.

He groaned involuntarily.

Despite the immense pressure on his back, he felt relaxed. He had often wondered how his life would end. Being suffocated by a carpet had not made his top ten, and yet here he was.

If dealing with parents was bad, dealing with a partner or spouse was worse. Or so he thought. Others would disagree. The old ones he could handle. People who had lived their lives. That seemed ok. It was the young ones. Those in their late teens or early twenties, who were just on the cusp of discovering the world.

Multiple vehicle pileups. A shooting. Alcohol poisoning. And the partner: hysterical, tears streaming down their face, begging them not to go. Begging them to hold on. That their world would end without them. A memory surfaced like a bubble, unbidden. A girl. Probably eighteen or nineteen. Her boyfriend had collapsed and had been brought in convulsing. No alcohol. No knocks to the head. By the time they had figured it out, he had arrested three times. When the fourth time came it was the end.

Undiagnosed brain cancer – two tumours at the back, the size of apples. It had probably been there for years. Sometimes it just happens like that. But that would have been no comfort to the girl. He remembered her face. The tears streaking down her cheeks. A nurse tried to hold her as she fell apart.

It was times like those that he realised how fragile it all was. How tightly we all cling to the edge of life. The girl had sobbed. Huge racking gasping sobs from her very soul. He could still hear them all these years on.

Cullum hoped that Amanda would not cry too much. She was still young enough to move on, although no doubt at the time it would not feel like it.

He felt a wet creaking within his chest. Another rib was going to go. Too late he tried and failed to shift what he could of his weight.

Cullum gurgled and then coughed. The other lung was filling up with liquid. His air of serenity began to evaporate and was replaced by a rising tide of fear and panic.

He was going to die here. He was going to drown in the fluid of his own lungs, as he was crushed from behind. Before, this had somehow seemed slightly humorous. Now? Now it felt very unfunny. Now it felt like a very bad joke indeed. There was a sense of ignominy.

He was Andrew Cullum. He was a doctor. He helped people. He was not a bad guy. Ok, he had done some things that, looking back on them, he was not proud of, but such had been the enthusiasm of youth.

He did not deserve this.

This was a death that should be reserved for paedophiles and murderers. Not for him.

He choked again, and he felt something come up. It was too dark to see what colour it was. But it did not smell good. He felt another gurgle inside himself. He spluttered, desperately trying to keep his airway clear. It felt like the pressure had grown, and he could feel the full force of the object on top of him bearing down on his head and back. Like a giant trying to pop a spot.

Another cough and splutter. More fluid this time. A lot more.

Something slid past his head. He instinctively tried to crane his neck to see, forgetting that he could not move. The thing slid back into his limited field of vision.

Black. Covered in dirt and dust. He squinted. It was a boot. A second later a face appeared. It was in a full gas mask, and the torchlight on the helmet made him squint. It was a fireman. Definitely a fireman. The torch beam swung through the dusty air, illuminating him.

Cullum heard a sound. With the ringing in his ears he could not make it out but he surmised that the fireman was talking to him. He made thumbs up. Sign of life.

The face disappeared. The fireman had seen it, right? He had seen him move his hand. He could not have missed it. Cullum felt a panic begin to rise up inside of him.

A scraping sound punctured through the ringing in his ears, and a black metal object slid towards him. A similar sound from behind him. A second one.

Another face came into view. This was a medic. Also in a full gas mask. The dust was stinging Cullum's eyes and he badly wanted to cough again. He saw a green tunic and white helmet, but could not make out if it was a doctor or a first responder. Either way, he guessed that this Major Event was not limited to himself.

The medic was saying something to him, but he could not make it out. Thumbs up again.

The face disappeared. The jacks began their slow work. The face reappeared. An arm reached through and held his hand. Not pulling him. Just holding him. *I am here. You're not alone. We'll get you out. Hang on.*

Cullum felt tears well up inside him. The hand gripped him, and he squeezed gently back. *I'm still here. I'm still alive. Thank you thank you thank you.*

The jacks creaked and crunched up. First just a little, taking the weight of whatever was on top of him. The mass could only have moved a fraction, but Cullum already found it easier to breathe. He tried to scramble towards the medic.

"NO!" The voice was clear and punctured through the ringing. Cullum froze. "DON'T MOVE!"

The jacks cranked up further. An inch. Maybe an inch and a half. The medic slid a thin piece of orange plastic along the floor to where Cullum was. It was just about as wide as he was.

"GET ON!"

Thumbs up. Cullum gingerly slid himself onto the sheet.

Very slowly it was pulled toward the medic. Cullum saw a second figure behind the first. And then a third. A fourth. All in gas masks. Air tanks on their backs. The place was swarming with them. He saw stretchers going past him. The emergency lights casting everyone into eerie silhouettes. Finally, he was clear of the mass that had pinned him. His eyes rolled to take it in. A length of wall. A very large, very heavy length of wall.

Cullum tried to get up, but the medic was already on top of him, gently holding him down. He felt a neck brace being applied. He was transferred onto a spinal board. He felt himself beginning to move. He was being carried.

His eyes followed the ceiling. *Towards reception. I'm getting out. I'm going to make it.* Relief swept through him like a dam breaking.

The cold night air slapped him hard in the face. There were fire trucks. A lot of fire trucks. Cullum counted six units. He had taken some residents on a day out a few years ago to visit the Hillingdon Fire Service. They did not have this many units. Extras must have been called for. Slough. Pinner. Staines maybe.

As he passed through what was left of the main entrance, he saw that most of the front of the ground floor had been blown in. All the windows had gone, leaving gaping holes, like some unknown soldier caught in the crossfire and sagging. The brickwork bulged inwardly, and in places it had already collapsed. Firefighters were trying to prop what exposed lintels were left with long metal scaffolding-type jacks, in a desperate bid to stop the upper floors coming down and pancaking the building.

Cullum remembered the footage of the twin towers coming down. This was not on that scale, but he still shuddered. He felt himself being put onto a trolley. Rain drops fell slowly from the sky. A few touched his parched lips. He felt like a child again, being blessed at Communion.

As he was manoeuvred down the driveway, towards an ambulance, he began to see what remained of the old building in profile. The upper floors appeared to be sagging dangerously forward, like some ancient drunk on a final and catastrophic souse. It was only from this angle that he appreciated how much of the ground floor had really gone.

In his daze, his eyes were drawn back to the night sky. He frowned. High above him, he fancied he could see a distant light, alternating slowly between white and purple, crackling and then fading, only to reappear a few seconds later. An aircraft? No. A helicopter maybe. With those heat cameras.

A medic leaned over him. No gas mask this time. "DON'T WORRY ABOUT THAT. LOOK AT ME. CAN YOU HEAR ME?"

Cullum tried to nod, forgetting his collar. He realised that he was strapped down, and was utterly immobile. With his hand, he made the thumbs up.

The medic spoke again. An unintelligible noise came through.

Cullum pointed upwards from his restrained wrist. *SPEAK UP!*

"CAN YOU MOVE YOUR TOES?"

Cullum waggled his toes and realised that he was shoeless. *When did that happen?*

"FINGERS?"

Cullum gave his best *playing-the-piano*.

A light shone in one eye, then the other. "NAME?"

Cullum tried to speak, but coughed and spluttered. "Doctor Andrew Ross Cullum," he eventually croaked.

Another spinal board was carried past him and his eyes followed it until it was put on a trolley not far from him. Kandian. Utterly lifeless.

"BREATHE IN FOR ME."

He felt the cool metal of a stethoscope on his chest. He sucked air in, and felt the dull pain, clawing away on the inside.

"OUT... IN... OUT... AGAIN". The medic did this another three or four times, and Cullum felt himself beginning to relax.

A loud braying, like an excited donkey, broke through his too brief reverie. His eyes flicked left. George Tate sat on the back of an open-doored ambulance, laughing maniacally. A blanket was draped over his shoulders, and as he threw his head back to laugh again, it slipped off.

Although dusty, there was not a mark on him. Not a bruise or cut or even an abrasion.

Two men flanked him. He recognised one of them immediately. The son. Devon. That was it. And the other? The face seemed familiar, but the name would not come, instead lingering at the bottom of his memory like a weighted corpse. He had seen him before. Not as often as the son. Or the nephew. But... *the nephew!*

Cullum knew that he probably would not have got out in time.

"George!" he said hoarsely. He spluttered, dribbling down his own chin.

Tate looked around wildly for a moment. The son pointed his attention toward Cullum.

"Andrew!" The old man beamed widely.

Cullum's throat was parched. "Your nephew?"

George Tate's expression darkened and the son looked at his father and then back to the prone doctor.

"He doesn't have a nephew," the son said.

Before he could say anything, Cullum felt his trolley moving and was loaded into an ambulance.

"I NEED TO GET YOUR CHEST X-RAYED."

*

103

"I don't get it," Danielle said.

"Don't you?" Freeman replied, smiling thinly.

"No. What blew up the nursing home?"

"Officially? Gas explosion from the derelict flats opposite. They were due to be demolished, and it looks like either kids or squatters got in... and well, boom."

"And unofficially?"

"Cause unexplained."

"What does that mean?"

Freeman shrugged. "There was an explosion either within or just outside those derelict flats. But there is no explanation how or why it happened. George Tate was the only one to come out completely unharmed. There were twelve fatalities, and nearly a hundred seriously injured. Houses in the immediate surrounding were completely destroyed."

"But I don't really understand how this links to anything. George Tate got lucky."

"Did he?"

"Well the evidence speaks for itself... doesn't it?"

"You tell me. George Tate is the only resident of Paternoster House to walk away without any injury. Not even a scratch. He was visited immediately before by a man who claimed to be his nephew, even though he has none."

"So who was he?"

Freeman touched his Plex-Pad, and a grainy CCTV photograph loaded onto the screen.

Danielle narrowed her eyes. "From the nursing home reception? This is the nephew?"

Freeman nodded. "A contact at the Justice got me a copy."

"So?"

Freeman touched the Plex-Pad again. Another photo appeared.

"That is from the Maiden Castle dig, nineteen-seventy-five. Back row. Second from the left."

Danielle paused. "Good grief!" she said, looking up. "It's the same man. He's not aged a day. Who is he?"

"Who do you think?"

"Celus Tuther?"

Freeman nodded again. "Probably."

"Was he in the explosion?"

"If he was, they never found his body."

Danielle sat back in his chair. "Well, this is the first piece of evidence I'll really accept. But on its own, it's not much. People will just say that it is a look-a-like. A coincidence. And George just got lucky."

"Maybe. But we also have Eric Kandian's visions."

Danielle was not sympathetic. "Visions? Really? That is going a bit far. The man was clearly delusional. Your witness as good as said that he had advanced dementia."

"Maybe. But how did he know about Doctor Cullum's new love interest? Or the mother?"

Danielle was not budging. "Like he said, maybe he overheard him. It's pretty flimsy to call it a vision."

Freeman paused. "What is your first memory, Danielle? I don't mean a birthday party or playing somewhere, but the first time you remember something outside of yourself. A news story. Something big."

Danielle thought for a moment. "Probably two-thousand-and-three. The shuttle disaster. What was it? Columbia that was it. I watched that with my dad. I was three."

"So the Paternoster explosion would have been when you were six?"

Danielle nodded.

"Do you remember it? Do you remember the story being reported?"

Danielle thought again and shook her head. "No. I don't."

"That's because it only made the newspapers. And there were no pictures. It never got broadcast on any of the news channels. Don't you find that a bit odd?"

"Maybe a little. But is it that they just couldn't release the footage? A D-Notice maybe?"

"For a residential gas explosion? No. And don't forget, the papers reported it." He pressed the Plex-Pad, and several clippings from various newspapers appeared. Danielle felt her interest being piqued.

"Even today, you still cannot record or broadcast from the site," Freeman continued. "After that explosion, not a single piece of recording equipment would work within fifty yards of that blast crater. Not the police, not the fire service and not the journalists. And I know why."

CHAPTER 6

Hunnin 1:4-18
The Darkness comprehended not Creation and reached for the Kingdom of God
Through the windows of sleep and death.
And Creation, in its innocence, reached for the Darkness with the promise of light.

God beheld the corruption that would be wrought and decreed that this shall not be.
He commanded that we servants of the sky bind the eyes of Creation,
That they shall not see nor reach nor touch the Darkness.
And their eyes were bound, that in death Creation would see and dream no more.

My name is John Lennox. I am a local and national reporter for the BBC News network.

Monday 4th December 2006
John knew it was early. Too early. His phone buzzed again. He rolled over. The red LED of his alarm clock mockingly informed him it was a little after five. It was still dark outside, with no hint of a sunrise.

The phone cut off. A few seconds later it started buzzing again.

In the morning gloom, he fumbled to his bedside cabinet, reached for his phone, and snapped it open.

"Yeah?" *This had better be good,* his tone said.

"It's Murph." Murphy King had been his camera operator last night.

"Murph." John's mind was still struggling to get into second gear. "Yeah. What?" he said eventually.

"I... your..."

John wanted to tell him to get on with it, but it was too much effort at the moment.

"The footage is... your report is knackered."

John's mind kicked up the revs and went into second gear.

"What?"

"The camera is bust. Everything is scrambled."

Third gear. The revs were climbing faster now.

"How much of it?"

"Everything. Everything is gone."

Fourth. Needle in the red. Sleep was a long way behind him already, and he was sitting up in bed, very *very* awake.

"Everything?"

"Everything."

"Does Will know?" Will Pitman was their producer.

"Uh huh."

Damn! Damn! DAMN!

"Where are you?"

"TVC." Television Centre.

"What are you doing there?"

"I've been here all night. Trying to recover your footage."

"And?"

"Like I said. Nothing. It's all gone."

And there it was. His mind slipped into overdrive and carried on climbing.

They had been at the site of the Milton Road gas explosion for nearly six hours last night. He had got some great interviews. Some teary old ladies. A few scared kiddies. The sombre Police Commander. Shots of body bags coming out. It was not award winning, but it was pretty good all the same.

"What happened?"

"No idea. I watched the VT back in the van and it was fine. It was when I came to upload it all at the studio… all I got was static. I've had the techs look at it. They can't explain it. They just said it must be a faulty unit."

"What does Will want us to do?"

"What does Will always want?"

John sighed, sitting on the edge of his bed now. All Will ever wanted was the report. On time.

"ITN owe me a favour. Will he accept licensed pictures?"

"Dunno. Maybe. Are you going to come in?"

"Yeah. Yeah, I'm on my way. Maybe an hour or." He looked at the sleeping form next to him, and his cock twitched. "Make it ninety minutes."

"Ok. See you then." The line went dead.

John went to put his phone down but noticed a text message. It was from Julie, his wife.

Cairo is lovely. Wish you were here.

The stab of guilt was enough to subside his stiffening.

He prodded the girl next to him.

"Hey. I got to go to work." She was one of his regulars. Pretty good most of the time. The ache in his balls reminded him that she had been on form last night.

The girl stirred.

"Hmm...?" her hair was a tousled mess, and slightly matted. They had really worked up a sweat, John thought rather proudly. The stiffening returned.

"I've got to go in."

"Ok." She still was not awake.

He slipped a hand under the sheets, over her tight belly, skimming her shaved pubis, and lightly touched between her folds.

I know how to wake you up.

She was still damp. His cock was now at full attention, straining against his own skin, trying to break free. The girl moaned a little. She was more awake than she had pretended. Sensing what was about to happen, she kicked the duvet off, opened her legs, and began playing with her already erect nipples. Her other hand reached for his cock.

John hated it when she did that. She was trying to tug him off rather than take him in.

Julie doesn't do that... but then Julie spits. And that is just rude.

He made a mental note to see if the agency had any new girls on their books. Someone absolutely filthy.

He took a step back, out of her reach, and grabbed a condom and rolled it on, grunting at the feel of the cool latex against his manhood. He felt a little precum on his engorged head.

Oh well. Still, she is bought and paid for. A quickie then.

Bending over the girl's prone form, he placed one hand on her shoulder, and the other cupped a buttock.

But damn she smells good.

And with that he buried himself up to the hilt with the first stroke, feeling her body arc underneath him.

*

The Tube had not been too busy, but any later and John would have struggled for a seat. He was glad to sit down. The quickie had turned into a longie, and he was a little sore.

He had tried Rich twice on the way from the flat to the station but had only got voicemail. He had been at college with Richard Davis and they had kept in touch over the years, eventually becoming uneasy friends. John had bumped into him last night at Milton Road.

Rich was with ITN now, and there was always jibing between the two of them about their respective employers. John won on standards, and then Rich would text him his latest bank balance.

John checked his phone as he came out of White City. A text message came through.

Got your v.mail. Call me back. VVR

Very *Very* Rich

John hit the redial.

"Johnny! You old whoremonger!" Rich was unreasonably cheery for a Monday morning. That meant he either had something you needed, or he wanted something from you.

John's second espresso had yet to kick in, and he did not much feel like engaging in their usual games, which would inevitably end with "And how much do you earn my PLJ?"

Poor Little Johnny.

John hated being called Johnny. It made him feel simultaneously like he was back at primary school, and that all his girls thought of him as a walking wallet. Which they probably did. But he wanted to believe otherwise. He needed to believe otherwise. They enjoyed it as much as he did.

Didn't they?

And he definitely hated PLJ. "Rich you cokehead! You're up early."

"It's a busy old world son. You know me. I'm like a shark. Always moving."

John winced. That old adage was not even true. "Listen. I need to beg a favour."

"Oh really. Need another alibi?"

This was starting to wind John up. But he kept his temper in check. "No. Umm... have you reviewed your footage from last night?"

There was silence at the other end of the phone. John started to walk on to the footbridge that would take him over the road.

"Rich?"

"Yeah. Err... not exactly."

"There has been a balls up with our camera. Scrambled everything we shot. Can we license yours?" John knew that this was going to cost him.

There was another pause. This was not like Richard. Not like him at all. Why wasn't he lauding it?

"Rich? You there?"

"Yeah. Um... ours is scrambled too."

"Serious?"

"Yeah. What did you get?"

"Dunno. Haven't seen it yet. Murph said he was on it most of last night. But he says we got nothing."

A third pause. Eventually Rich came back. "Do you know Kristi?"

"Who?"

"New girl. Does the Sky stuff for Channel Five."

Sky News had been providing the Channel Five content since two-thousand five, taking over from ITN. Most of the staff were still raw and did not talk about it other than to complain about how unfair it all was.

"No."

"Well... she and I..."

John knew what that meant. "Yes?"

"Well she was down there as well last night... her footage has gone too."

John had reached the other side of the bridge and the entrance to Television Centre was within sight.

"Three cameras...?"

"And the Police's. They've already tried to requisition our footage. I imagine the Fire and Ambulance will be the same."

"Have they got any explanation?"

"If they have, they're not saying. But I've got a man in Whitehall. He says it sounds like residual electromagnetic radiation."

"What's that?"

"The most obvious answer is that it's the left-over of either an EMP or a dirty bomb."

"A bomb?"

"Sure."

"In a very white, very middle class, London suburb? You're having a laugh."

"Why not? Some fundamentalist wanting payback for Saddam. You know, send a message before the big day. And what have we got here? A nice empty block of flats that the council never check. They get their mixes wrong and bang."

"You've been watching too much Bauer."

"Why not?" Rich asked again.

"Because if it was a dirty bomb, then where are all the bods in radiation suits... hang on, Murph's waiting out front for me. I'll call you back."

*

"There are guys in radiation suits all over the shop!" Murph gabbled excitedly. "Will wants us back over there now. The van is being loaded. Let's go!"

"Whoa. Hold on Tonto. Bods in suits?"

"Yeah. Will just got the shout from Reuters. He wants us to get the jump on ITN and Sky."

John decided to stay quiet about his conversation with Rich. "But we were wandering all around the scene last night. Have we been exposed?"

Murph stopped and thought, then shrugged. "S'pose so."

"This is nuts," John muttered. He dialled Will on his mobile.

"Are you on the road yet?" William Pitman demanded. The man was not so much a pit bull, more of a military experiment into testosterone overloaded gene splicing that had gone wrong.

"No. What if you're sending us into a radioactive hot spot?"

"Then your balls will drop off and your wife will thank me."

"To hell with you."

"I love you too. Now get going."

"No."

"What?" Will barked. He was not used to hearing that word.

"I'm very attached to my balls, and I'm not going to..."

"For God's sake, you whine like a girl. Look, Brunel University is up the road from the scene. I know their VC. I'll get him to send over some of his radiation protection chaps. They'll put those cards on you. If they turn red or blue or whatever, then I'll pull you out. Deal?"

John did not like it. He did not like it at all. But Will was using his reasonable voice, even though he was being anything but, and that made John doubly annoyed. "Mmm..."

"Good boy. Call me when you get there."

*

The traffic was its usual murderous Monday morning rush-hour self and it was after nine-thirty by the time they got to the scene. The dual carriageway had been at a standstill at the Hanger Lane gyratory. Why Highways did not do something about it was beyond him. John mused for a few moments on a feature on the capital's roads. Gridlock. Unfit for modern purpose. He gave up on it. Dull.

The December chill had bitten deep, and he had the thermostat in the van dialled all the way up, and now the hot air was drying out his contact lenses. John's mood was darkening.

The site had been completely sealed and armed policemen stood every fifty yards along a taped line, which was much expanded on last night's operation. John got out of the van and noted that Sky was already there. Kristi whatshername was talking to some local residents who *just couldn't believe it – you never think it's going to happen here.*

John felt himself groan inwardly. She was...what? Twenty-five at the most. Why didn't she just pop that last button and get those puppies out? Oh, and there she goes with the sympathetic nod.

John nodded at one of the officers. "Got press liaison?"

The officer jerked his head right. "Portacabin at the end."

Milton Road had been completely sealed off, and at its head sat three large portacabins. Police vehicles clustered around them like hungry children seeking sweets at a party.

Murphy began unpacking the van.

"I'll pop in and see what they've got," said John.

111

Murphy just nodded, absorbed in his equipment check. John stepped through the open portacabin door. There seemed to be three rooms. Each one its own separate hive of activity.

"Err... press?" he said. There were a lot of guns on show, and guns made John nervous.

An officer approached him, and he flashed his press card.

"Through here."

The officer took him into a side room. "Were you here last night? Reporting?"

"Yes..."

The officer cut him off. "What is the condition of your footage?"

"Gone. Just static."

"All of it?"

John nodded.

The officer handed John a sheet of paper. "This is our official statement. Current evidence suggests a gas explosion last night at the Woods Flats. They were empty, pending demolition, and we cannot say at the moment if the explosion was accidental or deliberate. We are pursuing all lines of enquiry. There has been some electromagnetic.... phenomena. We do not know if this is linked to the explosion but, as a precaution, we have evacuated these streets, and are conducting a thorough investigation."

The officer handed John a second sheet. It was a map of the area, with a red circle extending some two hundred yards from the now demolished flats.

"Milton Road is completely closed, as is Milton Court, Almond Avenue, Needle Close, Pepys Close, and The Woods. Ivy House Road and The Avenue are each closed from about half-way up. Swakeleys Road is open as is Long Lane and the Park."

"How many people have you had to move?"

"Just over five hundred. That includes those who had their homes destroyed last night."

John was making notes.

"It's all in the brief," said the officer evenly.

"Sorry. Force of habit. This electromagnetic phenomenon... is this linked to the lights in the sky that some witnesses have said they saw last night."

The officer looked at him hard for a moment. "Are you taking the mickey?"

John looked up from his notebook. "No," he said innocently.

"Then take your head out of your arse and have a look about you once in a while." The officer turned on his heel and exited, leaving John feeling bewildered.

He made his way back out to join Murphy and was surprised to find him deep in conversation with a young man.

"Hello?" John said. The two turned, and John saw that Murphy was fitting something around his camera.

"Hello," said the young man. "Lionel Orton, from Brunel. Your boss called my boss... and here I am." The two shook hands.

John looked Lionel up and down. He could not have been older than twenty-two or twenty-three.

"*Lionel?*"

"Yes. I know. A bit of bug-bear. Family name."

"So what have you got for us, *Lionel?*"

Lionel clipped a plastic tag on to John. "Film badge."

John looked at him blankly.

"Radiation detection. They're thermoluminescent. See this readout here?" He pointed to the small LED screen. "That number hits a hundred and you're done cooking. Time to get out the oven." The young man looked unreasonably pleased with himself.

John looked down at the small plastic frame. "That's it?"

"That's it."

"What have we got going on with the camera?"

"Lead-lined housing. Should try and prevent whatever it is that is stopping you recording. Or playing back. Whatever."

"It weighs a ton," said Murphy, trying to hoist the camera onto his shoulder.

"Uh huh," said John, and then back to Lionel, "So what can you tell us?"

"Not much. We have supported the police as best we can, but they have got their own division for this."

"Right. So what do you know?"

"At the moment, nothing.... oh except that there is no radiation. Well, nothing above background."

"No radiation? Then why am I wearing this?" John thumbed the plastic tag.

"Your boss told my boss that it would make you feel better..." Lionel replied, then seeing the look on John's face he went quickly on, "but they did think that there might have been something this morning. Hence the suits."

"Are they still here?" Some footage of the full radiation suits would have been great. Give his report a Hollywood feel.

"No. They went a few hours ago."

"What did they find?"

"Nothing. Well, nothing detectable."

John's frustration was rising, and his nostrils flared. This was feeling like a wasted trip.

"Has anyone else been in touch with you? Army maybe?"

"No, just the Civil Service."

"What did they want?"

"A couple of bodies to help carry equipment, set stuff up and make records..."

"Of what?"

Lionel looked at him as if he was joking, then clearly seeing that he was not, "You know..." he pointed skywards.

John and Murphy turned, and gazed at the grey sky. It was heavy with a brooding winter and looked like a sheet of recently hewn granite. For a moment they saw nothing. And then there it was. It started slowly, like a twinkling. It grew rapidly, pulsating from pure white to a deep purple before fading out and then back in again.

It was not spherical, but more oblong with jagged edges, and there seemed to be electrical discharges within it. They looked as if they were beating rhythmically.

The thing was about twenty or thirty foot across, and completely silent. John guessed it was no more than five hundred feet up and probably directly above the blast site. The three of them stood there, just watching the light display high above them. And then it faded completely, and the sky returned to its impassive grey. Snow was coming, and it was going to be a cold winter.

"Well that was very Close Encounters," said an awestruck Murphy.

John was equally shocked. "What was that?"

Lionel shook his head. "We have no idea."

"It wasn't here last night. We would have noticed that!"

"It was spotted about one in the morning, but it had probably been building before that. Whatever it is, the activity peaked at about four or five. Then it was coming every couple of minutes. And it was bigger. Now it is about every half hour, and the duration of the activity is much less. It was about fifteen minutes, and now it is maybe two or three. It's a lot smaller too. It looks like it is cycling down."

"Cycling down? To what?"

Lionel shook his head again. "We don't know. Other than its physical presence, we cannot measure it. No heat, no sound, no emissions. It looks like a mini version of a Borealis, but..."

"Starfish Prime!" Murphy exclaimed.

John and Lionel turned to look at the cameraman as if he had two heads.

"You know?"

The two men clearly did not. "Wasn't he the leader of the Autobots?" John asked eventually.

"That was Optimus," Lionel said on reflex.

John had the measure of him and smiled to himself.

"No, Starfish Prime was this thing the Americans were doing in the sixties," Murphy continued. "Super high altitude nuclear tests. Like on the boundary of space. They did a bunch. And then the Soviets did a few too.

They created these weird glows in the sky, like the Northern Lights... you said the Borealis right?"

Lionel nodded

"But they also created these artificial radiation belts in low orbit. Knocked out a whole load of satellites. Supposedly these belts have been slowly falling back to earth ever since."

John and Lionel were silent.

"How do you know all of this?" John asked.

"My dad was in the RAF."

This sounded familiar to John. He was sure Murphy had told him about his dad. Some sort of honour like an OBE or MBE or something. Apparently, he had been a big noise in the air force. He wished he had paid more attention now.

"He was always complaining about the belts," Murphy persisted. "He said that if they even came near an aircraft... well it would just lose power. No warning or anything. Just fall out the sky. There was a bad one in Turkey in sixty-three. Killed a lot of civilians on the ground. That was a Dakota I think. There was a Lockheed in May of the same year. That was followed by a couple of B-forty-sevens. I remember my dad talking about an awful one in sixty-seven. That was a Neptune.

"The last one I remember hearing about was in ninety-three. Hawkeye came down in the Ionian. The Soviets claimed a Sukhoi in ninety-nine, but no-one is really sure about that one. All the pilots described it as if a net had come down over the frame, and just sucked all the power out."

John was transfixed. He turned to Lionel. "Could this be true? A man-made radiation belt drifting back to earth?"

Lionel thought for a moment. "Don't know. Could be. It would certainly account for the physical manifestations. But after all this time? I know the mid-air tests Murphy is talking about, but they were low yield. I mean really low. Like a kilo-tonne. I could cook up something bigger in my bath today. And given where the science was in those days, I'd be surprised if those radiation belts stayed up there for five years. Ten at the most."

"What about if more went up than the Americans claimed?" asked Murphy.

"True," said John. "It wouldn't be the first time they've told stories. Maybe something exotic they were testing?"

Lionel shrugged. "It's possible. I mean, *anything* is possible. But if it was a radiation belt, then I would have expected to see drift. It wouldn't stay in one place. And there would be something to measure. Decaying particles. Heat. Maybe even some radio signals. Nuclear radiation gives off a very distinct radio signal. This isn't giving us anything apart from light."

"Could one of these belts have caused the explosion?"

"I'm not saying an absolute no, but I doubt it. That thing is too high up."

"What about if there was a second belt?" said Murphy. "What if there were two belts, one sort of on top of the other." He put his camera down and held his palms out, one over the other with a gap between.

"Like I said, *anything* is possible, but then surely everyone would have seen the first belt like they are seeing this one."

John had to agree with him there.

"What about if it was small? Really small? Like not even a meter across?" Murphy asked. John could see he was like a dog with a bone. No doubt he wanted to go back to his Old Man and finally have a story to swap.

"I... I really don't know. It's not likely."

"But not impossible. That's what you're saying, though? It's not impossible?" John interjected.

"John, nothing is impossible. Highly improbable maybe..."

John looked to Murphy who was trying to hoist his camera up.

"Want to go on the record? You'll be on the one o'clock!"

"What? No!" Lionel said, taking a step back, offended that he had been led on like this. "I'm really not allowed to. All this stuff has to go through our press office. You... you don't have my consent!"

"Hey, chill out," said John, turning his back and making the *cut* sign to Murphy.

It had been worth a shot.

"If there was a second belt, would there be an evidence of it? On the ground?"

Lionel was still rattled. "Err... not visibly. Your monitors would pick something up. Depending on the concentration, you might get a little heat from the soil."

"Can you get us to the blast site?" John was as keen as Murphy now.

"Are you kidding? No!"

"Come on. You must have some sway with the police. Just say that we're your assistants."

"Absolutely not!"

"Alright, can you show us a way in?" John produced the map the officer had given him. "Everything inside the red circle is evacuated and closed off."

Lionel sighed. "I went to school just up the road – there's a shortcut. See this here? Swakelys Road. That line of trees going north to south – that's the River Pinn. It's not on your map, but there is a footpath. Actually, there are two. The one on the west side of the river will bring you out in Swakelys Park. The one on the east side will bring you out three-quarters of the way down The Avenue, next to the tennis courts. You'll be about a hundred yards from the blast site. I've not been down there. My lot have just been monitoring the readings they give us. But they say that these flats here and here" he indicated on the map "have been completely destroyed. It's a straight run from the footpath. Best guess is that your badges won't pick anything up until you're nearly on top of the source. If nothing else, you'll be able to get a great view of... whatever that light display is.

"If you're lucky, the Police Commander won't be local, and he won't know about either of these footpaths. If not, you'll probably be arrested on the spot. This lot don't have much of a sense of humour today, so expect it to be rough."

"How far is it from here?"

"A two-minute drive. Not even that. You can probably park up at either Stedman Close or Irwin. You'll have to cross the dual carriageway if you park at Irwin."

"Thanks," John said absently, not really meaning it. His mind was already galloping ahead.

*

Ten minutes later, Murphy, had the van packed up, and they both sat silently in the front seats.

"What do you reckon?" Murphy said.

"I think we should do it. If whatever it is, is genuinely cycling down then we probably don't have much time. It could be completely gone in an hour. We can come back and do the old biddy interviews later."

"What if the Law catches us?"

"Blag it. Worse case we spend a couple of hours in a cell before Will springs us. We've been there before."

John was referring to an incident a few years ago when they had 'accidentally' wandered onto an army training range. They had been trying to film evidence of bullying and abuse and had some good footage before they were caught. The Army had not been pleased but had eventually agreed to let them go in return for their signatures on Non-Disclosure Agreements that were so water tight they made a ducks arse look like a sieve. Their footage had not been returned.

Those few hours in an army cell had been less than comfortable.

"And what if the site is radioactive?"

"You heard what *Lionel* said. It's probably not. And even if it is it won't be strong. We can get on, shoot a bit, and then get out. Pad it out with some shots around the village. Leafy avenues, that kind of stuff."

"What about if it's more than a little bit radioactive? What if it really is some freaky prototype the Americans put up there, and now it's coming back down?"

John shrugged. "Like Will said, our balls will probably drop off, and my wife will thank him for it. Are you up for it? If not, just say and I'll take one of the units..."

"The hell you will. You've already broken one of my babies. I'm not letting you touch another."

John could have objected, but he had deliberately pushed Murphy's button. And now he had him along for the ride.

A few minutes later they were parking up in Stedman Close. John could not see any police presence in the immediate area, but all the same, he had to chivvy Murphy along. They came out onto Swakelys Road and made their way along to the bridge that was flanked by thick trees on either side.

There was a small wrought iron gate that had once upon a time been black. John put his hand on it to push through and was disappointed that it did not squeak.

"It's the other one," said Murphy behind him. He was struggling to balance with the camera in its new heavier housing.

"What?"

"It's the next one. That is the west gate."

"Are you sure?" John pulled the map from his pocket.

"Yup."

Murphy was right.

They carried on to the next gate and made their way through. The waist-high ironmongery did squeak this time, but not enough for John's liking. It was a gate that lacked passion. Being December, there was hardly any leaf cover, and the branches reached out over them like so many skeletal fingers grasping out towards a sun that had forsaken them long ago.

The density of trees was not so much that they could not see through, but enough that what they saw was only glimpses. According to the map, it should not be more than three hundred yards to the tennis courts. The path was well used but narrow and they made their way along as quietly as possible.

"Are you on?" John said, turning to Murphy.

"Power's good. VT is good. Sound good. Green lights across the board."

"Tried recording?"

"I did in the van. Looked ok."

"Start it properly from now and we'll edit as we need to."

Murphy pressed the record button. "We're good."

John nodded and pressed on. The cool breeze of the winter day had begun to pick up. Heavier darker clouds were now skidding across the sky, like elemental bombers threatening to dump their frozen payloads.

The path began to narrow, and the mossy tree trunks clustered in like penguins in a blizzard. Ahead, John could hear a rhythmical thoc-thoc-thoc.

He turned back to Murphy. "Does that sound like someone playing tennis?" has asked incredulously.

Murphy nodded. "Yeah. Kinda does. Aren't the tennis courts supposed to be closed as well?"

"You would have thought. Still, this area is full of retired Majors who have been having their Monday morning constitutional since the ark."

"HEY!" There was a shout. Both men snapped their heads to the right. They could just make out a figure on the other side of the river, and he was in a police uniform.

"Come on!" John pulled Murphy forward. The officer would have to wade across the river or run to the top where the bridge was and back down their side to catch them. At best they could get a minute or so of footage from the blast site.

Both men made their way forward quickly. John a little ahead, Murphy struggling with the heavy camera. The wind picked up again, and the trees began to creak around them. John knew there was little danger of them coming down, but the noise added to his sense of urgency.

John felt his ears pop. He could see the end of the path ahead, and pushed forward. The thoc-thoc-thoc was louder now. They were almost there...

Both men ran through the end of the path and stopped dead.

For a moment neither one of them said anything. They barely dared to breathe. In front of them was not the suburban ideal they were expecting. No whitewashed houses. No tennis court. No tree lined avenue. And no demolished buildings.

They were about a third of the way up a gentle hill. Behind them, where they had just come from, was a thin copse of trees that thickened the further back they went. In front of them was a vision that would remain with them for what remained of their lives.

Thoc-thoc-thoc

The air was heavy, thick, as though pressing on their chests. For a moment, with the shock, their breathing struggled to adapt, and they felt the pressure of the atmosphere against the soft flesh of their eyes and ears, pushing in.

In the distance was a sea, black and choppy, casting sludgy dark grey spray high into the air. The vast sky was reminiscent of home, although the sunlight, such as it was, was weaker. Sicklier. Dark heavy purple-black clouds boiled and rolled high over them, like a pantheon of unseen gods mocking the insignificance and irrelevance of all mortality. That all must be purged of their sins before being washed away like grains of sand.

Thoc-thoc-thoc

For a moment, John thought he saw movement in the clouds. A thing. A colossal eye? No, some sort of arm of pure muscle. Thick and hundreds of miles across. And then the clouds swirled again and whatever half fancied outline he thought he saw disappeared back into the gathering vortex.

The spiteful wind bore down from the coast, bringing with it an acrid bitter tang that was familiar to both men, but that neither could place. It was more than a smell. It was a taste, and it hung at the back of their throats with a distant thought of pending vomit.

Thoc-thoc-thoc

Against the burgeoning ocean was the outline of a monstrous and distorted city. The part closest to them reminded John of a medieval castle, and he fancied he could make out the silhouette of a keep and a tower. But it seemed to act as a gateway to something so sinister then he did not want to look at it, and his mind recoiled as a hand may grasp for a hot saucepan handle, again and again, flinching from it each time.

The city was in darkness save for an occasional bonfire, giving an impression of a single solid stone from which the entirety had been carved. Thick black towers reached skyward, and from one, John could pick out an ethereal light against the darkening horizon, its highest spire lightly caressing the bottom layer of cloud.

Thoc-thoc-thoc

The domes and the minarets were all equally colossal in scale, and yet each one seemed deformed, mutated and curling at grotesque angles, as though they were reflections of some nightmare house of mirrors.

Despite this vision of perversion and the absurd horror of their situation, it was not these sights that had frozen them. In the immediate foreground, not more than a few hundred yards in front of them seemed to be some kind of rally. There were no seats, no stadium. Instead, thousands of what John assumed to be uniformed troops, stood silently in formation, as the steady rhythm beat out...

Thoc-thoc-thoc

The soldiers, if that is what they were, seemed to be dressed in dark grey close fitting slashed jerkins, and similar colour loose shirt and trousers. All had shoulder length jet black hair, and in their right hands held what looked like a stave or pole some five feet long. Some wore a short cloak or shawl that fluttered in the strengthening winds.

They were all standing to unmoving attention.

Looking down from the slight rise on the hill, the scene reminded John of the Nazi addresses given by Hitler. Badly made flags fluttered in the wind, and all eyes appeared to be facing away from them, towards the castle monstrosity, where there seemed to be a slightly elevated platform and some kind of pulpit. John could just make out a figure on the podium, which was flanked by another five individuals on each side. He was too far away to make out their features, but all looked as if they were dressed in the same uniform.

Thoc-thoc-thoc

It stopped. John and Murphy held their breath. The figure in the pulpit stood, raising his hands to the boiling sky. The soldiers began to rhythmically drum their staves on the ground, the beat rising like a crescendo against the increasing wind. A low chant came from the assembled masses.

Da da Danu ha,
Ka sa Danu ha
Ma da Danu ha

The chant began to repeat, increasing in volume, and building to a deafening crescendo.

Da da Danu ha,
Ka sa Danu ha
Ma da Danu ha
Da da Danu ha,
Ka sa Danu ha
Ma da Danu ha

Finally it reached its frenzied peak

Zhroma,
Zhroma!
ZHROMA!

The clouds above them boiled like the contents of a cauldron and crackled wildly. Although John could not see any lightning, the clap of thunder that followed told him that the storm was close. Probably immediately overhead.

The chant fell to absolute silence and for a moment even the howling wind seemed to pause. The figure in the pulpit dropped its arms. As one, eleven huge wooden crucifixion crosses were raised high above the assembled mass.

Even from this distance, John could see the naked contorted form of a heavily pregnant young woman on each and every one, eyes bulging in pain and fear. Heavy metal spikes had been driven through their wrists and ankles.

That's what that heavy knocking sound was, thought John. *It was the nails going through into the wood!*

A front line of the soldiers stepped forward so that they were just off centre of the crucifixes. In unison, they held their staves aloft, and in one fluid simultaneous motion lunged forward, smashing them like baseball bats across the legs of the women.

John winced, hearing the dull crack of breaking bone, and averted his eyes momentarily, as the crucified sank, no longer able to hold themselves up.

Why are they not screaming? It was then that John noticed that they all had rags stuffed into their mouths. Not like a traditional gag, but cloth actually stuffed down their throats. John could actually see some of them starting to choke on them.

The front row of soldiers had returned to their position in front of their respective crucifixes. The rest of the legions began to bang their staves on the ground, and once again the low chant struck up

Da da Danu ha,
Da da Danu ha,
Da da Danu ha.

The front row of soldiers had crouched, both hands clutching their staves as if they were about to pole-vault.

Da da Danu ha.

Da da Danu ha!
DA DA DANU HA!

At the crescendo, the soldiers lunged forward, driving the end of their staves up towards the exposed genitals of the helpless women.

The staves penetrated. Ripping and tearing, boring through the soft yielding flesh, the staves erupted in an orgy of blood and entrails from their engorged abdomens and chests.

Even with the gags, John could hear the screams. Some were still alive. He felt pale and clammy. Murphy vomited, falling to his knees.

The sky rippled like a sheet. The lightning was clear this time, illuminating distorted and brutal shapes behind the cloud.

The figure in the pulpit had raised its arms to the sky again. "Now they believe! The Third Twine has failed!" it cried out. It was a man's voice, thick and frenzied. "Now they believe! NOW THEY BELIEVE!"

The crowd chanted their strange invocation back.

DA DA DANU HA!
DA DA DANU HA!
DA DA DANU HA!

The sky crackled and briefly shone again in rapture.

Murphy vomited again and cried out. John turned to him and helped his colleague up. Blood was mixed in with puke. A lot of blood. Murphy gagged again, doubling over. Dark thick ooze dripped lazily over his lips. His stomach was empty, but this did not stop him continuing to heave.

John bent with his cameraman, taking his weight. In that instant, he heard a whirring sound. A stave smashed into the tree behind him, ripping out an enormous chunk of the trunk. It had missed his head by mere inches, and despite the force of its impact, the stave remained intact.

John jerked his head up. They had been seen.

Two more staves came whirring towards them, and John had to throw himself and Murphy to ground.

"We have *got* to move Murph!"

"Uh-huh!"

The two men scrambled to their feet and saw a small group of soldiers running up the hill towards them. Under a hundred yards and closing fast. John turned and sped back along the wooded path. Murph picked up the camera and did likewise.

Eighty yards.

Another stave smashed through the undergrowth on John's left.

Seventy.

The two men forgot all thought of pacing themselves and sprinted as hard as they could.

Under sixty yards.

John could hear the sound of pounding boots behind him as the soldiers gave chase.

Fifty yards to intercept.

Another stave smashed through just missing him. Lower. Around knee height.

Forty.

Already his lungs were on fire, and he could feel tears on the edge of his eyes as he powered straight through his burn.

Thirty.

Another stave. Inches from his knee.

Twenty.

Murphy cried out. An almost child-like shriek.

John turned to see Murphy falling, a stave through his leg at a sickening angle.

The camera skidded forward to where John stood.

TEN YARDS!

Murphy held a hand up to John. *Please!*

John did not even pause to think.

He reached down. Grabbed the camera. And ran.

"NO!" The scream was filled with all the rage and terror of the moment and then was silenced with a gurgle.

For the rest of his life, that scream would haunt John. In the small hours of the mornings, many years from now, he would wake, drenched in sweat, his skin prickling as he played that scream over and over again. A scream that knew that a brutally painful end was mere seconds away, but that also swore unrelenting unyielding undying vengeance.

It would loop over and over and over in his mind, like a scratched record. Always that scream. That way. Haunting him. Waiting for him.

John did not turn but barrelled along the darkening path, the bare branches scraping at him, clawing at his clothes and face. Harder and harder his legs pounded, lungs burning. The weight of the camera was extraordinary. And then he was at the familiar black gate. But he was not stopping. Hurdling the gate, he caught his foot.

The camera left his grasp, smashed into the pavement, and span onto the dual carriageway. His face connected with concrete with a dull wet thump. Pain flared through him like a supernova, burning all in its path. His mouth was filled with blood and bile. He could feel a couple of teeth free and floating within his now gaping maw. His nose was nothing but a tattered mass of ruined flesh, bleeding freely over his face.

He tried to breathe but just inhaled blood. He turned over, coughing and spluttering. The blood would not stop. His eyes were watering, trying to clear the fluid that was running into them, and he could feel grit in a cut above his eye as more of his life essence pumped out, blurring his vision.

He tried to get up. Fire erupted in his shoulder. Broken or dislocated. His left foot was still tangled in the top of the gate's ironwork. Dimly, he imagined this was how a cowboy felt having been thrown from his saddle, but still with a foot in the stirrup.

Except he was no cowboy. He was a coward. High above him, in the night sky, something twinkled dimly, distantly, removed from everything else.

And then the night swallowed him.

*

"He had no idea how long he laid there," said Freeman, "but the police discovered him early in the morning. He had been missing nearly thirty-six hours. Murphy was never found."

"That's some story," said Danielle after a pause. "Total rubbish. But some story."

Freeman raised an eyebrow. "You think so?"

"Come on. How does this even link to Tate? There isn't a single thing to corroborate it. Not one piece of evidence."

"Isn't there? There was an explosion. A strange light in the sky was seen by hundreds of witnesses."

Danielle paused. "Maybe, but the castle? The crucifixions?"

"Don't forget the assembled masses. Lennox's description of their look and attire is very similar to those of Dennis King and Harry Gordon."

"Your Raven Men? I'm not buying it. That camera must have been smashed."

"It was."

"So all that electromagnetic interference must have wiped it. Surely?"

Freeman slid another sheet across the table.

"Not on your pad?" Danielle questioned.

Freeman chose not to answer her question. "They were able to recover a single frame."

Danielle turned it over. The picture was slightly fuzzy, and there were occasional patches of white noise where the image had not been wholly recovered. But there, clearly against a stormy sea, was the outline of a small medieval castle that was a gateway to some architectural monstrosity of goliath proportions. The sky was a purpling bruise. In the foreground was a huge gathering of thousands, if not tens of thousands, of dark clad figures.

Danielle was incredulous. "It was real?"

"It *is* real." Freeman pulled out a framed canvas and put it on the desk.

"One of Kandian's?" Danielle asked examining the grotesque cityscape she had just heard about. She did not need Freeman to point the similarity between the still and the painting. The two were as identical as they could be. "Where did you get it? From the daughter?"

"Actually no. It turns out that having her father in that nursing home had put her massively into debt. She sold them to Doctor Cotrahens."

"Cotrahens? How on earth did those two meet?"

"He was the second man that Doctor Cullum saw Tate with. He would come by from time to time to see his one-time colleague. He met Amy Kandian the night her father died."

"And you got this from him?"

"Well, no. Cotrahens is a long time dead. His estate sold off most of his possessions – what was left anyway. The collection of Kandian's artwork was split up. Some went to museums. Others were bought by private individuals. This one," he tapped the frame, "was loaned to me by The Accipiter Corporation."

Danielle's eyes narrowed. "The charity that helped fund George's dig at Maiden Castle?"

"They're not a charity. Walsh got that detail wrong. But yes. Accipiter and Tate have a great shared history. But these are spoilers – we'll come back to Cotrahens later."

Danielle looked at the painting closely. It was both exquisitely beautiful and utterly hideous at the same time. She shivered. "So what are you telling me? John Lennox and Murphy King stumbled on... hang on."

Freeman smiled. "Go on."

"Who was Murphy King's father?"

"Who do you think?"

Danielle felt goosebumps rise on her arms again. "Dennis? The cadet from…"

Freeman just nodded.

"Ok," said Danielle. "This is starting to get better. Do you think it was a coincidence that Dennis was involved with the Falkland incident and his son with the Paternoster explosion?"

"I don't think that there are any coincidences in this story. I think that once someone gets involved, be it through chance or conscious intent, not only do they stay involved, but I think their descendants get caught in the wake too. It runs with the blood – like strands of a twine. Once you're in, there is no way out."

"In? In what? I still don't really understand what this is."

Freeman held up the photo. "The Land of Sumer."

"You think that John and Murphy found George's magic kingdom? Come on!"

Freeman's expression had become earnest. "Tate translated the steles at Maiden Castle, probably with the help of Tuther. They speak of a Goddess binding The Land of Sumer after it was corrupted."

"You mean like Eden? And the banishment?"

"Along those lines, yes."

"Ok, but I thought that George's work was shown to be a forgery."

"No."

Danielle was confused. "What do you mean no?"

"It was shown to be plagiarised. It was not shown to be a forgery."

"So you think his shipmate wrote a translation of the steles, and when he died George stole it? How did Jim Latter even know about them?"

"You're jumping ahead. But just think; what if both Tate and Latter were right? What if there was some sort of first land, but Man got expelled?"

"That's what you think this is? It's pretty similar to your other theories of a mother civilisation."

"True. But I think that with the help of Tuther, Tate was able to open a window or a doorway or something to Sumer."

"Ok. I'll suspend disbelief. What if Tate did open a doorway?"

"Don't you understand?"

Danielle shook her head.

"That's what the explosion was. The door swings both ways."

Danielle still looked blank.

"There is something on the other side. Something that knows about us. Something that does not want us to see. And It slammed the door."

"The door that George was opening?"

"The chanting that Cullum heard... that was the door being opened. Tate found a way to open it, and Kandian, with his grip on our reality slipping, was able to see it too. But he could only see it when Tate called it. When Tate was not invoking it, Kandian could not see it. He said to Cullum that it was behind a curtain. There but unseen."

"And the music Kandian heard was Tate's little mystic ceremony?"

Freeman nodded. "Something like that."

"And this Thing that closed Tate's door – what is it?"

"I'm not completely certain. But I think it's the Creator."

"Right... Danu?"

"DON'T SAY THAT!" Freeman had nearly lunged across the desk.

Danielle flinched, recoiling. "What? Why?"

Freeman seemed to struggle for a moment to find the right phrase. "Words are power. I'll explain more later. But remember what Kandian said – you must never, never say her name."

Danielle was bewildered. "Ok," she said slowly. "Why do *you* think the Creator slammed George's door shut?"

"Because in the Maiden Castle texts, it was Her that bound Sumer."

"Right, by turning three stars. I still don't understand the connection you have made."

Freeman handed Danielle a thick pile of papers.

"It's the same picture. From the camera still," said Danielle, shuffling through them.

"Is it? Look again."

Danielle shuffled through them again. "Yes. Same picture."

"I've used the same still, but each print is over consecutive days. Each printed at exactly three in the afternoon, for the last hundred and fifty days."

Danielle still looked baffled.

"Flick them. You know, like the old flip books when you were a kid."

Danielle knew the flips books well. She had made a great one when she was seven, of a stick-rocket flying. She half smiled at the memory. She flicked the pile and stopped suddenly half way through.

"You've done something to these," she accused.

Freeman laughed and held his hands up. "I promise you I have not done a single thing."

Danielle flicked them again, all the way through this time.

"How is this possible?"

Freeman shrugged. "Time and its effects are different in Sumer. I don't really understand it myself. I think that the moment that camera caught changes. It's not fixed. It's fluid. Time changes."

"Time changes?"

"Maybe not here, but in the Land of Sumer it does."

Danielle flicked the stack of paper a third time. All the figures remained static, yet overhead there was some movement in the cloud, and in the top right corner was a brightening that became three stars, before fading again, and the clouds swirled jerkily some more.

"What are the stars?" she asked.

"That's why I think the Creator is involved. The castle texts say that She bound the Land of Sumer by turning three stars. I think Kandian saw it too. He said *'three stars turn, she will come'*. There are your three stars."

Danielle checked Kandian's painting. The stars were an exact match for the camera still.

"I don't understand this at all. A still frame moving? An impossible print. Is this why the image is not on your Pad?"

Freeman said nothing, but let the young woman flounder in her own bewilderment. There was more to that story, but it would be told later.

Danielle flicked through the prints again. And again. "Are they a constellation?" she asked.

"Not one that is easily recognised. There are plenty of three-star constellations, and even more that have that configuration somewhere within them."

Danielle flicked through them again. Outside of the three stars fading in and out, there were lots of little movements. Now that she was looking for them, she could see them. Small formations within the blanket of cloud seemed to swirl a little. Some of the tree branches swayed as if in a breeze or light wind. A few of the figures looked as if they were shifting their weight almost imperceptibly.

And still, she felt as if she was missing something.

She pulled the first two frames and the last two from the pile. It was like playing a game of Spot The Difference.

She stared at the images. Something was wrong. Outside of the obvious, there was something very, very wrong.

"What do you see?" asked Freeman after several minutes.

Danielle did not lift her head but resolutely continued to examine the images. "I don't know," she said. "There is something, but I cannot put my finger on it. It's like part of the image is repeating, in a loop. Like the stars. They fade in and out a few times. But there are other parts that seem linear. This figure here," she pointed to one of the many dark clad soldiers in the foreground. "He sways a little, from left to right. Not back again. Just starting on the left, he shifts his weight to the right. And that's it. But his movement does not correspond to the same as..."

And then she saw it. The discrepancy that had been niggling away at her. She put the stills back into order and flicked through them again.

She inhaled sharply. And flicked through again.

There, right at the edge of the frame was half... no less than half of someone's back, walking away until it was completely off the page.

"There was someone else there!"

Freeman said nothing.

"On the hillside. There was someone else there. Look. You can see him. He could only have been ten yards from where John was..."

Freeman spoke quietly, almost mournfully. "It's not a him."

"But, you can see..."

"It's a her."

Danielle was shocked. "You knew?"

Freeman nodded grimly. "Her name was Anna Hyde. And she is very likely lost to us forever."

CHAPTER 7

Excerpt of a letter from Cardinal Muninn to Excellency Fürstenberg, Wewelsburg Castle, dated February 1798

Excellency. I leave Bern tonight by your command. The French will surely be within the walls by the end of the month. I have pleaded with Gottfried to come with me, but he resists. I fear we will lose him should the town fall. His paintings are something to behold. It is what he sees that no-one else does; he claims that the animals live of their own accord, and at times he even plays with and talks to them. I have witnessed paintings that were not as they were the evening previous. This is some new magic; something dwells within his brush.

My name is Ben Buckley. In 2006 I was a trainee Data Retrieval Specialist with Magnetic Information Systems, where I was briefly mentored by Anna Hyde.

Thursday 7th December 2006

Anna stirred, her eyes fluttering open. The alarm clock read six-sixteen and her baby laughed again. He was standing in his cot, blankie clutched in one hand, and, with the other was, trying to lever himself up and over the rail. And apparently he found this hilarious.

The Escape Artist Extraordinaire strikes again.

"Ryan."

Her sleeping husband remained in his comatose state.

"Ryan!"

Nothing.

"RYAN!" An elbow found his ribs.

"Wha...?" He sat bolt upright. "Is Chris ok?" He was still groggy.

Anna got up. She did not know why she even bothered. She crossed to the cot and picked Christopher up.

"Is it time for a feed and a change Little Man?" she whispered to her child.

"I'll do it," said Ryan blearily.

Anna just looked at him. *Like you did the five times last night?*

She wanted to be fair to her husband. Parenting had not come as easy to him as it had to her; not that 'easy' is a word that she would use. Maybe 'natural.'

But either way, these days he was barely making an effort.

They had been together since the end of university and married six years. Christopher had not exactly been planned, although they had talked casually about having kids *one* day.

Ryan had worked in The City for the last eight years as back-office support to a commodities trading company. He did not carry out the trades himself but had checked those that were made for any irregularities. He had never enjoyed the job per se and, after a few drinks, would become increasingly vocal about it.

But it paid the bills. It *had* paid the bills.

Ryan had suspected it for a while. Things were hotting up in the financial markets, and not just in the UK, but in America and Europe and Asia-Pacific. Prime yields had compressed from six percent, down to four, and then to three-point-five, all in a matter of two years. He would have liked to have said that he saw it coming, but the truth was that when he saw a flurry of three percent yields, all he could think about was how much money the company was making, and how big his bonus would be. It would be a lot. A helluva lot.

And then the engine seized. Somebody somewhere had forgotten to check the oil. Lending started to dry up. Bond rates moved out. LIBOR began to go crazy. Somebody somewhere was getting very rich by sucking all the capital out of the system, and it was not him.

But it was a blip, they had all been told. A correction in market values.

Ryan thought he had seen an opportunity. Take a whacking great redundancy pay out now, and in six months time, when the crisis is over, be gainfully reemployed somewhere else. He would be ahead of the curve by an extra year or two.

Except that it had not worked out like that.

Values had not corrected. Their angle of descent had increased. Net Asset Values began to stumble. EBITDAs fell through the floor. Two thousand and seven was not looking clever, but that was not what worried him. Two-thousand and three had seen some of the lowest ever rates for debt, and all those commercial loans were due to be repaid in o-eight. Just over twelve months away.

There were whispers of a bank or two going under. And not one of the tiddlers. One of the big American boys. Lehmans and Goldmans were probably insulated, but Merrill Lynch? They had heavy debt exposure. *Very* heavy.

This was arse-puckering time. Unless a shed load of equity came back on to the market, a lot of people were going to get shafted. *An awful lot* of people.

So where did that leave him? Sitting on a stack of slowly dwindling money, with little chance of getting a job in the next few years. And so Ryan had come to an agreement with his wife. She would go back to work, Chris would go to nursery, and Ryan would stay at home, do the chores, and write that book he had always been threatening.

Except Ryan had found out he was not really motivated. In his head, he knew how the story ended. And that was where his enthusiasm had run out. In the last six months, he had barely written ten thousand words and most of those he was not that impressed with. For the first few weeks he had stuck to the agreement with Anna, and he had cooked and cleaned and washed. But that was boring.

And he was boring. Maybe he was just tense. That was it. The future had become dangerously uncertain, and he was just a little bit stressed.

So, have a drink – just a small one to relax.

And that was how it started.

A glass of wine with dinner and a wee dram before bed. Except that he never had a good night's sleep with the alcohol still in his system. But he still needed to unwind, right?

Ok, so maybe a dram or two in the afternoon, and then a glass of claret with dinner.

Of course, when Anna came home she could smell it on him. She never said anything. Not about the drinking. But the chores not being done? She had something to say about that. And what was his defence? He did not have one. He knew that. He felt that voice rise up inside of him. It had been quiet for years, like a sleeping black dog, but always there.

Of course, you don't have a defence. You're weak and pathetic and your wife is carrying the family.

How long had it been since they had made love? Two months? Three?

Five and you know it! Why would she even touch something as disgusting as you? Look at yourself. Everything about you is a failure. Everything everything everything!

And so he had started going to bed later and later. Limiting the time around her. He only upset her anyway. For the first time, silence had entered their relationship. And it was not that comfortable easy silence that comes at four in the morning after the exuberance of youth has put the world to rights. No, this was the silence that said *I have nothing to say to you.*

As their relationship had become quieter, so the voice in his head had become louder and more persistent.

Everything about you is a failure. Everything everything everything!

And so he had drunk more to blot out that voice. It worked for a while. But then in the morning, or whenever it was that he got up, it was always there. Laughing. And he was always so much more fragile when he woke up.

So he would have a little drink. Just to get the motor running.

But the little drink in the morning had been growing. It had grown big, and the black dog in his head had grown with it.

Anna took the child out of the bedroom. Ryan heard her walking down stairs, and the kettle came on in the kitchen.

Tea. Yes, a cup of tea. That is what he needed. He tried to sit up on his elbows and half slipped. He was still drunk.

Everything about you is a failure. Everything everything everything!

He lay back down, closing his eyes, praying that the room would stop swimming. A car honked its horn outside. That was Jane from next door. Her boy was just a month older than Chris, and she was taking them both to the nursery.

It was half seven already. He had fallen asleep again.

Unconscious! Who are you kidding?!

The front door slammed.

Anna had left. He had not even heard her say goodbye.

She didn't. Why would she speak to something like you?

*

Anna waved to the retreating Espace, turned, and made her way up Norfolk Road. The line of bare London Plane trees seemed to almost blend with the leaden sky. A few leaves hung stubbornly on to the branches, refusing to succumb to the inevitable.

The walk to Southbury Station was cold. Despite the mild November, winter had ridden in on the coat-tails of December and was now biting, making up for lost time.

Although the platform was busy, the train itself was not so full that everyone could not take a seat. Many of the city workers had moved out to Cheshunt in the boom, and it appeared that more and more were choosing to work from home during these straitened times.

Anna looked out at the darkening sky. Snow was coming.

Seven Sisters was even busier than she expected. She supposed it was the build up to Christmas - people taking a day off to get presents. But even so, she had to fight harder than usual to get off the train. Why did people on the platform always stand in front of the carriage doors when they know people are trying to get off?

She was in the office by half-eight and had just finished making her first cup of coffee when Steve Sloman came into the staff kitchen.

"Morning," he said, starting to make his own cup of tea. Steve was one of the regional directors and was well regarded, not just amongst the staff but also with the clients. He had that quality that just made everyone think, *it's all going to be ok.* "How are things?"

"Yeah. Fine. You?"

"Pretty good. We've got a couple of big pitches next week. Hopefully, see if we can land at least one. See if we can't replace USS." The loss of the

Universities Superannuation Service had been a blow. Little work, and high return. "What's your load like at the moment?"

"A bit full to be honest with you. A few of the banks had backup centres in Fiji, and what with the coup, all the lines have been cut. We're trying to retrieve what we can from the European backup sites, but it looks like they'll have a lost a week's worth of data."

"What are we talking? Transactions?"

"No. Mundane stuff mostly. Email correspondence. Net traffic stats. Nothing that will cause a ripple out there." She nodded towards the window. *Out in the real world.*

Companies lost data all the time. Sometimes it could be retrieved, sometimes not. But what mattered was how sensitive it was. The more sensitive, the more they could charge.

"Any chance you could fit a job in for me?"

"Depends on what it is." she said, sipping her coffee.

"It's for The Met. Digital camcorder got fried."

"I didn't know we had the contract."

"We don't. Their usual contractor is backed up, and can't touch it for a week. We're the first reserve on their contractor list. Might be a good opportunity for us to try and raise our profile."

"Hmmm. How much data?"

"Hard to say. Somewhere between and an hour and ninety minutes of footage."

"Do you know the resolution?"

"No. But it'll be high. It was a Beeb job."

"I thought you said it was a camcorder?"

"It is. You know, one of those on the shoulder things."

"Steve!"

"What? What would you call it?"

"A film camera."

Steve shrugged. "Ok. A film camera."

Anna rolled her eyes. That was the problem with reps. They always promised the client the earth and then handed it off to the grunts with no thought as to if it could ever be delivered.

"What's the spec?"

"Not sure. Probably twenty-five frames-per-second."

"How much of it has been lost?"

"Looks like a hundred percent."

"Steve! Come on. I'm good, but I'm not a miracle worker."

"Anna. Please. We could really do with a win."

Anna paused for a moment. "Ok. I'm too soft for my own good, aren't I?"

"Thank you. Really appreciated."

"I'm not promising anything. I'll have a look at it. If there's nothing that I can do, or it's going to take more than a couple of days then that is just tough."

*

Anna was examining the broken camera casing when Ben came in at ten to nine. She did not even have to look up to know it was him. The tinny *tsh-tsh-tsh* coming from his earphones was so familiar to her that she often wondered how he did not permanently damage his hearing.

She remembered when she was discovering her own taste in music, in the grunge and Seattle sound of the early nineties. But what Ben listened to – well it all just sounded the same. She wished she was cooler. That she could *get it*. But she did not.

What was it this week? Slipknot? He had tried, bless him. He had played her some of the quieter tracks, and they were ok, albeit not her thing. But then he had tried the one about pushing fingers into her eyes. Or was it his eyes.

She had remembered what it felt like to feel that angry. To want to rise, resist and rebel. Killing In The Name still made her feel sixteen again. Now that was proper metal. But the truth was that she just was not that angry anymore. Not even at her feckless husband.

She just had to look at her little boy and she felt content. And when she was not feeling content she felt tired. God, when had she got this old?

"Hi," said Ben, in his typical borderline non-committal grunt.

Anna had sized him up when she first met him. At twenty-two, he was a recent IT graduate and still dressed as if he was studying. He made an effort, in so far that he wore a shirt and his shoes had been polished, but if he had ever been shown how to iron, he had long forgotten. It was not that he was not talented. Anna wished that she had been able to grasp concepts the way that Ben did. He made it look easy and was able to extrapolate protocols from one process to another, often in a myriad of combinations that would never have occurred to her.

It was his lethargy that bothered her. He was never excited. Never down. Never frustrated. He did his nine to five-thirty without complaint and then went off with his droogy mates on a Friday night. He had invited her along once, to some club. Slimelight. What sort of name was that for a club?

Anna knew this was unfair. Perhaps she was resenting Ryan for taking those years from her. She could have been free and single, and tearing London a new one every weekend. But it was much more sensible to save a deposit for flat, and then a house. She had chosen him and he her. And they had just sort of drifted along ever since.

"New Lost Prophets album," Ben said, offering her an earphone. It was caked in wax.

"You're ok thanks," she said, turning back to the camera. Ben looked disappointed, but then he always did. "They weren't the same after Chiplin left," she finished.

Ben looked stunned, and Anna felt proud that she had forced him to emote. *I'm still cool*, she thought.

"I've got the new Pearl Jam album on order if you want a copy," he said. Perhaps he had finally found a crack in Anna's seemingly impenetrable exterior. *She knew about Lost Prophets! Finally some common ground!*

"You're alright thanks. Ten was their peak. Come and have a look at this."

"Pretty banged up. What is it?"

"Blue Job."

"Wha..." At twenty-two, Ben still only thought about one thing other than music.

"I said blue," said Anna, half smiling. God, she had almost seen those unreasonably tight trousers twitch. She remembered when Ryan had been like that. All fire and raw passion. In those early weeks, they had both been little more than animals. They had missed so many lectures, just to stay in bed, exploring each other's bodies with an almost casual roughness, each pushing the other towards some unknown limit. After that first weekend, she had walked like John Wayne for a week. That memory gave her a warm glow.

And then of course real life had dared to intrude. Exams had to be taken and then careers started. What did that leave? A snatched dinner before crashing in front of the television in order to numb once sharp minds and then to bed where they were too tired to do anything other than grinding up against each other quickly once a week. In time that had become once a fortnight. And then less frequent.

Of course, it was not always mundane. Sometimes the weekends were better when they managed to get out and have some fresh air. But invariably it was a downward spiral, and she knew it. Christopher had come along nearly twelve months ago, and whilst she had no frame of reference, the pregnancy and delivery had been easier than most. But with all her attention on the little man, the distance between her and Ryan seemed to grow. And the child was not even demanding. He was a happy little boy. Maybe she used that relationship to hide from Ryan.

But it was his fault as well. What was once a fire was now little more than embers and he did little to stoke it back up. There was no suggestion of leaving him. He was her husband. The father of her child. But another forty or fifty years of gradually increasing indifference?

So what? An affair? Add a bit of spice back into her life? But where would she find the time? And with whom? There was not anyone at work that she would touch with a barge-pole, and she did not socialise anymore, or at least not like she used to. There was the Christmas get together with the girls, and then the works summer party. Hardly a social butterfly.

She suspected that Ben had a crush on her, but boys of his age had a crush on anything with a pulse.

"Oh, the Law. Right." Ben's comments brought her back from her brief daydream.

"Yeah. One of Steve's clients."

"So what happened?"

"You know better than that," she said, removing the screws that barely held the remains of the casing together. "We recover. We don't question. Here, hold this." She handed him the screwdriver and removed the case. "Have a look and tell me what you think," she continued.

Learn by doing, her eyes said.

Ben took his coat off, put his earphones on his workstation, and pulled over a large magnifying glass.

"The main circuit looks fried. There is impact damage on the sides. But I can't see any burns. Probably not an electrical short. Maybe mags?" Magnets were always a likely source of data loss, and Anna was secretly proud at how Ben applied deductive reasoning.

"Possibly. Look again."

Ben returned to his examination of the circuit. "Is that a bit of melting? There on the solder?"

"What would that suggest?"

"Someone microwaved it?"

"Some sort of microwave radiation, yes. So what would the next steps be?"

"Err... scan the hard drive. Copy it if we can. Find the longest piece of continuous data and try and see if anything can be recovered from there?"

"Good. Off you go."

*

It was about an hour later when Anna returned to Ben's workbench. "What have you got?"

"Not much," said Ben, sitting up and stretching. "Sector zero is intact, and I've got file sizes and locations. But the actual files themselves... well most of them are toast. The audio has completely gone."

"Ok. Have you got the File Allocation Table?"

"Yup."

"Good. So where is the longest set of unbroken data?"

"Looks like it is about the twenty-three-minute mark. But it's not a lot. Maybe a megabyte or two. Three at the most."

"Let's have a look at it." Anna leaned over Ben and called the file up. At best it was maybe a couple of frames. Probably less. "Ok. Create a separate directory. Now before you start processing, get familiar with it. You'll need to be able to tell the difference between a raw and part recovered file."

The file appeared in the window of the recovery application. White snow.

"See?" said Ben.

Anna smiled. It never ceased to amaze her what the untrained eye could miss. She took a sheet of paper and drew an outline on it.

"What's that?"

"That is what will appear on the first pass. Go on. Run it."

Ben set the recovery programme to run a single pass, and a few minutes later, the file reloaded into the window. White snow.

Ben looked at her, confused that his mentor could have got it wrong.

Anna smiled. "Do you see it?" She put the paper side-by-side with the monitor.

"No."

"There." Anna traced the outline for him on the screen. Ben looked from the monitor to Anna's drawing and back again. He saw the faintest outline on the screen, and it matched Anna's crude drawing.

"How?" he asked, bewildered.

"Just practice. Don't worry. You'll get there. Right set that for say another twenty passes, and then come and give me a hand with Fiji."

*

It was after lunch when they returned to Ben's station. They had both brought sandwiches from home, but Ben had chosen to sit with Fiona in the staff room. Anna had decided that that Fiona was odd.

It was not that she was the only other woman in a company of nearly a hundred borderline autistic socially inept men, but it was her evasiveness. She never answered a question, and she had never met Anna's eye. Not once.

Fiona had started at the same time as Ben, but she had a more natural flair for the discipline. Anna knew that she would pass her accreditation exams the first time. Ben, on the other hand, was a fifty-fifty. She was a few years older than Ben, possibly mid-twenties, but she had never confirmed her age to anyone. Her pale skin and shoulder length black hair had set all the trousers twitching. Not that any of the men would actually know what to say to her, let alone do to her, assuming she even let them within ten yards.

She was smart, efficient, and in every way a model employee, and possibly a role model for every other woman in the industry. And she only had eyes for Ben. Anna knew that Ben thought it was sexual - that there was at least a chance he could get into her knickers. Anna had to have the chat with him very early on, about what was and was not acceptable material to email. He had looked suitably chagrined.

Anna did not dare to think when was the last time Ben had got any. Certainly not since he had started with her. Poor boy must be rubbing his palm raw. But Anna also knew that, for Fiona, the last thing on her mind was sex. It was not just that she was out of Ben's league, although it was like comparing the Premiership with the Nationwide Conference. It was that she was playing with him.

Anna had watched Fiona flirting by numbers. Flicking the hair. Tilting the head to expose her neck. The kitten laugh. It was the smile that gave it away though. The smile that was far from innocent and said *let me in or I'll huff and puff.*

A predator's smile.

She suspected that Fiona was building up for a sexual harassment case, and she had already put Steve and HR on notice. Of course, there was not much that they could do other than monitor the situation. The Christmas Party was only a few weeks away, and it would not be the first time there had been a sticky ending to that event.

When Anna had first started with the company, there had been another Anna who started at the same time. They were known as Big Anna and Little Anna, and she did not like being Big Anna. At the Christmas Party that year, Little Anna was not seen much after nine, and the next morning an embarrassed-looking director was seen leaving her hotel room.

Ultimately, no-one had cared, but it had provided reasonable office banter for a few months, and it was due to this that Little Anna had later sued, and won, on the grounds of harassment. It did not make it to court, and there were rumours of a *substantial* payout. Needless to say, the company did not meet its targets that year, and Big Anna did not get her bonus. Well, she was not going to let some trollop take her bonus away again. No way.

"Have a nice time with your little friend?" she asked.

"Hmmm..." Ben said noncommittally. He knew that his manager did not like his crush. Probably because she was old and lumbered with a kid, and Fiona was young and *so so so* hot. He had once seen Anna's breast leak milk through her top. She had been apologetic, but Ben felt traumatised. He did not know they could do that.

Whenever Anna mentioned Fiona, he kept his own counsel, just like Fiona had said he should do. At lunch, Fiona had confided in him. Ben *knew* that she had a secret. For months he had sensed that there was something that she was not telling him. Something that absolutely needed to get out, but was held in check. And over a coffee at lunchtime, Fiona had finally told him.

She was a Born Again Christian and had invited Ben to her Church on Sunday. He had thought about saying no for a moment. He had met a few BAC's at university and they were not his bag. But, he remembered that by the end of their third year, all that pent up sexual frustration had been absolutely bursting to get out. He had not seen any of that action, but two of his friends had got hook-ups at the Summer Ball. They had not stopped talking about it for weeks.

Fiona had been going to her church for a few years. The way Ben saw it, she was just about to ripen and, for once, he was in the right place at the right time.

So he had agreed that he would go along and see what it was all about. It was not in a traditional church, but rather in a central London theatre. The church had the use of it in the morning, and in the afternoon it was turned back over to whatever production was on that season. That left plenty of time for lunch, a few coffees in Leicester Square, then maybe some dinner. He knew this great Persian restaurant on Garrick Street - all mezes. For some reason, girls loved the whole eating-with-your-hands thing. He knew the secret; make her happy and relaxed, and then don't make a move. Her own insecurities would make her throw herself at him. His older brother had taught him that after too many beers.

Anna could see that she was not going to get anything out of her student, and turned to the monitor. "Right, let's see what we've got."

The image resolved on the screen. It was still mostly snow, but faint outlines could be made out. On the right, the silhouette of a forest was forming, and to the left there seemed to be the impression of a body of water – possibly a large lake or a sea. Shadowy figures seemed to be focussing on a central point near an unidentifiable building, and in the foreground, these eldritch forms gained solidity.

"Do you see?" Anna asked. "The program is finding uncorrupted data from the other frames and marrying it into this one. Position...colour gradation."

"Won't that just create a jumbled mess?"

"No. It'll only look five seconds in each direction, but with a camera running on twenty-five fps; it should give us just over two hundred frames. It'll still be a composite, but it should be enough to start filling in some of the other frames. We may even be able to get a short sequence out of it."

Ben shrugged. "This is the longest set of unbroken data. All the others are pretty mashed."

"You'd be surprised what the program can do. Now, how many more passes will it do between now and say, four o'clock?"

"Hundred?"

Anna smiled. "Half that. Remember, it's picking pixels from the surrounding frame. It'll go for the easy ones first, so each successive pass will take longer as it has to work harder. Go for," Anna looked at the clock, "say forty-six." She would like to be back at the station as it finished the last pass, just to say *ta-da!*

Ben was looking at the image on the screen. "Does this look a bit weird to you?"

"Ben!" Anna's voice had an edge. "You know the rules. We just recover the data. Nothing more. No reading emails. No gazing at whatever porn they've got stored on their hard drive," *and there was always A LOT of porn.* "Just do the job."

"But... just look."

"Ben. No buts."

"Please," there was whine to his voice. He was still twelve years old underneath all those spots and lank greasy hair.

"Ok." She was exasperated, and wanted to get on, but if it never hurt to give in to a student's pleadings. Once in a while, they saw something she missed. She had learnt that the hard way.

She looked at the image. There was still a lot of snow, and what had been resolved was blurry and out of focus.

"What am I looking at?"

"There," he pointed to the far right of the screen. There seemed to be a figure, standing side on, half in and half out of shot, in the foreground.

"What?"

"The pattern on that blouse. On the cuff."

"Yes?"

"Don't you have a blouse like that?"

Anna turned to look at the boy, her frustration threatening to boil over.

"Ben! Can we get on now?"

"What? It is! That's your blouse!"

"Well I'm very flattered that you pay so much attention to what I wear, but perhaps you might like to think how many women also buy their blouses from bloody Primark!"

*

Four o'clock came around too quickly. Ben had worked with Anna for a few hours on the Fiji problem before Steve had called on him.

Anna had worked quicker without him. She knew how important training was, but why did she have to be the one to give it? She had her own workload.

Ben was late. Anna was half relieved as it meant that she could get on without having to explain everything, but also half annoyed. This was part of his training.

She called up the retrieval programme, and the system clock told her that the last scan would be finished in three... two... one.

And Ben was not there to see it. *Damn!*

The image resolved itself on the monitor. A few patches of snow remained, but on the whole, it was clear, albeit not entirely in focus. A number of areas were sharper than others. She could make out the sky, some sort of coast, odd looking buildings, a large crowd in the mid and foreground.

Her eye was drawn to the figure Ben had pointed out before.

That's not right.

Anna felt an involuntary shiver.

It had moved. It had turned towards the camera.

Anna could see more of the features now.

There has got to be a glitch.

Anna opened up Ben's working folder.

There was only one file it.

"Ben!" she exclaimed to herself, more in frustration than anger.

"Yes?"

Anna spun around. "Where have you been?" she demanded. "It's ten past four. You're late!"

"Sorry," he mumbled. "I was with Steve."

"We'll talk about that later. Right now, I want you to explain this to me. You've not been backing up your work!"

Ben looked baffled.

"You're supposed to create an individual file every time a pass is completed."

The look of confusion did not leave Ben's face.

"Ben, you've been overwriting the same file. There is no way to go back and undo any mistakes!"

Ben flushed. The option had been there, on the menu. 'Create new file after each pass'. But Anna had been with him and she had not told him to check that box.

"Sorry," he muttered, looking at the floor like a naughty school boy.

Anna wanted to remonstrate with him again but held herself back.

"Did you do anything to the program whilst I was gone?" she asked, half accusingly.

Ben frowned. "No."

"Sure?"

"Yes." He remained defiantly firm.

Anna turned back to the screen with a huff. She knew it was unlikely that Ben had interfered with the program. In all likelihood, the program had just reconstructed a composite image from the surrounding frames, and in those, the woman in the blouse had been turning. Those frames had just contained more recoverable information.

She ran a single pass, this time, making sure to save the file.

A minute or so later, the image resolved itself.

Anna felt her stomach knot, and her chest constricted as though someone had tightened a steel band around it. The figure had moved, again. It was now staring right at whoever had been holding the camera. It was staring right at her.

Anna divided the desktop into two, keeping the newer image visible at all times. She opened the previous file.

It was more than a winter chill that crept into her blood, and she felt the hairs on her neck begin to rise. The position of the figure in the older file was exactly the same as the newer one. It was not possible.

She had seen, with her own eyes, where the figure had been. She ran another pass, feeling her heartbeat begin to rise with the urgency of a drummer boy dictating the beat of the final charge.

The image resolved itself.

It's not possible!

The figure had moved forward. She could make out the features more clearly now. A woman in her early thirties. Blue jeans. White blouse. With a pattern on the cuff. Just like hers.

Her heart was pounding. She ran another pass. Despite the cool of the office, she could feel her back begin to bead with nervous sweat.

What the...?

The figure had moved forward again. Her hair had lightened. Almost to Anna's shade of brownie-blonde.

It had been dark before! I know it was dark before. Almost black.

She called up the previous files. They all showed the same woman in the same position. And she had always had the same brownie-blonde hair.

This is a joke. This has to be a joke. Someone is in the server room, rewriting the files as I go along!

She turned around. Ben was still there, looking sheepish and offended at her last accusation. Everyone else was at their workstation. Heads down, and desperately trying not to meet her eye. They all knew when their team leader was in a mood and they had no wish to be the next victim of her well-known temper.

Everyone else was there. Except Fiona.

"Where is your little friend?" It was not a question. It was a demand.

"Who?"

"Don't play with me." His voice was like a sharpened blade.

Ben shrugged. "She was waiting to see Steve as I left his office."

Anna punched in Steve's speed dial on her phone.

"Wotcha," Said the voice at the end. "How is that police..."

"Is Fiona with you?"

"Yes."

Anna did not know what to say. She had not thought this far ahead in her fog of bewilderment and frustration.

"Do you want me to send her out?" Steve asked.

"Yes. No, I mean no."

"You ok?"

"Yes. Fine." She paused. "There's a problem with your blue job. I don't know if it's the programme or the data, but the best I can...."

"Hang on. We'll be right out."

"No. Wait..." The line had gone dead.

Anna ran another pass. The image resolved.

Anna felt sick. The figure was much further forward now. Anna could start to make out features. A long oval face. A slightly hawkish nose.

Anna caught a smell. Bleach?

She turned around again. Had someone used a table wipe? She could not see anything other than her team hunkering lower and lower behind their monitors.

"Do you smell that?" she said to Ben.

Ben grunted and nodded. He looked around but likewise saw nothing. Anna turned back to the monitor. Steve would be there any minute.

She ran another pass. The image resolved itself.

For a moment Anna thought she had heard something. Distant chanting. Like one of those Gregorian monk CDs she'd bought and then listened to once, because she thought that by just having it in her collection Ryan would think she was intellectual.

She opened the background file and looked for any semblance of a partially recovered audio track. She was not surprised that there was none.

The figure had moved forward again.

I'm losing my mind, she thought. *I've actually gone crazy.*

The door at the end of her floor opened and she saw Steve. And of course, Fiona was with him.

Of course. They were both in on it. And Ben too probably. Ha ha! Ha ha DAMNED HA!

Anna ran a final pass. The program was still running as Steve approached. With Fiona.

Anna felt her insides grind like cogs that had run out of oil. God alone knew how much she detested that woman, all smug and pert. Bile and vitriol rose up inside her like a leviathan from the deep, roaring at the heavens before devouring all around it.

"So? What have we got?" Steve said cheerfully.

The image resolved once again.

The figure was almost on top of the camera, taking up nearly a third of the screen, her hand held out. A single finger was raised as if reaching out or beginning to grasp.

Anna could hear Steve breathing behind her, waiting expectantly.

The smell of bleach came again, and with it came that brief distant chant, somehow guttural and full of resonance.

The woman in the image was looking right at her. Directly into her eyes. There was something there. An imploring. An unspoken cry. It was almost primal, a wild last desperate begging for... for what? She felt a deep sadness well up, dousing her anger and frustration.

All is lost, came an unbidden thought.

In the days to come, Ben would struggle to really understand what happened next. He could remember the smell of bleach. Like toilet cleaner.

Steve had been standing there. "Well?" he had asked.

Anna had half turned to answer but had then turned back to the monitor. She had looked as if she was about to cry.

And then she touched the screen, meeting the hand of the frozen figure.

Ben's ears popped and he felt sick.

The smell of bleach made his eyes sting, and they watered. In that moment, Anna looked like she was two-dimensional. Flattened and without any depth. And then it was gone.

His eyes stopped watering, and he worked his jaw to clear the uncomfortable sensation from his ear.

He could see just over Anna's shoulder. The figure of the woman was still there. Side on, but with her head turned slightly towards the camera. Looking slightly confused. Just as she always had been.

He realised that his first impression that it had looked like Anna was wrong. The woman in the image had browny-blonde hair, whereas Anna had always had black hair. He suspected a dye job. No-one had hair that black.

Anna turned around and looked through Steve to Fiona. She smiled her usual hawkish grin.

"It's alright," she said sweetly. "I've fixed the problem."

*

Danielle was quiet for a moment.

Freeman added nothing more and let the silence grow between them.

"What happened?" she asked eventually. "Possession? A body swap?" Her sense of incredulity had long since left her.

"All of that. None of that. Who knows? But I think that *something* crossed over."

"Crossed over? From where? And what was it?"

"What crossed over? Who can say? But from where?" He held up Kandian's canvas, and one of the stills. "The Land of Sumer."

"You're still going with that?"

"Aren't you?"

Danielle paused again. She could feel the romantic part of her mind wanting to believe. Yet her rational brain reminded her that it was the twenty-first century, and the world had long ago stopped believing in fantasy realms and unicorns.

She caught herself. She had not though - she still believed. Maybe not in Narnia or Castle Rock, or Mossflower. But she did believe. Deep down in the secret court of her heart. She believed in... what? Something more. Something else. The next place. Maybe.

She put the thought from her mind and avoided Freeman's question.

"I'm not biting," she lied. "If something did genuinely come through and either possessed Anna Hyde, or swapped bodies with her, or whatever, then her behaviour would have changed. Somebody would have noticed."

Freeman answered slowly. "It did and they did."

Danielle frowned. A story that was corroborated? Well, there was a first time for everything.

"Who?" she asked, leaning forward.

Freeman paused, mulling his answer. "Before I tell you, I want you to consider something."

Danielle did not like this delaying tactic. "What?"

"What if words have power?"

"Of course they have power... the written word is..."

"No," Freeman interrupted. "What if the spoken word has *actual* power? Tate's translation of the steles frequently speaks about Words of Power. Gravity is powerful enough to bend light, and everything we know in the universe has a gravitational field, albeit a weak one. A single photon of light leaves a gravitational wake."

"What does this have to do with your source?" Danielle asked.

Freeman's tone was sombre. "My source... he's a tortured man, and he was brought to do certain things that he can barely live with. You will ask why, if he knew what he was doing was wrong, he just did not leave, and I will tell you that it was because he unwittingly agreed to a life of servitude. And because he agreed, he was bound."

"And you're telling me this because you think he was under the influence of these Words of Power?" Danielle tried to suppress her incredulity.

"Yes. I know that you don't believe it but just think about it; every time someone sees Sumerland, they hear chanting. Before the explosion at Paternoster House, Andy Cullum heard George muttering in some arcane language... probably to rend a hole between worlds.

But it is more than that. Every time someone has... has an experience, they have a physical sensation. John Lennox told how his ears popped as he crossed over. Dennis King and Harry Gordon made similar comments. Ben Buckley said he felt his ears pop as Anna and the thing from Sumerland swapped places. I think that they feel their ears pop when... when something about our reality changes, and I think that these Words of Power can do that. They can actually change our reality. Just think about it. The creatures that have come through... they know how to use these words and they can make you believe in anything, just by forcing you to agree with them."

Danielle was intrigued by the premise. "These would be your Raven Men, I suppose?"

Freeman nodded. "Yes. I think that's what came through Anna Hyde's monitor. Or maybe its essence."

"Ok," Danielle replied. "I'll buy it. So if something did come through, and her behaviour did change, who noticed?"

Freeman's pause was longer this time. "Her husband," he said eventually. "And Anna made him do terrible things."

CHAPTER 8

Matthew 27: 4
"I have sinned," he said, "for I have betrayed innocent blood."
"What is that to us?" they replied. "The responsibility is yours alone."

My name is Ryan Hyde and I am an alcoholic. It has been fifteen years since my last drink, which was on 16th April 2010. It was the day that I left the things that had once been my wife and child. I would never see them again.

Thursday 7th December 2006
Ryan was down in it.

The day had not started well, and it was not until after lunch that he had got out of bed. He was in a black mood.

How dare my wife not say goodbye to me. How dare she!

Of course, the other voice had answered, even though he had not asked it to.

Why would she?

And so he had a drink. Just a small one. To get warmed up. To get the old engine going. To quieten the voice a little. That had been around twelve-thirty.

It was now gone six and he still had not showered. And there had been a few more drinks. Quite a few more drinks. Ok, a lot, even by his standards. But he was alright. He would just have a coffee and some toast before his darling wife came back. Maybe wash his teeth too. For his darling wife.

The little bitch! It's gone six! Where is she?!

The dirty dishes from last night's meal looked back at him. The washing machine winked accusingly, reminding him that it had done its job some hours ago and he would do well to do his.

He did not move but looked at his laptop screen. His document was empty. He had not written a single thing that afternoon. He was reminded of that Kubrick film with Jack Nicholson. It would be easy to copy and paste *All work and no sex makes Ryan very VERY angry.*

He hit the keyboard briefly, deleted it, and looked around. He did not mind the house. It was a small Victorian mid-terrace three bed. But the third bedroom was really a box room. Ryan thought it had once been the bathroom that had been converted when the extension was put on the ground floor.

And wasn't that a bodge job!

Single skin brickwork, mouldering wooden frames. Anna and he had taken it on as a project. With the rise in the property prices, they could do it up and make a quick buck. But then Anna had got pregnant.

Little bitch did that on purpose! To trap me!

Ryan knew that was not true. Not even lying to himself made him feel any better. He wanted to rail against everything. To blame everything. Everyone.

This is not the way things were supposed to be.

This is not who he was supposed to be.

In all honesty, he wanted to cry. He felt the bubble of shame well up inside of him. He felt that a lot these days. As if everyone had somehow swum away from him, leaving him bobbing on an ocean. He could see them all in the distance. Getting smaller. Not even waving goodbye.

Of course, he knew that his life had not left him. He had left it. And it was not that everyone was getting smaller. He was just getting further away. He quite liked that idea and typed that last thought onto the screen.

It sounded self-pitying, and he deleted it.

The empty document stared back again.

He took another noisy slurp from his tumbler. The harsh alcohol did not even burn anymore. He felt the comforting warmth slide down into his belly where it rested for a few minutes before slowly fading.

What? It's not like I'm on hard drugs. It's just a little drink.

Somewhere deep inside him, Ryan knew the truth. It was not the one little drink that was the problem. It was the nine or ten that followed it that was the problem. And it was a big problem.

But when is a problem a problem? I'm not hurting anybody, he reasoned.

You're hurting yourself. That was his grandmother's voice. God, he missed her. She had been that kindly silver-haired woman who had always told him stories of the blitz and working in a munitions factory and how his grandfather had been ground crew for the RAF in Egypt, and would show him the one telegram she had received from him, now yellow and brittle with age.

Gran, how come paper goes yellow with age, but people go grey?

His Gran had laughed. She was not the most educated woman and she knew it, having left school at twelve. Yet she always had a way of empowering him - making him feel that he could do anything. He had always imagined her stories in black and white, like the old films they had watched together. She had cried at Brief Encounter. He did not understand at the time. He did now.

He heard the front door unlock.

He still had not tidied the kitchen

Or had a shower.

And yet still he was relieved. His wife was home. His darling wife was home!

Anna stood in the doorway to the lounge, surveying both the state of her husband and the kitchen beyond. Ryan stood and went to hug her. The room swam and he sat back down. Hard.

He looked up at his wife, expecting another angry monologue born of frustration. Something was different about her. He could not put his finger on it. Was she taller?

People don't just get taller! The voice inside mocked.

Paler? What was it?

"Ryan?"

Ryan frowned and tried to focus. "Have you had a haircut?"

Anna did not reply but carried on looking at him curiously as if she was not entirely sure what it was that she was seeing.

"Anna? You ok?" He stood up and was able to counter the slow spin of the room this time.

"Yes. You are my husband."

That's odd.

Ryan grinned. "Yes, I am," and made an overblown attempt to bow. His ears popped and he felt the room shift around him. He sat back down quickly.

"I am your wife," said Anna. She had half cocked her head, as though listening for a distant voice.

"Uh-huh," he replied, rubbing his eyes. His ears popped again, and he felt the room's spin resume. He closed his eyes, and tilted his head back, fighting a wave of nausea. Ryan heard the footsteps of his approaching wife on the carpeted floor and then felt the warmth of her body as she straddled him, pushing her hips into his.

Ryan's eyes snapped open. They had not touched like this in months.

His wife was looking down at him, unblinking and impassive. "I am your wife," she said again and ground her hips into his. Her kiss was savage, more teeth than anything else. Ryan tasted blood in his mouth and some primitive part of him, long dormant in a lagoon of alcohol, stirred and then rose. He went to flip her over so that he was on top, but she remained firm, pinning him to the sofa.

*

That night, Anna moved Christopher's cot into the nursery. Ryan noticed how sinewy her arms had become, bristling with definition. Had they always been like that?

The child had seemed ill at ease with Anna at first, but they put it down to a difficult day at nursery, and some late teeth that were still making their way through.

In bed, their bodies entwined again. Anna was as vigorous and insistent as she had been earlier. Again Ryan tried to turn her over, and again she pinned him down, making him work from underneath.

Her hands pressed down his chest, and one of them worked its way towards his throat. "You love me, don't you?" she said between exaggerated gasps.

"Wha...?" his reverie broken.

"You love me, don't you?" Her hand began to paw at his throat.

"Yeah sure."

"Say it!" She tightened around him.

"I... I love you!" He gasped, eyes bulging.

"And you would do anything for me." Her grip had not relaxed.

"Yea..."

"Say it!" She carried on squeezing.

"I would do anything for you." His ears popped for the third time that day, causing him to wince.

With three quick thrusts, she finished him off and dismounted.

Ryan barely slept that night. He felt something inside of him - cold like thousands of tiny snakes slithering through his veins. During the snatched interludes of sleep he dreamed of a home that was not his own, and yet there were similarities. The doorways were distorted; twelve feet high, culminating in crude and brutal misshapen peaks. Around him were once members of his family, long since dead. His father, serenely gazing out of a kitchen window, bathed in a faint purple light, turned to face his son.

"The Third Twine has risen. The key is joined. Find the gate," the old man said, and then turned back to the window, oblivious to his son's presence. Outside, his garden seemed to stretch to an impossible distance. Below him the ground had opened, revealing an immense pit, with steps that wound down into the darkness. As he went to place his foot on the first step he realised that it was not a hole in the ground at all, but rather that his garden had become an immense pool, perfectly reflecting the sky above him. Dark and thunderous clouds hinted at impossible horrors within, and the air felt greasy against his skin as he realised that the yawning chasm that had been in front of him was now in the heavens above him.

Ryan was startled from his doze and saw that Anna was awake, eyes open and looking at the ceiling. Looking through the ceiling. In the shadows of their bedroom, even her irises looked black.

*

At seven-thirty the next morning, Anna saw Christopher into Jane's waiting car, and then returned inside.

Ryan had awoken and was painfully thirsty. "Are you not going to work?" he said, gulping water noisily.

"No. I quit."

Ryan was stunned. "What? Why?"

Anna looked at him coldly. "It was not what I wanted to do."

"But what about our agreement? What will we do for money?"

Anna tilted her head to one side as if she was listening to a distant voice.

Ryan realised that she was looking through him to the pile of dirty dishes behind him. He felt a felt a flush of shame and anger rise up within himself. He reddened, began to protest, and then thought better of it.

"Come with me." She barked. It was an order rather than a request and her new puppet obeyed without thought.

Wordlessly, they dressed, and then headed out into the crisp morning. There had been a light frost the night before, and the cobwebs in their neighbours' holly bush were picked out like constellations from another time and place.

They spent the morning walking. Occasionally Anna would stop, look around herself, as if she was seeing Enfield and its residential sprawl for the first time, and then carry on. The silence grated on Ryan. He felt like a chastened dog. He wanted to protest, to say something, anything, but the words caught in his throat.

It was just a few minutes after noon when they came into the town centre. They had zigzagged through the back streets, avoiding the arterial roads, except when they had to cross the Great Cambridge Road, until eventually they had come through Bush Hill Park, and passed the children on the swings. A small group of them, no more than half a dozen, all three or four years old, laughing and running about. Pre-schoolers.

It was here that Anna had paused longest. Just watching them with no emotion on her face. The intensity of her focus made Ryan uneasy.

After a short time, she had moved off and Ryan had followed. Now he could see the pub. "Lunch?" he said, as cheerily as he could.

Anna looked at him coldly. "Have you been good?"

"What?"

"Have you been good?" irritation had entered her voice.

"Of course..."

"Have you been faithful?"

"Wha..?"

Anna walked up to him on the busy street, grabbed his crotch, and began to squeeze. "Have you been faithful?" She was looking right up at him now, demanding an answer.

"Yes, Jesus... Yes!"

Nearby shoppers turned at his last yelp, noticing how Ryan had come up onto his toes.

Anna did not let go.

A hooded teenager called from across the road. "Go on love! Woo!" She had brought out a mobile phone and was holding it up, presumably recording the spectacle.

Anna half turned, realising for the first time the very public nature of her actions, and released her husband.

*

The George Public House was one of the oldest establishments in Enfield, and even though it had been through numerous refurbishments over the years, it still managed to hold on to the smell of old sweat, fetid beer, and stale smoke. Given that it had been a full six months since anyone had been allowed to light up inside, Ryan thought the lingering smell of stale nicotine was impressive.

At first glance, the pub's most recent incarnation looked quite modern with a number of booths lining two of the walls, and big sofas in the middle. However, a closer inspection revealed well-established glass marks on the table tops, and worn seats with stuffing trying to escape through holes that had once been cigarette burns but were now more sizeable. The floor had that tacky feeling of too many spilt cocktails from Friday night's Happy Hour, and no amount of cleaning would ever change that. It had become part of the fabric of the old building, just as the silence had become a part of Anna and Ryan's relationship.

They sat in a booth by the window, watching the pedestrians wander by, bracing themselves against the chill December wind that had arrived without warning only a few hours ago. Ryan was nursing a half-finished pint, and looking forlornly at the three empty tumblers that had been chasers. Just enough to dull the edge, but not enough to take it away completely.

Anna sat, gazing through the pane of glass, her wine completely untouched.

Few words had passed between them. Whatever Anna had asked, Ryan had agreed to. His balls were still sore. If he had suspected that the balance of power between them had been shifting, he was now in no doubt that the process was now over. He felt like a dog that had been kicked but still returned to its master.

Outside, it began to rain a watery half-sleet. Slowly at first, and then increasing in intensity. A real December downpour. Visibility quickly fell until neither of them could make out the other side of the road.

The wind picked up, trying to drive the deluge to a horizontal angle, rattling The George's single-glazed window. Pedestrians quickly got undercover as umbrellas were turned inside out in an instant.

It reminded Ryan of the weather they had experienced when they lived in Edinburgh, just after they had graduated. It had only been a year or two, working for small companies before London called. What had it been? The Christmas Storm of ninety-eight? Their flat had lost power early on. They were luckier than most. Chimney stacks had been blown down, caving in a neighbours' roof. Advertising hoardings had been ripped from buildings and had gone through windows. Fences had blown down as the East Coast had been battered by the most severe storms in living memory. But they had not cared. They had each other and for three days had done nothing but snuggle under the duvet in the darkness. He had almost been disappointed when the lights came back on.

Now Anna looked out at the rain, a sense of wonder on her face as if it was the first time she had seen such weather.

"How long will it last?" she asked, her hand reaching out to touch the cool glass.

Ryan frowned, shrugged, and looked down into his pint. "It can't rain all the time," he muttered.

Anna looked baffled. "Of course it can't."

Ryan felt something rise up inside of him. A bubble of fear that made him feel sick. "It can't rain all the time," he said again, more cautiously.

Anna continued to look at him blankly.

Now Ryan knew. Something was wrong. Something was very wrong indeed. Their first proper date, away from the University, Halls, and big woolly jumpers had been to see an afternoon re-run of The Crow at the local cinema. It was Brandon Lee's last film and Ryan had loved every minute of it. He knew that Anna had been less keen, but enjoyed it because he enjoyed it.

During a scene where things had looked desperate, one of the characters has said "It can't rain all the time," and the theme had been repeated.

Their first year after university had been difficult. They were suddenly facing the prospect of having to budget. No longer receiving their grants, they had to find the money to pay the rent, the council tax, the heating, the electric, the food. Early jobs had not paid enough, and there were more than a few times when they had sat around what they called a dining table in the small galley kitchen, with nothing but a single light on, and a lonely crisp sandwich between them. And that line – that theme – had become theirs. "It can't rain all the time." Things will get better. It had become the motto of their relationship.

Ryan had no idea how many times they had said that to each other over the years. Hundreds probably. "It can't rain all the time," followed by a big hug. And now Anna was looking at him like he was an idiot whilst the rain pounded against the window pane incessantly.

Maybe that is because you are an idiot, his black dog growled to him.

Ryan wanted another drink to choke out that voice. He wanted a very large shot of something very strong. Anna continued to stare at him unblinking.

He excused himself and went to the toilet. His bladder was suddenly desperate to be relieved. As he washed his hands, he caught himself in the mirror. Even underneath the four-day stubble, he could tell that he looked old. Old, and very, very scared. His imagination took flight.

It looks like my wife. But she doesn't act like my wife, and she certainly doesn't screw like my wife.

Ryan rinsed his face with cold water. Now he wanted to be sober. He wanted to try and wrest back some control.

He felt the same icy tendrils in his veins that he had the night before, sliding along his being, caressing his organs before wrapping around them like some knotweed that began to slowly squeeze.

He wanted to think, but his mind was fuzzy from the alcohol. Almost involuntarily he walked back out, straight to the booth where Anna was, and sat back down. He had not meant to do that. He had wanted to take a minute and… The rain had stopped, and Anna was staring at a small child who was dancing in a puddle before her mother took her hand and pulled her away.

As he sat, Anna turned to face him. Something about her demeanour, the way she shifted told Ryan that she knew that she had slipped up.

"I remember everything about us," she said, "don't I?"

A clever slight made its way to Ryan's lips and waited. *Do you? Do you? Do you remember? Or are you pretending to remember?*

Ryan took too long to answer. Anna looked at him hard, eyes ablaze, and through near gritted teeth. "Say yes. I remember everything about us, don't I?"

The look reminded Ryan of the Medusa - a seething endless rage behind a wafer-thin visage of beauty. "Yes," he muttered and, feeling his ears pop, worked his jaw.

Anna relaxed, and almost smiled. "I like you, Ryan, I really do," she said in an almost monotone. "Now I am going to ask you to do some things, and you will do them, and we will be together. Do you understand?"

"Yes." It was automatic. Ryan had barely even registered the question, and the rapidity of his own response had surprised him.

"Good. And if you do them well… we will do Things."

Ryan knew what she meant. Ryan knew exactly what she meant. During that first year after University, when they had struggled for money, Anna had written some short stories. Adult erotica. They had been published in a number of men's magazines, and whilst the money had actually been very little, it had always just been enough to get them through.

The stories had been in the tradition that the readerships had enjoyed. Cock-hungry cum-sluts in leather and lace taking it every which way. Candle wax. Toys. Bodily fluids everywhere made for the usual happy endings.

By contrast, their own sex had been staid, and when Ryan had pressed his wife to be a bit more adventurous, thinking that what was in her stories was actually her real sexual self trying to be set free, she had laughed. She had given the readers what they had wanted, and those 'Things' did not interest her.

And so 'Things' had become another part of their secret language. The hidden poetry innate to all relationships. Little words or phrases that mean something completely different. An in-joke that mystifies the rest of humanity.

Anna was offering 'Things'. Ryan remembered the stories about the uniforms, baby oil, threesomes, the restraints, and teasing. And of course the glorious climax. When he had first read them, he often did not make it halfway through before he had to take his wife. Then he had to read the second half and be relieved again. Anna had always taken this as a compliment, that her stories were having the desired effect on at least one reader.

Except now, Ryan was not turned on. Fear flowed freely through him, like a caustic tide, burning and scarring all in its path. Anna had been very insistent. These were stories. They were not to be made real. He had tried to force her once, and that had ended in one of their very rare shouting matches. He had not tried again.

One part of him told him to be excited. *Things! You're going to get Things! Do whatever she says!*

The other part of him was telling him to run. *Get Christopher from the nursery, and just run, and don't stop running. Ever.*

Because whatever it was that sat across from him, Ryan knew it was not his wife.

Anna tilted her head. "You are not turned on?"

Ryan mumbled something deliberately incomprehensible and looked down into the remnants of his beer.

Anna turned to survey the pub. The barman was just leaving, heading into the back office. Otherwise, The George was empty and the pedestrians who had sought shelter had decided to the brave the December day once again.

She turned back to her husband. "Stay there."

Anna slipped underneath the table, and Ryan realised what she was doing. He tried to flinch, to move but found himself rooted to his seat.

He felt his fly unzip, but his cock reminded defiantly limp. Ryan felt her take it in her hand, and almost immediately it began to engorge. Then came that feeling, as it found a warm wet hole. Ryan loved that first feeling. Of sinking in.

Anna worked on him, and Ryan felt himself disengaging from the world and going into his primal place, where men snort like rampaging bulls in the dark before bearing down like a conquering horde.

Quickly he felt his other self fill, and he positioned himself to release.

Anna stopped, pulled away, and slipped back onto her seat.

The barman came back in.

"Now you're turned on."

Ryan stared at her incredulously as she delicately wiped the spittle from her chin with a napkin, his cock demanding immediate attention. Demanding immediate relief.

Anger began to well up inside of him, and his face flushed with something other than alcohol. He went to remonstrate, to berate the thing that was now his wife. The words caught in his throat and no sound came.

Anna smiled. "Now. Do the things I tell you to..."

*

Even though it was just before four, it was already dark as they made their way east along Lincoln Road, heading back towards their home. As they approached the dual carriageway, the noise of the rush hour traffic greeted them like so many snarling dogs.

Suddenly, a little girl rushed passed them. Ryan guessed she was about seven or eight, and judging by the outsized rucksack on her back, had probably come from the nearby Bush Hill Park Primary School. Ryan had not toured it but had assumed that it would be where Christopher would eventually go. He had heard that it was improving.

Anna stood stock still, watching the little girl intently as she approached the pedestrian crossing and waited patiently for the lights to change.

There was an unsettling glint in her eye when she asked, "What is she doing?"

"Going home I imagine." Ryan was confused. He hoped that the thing that was his wife was not brooding.

"Where are her parents?"

"At work probably."

"She goes home alone?"

"Looks like it." Ryan wanted to say more, to ask her what her interest was, but the words would not form.

"Come on." Anna took her husband's hand and pulled him forward.

"What are we doing?"

"Following her."

Ryan wanted to panic. This was not right. Using sex as a weapon was one thing. Following little school-girls was completely another. He trotted along with his wife, his feet moving as if of their own accord.

"What are we doing?" He managed to wrest control back and stopped.

Anna looked at him and smiled insincerely. "Just making sure she gets home."

She resumed her walk, and Ryan followed unwillingly. Whatever it was that Anna was doing, Ryan knew that it was not making sure she got home safe and sound. The light turned green and the girl trotted across the busy road. Anna and Ryan followed, crossed to the opposite side, and followed discretely. They passed the rubble of the recently demolished GE Lighting Factory, the industrial warehouses that stood empty, letting signs that begged for some interest, and under the railway bridge.

Ryan felt panic return. This was not right. They were stalking her. This tiny, fragile, innocent little girl. They were nearly at their turning. He would be able to say "Stop", that their home was down there. They could let the little girl go.

Abruptly, the girl turned right, into Suffolk Road. They reached the top of the street and Anna stopped, watching the little girl half-walk, half-skip on. She trotted up to a door, reached into her coat, pulled out a set of keys, and let herself in.

The door closed, and Ryan let out an audible sigh.

Anna turned to him. "There are no adults in there?"

The house had been in darkness. "Like I said," Ryan replied, "her parents are probably still at work."

Anna said nothing but continued to stare intently, a half-smile playing on her lips. "Come," she said eventually, and they walked on to their turning.

*

That night Ryan dreamed again. He was in his house, and yet it was more. In reality, it was a mid terrace, but here it had two immense industrial warehouses added on to it, like aircraft hangars. These impossible extensions were old, and in places the roofs had buckled and started to come down. In one was a gargantuan boiler, the type his parents had in their old house. Encased in a flimsy red jacket, rotting pipes zigzagged across the walls and floor.

The other hangar was empty, save for an assortment of strangers who seemed to mill around without purpose. Ryan could see that there were holes in the concrete floor, through which he could see a variety of cardboard boxes. The strangers talked amongst themselves and when Ryan approached, they accused him of scratching their car when he had been moving boxes.

Ryan thought he had done this but could not remember when.

And then Anna was by his side. This time, it was his Anna, not the cold creature of yesterday. He tried to tell her that this was all wrong. That their house should not have two hangars let alone a basement filled with boxes. She smiled and held her finger to lips, and then pointed to the ceiling.

A silver mobile hung, lonely and caked in dirt, from one of the hangar beams. It was tiny against the size of the roof, but as it turned, Ryan saw that it was made up of three circles, one inside the other inside the other. Underneath the grime, he saw a brief shard of light, as a pale sunbeam found a rare clean patch and gleamed.

Ryan thought it was beautiful, and stared, as the three circles turned slowly and independently of each other, playing a little sparkling dance. And he forgot about the hangars and the basement and his wife. He watched the twinkling mobile.

*

The next morning Ryan woke up sober. It hurt.

It was Saturday and he could hear cooking noises coming from the kitchen. Christopher was laughing and babbling. The clock read ten-thirteen. Footsteps on the stairs told him Anna was coming. Involuntarily he tensed. His wife appeared at the bedroom door.

"Here you are." She handed him a bacon sandwich with crispy rinds and brown sauce. Just the way he liked it. A cup of coffee was placed on the side cabinet. "What are you going to do today?" she continued.

"Umm... I was going to carry on writing," he replied, not meeting her eye.

"Good, but I need you to take Christopher this afternoon."

"Ok. For how long?"

"An hour. Maybe two."

"Why?" Anna's face became impassive, and Ryan instantly regretted asking the question.

"I have a job interview," she replied, softening and then smiling.

"On a Saturday? For what? And when did you apply for anything?" Ryan felt more confident now.

Anna's smiled faded. "There was an advert for a minicab controller in the local paper. I gave them a call, and they've invited me in."

Ryan wanted to ask what she knew about co-ordinating minicabs but thought better of it.

"And besides," she continued, "it is only just around the corner, which means I can keep an eye on you."

*

Ryan played with Christopher for most the afternoon and marvelled at how much the child looked like his mother. The pale skin, slightly hooked nose, thin face, and that black-black hair that was already growing into his mothers' style.

His mind had returned to the events of the previous day, and he had briefly reflected on his feelings of fear in The George and the urge to get as far away from Anna as possible. Looking at Christopher, he knew that it would never happen. If he took the child, his wife would hunt him relentlessly. They could run and she would always find them. He would just die tired. And Ryan could not leave without the boy, even though he had been largely indifferent to his father all day.

Anna was treating him like a pet. In some ways, it was better than before. But in others...

The front door opened and then closed. Anna had returned. Ryan was not surprised when his wife brought the news that she had been offered the job on the spot, and it did little to assuage his growing sense of unease.

*

A semblance of normality returned to the house over the next few weeks. Jane picked the child up in the mornings, Anna left for the minicab office where she worked until six or seven, and Ryan returned to drinking.

Anna was indifferent. When at home, her attention was wholly consumed with her child, and she took on the bulk of the household chores without comment or complaint. And yet Ryan felt that much was undone. Whatever changes his wife had been through that Friday was not over. It was still there, and he had the sense that even now, cogs were still turning, invisible and behind the scenes.

Her mobile phone would ring at odd times of the day, and she would always take the call outside, speaking in low whispers that Ryan could not make out. When he asked her who it was, she casually told him it was just a friend, or work asking her to take an extra shift. A few times she told him to mind his own business.

Ryan began to suspect that more was going on. That another man was involved. The voice of his black dog rose up again telling him that of course, Anna was looking to leave him.

Who would want to stay with something as wretched as you? Who?

One day, he went to the minicab office to check that his wife was really there. She saw him as soon as he walked through the door, a radio headpiece to her ear, clearly relaying instructions. She just stared at him, and he quickly left. That night she made no comment about his impromptu visit, and he did not repeat it.

*

It was a few days before Christmas when Anna came home unexpectedly early. Ryan had passed out on the sofa, his drinking having increased since the incident at the minicab office. She slapped him. No response. She slapped him again. Hard. Very hard. Ryan started, the taste of blood from his split lip already in his mouth.

"Stand up," the command was barked.

Ryan shakily got his feet. The room was spinning but he knew that non-compliance would not be well received. He was feeling ashamed and embarrassed at having been caught.

"I want to move."

Ryan frowned, trying to process her words. "Now?"

"After the holidays. The second week of January. You will need to start packing boxes."

"Uh, where are we moving to?"

"Fife."

"What... back to Scotland?" Ryan knew it was unwise to question her, but his mouth responded before his mind could apply its usual filter.

"Yes."

"Where in Fife?" *Bad idea Ryan, very bad idea.*

"Falkland. The company is expanding and wants me to run the office there."

Ryan wanted to protest. Did he want to question what minicab company went from London to Falkland? He had been walking there a few times with Anna when they had started dating. It was a cheap day out, but the village, such as it was, was no more than a few hundred people. A thousand at most. How could a minicab company operate with those numbers, especially when the majority would have their own transport?

The words died on his lips.

"What do you want to do with the house?" he asked eventually.

"A woman at work will buy it. She will give us a very good price for it. Double what we paid. It will fund you and..." she looked at the nearly empty bottle of vodka by the side of the sofa, "... and your hobby."

She doesn't care, thought Ryan. *She doesn't care about the drinking.* It had dawned on him how much he needed Anna to care. Even if it was unspoken, he needed to be needed. However, Anna's ambivalence only served to reinforce how redundant he was in his own life.

The black dog laughed.

"Ok," he said weakly and sat back down.

*

It was late February and Ryan was struggling to unpack boxes with one hand. His left hung limply by his side, the fingers taped together roughly. As he continued to unpack, Ryan had not realised until now how much rubbish they had. Old VHS cassettes when they had bought the DVD version only recently. Guitar tab books that had never been opened for albums they seldom played. Boxes of odd wires. A dusty bag of Drachmas and Francs. Ryan could not remember when they had last been legal tender. But Anna had been insistent that nothing was thrown away. So, dutifully, he had boxed everything, and one day, not long into the New Year, he had been presented papers to sign. He had not read them, but scrawled his name, and that was it. The house formally completed a week later.

Events had moved with such speed that they had seemed to take on almost dream-like quality. They had left London, moving into a three bedroom house on Liquorstane Lane in Falkland - the irony of the name was not lost on him.

Christmas had been spent without a tree, and what had once been a traditional dinner was a ready meal from the supermarket. More and more dinners had been like that of late, but Ryan had again not said anything.

The truth was that violence had entered his marriage almost as casually as the alcohol had. What had started as a slap or a grab was now a well-aimed kick whenever Anna was displeased with him, and that was becoming increasingly frequent. He struggled to know what to do. It was not as if he could hit her back. And she had always been apologetic after. Apologetic in her own way.

Do you see the things you make me do?

It's for your own good.

I'm just trying to help you do it better.

And then there was always the promise of 'Things'. A colleague of Anna's had come back one evening and had dinner with them. Ryan was amazed at how alike they looked and fantasised that in another life they could have been sisters.

After she had left, Anna told her husband that Irene might be interested in 'Things' with them. Deep down he knew it was a lie, but that did not stop him thinking about her. Irene had hugged him goodbye at the door, and he had caught the smell of her. Like wildflowers in summer and pink champagne. It made him ache.

The sound of the letter-box made him stop, and he stood wearily to collect the mornings' newspaper and mail. They always came together. In a village as small as Falkirk, people often had more than one job and would frequently do them both at the same time.

The Postman was actually a Postwoman who Ryan had spoken to once. He struggled to remember her name, even though she had introduced herself. The village as a whole was very friendly, but when Ryan told his wife about her, it was made clear in no uncertain terms that he was not to communicate with any of the locals other than a cursory nod if he was out.

There would be consequences if she found out he had done otherwise.

Ryan picked up the small pile of mail from the doormat and froze. The letters drifted back down to the floor like autumn leaves, but he held the newspaper tightly.

KIDNAPPED!

Eleven girls from seven primary schools in North London were simultaneously abducted last night...

Ryan could not read the rest, and slumped against the wall.

All of their photos were plastered across the page. The third one was the girl that he and Anna had followed home less than two months previously.

NATIONWIDE MANHUNT!

He felt sick and only just made it to the toilet where he emptied his stomach. He lay there for a moment, shivering and shaking, more through shock than the winter cold that only Scotland knew.

That girl. Her smiling face. Her muddy blonde hair.

He forced himself up, and into the kitchen. He went straight past the fridge, to the alcohol cupboard, and poured himself a large measure. It went down in one, and he poured another. He briefly felt his stomach complain, and then subside.

Gingerly, he went back to the hallway, picked up the newspaper and went into the TV room. Sitting on the sofa he began to digest the story. Eleven girls had failed to return home from school last night. The youngest was six, the eldest was eight. All had left school later than normal, and all were latchkey children. The schools were all close to each other, and despite reports of a number of minicabs in the area, the police had been in touch with their dispatch offices and all had genuine reasons for being in the vicinity. The detective in charge of the case appealed for witnesses in the area... Anyone acting strangely... Anyone new...

Ryan's stomach turned. He could feel himself beginning to sweat and shake again. He put the paper down. He knew that Anna was involved. He *knew* it. He could not prove it, but he knew nonetheless. He leaned back and closed his eyes, letting a wave of nausea roll over him, then away.

What to do?

He could call the police, perhaps evenly anonymously. But what would he say? That he and his wife and followed one of the girls home eight weeks ago? They had not been in the area yesterday and had never spoken to her.

And Anna being a minicab controller? It was all too much of a coincidence.

He opened his eyes. Above him, Anna had hung a silver mobile. Three concentric circles were suspended from the ceiling of his living room, gently twisting and turning.

Ryan knew that he should find this strange. But it was pretty; the way the light was caught and then reflected softly. He felt his heart rate begin to slow, and Ryan relaxed. The mobile continued to turn lazily in the drafts and eddies of the old house.

There must be a rational explanation.

Still, he should call the police.

Despite it not yet being noon, Ryan felt sleepy, and even as the mobile continued to turn, his eyelids began to droop.

*

His dream was fragmented. Half-images and imagined conversations rose and fell like waves. At one point he fancied himself to be sitting on a raft on a dark sea. It was night and the water was as black as the sky. He felt the low soft rocking underneath him and found it comforting.

He could hear distant sounds, but these were of no consequence. High above him, where the moon should have been, a celestial-sized version of the mobile spun lazily.

For reasons he did not understand, he smiled, and then drifted along.

*

It was after six when Anna came in with Christopher.

The sound of the key in the door startled Ryan into wakefulness, and when Anna noticed that very few boxes had been unpacked, the look on her face told him that she was most displeased.

And that would never do.

Christopher mewled and Anna took him upstairs to his playroom. Ryan heard the returning footsteps and was desperately trying to think of an excuse when his wife walked in. Her eyes blazed with rage, and he instinctively flinched.

She noticed the paper on the sofa and relaxed. "It's been on the radio all day." She turned, and headed into the kitchen to make dinner. She did not ignore the vodka bottle but looked accusingly at Ryan. He made no reply. Anna said nothing further but began opening cupboards to get saucepans.

"Do they have any leads?" Ryan asked, trying to deflect the subject away from the empty bottle and on to the missing girls.

"No. But they think it might be related to a case in Portugal; a paedophile ring tried to snatch girls from a school en masse. That was a few years ago, but apparently, they did not get them all. The police think that maybe some of them came over here. Or it's a copycat."

"Poor lasses," said Ryan, half to himself, as his wife began to chop vegetables.

"Oh I wouldn't worry."

Ryan stopped dead. *Not to worry? Eleven girls go missing, and she says not to worry?*

Anna continued. "They were from broken families. They all had stepfathers or their mother's boyfriend of the week living with them. Some were in foster families. You know what that's like."

Ryan had been briefly fostered as a child. His father had worked on the rigs and was away a lot. He and his sister... well, even Ryan would admit that they had been a handful. His mother had some sort of breakdown in one of the local shops when the cashier asked how she was. He was sketchy on the details.

The fostering process.... well, there had been nothing wrong with it. He had never been abused or anything like that. But still, it had been a strange house with strange smells and a strange family with strange ways.

He and his sister were returned to his parents after nearly six months, when his father gave up working on the rigs, and took a job locally. But still, it had been one of the most unsettling episodes of his life… apart from these last few months with Anna.

"They are probably better where they are," Anna went, oblivious to her husband's expression of incredulity and revulsion. She turned to fill a jug with water and finally saw the look on his face. "What? There is no evidence that anything has happened to them. You know what silly little girls can be like. They've probably just all run away together."

Ryan wanted to rage at the thing that was his wife. He wanted to shake her. He wanted to slap her. "Yeah," he muttered, his bravado giving way. "They'll probably turn up." He looked at the floor.

"Oh, I doubt that," Anna said cheerily. "If someone wants to stay lost, they stay lost, schoolgirls or not."

*

The summer entered limply in Scotland as it had been doing more and more often in recent years.

Ryan had finished the unpacking of the boxes and Anna began instructing him in the decoration of the small playroom for Christopher. The process was slow as his alcohol intake continued to grow and it was late August by the time he had finished.

It was one evening, with the sun still on the horizon, when Anna came home with an unexpected guest. Ryan had been having one of his better days and was not unconscious when he heard the key in the lock. Anna came in, and a man followed her.

"Ryan, this is Mr Kethron." *No hello darling, how has your day been?*

"Err… hello." Ryan leaned forward to shake his hand.

"Hello." The man was immense, nearly as wide as he was tall. Ryan had the sense that Mr Kethron was someone you would want on your side.

Apparently, in his mid-thirties, Kethron had black hair that was closely cropped, revealing ears that seemed a little too pointed. They reminded Ryan of a Vulcan or an elf. His sheer size suggested that he was a very physical man, and Ryan had no wish to find out how physical.

"Mr Kethron has a job for you. I told him that you would be more than happy to help."

"Yeah, sure," Ryan said too quickly. "What do you need?"

"I've got a civils job at Edinburgh Airport. I need some labourers."

"Oh right. What's that?"

Kethron looked to Anna as if Ryan was the village idiot.

"Edinburgh Airport. It's a…" he began.

"No. I meant the civils. What are they… these civils?"

"Think of it as groundwork."

"Like digging?" Ryan asked.

"Aye." Ryan was getting the impression that Kethron was not a man of many words. "Except that you'll be filling in."

"Filling what in?"

"Doesn't matter. You got any criminal convictions?"

"Just three points for speeding. But that was years ago. They might have expired by now."

"Good. You need to get CRB checked. Fill this in." Kethron handed him a form and turned to leave. For a moment he paused as if having second thoughts. "And pal, turn the sauce down. You stink."

His words hit Ryan like one of Anna's slaps. He went to say something, anything to defend himself, but Kethron was already out of the door. Anna followed after him, and Ryan could hear them talking on the pathway.

*

Six weeks later, Ryan received a letter informing him that he had been cleared by security for work at the airport. He thought about having a drink to celebrate. The look on Anna's face told him that he should think better of it, and he did.

He was unsurprised that it was Kethron himself who picked him up in a regulation white van early one cold Monday morning in October. He was also unsurprised that the hour and a half journey was conducted in total silence.

Once at the airport, Ryan spent the morning in an old leaky office, watching a video about health and safety, whilst the wind blew with increasing fervour against the rusting Crittall windows. This was the part of the airport that the passengers did not see, and as such the airport operator was content to let it rot for the time being.

From his uncomfortable plastic seat, Ryan could see the small airplanes moving slowly from the main runway to the Business Aviation Terminal. To call it a terminal was like calling a sandcastle a mansion. Two squat portacabins sat next to an equally dejected single-storey brick building that showed every sign of needing a new roof. Once in a while a fuel truck would come around from the main terminal and fill up one of the Lear Jets before trundling off to service the more sizeable aircraft.

Considering it was Scotland's busiest airport, as the video repeatedly reminded him, Ryan felt... that it should have been grander. But he had never worked at an airport before, and this was his first time seeing the behind-the-scenes operation. His induction completed, Ryan crossed the potholed road that led to the Contractors Compound, and met with Kethron and the rest of the men he would be working with.

The job seemed simple enough. Edinburgh Airport, although spending its early life as an RAF base, had been converted for civilian use in the fifties, and in the seventies had benefited from a new longer runway and what was at the time a state-of-the-art terminal. It did not look state-of-the-art now.

The problem was that, unknown to the designers and engineers at the time, the new runway went over an old coal mine. The runway was inspected several times a day, for rubbish and debris, and for a number of years it had been noted that a depression was forming in the grass just to the north, along the boundary with the Almond River, where water would collect in a pool before draining mysteriously away.

A survey team had eventually been sent out, and as they were examining it, the whole thing had collapsed, revealing a ventilation shaft some twenty foot across.

Fortunately, it was sufficiently distant from the runway not to impede the operation of the airport. Unfortunately, it was close enough that every pilot and passenger could see it on takeoff and landing. The press had a field-day.

A flurry of letters between the airport operator and the Coal Board had yielded a map that showed a network of enclosed mine tunnels at a depth of several hundred feet, all which dated back to the eighteenth century.

The airport operator had gone to exceptional lengths to emphasise to the public that their operation was safe, but as a precaution had closed their secondary crosswinds runway. Looking at the map, Ryan was not convinced that the main runway was any safer, but held his tongue.

Kethron's job was two-fold. Firstly get in, and survey the extent of the mines. Secondly, make them safe and fill them up with expanding concrete. The first part had already been undertaken and now came the part of marshalling a fleet of concrete mixers across a busy runway, and filling in the mine.

Even before Kethron said it, Ryan knew there had to be a catch. Not fifty yards from where the first ventilation shaft had collapsed was a standing stone. Allegedly dating to Neolithic times, the Cat Stane was later adapted to be a sort of war memorial to the Pictish dead who had repelled a Roman invasion. And the mines had of course gone straight underneath this, threatening to bring the series of graves and the five tonne stone crashing down.

As Kethron explained, the problem was that the stone was a scheduled ancient monument and could not be moved, so the team had to take additional measures to ensure that the mine did not deteriorate causing further ground collapse and the loss of the stone. The emphasis on its preservation had been firmly put on the airport chiefs, who had likewise impressed the severity of any possible damage on Kethron.

Given the extent of the mine, the standing stone, and that a substantial river ran through the middle of the main runway, Ryan could not help but think that this had been a particularly bad place to build an airport.

*

Several weeks after his induction, Ryan found himself standing at the mouth of one of the vertical ventilation shafts. Nine had been opened up in total and the mine network had been divided up into cells, the intention being to fill each one independently with expanding concrete. Ryan was not sure, but this did not sound like the method traditionally used to fill in a mine.

Again, he kept quiet. Anna would not be pleased if she heard that he was asking difficult questions.

Because of the poor quality of the earth, they would have to do it in layers and, when dry, someone would have to go back down to confirm that the earth had not moved before the next layer could be applied. Each layer of concrete would take three months to cure, and a minimum of three layers was needed per cell. There were eighteen cells – two off each ventilation shaft - and this had quickly quashed Ryan's hope that they would be finished by Christmas. The Scottish winters could be brutal, and Ryan was not looking forward to working outside if a freeze came.

Kethron had laughed at him when he had asked how long the job would last. "At least a year. Maybe more. Don't worry little man. We'll look after you."

Ryan had not liked the way that had sounded, and right now, it did not feel like he was being looked after. Watched, yes. Looked after, no. He stood a little way back from the terminal and the wind picked up again, buffeting Ryan so hard that his eyes began to water. As he would have expected, the main runway- and associated taxiway network - was on a flat plateau. What he had not expected was that there were very few trees to break the wind. Trees attracted birds, and birds led to aircraft engine strikes.

So why build an airport next to a river where all the birds come to drink and feed?

The winter chill bit deeper. Ryan shivered, as he stood by the pump watching as the first load of concrete descended through the pipe - like some monstrous vein - to the mine floor below. The pressure and flow of the concrete remained constant, and firmly in the green, and Ryan allowed his eye to wander. He could see the remnants of what would have been the original part of the airport. Old RAF buildings lined the airside-landside boundary of the airport, their once proud green paint now mouldering and flaking. They had stood since the thirties, but were now functionally obsolete and of course riddled with asbestos. The airport operator had bought the final parcel of land from the MOD nearly fifteen years ago and then done nothing with it. There was a rumour that they were trying to recruit some hot-shot development surveyor from London to lead an air-cargo regeneration programme, but Kethron had harrumphed at Ryan when he had asked if they would be able to get involved in that contract too.

"We're here to do this job, so let's focus on that, alright pal?"

The needles were still in the green, and Ryan looked over to the main terminal building. It was almost completely encased in scaffolding, as another extension was added. Supposedly there was more retail space being added, but Ryan did not see the attraction.

It's a glorified bus stop, not a shopping centre. Who buys this crap?

He had become friendly with the airport's lead engineer, a big man with an even bigger sense of humour, affectionately known as Kiwi.

"You wouldn't believe how much the retail operation brings in," Kiwi had told him. "Nearly forty million a year." No wonder they wanted more of it.

Ryan's radio squawked, bringing his focus back to his dials. "Go ahead."

"Looks good. Shut it off." That was Tom. He too had come up from London, having decided that teacher-training was not for him. He worked as a DJ a couple of nights a week at one of Edinburgh's lesser clubs, and Ryan had suggested to Anna that they go along one night. Her look of utter contempt gave him his answer.

Ryan pulled two levers and the dial needles gently fell to zero.

"Ok. Bring me up," the radio squawked again.

Ryan punched another button and the pulley mechanism whined into life, bringing the temporary lift platform up from the tunnel below.

"How does it look down there?" Ryan asked once Tom was up.

"That layer's gone down ok I think, but I don't like the soil. It's flaky. The whole place is absolutely soaked..."

Tom broke off as the sound of a landing aircraft drowned him out. They came in every couple of minutes, with only the briefest lull around lunch time, and the noise of the engines often made it impossible to hear the radios.

With a squeal of tyres and a roar of reverse thrust, the plane taxied to its stand. Ryan was still in child-like awe of how these machines, that weighed so much, could get off the ground, let alone stay in the air.

"Looks like there is water getting in somewhere," Tom continued. "If we don't get the props right we'll lose a wall."

Ryan wondered how a failed teacher and part-time DJ knew so much about the effects of water in mine-sealing operations. But then how did he know? He had learned as he had gone along. Little snippets here and there. Maybe he could use it in his book.

The truth was that, with the exception of Kethron and his two senior managers, there was very little experience on the team. Ryan supposed it was cheaper that way, but he had been tempted more than once to ask Anna why she had put him forward for this job. The pay was a pittance, and he suspected that it was an attempt to get him out of the house.

Maybe Anna does care.

Ryan considered that thought and dismissed it. If Anna had been cold before, these days she was positively frozen. Communication, such as it was, was brief, direct, and without depth. He knew that Kethron was giving her daily reports on him.

He suddenly wanted a drink. A proper drink that would take away all these feelings and let numbness enter, if even only for a little while.

Another plane landed, and Ryan waited for the engine noise to abate before he replied to Tom.

"Best to let Kethron know. He's already made it clear how thin the margins are on this job. He won't want any surprises."

*

When winter came Ryan was not disappointed that the work was suspended. The ravaging wind had been picking up, and even under his thermal gloves, he was losing sensation at the end of his fingers. Several times he had tried to pull the levers to "Off" and slipped, only to grasp and scrabble at them again before succeeding.

Nor was he surprised that Christmas came and went without any kind of marking of the celebration. No tree, no Christmas dinner and no presents. Christopher seemed indifferent. Now nearly two, he was developing a good vocabulary, although the practising of it seemed reserved almost exclusively for his mother. Ryan thought the boy eyed him with suspicion and was not interested in playing with his father when he tried to make the effort.

What did surprise Ryan was the arrival of two police officers in the middle of January. He saw them walking up the short path to the front door, and despite his intoxication, he felt his bowels turn to water.

This is about the girl. The one you followed home. They know. They know what you did. Anna told them. She put it all on you, and now they know and you are going away for a very long time. And you know what they do to men like you inside. Oh yes, you know, and now you are going to find out exactly how loud you can scream.

The door bell rang, and Ryan let out a little yelp.

He looked to the back door. He could run. But they would see him. Over the fence maybe? It was still too cold to be out long without several layers of clothing, and there was no time for that. Perhaps he could pretend to be out. He could just lie on the floor.

The doorbell rang again.

Anna was back at work already, after the festive break. She need not ever know the police had been here. If she did she would be angry. Very angry indeed. Maybe if he told them the truth she would be put away, and he could start over with Christopher. Somewhere new.

The heavy door knocker rattled.

"Mr Hyde. It's the Police. Open up please."

Ryan crept towards the door.

Were they really the police? They were in uniform, but were they real? Maybe Anna had made more friends. Maybe he would be arrested and get in the car and never be seen again. This was her way of getting rid of him. He knew it.

He put his eye to the spyhole. "Can I see some ID?" he asked weakly.

Ryan saw the two officers look at each other in bemusement, reached into their jackets to produce their warrant cards, and held them up to the spyhole.

They could be fake. They could be fake cards for fake policemen in fake uniforms.

Ryan realised that he did not even know what a police ID card looked like and that he was probably out of time to make his escape. They knew he was in the house, and could kick the door down. He had seen enough police dramas on the television.

Gingerly he slid the bolts back, turned the key and opened the door.

"Hello, Officers."

"Mr Hyde?"

"Yes."

"Ryan Hyde?"

"Yes."

"I'm PC Parry. This is PC Cooke. May we come in?"

"Umm... sure." Ryan led the two officers into the lounge. Cooke said nothing, but looked around the house, taking all the features in, before settling on the small mound of empty wine and vodka bottles.

"A good Hogmanay Mr Hyde?" Parry asked, following his colleagues line of sight.

"Umm... yeah," Ryan replied weakly.

"Have you been drinking today Mr Hyde?"

"Yes." There seemed little point in hiding it.

"Are you drunk or can you help us with our enquiries?"

"I wouldn't drive, but I'm not drunk," Ryan said a little too defensively. "What enquiries? What is this about?" He sat down before the shaking of his legs was noticed.

Cooke and Parry had seen his condition at the door but said nothing.

"Do you know Thomas Cullum?"

"Tom? Yes. What's happened?"

"How do you know him?" Parry ignored Ryan's question.

"We work together at the airport."

"Which airport?"

"Edinburgh."

"And what do you do there Mr Hyde?"

"I'm filling in the mine. The one that is under the runway. It was on the news a while back."

"And who is it you work for, Mr Hyde?"

"It's a contracting firm. Corax Ground Works. Mr Kethron runs it, but we're part of a larger company. Corvus Group Holdings. They do a bit of everything. What's happened to Tom?"

"When did you last see Thomas Cullum?"

"Umm... probably a month or so ago. Work has stopped because of the weather."

"Did you speak to him over Christmas?"

"No."

"Text?"

"No.

"Email?"

"No."

"Have you ever bought drugs from your friend Tom?"

Ryan's alarm was giving way to anger. "What? No! Look, what's going on?"

"Mr Hyde, I am sorry to tell you this, but Tom Cullum passed away on New Year's Eve."

A wave of shock enveloped him, briefly giving everything a dream-like quality. "Oh my god," he whispered. "What happened?"

The two officers looked at each other.

"Mr Hyde, did Tom ever mention a girlfriend?"

"No."

"What about a Charlene Jefferson? He might have referred to her as Charlie."

"No. I thought he was single."

"Did he ever mention that he was having trouble with someone?"

"No."

"Someone was hanging around his flat?"

"No. Nothing like that."

"Nuisance phone calls?"

"No. He invited me to a club once where he was DJ-ing."

"Did you go?"

"No."

"Why not?"

Ryan considered mentioning his wife's reaction to the suggestion but thought better of it. Anna would not like her name being brought up in this conversation.

"I have a young child. He's nearly two. My clubbing days are behind me." He smiled weakly.

"Where is your child now?" The officers' gaze had returned to the pile of empty bottles.

"He's at the nursery."

"Did you know that Tom was into drugs?"

"No."

"Was he ever late for work? Absent for a few days perhaps?"

"I don't think so. Mr Kethron would be the best person to ask about that."

"We've already spoken to Mr Kethron. He said that you two were quite pally."

Ryan shrugged. "Tom was ok. But he didn't confide in me or anything."

"How long had you known him?"

"We met on the job. In October. So... about three months maybe."

"Did he ever come here?"

"No."

"Did you ever go to his flat?"

"No. I usually come home straight from work."

"Why?"

"We don't have a second car, and my wife needs hers."

"How do you get to work?"

"Mr Kethron picks me up. How did Tom die?"

"The enquiry is ongoing Mr Hyde."

*

After the police had left Ryan turned on his laptop and began looking for details of what had happened to Tom.

Between various news reports, Ryan was able to piece together that Tom had recently started seeing Charlene "Charlie" Jefferson. The problem was that Charlie's former boyfriend had not taken this well and had hung about Tom's flat resulting in the police being called a number of times, although all the trouble had been verbal and there did not seem to have been any physical altercations.

On New Years' Eve, Tom had been due to play at a small club and had reversed his Corolla out of his usual spot in the tenant's basement car park. The car park was not pass-controlled, and unknown to Tom, Charlie's ex had been underneath, presumably tampering with the vehicle. He was crushed when a wheel went over him and died of internal injuries.

What followed next was unclear, and the media speculation had made events even more so. Tom had fled the scene – that much was known from CCTV footage. The body had been discovered some hours later when neighbouring residents returned from the evenings' celebrations. The police were called, and it was quickly established who owned the vehicle, and also that Tom had not arrived for his DJ-ing slot.

Tom was found two days later in woodland near Pitlochry by dog walkers. He had apparently died from exposure but also had a quantity of Ecstasy on him. How he got there was unexplained, and both his car and Charlie remained missing...

Ryan sat back letting out a sigh. Tom's Facebook page was filled with condolence messages. At the top, was the "Photos" tab, and idly he clicked it. A myriad of albums appeared. Ibiza 2002. Ayia Napa 2004. Benidorm 2006. Scotland 2007.

Ryan clicked the last tab and began to scroll through. Various club nights. A host of increasingly sweaty faces pushed up against the camera with almost caricature-like leering grimaces. Halfway through his breath caught, and he heard himself choke, cough, and then splutter. But the sound was very far away as if he was listening to someone else. His attention was now wholly on the screen.

There on the monitor was a photo, and the caption read "Tom & Charlie".

Except Ryan knew that woman. And her name was not Charlie. It was Anna's friend – Irene. Ryan shivered. It could not be. But it was. He looked again at the photo. It was definitely her. He quickly scrolled forward through the rest of the photos, and there she was again. And again. And in the background of the group shot. There was another of her, half-hugging Tom.

Ryan felt sick. Very sick. Putting the laptop down, he crossed to the kitchen. No vodka. Opening another cupboard, he found the whisky. He usually did not touch this until the afternoon, but these felt like desperate times.

He poured himself a measure, his hand shaking so that it became a double, and then a treble. He downed it in one and poured himself a second. From the kitchen's open door, he could see his laptop. He shivered again and poured himself a third.

What would he tell Anna? Kethron would no doubt inform her that the police had interviewed him and that he had given Ryan's name. He could not say that he had not spoken to them. That would displease her to start with.

But he did not have to tell her about Irene. She did not need to know that.

Except that she would check his internet browsing history. She was doing that more and more often now. Checking what he was looking at. And she would see. And she would know.

Ryan quickly went back into the lounge and told the browser to clear the viewing history and all the temporary files. A minute later the program confirmed that the operation had been completed.

Except now it says that you have never looked at anything. Anna will know that you cleared it. And she will want to know why...

Ryan began to panic.

It was running slow. That's it. The computer was running slow. Needed a clear out.

But Anna would know.

It had not run slow when she used it. Why was it running slow for you Ryan?

Ryan began to sweat and again considered the possibility of fleeing.

Leave the boy – he's his mother's child anyway. Run. Get out. Get away. Just run!

Ryan stood still, despite the screaming voice inside his head. Where would he run to? He did not know anyone in the village. Anna had made sure of that. Maybe someone from work would take him in, but then Kethron would find out and he would tell his wife. And with no car, how would he get away?

The train station. But he had no money. Anna had taken his wallet away when they had first moved up to Falkland. He had no cards, no cash. And apart from his airport security pass, he had no ID.

Maybe there is someone you could call. From before.

Ryan picked up his mobile, before remembering that Anna had deleted most of his contacts. The same was true of his friends' email addresses. It dawned on Ryan how utterly trapped and helpless he was. There was nothing he could do to get away. With this last heave of resignation, his panic evaporated.

He would just have to tell Anna the truth.

Ryan began to cry silently to himself, imagining the punishment that would be wrought on his already bruised frame. Curling up on the sofa, he found himself exhausted, and sleep came like a wave, rolling over him.

*

"I know," was all Anna had to say after he told her what had happened and turned to make dinner.

"But... but... what about Irene?"

"What about her?"

Ryan gawped. "But she knew Tom. And she is missing. And the police think she's called Charlie!"

"No."

"What do you mean 'no'?"

Anna spun around to look at him, her eyes telling him he should really not have used that tone. She crossed the room quickly and was suddenly very close to him. Too close. Ryan's hands instinctively went to cover his groin.

"It was not Irene in those photos, was it?"

Ryan wanted to protest the point, but self-preservation kicked in. "No," he said weakly and felt his ears pop.

"Irene did not know Tom, did she?"

"No," Ryan whined, feeling the tears creeping up, as his ears popped again. Harder this time.

"Tom was a lazy worker, wasn't he? He probably had it coming."

"Yes," was all that Ryan could whisper. His ears popped so hard that he let out an involuntary cry.

Anna smiled. "Good boy," and patted him on the head.

Later that evening, as the alcoholic vapours rolled off him like smoke from a fire, Ryan heard Anna on the phone. The voices began to muddle as unconsciousness bid him welcome, and he could not tell if it was Kethron or Irene she was talking to. But she did not sound happy. And that frightened Ryan.

*

Work at the airport resumed in February, which was later than expected due to the winter snow. The runways constantly had a small fleet of snow-blowers moving up and down them, and whilst they kept the tarmac clear for the aircraft, the cleared snow was deposited along the edges where Kethron and his team had been working. The melt had been slow.

"This is Rooksby," said Kethron on their first day back. "He'll be taking over from Cullum."

"Hi," said Ryan.

173

The man, who was nearly as big as Kethron, grunted a monosyllabic acknowledgement.

Ryan turned back to Kethron. "Did Tom tell you about water in the number three cell?"

Kethron looked at him hard. "No."

"He thought that there might be some ingress. Maybe from the Almond or from the Gogar Burn. He thought that the props might need adjusting, otherwise, we're at risk from losing a wall."

Kethron continued to look at him but made no reply.

"I'll check it out," Rooksby said eventually.

Ryan was not surprised when Rooksby came up and told him that he could see nothing wrong. He was Kethron's man through and through.

Ryan noticed that a lot of the faces that had been familiar before Christmas were now absent, replaced by hulks who were similar in appearance to Kethron. He had heard gossip that Kethron had been in the Forces, seeing action in Iraq and the Balkans, before going into 'private security'. How he had wound up at Corax was anyone's guess, but there seemed little doubt that he had built up an extensive network of contacts along the way. The replacements were all his men; strong, disciplined, and for the most part silent.

*

The winter grudgingly gave way to spring, and it was late April when work began at the southeastern extent of the airport's four-hundred-acre estate.

Aircraft stand two-hundred-and-ten through to-two-hundred-and thirteen had been designed for the big cargo planes. In their hey-day, they had seen some of the larger Antonovs delivering submarine parts, and the hope was that with the regeneration of the old RAF site into a cargo hub, the airport operator could win some of that business back from its southern competitors. They also had shallow mine workings running right underneath them.

Ryan watched as girders were brought in to line the walls and then brace against each other.

Kiwi stood next to him. "That's a lot of metal going in there," he said, pulling out the plans.

Ryan looked cursorily at the drawings and then back to the operation unfolding before him. He was learning that silence was golden when dealing with his wife or Kethron, and the lesson was spilling over into other relationships. *Just shut up and get on.*

It had been nearly a fortnight since Anna had last struck him. He wondered how long he could make this run last.

Kiwi turned the paper around again, closely examining the proposed design. "You could build a skyscraper with what they're putting in there," he said to no-one in particular.

Ryan's eye was drawn back to the plans.

"What are all these?" he asked, unable to help himself, pointing to a small protrusion on the page.

"New vents we're going to sink in for each cell. In case there is a build-up of gas. The concrete will expand, and push it out. Without it... well, there could be a bang."

"An explosion?"

"It'd be underground. Probably. But yeah."

"What are they doing about the Northern Shafts?" Ryan asked, trying to sound casual. He knew that there was substantially less metal going into the Northern Cells, and the mines were more extensive there. Less support meant an increased risk of a wall or ceiling slipping. Or worse, caving in completely.

Kiwi unfolded the page and looked at the area Ryan had asked about. "Similar design," he said. "But not to take as much weight. The shafts there haven't got aircraft stands over them. Just the grass. And the Cat Stane."

Ryan knew that was not right. There was something wrong about all of this. The job. The airport. The Cat Stane. And it was bigger than Kethron and Anna.

*

It was a few weeks later, and Kethron was standing too close to Ryan, making him feel uncomfortable. They were getting ready to fill the mine under the cargo stands, and it was one of the few occasions that the weather was on their side.

"Ok. Start it up," the radio squawked. Rooksby was down at the shaft bottom watching the first layer going in.

Ryan looked to Kethron who nodded and brought both levers down.

The pressure and flow dials jumped for a moment and then settled in the green. The sound of the compressor told them that they were up and running.

"Looks good," the radio called again.

Fifteen minutes passed. Thirty. And then an hour.

Ryan looked to Kethron. They were not meant to be putting this amount of concrete in. And where was Rooksby? He had known the radio to be silent for anything up to half an hour, but never this long. Even the men at the batching plant were getting nervous, and they were Kethron's own.

"Kill it," Kethron said darkly.

Ryan brought both levers up.

"Rooksby?" Kethron was on the radio now.

"Aye? I've lost flow. What are you doing?"

"Taking a breather. You ok?"

"Aye."

"Have we got much more?"

"Dunno. Nothing has come forward yet."

The pipe had been laid to the back of the shaft. The intention was to fill to the forward stop, and pull the pipe through before the concrete set, effectively creating a single slab that the second and third layers could be applied to.

"Go and check it out," Kethron growled.

"Ok."

The mine had not been as Ryan had imagined. In his mind, he had pictured the high vaulted tunnels that he had often seen on television. Whilst this was true of the majority of modern mines, those from the eighteenth century were little more than man-made rabbit warrens.

Ryan was five foot six inches tall and had to hunch himself nearly all the way over when he had gone down with Tom. There had been any number of forks and blind alleys which were a lot smaller and could only have been made by made by children on their hands and knees. Ryan remembered reading about the working conditions of the eighteenth century, how often there was no light, no health and safety, and little in the way of ventilation. Accidents were an all too common occurrence, and the lucky ones were just badly maimed.

Ryan did not envy Rooksby as he imagined him making his way along, bent double against the roof of the tunnel.

"We got a problem," the radio crackled a few minutes later.

"Go ahead."

"Looks like... I dunno. We've got a hole. Looks like a well or something."

"How wide?" Kethron barked, his demeanour was darkening noticeably, and suddenly Ryan wanted to be very far away indeed.

"Ten, maybe twelve foot. And it's deep."

"How deep?"

"My torchlight isn't hitting the bottom. But I can hear running water. Like a river or something."

Kethron was silent for a moment, thinking what to do next. "Ok," he said eventually, "come back up."

"Aye."

"And you, Wino," Kethron had turned to Ryan, "go and get me a set of those mine drawings."

*

It was later in the afternoon that they all sat around a table in the airport's main Administration Building.

Built in the late seventies, it was another example of out-of-sight-out-of-mind. Despite housing the Managing Director and various commercial departments, little had been spent on it in the intervening years. The two-storey brick building had a flat roof and the smell of damp only seemed to underline the already tense atmosphere.

The Development Director sat next to Kethron, and Kiwi came in shortly after and positioned himself on the other side.

"And it wasn't there before?" the Development Director said. Ryan had forgotten his name.

"Can't have been. The men wouldn't have been able to lay the pipe to the end of the section. It takes up the whole width of the tunnel," Kethron replied.

"Do we know where it goes?" Kiwi asked.

Kethron brought out the plan of the mine workings. "I've got three thoughts," he said, fingering the area where the hole had opened. "First is that it's a subterranean river. Second, is that it is another deeper mine that runs in parallel with the one on top, and we did not know about it because it's not shown on the plan. Or third is that it is something archaeological."

"Something archaeological? That's pretty broad." the Development Director said. "What do you think?"

"It could be anything," shrugged Kethron. "With that standing stone... well the whole area is full of Neolithic artefacts..."

"Don't say it," the Development Director snapped. "If Historic Scotland gets involved we'll lose years. Do you know any tame archaeologists? They can say it is a plague pit and we can just fill it in."

Kethron shrugged again. "We need to know how much we're filling in. It could be nothing more than a small depression. Or it could be a waterway that runs for hundreds of miles. I'm trying to source a camera now. We'll rig something up so that we can send a man down." Kethron looked at Ryan.

Ryan shifted his gaze to the table. He really did not want to go down there.

"What about if we put some dye in?" Kiwi asked. "If it is a waterway, we might be able to trace its path if we can find where it comes out."

Kethron nodded. "Could do. You'd be hoping it comes out somewhere local. Best case is that it comes out in the Almond, before Crammond. But it might discharge anywhere. We don't even know which way it's flowing."

The Development Director sat back. "Could we put some of the girders over the hole, and just carrying on infilling? Like a plug?"

"I'd be against that. Whatever this second network is, we need to make sure that it is not undermining anything else. If it is, then there is no telling if or when it might collapse."

"The airport has been here ninety years. If it was going to collapse into a hole it would have done so already," the Development Director said.

Kethron shook his head. "It could be eroding your main runway right now, and you wouldn't even know until one of those big heavy commercial liners landed heavily. The strength of the runway might hold, but if the ground underneath goes, and then your plane could cartwheel."

The Development Director did not need further convincing. He had seen a Cessna go tail over once, breaking its back. The sound had been sickening. He did not dare to think what would happen if a fully laden 747 went that way.

"What about the other cells?" the Director asked. "Can you continue those?"

"I'm not keen. I'd rather find out how big this thing is and where it goes before we carry on. You wouldn't want us back in a couple of years doing the whole thing over from scratch because of a shaft collapse."

*

That night Ryan told Anna about the events of the day, and in a rare move, she showed an interest, wanting to know what was at the bottom of the newly discovered duct. Ryan gave the sketchy details as best he could, but when he said that he thought that Kethron had him in mind for the survey her countenance changed.

"I don't think so," she said enigmatically.

"I don't want to do it either, but the way he looked at me..."

"I'll speak to him," she continued as if she had not heard his bleating. "You're not ready yet."

Later that night, despite the alcohol in his system, sleep did not come easily to Ryan. What had Anna meant, not ready... yet?

Like there would ever be a time when he would be ready. Once again, Ryan had the sense of things moving behind the scenes.

*

The next morning Kethron picked him up as usual. Readying himself for the customary silence, Ryan was surprised when Kethron addressed him.

"Don't worry Wino. It won't be you," he half-smiled, before crunching the van into gear and setting off.

Ryan made no reply but was silently grateful that Anna had come through for him. In that instant, he felt his emotions conflict. At one level he had grown to hate Anna in a slow burning resentful way. She had deprived him of friends, means, and confidence. But she had got him this job when it was painfully obvious that he was drinking instead of writing, and now she was protecting him from Kethron.

Of course, she was his wife, and the mother of his child, but Ryan felt detached from all of that as if it had happened to someone else. He pondered the dichotomy and wondered if Anna was re-moulding him. Making him as she would wish. It would explain the recent cessation of beatings. No doubt he would do something to warrant their reintroduction. But had he changed?

He looked at himself in the passenger mirror and realised how haggard his looked. Puffy sacks hung under his eyes like deployed airbags, and the whites of his eyes had long turned yellow. Where had once been laughter lines, now there were deep crevices of worry and his three-day old stubble was heavily flecked with gray.

"Yeah yeah, Wino, you look beautiful this morning," laughed Kethron.

Ryan looked at him but said nothing.

He returned to thinking about Anna, and the ghost of the abducted girls rose before him. Like so many other things in his life, it was still unresolved. The case had quickly gone cold and had been replaced completely in the news when Madeleine McCann had disappeared five months later. She had been missing nearly a year now, but Ryan often thought about the other girls. The Enfield Eleven.

Anna had never mentioned them, and if a news story or documentary was on the television which in any way referenced them, she turned the channel over. And yet still they haunted him. In particular, the one they had followed. He occasionally dreamt of her, looking up at him from an open grave that was filling with water. Except in the next instance, it would not be water, but blood. And she would just stare at him, soundlessly, until she was covered. Then would come a movement in the liquid filled grave, like some huge beast from the depths had risen too close the surface, sending forth a pulse from the deep.

As they approached a junction, Kethron uncharacteristically waved a silver Nissan in front of him. The driver flashed his lights and sped on.

"Friend of yours?"

Kethron smiled. "New airport managing director."

"Mr Johnson is leaving?"

"The parent company has picked him up. He's moving down to Heathrow to do something with marketing or purchasing or something."

Ryan was disappointed. He had only met Mr Johnson once, but he was well regarded and had made Ryan feel like what he did matter.

"So who's the new guy?"

"Glasgow's MD."

"What's he like?"

"I only met him once. Last year, before you joined, there was a terrorist bomb. Blew up part of their terminal."

Ryan's recollection was hazy, but he distantly remembered something about a 4x4 being driven into the terminal building before exploding up.

"Mr Johnson called all the contractors," Kethron continued, "and got them over there to help sort it out. We had the terminal open again within twenty-four hours. Glasgow's MD was new - only one week into the job."

Ryan whistled. "Trial by fire."

"You're telling me Wino. He was there the whole time. Never went home. Worked on the floor with the rest of us. He made a lot of friends that day."

Ryan realised that this was probably the longest conversation he had ever had with Kethron. "Does he know about our job?"

"I've got to give him a briefing this afternoon."

"Do you want any help? I don't mind coming along."

Kethron looked at him incredulously, broke into a toothy grin, and chuckled to himself. "Help? Not from you Wino, not from you."

*

Ryan hit the green button and the lift mechanism began to whine, bringing Rooksby up to the surface.

"So?" Kethron said.

Rooksby handed the video camera to Kethron and began to peel himself out of his safety harness. "It's a cave."

"How big?"

"Difficult to stay. The winch ran out before I got to the bottom, but I'd guess a couple of hundred feet across. Maybe sixty or seventy high."

"The water?"

"Not as bad as it could have been. It's more of a trickle, but the cave is causing the sound to echo. It drains out in a small hole at the bottom."

"Did you see any of the dye?"

They had put some soluble dye in the Gogar Burn to determine if it was the origin point for the water they had heard the day before.

"Aye. A little. Not much."

"Can we patch and fix it?"

"Yeah. It's too big to fill with concrete. We'd spend months if not years on it. Plus the water would just eat through it. I'd say girder it – make sure the walls and roof aren't going to shift. Then whack a plug where we broke through."

Kethron grunted an agreement.

Ryan was not an expert, but the idea of sealing a previously unknown cave on the basis of a single inspection did not sound right to him.

*

By all accounts, Kethron's meeting with the new Managing Director went well, and the budget to stabilise and seal the cave was approved. It was late September by the time work recommenced on the previous cells.

"Flowing well," the radio crackled.

Ryan was back at the cargo stands, seeing the cell taking its first layer of concrete.

Rooksby was down in the shaft but had been on extended leave over the summer. Ryan had asked him if everything was alright, but the man had just nodded, and it did not seem right to push the subject.

"Check your pressure," the radio said again.

"Green on forty," Ryan replied.

"I've got build up here."

"What are you on?" Ryan asked. There was a second meter at the end of the pipe that measured the pressure in the immediate environment.

"Just hit fifty." The difference in pressure between the two gauges suggested that gas was building up somewhere.

Ryan brought his levers up.

"I've shut it down."

"I'm still climbing. Fifty-four. Can you vent?"

Ryan signalled to the crew by the batching plant who activated the vent. The sound of the turbine powering up, sucking the air out of the mine filled the surrounding with a dull thudding.

Thoc-thoc-thoc

This was the third time that day that they had to break to clear the mine of gas. The concrete needed to go down as smoothly as possible, preferably in one application, and the constant need to stop and then restart was beginning to put a strain on the work crew.

"What are you at?" Ryan asked.

"It's coming down. Give it another minute or so."

Progress was slow and when the Christmas shutdown came, Kethron guessed that they were three to four months behind schedule. Ryan did not need telling how much this displeased the man. Kethron wore an almost permanent scowl.

The snows were not as bad as they had been the previous year, but Ryan thought it was icier. Little had changed at home, other than Christopher had got bigger and was relishing starting primary school in September.

By May all the cells - except the one underneath the Cat Stane - had received their first layers, and some their second. But the team was tense. There were increasingly frequent pockets of gas that needed to be vented and, whilst no-one admitted it, there was growing sense that there must be movement in the earth for there to be this much gas escaping.

It was August and the team was preparing the Cat Stane cell for its first layer. Looking up, Ryan sighted a figure in the regulation high-visibility jacket, similar to those he and the team wore, moving in and out of the old RAF buildings, near to the batching plant.

"New boy?" Ryan asked. He was sitting on the grass with Rooksby, eating his sandwiches, and watching the planes take off and land. After nearly two years on the job, he still found them fascinating to watch.

Rooksby shook his head. "Not one of ours."

"It's the airport's new development surveyor," Kethron said, from behind them.

"You met him?"

"Aye."

"What's he like?"

"Bawbag!"

Rooksby sniggered.

Ryan turned to face Kethron. "Why?"

"Reckons himself."

"How do you mean?"

Kethron narrowed his eyes. "Whatever he says, he believes it, likes it true."

"I don't understand."

"He says he's lucky. And he is. Says he can get a quote for an industrial spec build at ten quid a square foot, and he can. Says it'll rain, and it does."

Ryan was confused. "What? So whatever he says will happen, does?"

"Aye."

Ryan thought for a moment. "Isn't that new development going to be over that cave?"

"Let him find out for himself," Kethron replied. "You'd do well to steer clear of him."

Ryan nodded, still not understanding what was wrong with the airport's new employee. A flash of colour caught his eye, and he squinted. A second figure was with the first.

"Who's that with him?" Ryan said, pointing over to the derelict buildings.

"Kiwi. Best mates now."

Ryan felt a childish tug inside of himself. He thought he was friends with Kiwi. He did not want the new boy stealing him away.

That night, Kethron let MD's Nissan out again. Ryan spotted a figure in the passenger seat.

Kethron answered his question before he could utter it. "Aye," he said.

"That development guy?"

"Gets everywhere. He's been out with the Big Man a lot. Got some suits up from London. Next week, they got some Shaq or other over. That Bawbag has got some gift. People just follow him; give him whatever he wants, like he's the second coming."

Ryan instantly thought of Anna and the way she got what she wanted from him. But they were husband and wife. It was different. Wasn't it?

*

October was cool, but not as cold as it had been the previous year, and Ryan was working with Rooksby around the Cat Stane, beginning the preparatory works for when the mine underneath the standing stone would be filled in.

He had finally become used to the constant noise of the aircraft and proceeded without having to turn around every few minutes to admire the sleek hull of an approaching jet. Ryan was checking the integrity of the ventilation shaft in preparation for the testing of the gas extractor. Rooksby was not one for small talk, and the two men had worked in silence for most of the morning.

"Ok," Ryan said, connecting a power cable to the compressor. "I think we're ready for a test."

Rooksby was looking down the ventilation shaft. "Aye. What did that last sensor have to say?"

The sensor was a long rod that was sunk into the ground and tested for movement as well as gas pockets.

"Looks good," Ryan said. "Little bit of gas in the first hundred feet, but nothing we can't handle. No movement..." Ryan stopped and wrinkled his nose. "Do you smell that?" It was like the faint whiff of ammonia.

Rooksby looked at him and shook his head. "No. Is it coming from the vent?"

It was Ryan's turn to shake his head. "No. I thought I smelt bleach. It's gone now. Anyway... err, yeah. No movement recorded at all. What do you make of that temperature reading? Seems a little high."

Ryan's ears popped and, as he tried to clear the pressure, he heard a muttering. Thinking that Rooksby had replied he looked up and froze. Rooksby was gone. The airport was gone. Around him was a thick wood and through the canopy, he could see the purple bruise of a day that had been beaten into submission.

In a panic, he turned, and saw the Cat Stane. The standing stone was still there, but it seemed to be surrounded by a small group of men, dressed in dark tunics and rough leather pads that had been sown together like some kind of armour.

"I'm telling you," an oriental young man was saying fervently. "We need to send Celus' troops across the river. His archers can then flank..."

A second shook his head. He was Caucasian with sandy hair and was a similar age to the first man. "You'll leave Devon and Leo exposed. Let Celus cover their cavalry attack and then he can..."

"George!" the oriental said again, "you're not hearing me. We've not heard from either Devon or Leo's platoons in the last three days, there is no guarantee..."

The second paused, no longer listening to his comrade, straightened and turn to face Ryan.

"What is it?" the first asked. The rest of the men had put their hands on the assortment of weapons that Ryan now saw to be strapped to their sides. Crossbows. Swords. Guns. "Do you hear something?"

The second man continued to stare at Ryan – almost through him. "Master Otsuno, I'm not sure... I thought I..."

"I know that expression," Otsuno said. "One of them's near. A Twine. George?"

The man they called George shook his head. "No. This is different. I think this is a Waker..."

"One who looks *and* sees?" one of the soldiers from the back said. "We've not come across one of their kind in years..."

George was no longer listening but had stepped forward, towards Ryan. "Are you there? Are you…"

Ryan turned to flee in panic and Rooksby took hold of him.

"Whoa. Easy. You ok?"

Ryan looked around him, disorientated. He was back at the airport. "Err… yeah."

"Where did you go?"

"What?"

"I was talking to you, but you were miles away. Did you hear what I said?"

"I… sorry, no. I thought…"

Rooksby gently slapped him on the cheek. "Get it together. If Kethron sees you slacking… you don't want to know what will happen."

*

It was November, and an early frost had stripped the trees of their leaves. The first layer of concrete had gone into the Cat Stane cell, and all of the other second layers had been finished. Work even had begun on some of the thirds, and it looked like the team was making up some of the earlier lost time.

But the Cat Stane was where the focus now was. There was a sense of tension in the air. Even if the other cells were flawless, the team would be remembered and judged by how this last one went.

Additional girders had been ordered, and these were being fitted. It had begun to sleet, stinging Ryan's skin like tiny insect bites. Kethron stood next to him as he activated the lift and watched more girders being sent down.

"Do you want to start pumping the second layer before the Christmas break?"

Kethron shook his head. "It won't cure right. We'll break early and start back in January if the weather holds."

They broke in December, and the weather did not hold. The worst winter for twenty-five years surprised Scotland that Christmas. Trains had to be pulled out of snowdrifts, planes were grounded, and gritting salt ran out after the first week.

In the relative isolation of Falkland, the power went out after the first day, and water froze in the toilets, splitting the cisterns and flooding homes. Anna claimed to have been watching the long range weather forecasts and had bought nearly a dozen propane tanks and gas fuelled heaters. It was not a comfortable Christmas, but the three of them survived better than many of their neighbours, some of whom did not live through it.

It was New Year's Eve when Anna came through to the lounge and told Ryan that Kethron had called. The snow-blowers at the airport had deposited their loads all over the cells. The banks were twenty foot high in some places.

"Kethron says that you won't be back until March at the earliest. You can do some more of your book," she said smiling and handed him a generously-sized glass of neat vodka.

In the end, it was April when the team returned to finish filling the mine.

*

Despite being warm, the mid-April morning was not being kind to Ryan. He had a hangover. And it had lasted over two weeks. He could feel that his bloodshot eyes were dry, and he hurriedly drank some water from his bottle, feeling the cool liquid on his parched throat.

"OI! Wino!" roared Kethron. "That better not be vodka!"

"It's just water," Ryan muttered, showing him the label.

Kethron did not believe him, crossed to where he stood, and took the bottle, sniffing it. Without a word he thrust it into Ryan's chest and walked off.

They were trying to apply a second layer of concrete to the Cat Stane cell, and there had already been two gas releases already. The first one had not been too bad, but the second one had taken nearly half an hour to disperse, and Ryan had been worried that the turbine extractor was not sucking it out fast enough. Judging by the look on Rooksby's face, Ryan was not the only one.

"Alright," the radio squawked. "Start her up."

Ryan brought the two levers down and watched the needles creep up, settling mid-way in the green area.

"Pressure and flow are good."

"Ok, keep her coming nice and slow."

Ryan's attention drifted to the standing stone, less than forty yards from him. The inscription was away from him, and if he had not been told its significance he would have assumed that it was just a boulder. He was not the only one looking at the five tonne stone. At least half a dozen of his own team was watching it intently for the first sign of subsidence, and Ryan suspected that the bigwigs from the airport operator were watching from the terminal.

For a moment, the memory of the forest from the previous autumn rose unbidden. He could almost hear their voices.

"What pressure have you got?" the radio crackled, snapping him back to reality.

"Twenty-five."

"Drop it to twenty."

Ryan twisted a dial. "Any better?"

"No. I got thirty and rising."

"I'll shut her down." Ryan brought both the levers up.

"I got thirty-five. Fire up the extractor."

Ryan signalled to men around the compressor, and turbine extractor kicked in.

Thoc-thoc-thoc

"Is it on?"

"Yeah. What have you got?"

"Forty-five. Bring me up!"

Ryan punched the green button hard.

Kethron was standing behind him. "JUICE IT!" he roared to the compressor operator.

The extractor audibly kicked up several gears.

Thoc-thoc-thoc

The head of the lift cleared the mouth of the hole, and Rooksby jumped out.

"Seventy!"

"Down down down!" Kethron motioned everyone to lie down. They needed no second bidding.

For a moment all was silent, and then Ryan heard a sound like a cave whispering, followed by a wet tearing as if raw flesh was being stripped from bone.

A second passed. And then there was another sigh. The wet tearing that followed was louder this time, and Ryan swore he felt the ground rise and fall slightly.

Silence returned briefly, only to be broken by a plane landing, tyres squealing.

Ryan sat up. He was not the first, and everyone was looking at the Cat Stane. It seemed unmoved.

"Ten," Rooksby said, looking at his pressure dial, and then up to Kethron.

Kethron nodded. "Get down there and let me know how it's looking."

"Keep the extractor on, yeah?"

Kethron nodded again.

Ryan punched the downward release and watched Rooksby descend slowly down the shaft.

"Er... K?" the radio crackled.

"Yeah."

"We got movement down here."

"How much?"

"A lot... err... some of the girders have shifted. It looks like the wall was too wet to hold them. Err... hang on. Can you see anything topside?"

Kethron looked over to the Cat Stane. "Nothing," he said.

"Err... don't lose it, but I've got skeletons down here."

The graves around the Cat Stane had been examined once in the nineteenth century, and again just before the new runway was laid in the seventies. There was disagreement as to their nature with some claiming them to be Pictish, whilst others claimed there were some early Christians mixed in with them. A few claimed they were even older still. Regardless of who was right and wrong, the decision had been made to leave the graves in situ.

"How many?" Kethron said. Ryan was surprised at how calm he was.

"It's difficult to tell. I don't know. It's too dark. Can you send a light down the vent shaft? See if I can pick the outlines."

Kethron motioned to the compressor operator, who cut the power. A torch was quickly found, a rope attached, and lowered down the opposite shaft.

"What's your pressure?" Kethron said.

"Still at ten. Did you get a torch?"

"Aye. Coming down now."

"Got it. It's a mess down here."

"How many skeletons Rooksby?" There was an impatient edge to Kethron's voice.

"Seven, eight, nine... ten. I can see ten. No, wait. There's eleven."

Kethron smiled. "You're sure?"

"Sure as I can be. We've got a couple of tonnes of soil over... ninety or a hundred feet, but I can see the skulls just fine."

With a speed that surprised Ryan, Kethron turned on him.

"Ok Wino," he said, moving towards him, "Now you're ready."

"What?" Ryan took a step back just as another aircraft took off, almost drowning him out.

Kethron thrust a black metal box into his hands, and it felt unusually cold to the touch.

"You're going down there. Rooksby will direct you to the skeletons. You'll find a pendant or a stone around each of their necks. Put in the box and bring it back up."

"What?" Ryan yelped again, not comprehending what was being demanded of him. Fear flowed through his veins and he felt paralysed by the commands being given.

"You heard, Wino."

Kethron grabbed him, pinning his arms to his side and deposited him onto the lift.

"But... but... but...the tunnel, it's collapsing!" Ryan blabbered.

"That'll be the least of your problems," Kethron smiled and was joined by several members of the team, each looking sternly down at him as he descended into the shaft.

The darkness enveloped him like a sinister lover, and he watched the portal of light above him fade away to a dot. The smell of old wet earth invaded his nostrils, clawing its way to the back of his throat. Below him, he could see Rooksby's head-torch, and the sodium lamps around him gave off a weak light casting the outline of Kethron's men into seemingly impossible contortions.

Ryan was beyond panic. Terror raced through his system, mixing with adrenaline and alcohol into a heady cocktail. He felt light-headed, and it was only the sense of rising nausea that stopped him from passing out completely.

It was warmer the further down he descended, and a musty smell, like stale urine, began to mix with that of the wet earth. Ryan knew that this is what Anna had planned all along. She had planned it with Kethron. Always just leading him on enough to get him to do what she wanted. Hate mixed with fear.

He would get out of here. He would...

What? Stand up for yourself? The black dog was back. Ryan wanted to scream at it. Scream at himself. Scream at Kethron. He wanted to throw himself from the moving platform, but he was already too close to the bottom, and he knew he would survive. He wanted to do something. Anything to just not be here. In this hole. With all the earth... and death.

Death. The word ballooned inside him.

If this is what Anna had planned for him, then he would not be needed after this. Kethron would only need to bring Rooksby back up... and then he could just start filling in. Who would miss him?

Ryan imagined the wet earth filling his mouth and his ears with worms, as the white dot of daylight above him faded out. The girl, the one from his dreams, the one he had followed, mocked him from her dream grave.

Join us join us join us.

She disappeared again under a wave of dark, almost fetid, blood.

The lift platform hit the floor with a jolt.

Rooksby was waiting for him, leaning against the shaft wall, arms folded. In the half light, he looked almost identical to Kethron.

Ryan instantly made for the emergency ascent button.

Rooksby was quicker, slapping his hand away, grabbing his elbow, and twisting it behind his back. Ryan careened into the earth wall, his mouth instantly trying to expel the dirt that had been forced in.

Rooksby held his arm as if he were holding a pencil. "Stop it!" he barked.

Ryan did not stop and continued to struggle against the bigger, more powerful man. Rooksby raised Ryan's arm behind his back and began to twist. It felt like his shoulder was being torn from his socket, and Ryan screamed. Rooksby deftly kicked the back of Ryan's knee, and he sank to the ground with another cry.

"Stop it!" Rooksby ordered again, raising Ryan's arm by the wrist high above the prone man's head, his other hand on the elbow. He would snap Ryan's arm clean in two if he had to.

Ryan felt his arm lock and then reach its break point. Rooksby held it there, right on the edge, and Ryan stopped struggling.

"Good monkey. Now listen to me very carefully." Rooksby was whispering into his ear. "You're just going to go into the tunnel and get the pendants and that's it."

"Screw you!" Ryan spat back.

Rooksby tweaked Ryan's arm another millimetre towards breaking, and he yelped again.

"It'll be easy. Get in. Get out," Rooksby hissed.

"No. The tunnel will come down on me."

Rooksby steered Ryan by the arm to the tunnel entrance. Some earth had come down, but not as much as Ryan had thought, and he could clearly make out skeletal forms picked out against the sodium light that had been dropped down the opposite ventilation shaft.

"It won't. See?"

Ryan saw.

"Just put the pendants in the box and this will all be over."

"No," Ryan whimpered. "You'll kill me."

Rooksby laughed and released Ryan's arm.

"I don't think so. Anna is not through with you yet my little monkey."

He stared at Rooksby. Ryan had taken a leaf from Kethron's book, and since Tom had died he had not discussed his family with anyone. He had come to work, done the job and that was it. No small talk. No banter. No "how was your weekend?"

So how did Rooksby know his wife's name?

"How... how do I know I can trust you?"

Rooksby laughed. "You have two choices. You either do as you're told or..." Rooksby pulled something from behind him and began to absently toss it in front of him, catching it before gently throwing it up again. In the half light, it looked to Ryan to be some sort of dagger. The blade was dark, almost black, and the grip looked to be twisted and distorted. Ryan was in no doubt that the man was able to use it very effectively.

"We could find out," Rooksby continued, "if your screams can be heard above all that traffic." He pointed the blade upwards, indicating towards the constant movement of aircraft above.

Ryan turned, and from where he stood, he could see a skeleton less than two feet from the tunnel entrance, and despite the fist-sized lumps of dirt surrounding it, he could clearly make out the worn leather thread of something around its neck. He turned back to Rooksby.

"I get them, and then we both get out?"

Rooksby nodded. "And you never have to see me again."

Ryan looked into the tunnel again. His eyes had grown used to the gloom, and he could make out the shapes better. His mind was reeling. So much of this did not make sense. Why could Rooksby not get the pendants? Or Kethron? Why this huge saga just to get him here? He was in no doubt that

189

the partial collapse of the tunnel had been engineered. Tom had warned Kethron about the wall, Ryan was sure of it.

The face of the little blonde girl he had followed that cold December day rose again in his mind.

Join us.

He turned back to Rooksby. "They're the girls," he said indicating to the skeletons, "aren't they? They're the girls you kidnapped from London."

Rooksby frowned.

"The Enfield Eleven. Anna had them taken, didn't she?"

Rooksby laughed again and shook his head. "Stars! You monkeys. Always trying to find patterns where there are none. Look how far down we are. Why would anyone bury eleven school girls down here just to have some wino dig them up two years later?"

"You didn't answer my question."

Rooksby stopped laughing and was suddenly glaring at Ryan. "If it makes you feel better, no. They are not those girls. Now get in there."

Rooksby jabbed his blade first towards Ryan and then the tunnel entrance.

"I dropped the box," Ryan said. "The one Kethron gave me."

Rooksby looked across the shaft floor, saw the box, and indicated to Ryan to take it. Ryan had hoped that he would pick it up to toss it him so that he could get a jump on him, but Rooksby was better than that, and he knew it.

Ryan picked the box up and made his way to the partially collapsed tunnel entrance. Looking at it, he realised that he was probably going to have to crawl on his belly. Clambering in, he could hear the distant sound of the extraction turbine still working away.

Thoc-thoc-thoc

That was something at least.

He felt the earth beneath his chest, soft and wet. The first skeleton was easy to get to, and he quickly found the pendant around its neck. It was about the size of an old fifty pence piece, but in the gloom, he could not make out any details. It felt hard, like a stone, but also slightly warm.

Ryan put it in the box and worked his way to the second skeleton. Again he found the pendant, and again he put in the box. The third was nearly ten feet from the tunnel entrance, and had more earth on top of it than the others, and despite sweeping away what he could, there was no pendant.

"It's not here," he called back to Rooksby. He could see that the man had sat down on the earthen floor.

"It is," Rooksby said absently, still tossing his knife, and not looking up. "Try harder."

Ryan swept some more earth away. "I'm telling you, it's not here."

Rooksby sighed. "Move on to the next one. You can look for that one on your way back."

Ryan moved on and found the remaining pendants. Most were still around their owners' necks, but some had become detached and were in the earth filled chest cavities. He was soaking wet and chilled to his core when began to make his way back some forty minutes later. His hi-vis jacket had done little to keep the water out, and he could not tell if he was shaking from the cold or from withdrawal.

As he returned to the third skeleton he started to dig around again. His hands were frozen, despite the warmth of the tunnels, and he was able to make little more than claws with them. Even though the turbine continued to whirr, the air still tasted stale and fetid, and Ryan had to stop more than once to dry-retch.

He dug around the skeleton, and then into the chest cavity. There was no pendant.

"I'm telling you," he called to Rooksby, "it's not here!" He was tired, frustrated and still very, very scared.

Rooksby had been watching him intently since he had begun his return journey, like a buzzard perched on a fence, watching its prey in the field.

"Keep looking. It'll be there."

A sound came from behind Ryan. A skittering clicking almost clacking. Ryan turned over in a panic, desperately trying to focus on the source of the sound that had come from the ventilation shaft behind him.

"There's something in here!" Panic was in his voice. "There's something in here with me!"

Ryan began to scrabble towards the lift. In an instant Rooksby was on his feet and at the tunnel entrance, his dagger drawn and pointed straight at Ryan.

"Get the pendant!"

The clacking came again, distinct above the sound of the turbine.

Thoc-thoc-thoc

"But there's something in here!"

"There's something out here too monkey child!" Rooksby was almost spitting. "Turn the skeleton over."

Ryan paused, desperate to get out.

"DO IT!"

Ryan scuttled backward and hauled the skeleton over. The pendant was directly behind the spinal column, which came apart in his hands like old wet cardboard.

Grabbing it and throwing it into the box, he thrust himself forward as fast as he could and lay panting on the lift shaft floor.

"Good monkey." Rooksby was standing over him.

Ryan was cold, exhausted, and trembling all over. He did not care if Rooksby killed him now. He would be happy just to end this nightmare.

He held the box up to Rooksby. "Take it."

Rooksby recoiled and took a step back. "That's not for me. Get on," he said, indicating to the lift platform. "Time to go home."

Home. Ryan laughed to himself. He was lost and damned and who knew what else. Wherever his home was, it was very far from this place, and he had neither the energy nor the will to find it.

Ryan climbed onto the platform. Rooksby pressed his radio. "Bring him up."

No response came, but the lift began to rise. Ryan tilted his head back, watching the daylight grow ever closer, and feeling the warmth of the spring day reaching down to caress his tired worn face. Already the events of the last hour seemed somehow distant and surreal as if they had happened to someone else, and he had just watched a video of it. But the waiting figures of Kethron and his men at the shaft head told him it was not over yet.

As soon as his head and shoulders had crested the lip of the lift shaft, Kethron's men grabbed, him, hoisted him clear, and held him tightly.

Kethron looked at Ryan and then to the box.

"You want it?" Ryan asked. "Take it." He offered the box to Kethron who, like Rooksby, recoiled, but made no reply.

A few minutes later the lift platform returned with Rooksby.

"Take him landside," Kethron said to Rooksby. "We'll get this lot finished up."

Ryan got into the waiting van, and Rooksby climbed in.

"Told you we weren't going to kill you," he said, smiling.

Ryan felt numb. "What are these?" He shook the box and the stone pendants rattled inside.

Rooksby looked at him, and then out through the windscreen. "Here's how this is going to work monkey-man," Rooksby said, ignoring his question. "I'm going to take you back landside. We will go and get lunch like we normally do. If you make a scene or try to escape, I will hurt you. I may even kill you. If you make a scene in public, well I just might have to kill all the witnesses as well."

The airport handled around twenty thousand people a day. Around fifteen hundred an hour. There were *always* people around. Ryan knew that Rooksby was fast, but he was not that fast... was he? Still, he had no desire to put the man's claim to the test.

"Kethron will be back between three and four. He will take you home like he normally does. You will hold onto that box like your life depends on it, because it does. You will not try to talk to anyone. You will not try to divert my attention. And most of all, you will not speak to me unless I tell you to. Are we clear?"

Ryan nodded but said nothing. His body was beginning to ache from the physical exertions of the last hour. Hunger pangs reminded him that, despite his recent ordeal, it had been a long time since he had eaten, and he felt himself shaking again.

"Good monkey. When you get home, you will give that box to your wife's friend, Irene, and no-one else. Understand?" Rooksby said. Sliding the van into gear, Rooksby gunned the engine and followed the airside road to the control post.

The guard waved them through, and it occurred to Ryan that Rooksby had snuck the knife through the metal detector. That meant it either was not metal, or he had someone landside toss it to him over the fence. There was no CCTV along the boundary, and there had been numerous attempted breaches over the years, mostly by environmental protestors who had simply used bolt cutters but had then been caught when the roving patrol had spotted them.

But there had been more suspicious episodes, where holes in the fence were discovered, but no culprit or group was ever identified. The grass was always kept short, and Ryan suspected that this was as much about discouraging birds as it was ensuring that intruders had no place to hide. Despite this, there were plenty of nooks and crannies on the airfield where a holdall could easily be stashed.

Rooksby raised his hand in thanks to the guard and drove towards the Contractors Compound.

*

It was nearly two o'clock when Rooksby and Ryan sat down in the landside Wetherspoons. Rooksby had cleaned his captive as best he could by spraying him down with the water-jets from the carwash and had given him fresh overalls.

But Ryan still looked as he felt. Bedraggled, cold, and tired. And very, very afraid.

He had already guessed that Anna and her friend would be waiting for him when he got home. And then what? He had no idea and felt adrift on a sea of confusion.

"What do you want?" Rooksby asked, handing him a menu.

Ryan looked at it and pointed to the burger.

"Drink?"

Ryan pointed to the whisky and held three fingers up.

"Don't push it monkey."

Ryan lowered one finger.

"Well, I suppose you've earned it today." Rooksby signalled to the waitress who took their order and returned shortly with their drinks. A double for Ryan and water for Rooksby.

He's keeping a clear head, Ryan thought. Looking around him, he could see the passengers milling around. Families getting to ready to go through security. Loved ones saying goodbye to each other. Business men and women returning from Edinburgh City, boarding their plane back to wherever.

They and the rest of humanity may as well have been a million miles away for all the help they could offer.

Ryan saw the waitress returning with their food, and he downed his drink, savouring the sweet burning.

"Can I get you gents anything else?" the chirpy blonde said.

Ryan did not feel chirpy. Ryan felt anti-chirpy. The complete opposite of this youthful, enthusiastic, pert...

He tapped his tumbler and held it to the waitress without looking up. He could feel Rooksby's eyes burning into him, but he did not care.

"Same again? I'll be right back."

Ryan could see clouds were building up, threatening rain. He ate his burger. The meat was dry and tasteless, the salad limp, and the chips were more fat than they were potato. He ate it all regardless.

Rooksby chewed away in silence, never once taking his eyes from his charge.

If your last meal summed up your life... he mused. That would have been a great concept for a book, but Ryan felt that it was probably too late for that now.

He felt the alcohol begin its work, and a low level numbing began to take hold, dulling the edges of his vision. It did not make him feel any better. It never did. It just made him feel... less. But all those minutes of frozen feeling, of holding the world way, well they had to melt, and clarity would come rushing back eventually.

Rooksby's mobile buzzed. The outsized man picked it up, grunted an acknowledgement, and hung up.

"Time to go. Kethron is waiting for you outside."

Ryan stood with his eyes cast to the ground.

"Got the box?"

He raised his hand and shook the box unenthusiastically. He was being handed over to Kethron, and then to Anna. And then what? He did not care anymore. He just wanted whatever this was to end. He did not want to be constantly guessing how he should be, what strange machinery was working away in his life, or what new fear would be lurking at the threshold of his vision tomorrow.

Rooksby took him by the arm, and began marching him towards the escalators that would take him down to arrivals, and then out onto the airport road where he would be put into a van.

Except that did not happen.

As they approached the escalator, for a brief moment the cloud broke, and the spring sun shone through, bright and majestic, catching the pepper-pot shape of the new control tower, and reflecting in a thousand directions, illuminating the terminal building, and bathing him in purifying white fire.

He paused just momentarily, as the warm sun caressed his faced, like a parent's forgotten touch. Somewhere deep inside him, something broke, and he knew he was going to die. And it would be soon and it would be painful. Tears welled up, as Rooksby dragged him bodily towards the escalator.

And as he went with his captor, he saw a figure cresting the opposite escalator. It was a face he had never seen, but it spoke directly to him.

I've seen what you've seen. I've been where you've been. I've done what you have done... you are forgiven.

Ryan took a step out of Rooksby's intended path, meeting the stranger's eye, reaching for him.

A wave crossed the stranger's face, akin to recognition, and he too took a step forward.

"No, you don't!" Rooksby barked and went to grab Ryan, missing as his charge took another step forward.

Rooksby slid the knife out, and someone screamed.

The stranger saw the downward arc, and rushed forward, first hugging the now freely crying Ryan, and then sending him sprawling to the floor.

The knife grazed his cheek but carried on its sweep missing the target's kill spot.

Someone else screamed and an alarm sounded. The passengers stood frozen, staring at the unfolding scene.

Ryan registered the sound of pounding feet as uniformed bodies raced from the security area to the source of the commotion. But he was away, floating, and safe.

Rooksby knew he had a second at most to react. He could not handle the box, so it was kill the monkey or escape. From his vantage point, he could see across the airport forecourt to where Kethron was waiting with the engine running.

Pushing the passengers in front of him out of the way he left Ryan, bounded down the escalator and out to where the white van was, noting the rapidly approaching blue lights from the onsite police station.

Ryan heard the squeal of wheels but no longer cared.

The stranger raised himself from Ryan's body. "Are you ok?"

Ryan nodded. Tears streaking his face. "Thank you," he whispered.

The stranger held out his hand and pulled him up, and then embraced him.

"It's ok," he whispered in Ryan's ear. "I've got you. You're safe now."

*

Danielle looked at Freeman slack-jawed. "So what happened next?"

"That's it. Ryan Hyde's account."

Danielle struggled to know where to begin. "I thought you promised me no stoners or dropouts."

"Come on, he was an alcoholic, and when I interviewed him seven or so years ago he had been sober fifteen years. I still hear from him from time to time. And he's still clean."

Danielle still did not like it. "How much of it can be verified?"

Freeman smiled. "Anna Hyde did quit her I.T. job. And she did work in a minicab firm in Enfield. You'll remember the Enfield Eleven case. Edinburgh Airport really does have mine workings running underneath it, and they really were filled in by Corax, which is a subsidiary of Corvus. There really is a Cat Stane standing stone that marks an ancient graveyard, next to the main runway. And Tom Cullum really did die in the way Ryan described."

"Tom Cullum? Andrew's brother... from Paternoster?"

Freeman smiled. "Funny the way these circles move. There is always... a ripple effect. Things get caught in the wake."

"What about the cave?"

"That I cannot prove. There is no record of it. But the cargo development never happened. The cave would have been right under those old RAF buildings. Maybe it put paid to the development. The airport operator really did hire a development specialist, but they laid him off in two thousand and eleven when the airport was being sold."

"Did you track him down?"

"Yes and no. It seems that he got an extraordinary windfall a few months after he left the airport. He *bought* an island in the Pacific and retired there with his family. He won't return my phone calls."

Danielle frowned. "He bought an island?"

Freeman nodded. "Uh-huh. In cash."

"That's some windfall. What about Anna and Christopher?"

"It turned out that the house in Falkland was only rented. They went to Russia first, and then the US where they stayed in Seattle for a few years. After that, they moved around a lot, and I lost track of them both. The boy did come back to England to complete his Further Education. Youngest ever graduate in a Masters in Politics, Law, and Economics. But he moved on, and lived in California, working as a lobbyist, until they declared independence. Then I lost track of him too."

"Rooksby and Kethron?"

"Rooksby is still wanted on a wounding charge, but he was never seen again. As for Kethron... well no-one saw him driving the van. He was interviewed but never charged. He finished the job of filling in the mine, got promoted to the parent company and still works for Corvus today. He did not want to talk to me. Corax is still going, but it's half the size it was when Ryan was working there. Given the economic climate for the last twenty years, that is hardly surprising. Corvus went on to diversify. Today they manufacture the majority of the electronics for Net Station and even dabble in some software once in a while. They've even been known to pick up one or two military contracts in their time."

"Military contracts?"

"They acquired a small pharmaceutical company that had a CIA contract in nineteen-forty-eight, and have been growing it ever since."

Danielle looked the old man. "There's more to that story, isn't there?"

Freeman said nothing but continued looking at his publisher.

"What about Irene? Or Charlie? What was happening there?" Danielle continued.

Freeman smiled. "You do like to jump ahead. We'll come to her later."

"Come on. Tell me now. She's the same as whatever Anna is, isn't she?"

"Patience my dear."

"Ok. What about the pendants?"

"You held one. Well, one like it."

"That thing? That's it? That was what came up from those graves?"

"Well no. Mine came from a temple in Japan – a colleague sent it to me, although I cannot explain why such intricate craftsmanship was replicated hundreds of years and thousands of miles apart. But it's identical to the ones that Ryan brought up. His rescuer still has them in the box."

"So who was it that came up the escalators? And how did he know Ryan was in trouble?"

"Have a guess."

"Celus?"

"Nope."

"Well, it can't have been George. He would have been too old to wrestle anyone to the ground. The son – Devon? Or the grandson?"

"Not even close."

"I give up. Who?"

"John Lennox."

Danielle was stunned. "What?"

"It was John Lennox," Freeman repeated.

"The sleaze-ball reporter?"

"Yup."

"But why... how did he get there?"

"After he was picked up by the police, following his reappearance from Sumerland, he was interviewed – that's where that account came from - and then he quit the BBC and got a quickie divorce. The police still have a cold case on Murphy King. After the breakup of his marriage, Lennox disappeared for a couple of years. But he popped up again a year or so before meeting Ryan, and became a priest."

"You're joking, right?"

"No. He took orders."

"Where? Who would have him?"

"Well, that is where things get interesting. A little-known Christian sect called the Céli Dé. They had a small but notable following in Ireland and Scotland about twelve hundred years ago, but then got absorbed by other factions. As far as I can tell, today there are only a handful of practitioners left. And John Lennox is one. He has a small ministry in Dunfermline and is allowed to preach a couple of mornings a week at the abbey. He just happened to be going through the airport that day. I think he recognised something in Ryan. That he had been touched by the same thing he had… and stepped in."

"That doesn't sit right," said Danielle. "You said that there is no such thing as coincidence. There's more to it than that."

Freeman smiled knowingly. "There certainly is. Despite its relatively small size, the Céli Dé has significant business holdings. Valued in the trillions."

"What do they do with it? They certainly don't use it to raise their profile."

"They don't operate the business themselves, but rather make awards and grants from the income. The charity is known as the Chuldees Trust, which is just an Anglicisation of Céli Dé. The principal company the money is moved through is The Accipiter Corporation."

"Isn't that the company that funded Tate's dig at Maiden Castle?"

"Tate's *first* dig. A bit of a coincidence, eh?"

Danielle's eyes widened. "There was a second dig?"

"Oh yes. But again, you're jumping ahead."

"What is Accipiter? Sounds vaguely Freemason-y."

"No. But someone was clever enough to make it look like them. Their registered address is even on Great Queen Street."

Danielle loved the ingenuity of it. "Clever. A secret society pretending to be a secret society. So what happened to Ryan after Lennox found him?"

"Wherever it was that Lennox was going, he cancelled it there and then. He took Ryan back to his flat and got him a job as a cleaner at the Abbey. He still works there three days a week, and the rest of the time he works for Lennox."

"Doing what?"

"Mostly PA-type stuff. Diary management. Making sure the bills get paid. A bit of research…"

Danielle's brow furrowed. "Researching what?"

Freeman smiled "You're jumping ahead again. Right now, that is not the pressing issue. You have overlooked something important from Lennox's story."

Danielle thought for a moment. "What?"

Freeman placed a small plastic frame on the table. "That is the film badge that Lionel Orton gave John Lennox. Lionel was just doing his job at the time, and he didn't realise how important it would be. You see, a regular film badge gets sent away to determine how much radiation it has been exposed to. Have a look at the LED readout."

Danielle leaned forward, not wanting to know how Freeman had acquired the film badge, and took the piece of plastic between her fingers. "Minus two-thousand-three-hundred-and-twenty-three?"

"That thing should absorb radiation. It should be a positive number. Not a negative," Freeman said.

Danielle put it back down on the table. "You're going to tell me it's not broken or malfunctioning, aren't you?"

"Correct. But this film badge can actually trap particles of radiation that can be analysed later."

"Let me guess. Something that had never been seen before?"

Freeman laughed. "Far from it. It's a form of naturally occurring background radiation. There are hot spots all over the world of course, like Cornwall and Aberdeen which are high in radon. But that is because of the geology of the area. The rock types in the ground. This…this is something different. And it is rarely ever captured in the concentration that Lennox stumbled on. We've known of its existence for decades from observable effects on other materials, but it is only in the last few years that the scientists have been able to actually measure it in any meaningful way. However, its source remains a complete mystery."

Danielle could almost guess what was coming next. "You said hot spots, right? Let me guess. The Lomond Paps. Maiden Castle. Paternoster House. Edinburgh Airport."

Freeman laughed again. "Very good. There are of course many more. And not just on this planet, but throughout our solar system. Mars and the asteroid belt have levels many times higher than here on Earth. Later, I'll show you that it occurs throughout our galaxy if not the entire universe."

Danielle could feel that a point was being made, but she could not see it. "So if it's so common, why is it so important?"

"Radiation particles get emitted from a decaying element. This… well it's an energised particle, but no-one can understand what element it came from. Energised particles… their vibration decreases over time. It's like driving a car – take your foot off the accelerator and you'll slow down until you stop. Right?"

"Yes."

"Except this particle – Khronusium – doesn't. It will slow down, but then it will speed back up again, and then start slowing down again. But it never actually stops."

"Like it is being re-energised?"

"Exactly," Freeman smiled.

Danielle thought for a moment. "The light above Paternoster House?"

"It can't be proved, but very likely. Of course, our history, both modern and ancient, is riddled with tales of lights in the sky. It is difficult to tell for certain what can be attributed to this Khronusium and what is down... to other things."

"Over-eager imaginations?"

"Possibly."

Danielle considered this. "What about Ryan's vision. At that standing stone. Did he see George?"

Freeman held up his hands. "I'm not certain. I can make an educated guess, but that will have to come later. We need to build to that."

Danielle sighed. "So what does this account prove?" she said eventually.

"Two things; firstly words have power," Freeman answered. "That's why Ryan Hyde could not leave of his own accord. The Anna-Creature made him agree with her from the outset... well, to all sorts of things; that she was his wife and he loved her and he was faithful. I have no doubt that her real behaviour was far more sinister than Ryan relayed, but whatever force of domination he was under prevented him from seeing the truth. It is almost as if, by agreeing, the victim's local reality becomes warped. Everyone else is unaffected unless they agree too."

Danielle was unconvinced. "That's a bit of leap. He was weak and an alcoholic. What's your second point?"

"Fine fine," Freeman replied. "There is another story later on that will validate this particular hypothesis. My second point is that The Raven Men are already here. What Dennis King found under Lomond Pap in Falkland..."

Danielle frowned. "Hang on, wasn't that where Anna Hyde moved the family too?"

Freeman smiled and nodded. "Coincidence? I doubt it. Anyway, my point is that *they* are already here. Dennis King probably found one of their hatcheries... but Kethron and Rooksby and Anna's friend, Irene..."

Danielle interrupted again. "You're not going to tell me that was Irene Tate, are you?"

Freeman shrugged. "I can't say for certain. But the fact is that they are here, and the image from King's camera showed thousands of them. A whole army who are slowly making their way through to our world at the behest of whatever it was that Harry Gordon saw in the sky."

Danielle could see the strands beginning to weave together. As insubstantial as each piece seemed on its own, the whole was growing in both substance and weight. "Ok," she said eventually. "Let's assume that Sumerland is real. Let's assume that all of your sources who claimed that they crossed over really did, and let's assume that there is something on the other side sending through these Raven Men of yours. What does any of this have to do with George Tate? How does he fit into this?"

"Don't you see?" Freeman replied, leaning forward with an urgency that belied his age. "Tate leaves a wake behind him. And people get caught up in it, often without knowing that it is even him, and then... well, you can see that their lives take a right turn. His actions at Paternoster led to Murphy King's death, John Lennox' religious conversion, Anna Hyde, Ryan Hyde... the list goes on. All of them have been affected by Tate, even if they don't know it is him. Do you understand?"

Danielle thought for a moment. "Sort of... this is The Twine that the disciplinary panel found in George's notes at The British Museum? What Celus was looking for in the cave? What The Raven Men were running from in Harry Gordon's vision?"

Freeman nodded. "Tate *is*... something. He calls it a Twine, but I don't know what it is. But his story weaves through so many others... and no one can deny his effect."

Danielle found herself agreeing and on reflex tried to rationalise the evidence. "Other than Paternoster House, can you link George directly to any other sightings of strange lights?"

"Oh yes - several. Let me start with a contentious one. But I warn you, this one is a real humdinger."

Danielle loved the old man's turn of phrase. "Go on," she smiled.

"The Jonestown Massacre."

Danielle was impassive for a moment. "Never heard of it."

Freeman was incredulous. "Honestly?"

Danielle's response was cool. "Honestly."

"In nineteen-seventy-eight," Freeman began, "more than nine hundred US citizens committed suicide at a commune in what was then Guyana. It remained the single worst loss of civilian life until nine-eleven, and still the third worst today."

"You've been to South America? You broke through the quarantine?"

Freeman shook his head. "No. There was a formal investigation held in the US, and I managed to get hold of a copy of the report. The appendices are full of eyewitness accounts, wills, and some recorded last testaments of those who died there."

"And George Tate was there?"

"Celus definitely. And another man, who matches George's description, was with him. We know for a fact that George was on annual leave from the Maiden Castle dig at the time and that he was in Guyana. The night before the suicides, a super-massive Borealis was seen over the area. It is a matter of public record that aircraft were diverted around it. You'll be unsurprised to learn that even today, not a single piece of electrical equipment works in the area of Jonestown," he said, pulling a roll of magnetic tape from his satchel.

"What is that?" Danielle asked.

"It's a cassette… oh never mind. It's what was used before the Digital Information Service. Anyway, the day after the light display over Jonestown… well I'll let the dead tell this one."

Freeman pressed the play button and the sound of the tape hiss filled the room.

CHAPTER 9

Falling visions and rising voices, burn behind my eyes,
Fractured sight and creeping shadows, an enemy in disguise.
Reality turns and the mirror breaks, mainline the mainstream,
Living up is a living lie, an echo from a dream.

"In Search" by Even The Lost. © G & L Tate 1978

Saturday November 18th 1978

There is a click as the recording mechanism engages. For a moment there is nothing to hear and then comes the sound of distant voices and people moving about.

"Is it on?" a woman asks. She sounds strained as though she has cried until her throat is raw.

"Uh-huh," a man replies, sounding gruff and weary. "It's recording."

The woman begins. "My name is Isabelle Maria Fernandez-Pitman – Izzy to my friends - and I've been a resident of Peoples Temple Agricultural Project – more commonly known as Jonestown – for the last three years. Within the next few hours, I shall be no more, extinguished by my own hand.

"I go to my fate freely, voluntarily, and of my accord, as do my two children. I don't know how long we have until They get here. Maybe hours. At best a day. I won't let them take me or the children alive. I know what they will do to us.

"I'm certain that there'll be an investigation, and that we'll be written off as communists, or druggies, or paedophiles, or some other folk-devil the government wants us to be. If you've been reading the Press, you'll not be surprised by this, but I ask that you accept this recording as my last testament.

The people of Jonestown aren't evil. After the revelations of last night, we know that we were set up from the beginning. We are responsible. But we are not to blame. The Man is coming. He'll be here soon with his guns, and he'll try to take our children and if we fight he'll put us down like dogs. Better to go out by our own hand than his.

We never meant for it to come to this. We're all so very sorry. We didn't mean it. We believed that our work was for the greater Glory of God. None of us realised that we'd fallen so far.

It'd be easy to blame our leader, Dad - Jim Jones as you know him - but I honestly believe that he's been deceived as much as the rest of us. We don't condemn him. You probably think that it is creepy that we call him Dad. But it is just an affectionate name for him and is no different than 'Vicar' or 'Reverend'.

It's difficult to know where to start. We all have different stories that begin at different times, and so I'll settle for telling mine. A number of my companions are recording similar statements, and it's my fervent wish that the combined whole provides some illumination.

It was the summer of seventy-one that I came to Guyana, as a nurse and a missionary, with my husband, Randall Pitman. He'd been a chaplain at Kirtland Air Base, but had left after becoming disillusioned with the establishment. I don't know where he is now. If he's lucky, he'll be dead.

I was born and raised in Los Lunas, New Mexico. I met Randall in the summer of sixty-seven, and I know what you are thinking; a little catholic girl, a repressed USAF Chaplain and the hedonism of The Summer of Love. But that was not Randall and me. That summer was what happened to other folks. Those on the coast and those heathen European types. Ours was a simpler relationship. My younger sister knew his brother, a college grad who had hopes of going on to read physics at MIT. He was a sweet kid. Green as they come, but sweet all the same. So a double-date was arranged, and that, as they say, was that. Randall and I stuck. We were married the next Fall, and a few months after that Randall left the Air Force to join The San Clemente Catholic Church as an outreach worker.

Miguel was born to us in the spring of seventy-one, and when an opportunity came later that year to be part of a new Mission in Guyana, it felt as if God's Plan was being shown to us. To borrow from a Presbyterian, there are none as blind as those that refuse to see.

Our mission was based on the southern outskirts of Georgetown, and the Lord rewarded us with a plentiful bounty. It was hard. It was plenty hot in the noon heat, but we would all work on. Once off the single main road that went in and out, it was nothing but dirt tracks, and reaching a community most often meant having to borrow a mule. Randall taught at the Mission during the day and helped to sink wells in the evening. I tended the local women in matters of childcare and midwifery, as well as rudimentary general medicine.

Our congregation grew from a handful of hungry parishioners to three full services each and every Sunday. We were happy.

The people grew too – spiritually, I mean - with a number becoming active during service. That is not to say that there weren't difficulties because there were. We were often hassled by a local gang who stole our food and vandalised the corrugated iron shack that we called a church. Similarly, local officials would impose "fines", claiming that our visas weren't valid or that the church wasn't built within the grounds specified by the government lease. We came to expect such treatment, and in time there was grudging recognition for the work that we did. We never blamed our tormentors. They were poor boys, with no education or knowledge of the gospel. They didn't know any better. Maybe it would be better for all of us if we lived like that. In ignorance.

*

It was mid seventy-three that we heard of another mission coming to Guyana. This one was not backed by the Catholic Church but was a splinter of the Baptists. The proposed site was far from Georgetown, out in the Barima-Waini Region, and as such, we didn't pay it much attention. Randall said that there was less than ten thousand souls spread over some twenty-thousand square kilometres, all of it inhospitable jungle, and as such, we did not see that there would be any overlap between the two missions.

By early seventy-four, the story had changed. It was no longer a mission that was being established but a commune, and work was to begin in the spring. What information we did receive was not encouraging, and we heard tales of political scandal, fraud, and that the leader, Jim Jones – Dad to his followers - was being forced to flee America because of drugs and sodomy charges.

Randall, me, and the other mission members had worked for nearly three years to build our reputations as Americans and now it looked like all the goodwill we had earned would be squandered if we were in any way to be associated with this interloping hippy rabble. Needless to say, we were all deeply concerned, and several of the menfolk went to the US embassy... I say embassy. It was no more than a single storey brick building. No plaster or nothing. They came back more worried than when they left. It was a commune *and* a new mission. It was a done deal, and there was nothing we could do to stop it.

The central government had agreed on a lease of nearly four thousand acres of jungle near Kaituma, a remote gold-mining colony. Even though this was some hundred-and-fifty miles from Georgetown, and across dense and unforgiving jungle terrain, we all felt uneasy at the prospect of what this commune may bring.

*

In the April of seventy-four, Randall told me that a delegation from San Francisco was coming to begin preparatory works for the building of the commune and that they had agreed to meet with us to discuss our concerns.

When Randall told me that it was a 'delegation' I was expecting a small group of maybe a dozen men. I was not prepared for the five hundred souls that I met outside Timehri Airport. They were all so smart with their open neck shirts and big smiles - not the rabble of students and dropouts I had been expecting.

That was the first time I met Timothy Stoen of The Peoples Temple, and initially, I was suspicious of him. Of the five hundred delegates, he was one of the few white faces, but they were all at ease with each other. Africans and Mexicans and the white men. Some Afro-Caribbeans too.

When I asked him about this, he laughed and told me that was part of The Temple's problem. The Temple was an integrationist utopia and saw no distinction in race, colour, or creed. There had been some mighty opposition to them from the hicks in Indiana, and they had driven Dad and his congregation out to San Francisco. Despite the relative liberalisation of California, there were plenty who did not like what Dad was doing, and the police had set him up on charges of homosexual solicitation. Timothy also told me how the fascist right had infiltrated the organisation and then tried to discredit it, showing me a newspaper article from the previous September. Looking at the happy smiling faces around me, it was hard to relate to the 'abuses' and 'mind control' that the newspaper talked about.

Randall and I had certainly had our fill of segregationist views and violence. As a mixed-race couple, our windows had been put in more than once when we were first married. That was until Randall asked his Air Force friends to speak 'nicely' to those responsible. But we knew about living in fear. Fear of being spat at on the street; of being called lazy even though those folks knew nothing about us or our living. Once we even had a dead cat thrown at the house and threatening phone calls were not uncommon.

I won't say that Tim won us over there and then. Our minds were still too cluttered with all our preconceptions. But he did make us feel relaxed. Kaituma had an airstrip that could only handle the smaller aeroplanes, and Tim arranged for the ferrying of the other delegates to begin. It was then that we learned that the delegation was actually the first wave of immigration, and they were there to start the construction work. The building materials had been ordered and sent by boat a few weeks previously, and should be arriving just in time.

The ferrying of the delegation that day was slow. It was nearly a three-hour round trip to Kaituma, and only two airplanes that had been chartered, carrying no more than a dozen or so men at a time. Tim said that he thought they had hotel reservations, but I could see from the look on his face that he had underestimated how long the process would take. Randall offered him and some of his men the hospitality of the Mission, and they graciously accepted.

Their company that night was most congenial, and we learned more about their mission – a form of Pentecostal Socialism. They described a system, based on the gospels, where no man owns anything but contributes selflessly to the greater whole. I could see that Randall was unconvinced, but the way Tim described the communal way in which the children were raised, and the elderly cared for appealed to me. It seemed a good way of sharing both the bounties and trials that life brought.

As the evening wore on the conversation grew more theological, and wearied from the day's exertions I retired, leaving the men-folk to debate the mysteries and secrets of God's infinite universe. I truly wish that they had stayed secret.

*

The next morning, my husband seemed electrified. The men had talked until the small hours and had told Randall about their sermons. It seemed that Dad would often lapse into talking in tongues, and when he did some of the congregation would experience visions of heaven and God's Great Kingdom. Tim had invited us both to see the settlement in Kaituma, and Randall was keen. It had been many years since I had seen him in such fervour, and I agreed to go along too.

That morning, Timehri was still crowded with more than two hundred delegates, and it was evident that the ferrying operation had gone on most of the night. Despite having had to sleep on the airport's hard floor, all seemed to be in high spirits, and it was not long before an airplane returned that we were able to board.

The ride was bumpy, and combined with the sticky heat, I felt sick almost from the moment we took off. Randall barely seemed to notice, so deep in conversation was he with Tim and the other men.

My period was late and I strongly suspected that I would have to tell my husband. He would be happy, I knew that he would. But Miguel was going through a difficult phase of saying "No" to everything, and it had been wearing on both of us.

It was maybe a half-hour into the flight, and I was deep in my own thoughts when I heard the pilot say something. Randall leaned forward, looking to where the pilot was pointing and was joined by Tim and another member of the delegation. I craned forward, and could just see three dark objects moving across the canopy of the dense jungle. Steam was slowly rising in places, where the morning heat was meeting the night dew.

Tim said something to Randall, who nodded, but over the noise of the engines I could not make it out.

"What is it?" I asked him when he sat back down.

"Three helos." Helicopters. Randall often lapsed into his Air Force slang.

"What are they doing out here?"

"Tim said they are most probably from a gold prospecting company. They've established a site ten kilometres or so from the Temple compound and have an agreement that their staff can use the Temple facilities. In exchange, they make some donations."

Tim waved to the helicopters, even though there was no way they could have seen them. If I had known then what I know now, I would have kicked him out of the airplane, God forgive me for saying such a thing. It seems funny saying that now. Reflex I guess.

*

We circled the area that was to be the Peoples Temple Agricultural Project before flying the two miles back to Kaituma. As we came in to land, we saw a convoy of trucks driving down the mud road, taking supplies toward the site. It had been raining on and off for weeks, and the trucks seemed to be making heavy work, churning up the road. We flew low, seeing men trying to secure a load where the back-end had slid, and another filling around the wheels with what looked like sand or sawdust.

The Kaituma airstrip was just that – a length of compacted mud that the airplane landed on far too heavily. The residents of the nearby village eyed us with some amusement, assuming that Randall and I were part of the Temple. Their village was small but attracted enough transients, who worked for the gold mining companies, to be self-sufficient.

We were greeted warmly and joined the queue of trucks heading towards Jonestown. In front of us was an old rusting tanker, and Tim told us that this was carrying chemical supplies for the gold prospectors.

Jonestown at that point was little more than a small square of earth where the jungle had been cleared, but the sound of construction was all around us. Chainsaws whined and trees creaked before coming crashing down. Trunks were stripped and the wood sawed before being quickly whisked away to be fitted to the skeletal frames of what would be huts. The concept of 'homes' did not exist. All the huts were communal, and no-one had one any bigger or smaller than anyone else. Not even Dad. The makeshift canteen was serving cooling sweet tea and, under its canopy, I saw that Randall's eyes were alight. He could see the potential for Jonestown and his enthusiasm was infectious. I could see it too. It was like a song – everyone living in harmony. Living as one.

Whites worked alongside blacks. Hispanics prayed alongside Koreans. Children of all colours were playing together, running in and out of the building site, laughing. Even thinking about those early days brings a joyful tear to my eye.

Randall was unusually quiet on the flight back to Georgetown. I knew what he was thinking. He had pitched in for a few hours with some of the workers, clearing an area that was to be a field for wheat and rye. I loved seeing him so alive.

Almost instinctively, I found myself rubbing my belly. Randall looked at me, looked to me belly and then back to me.

"Oh, baby. We need to talk."

Randall broke into a big grin, the sort that went from ear to ear. "Really?"

"Uh-huh. I think so."

"How far?"

"Not far. Maybe four or five weeks."

Clambering over the airplane seats, he came and hugged me. I can still smell the mustiness of his sweat. I felt warm all over. And so safe.

Back at the mission, we barely slept, talking in low whispers for most the night so that the other members would not hear us. Randall wanted to join the Temple straight away, but I wanted to wait, at least until the child was born. Whilst medical care was basic in Georgetown, it would be non-existent in the jungle. And of course, I wanted to find out more about the Temple, and about Dad.

*

Winter did not really come that year. It seldom did. Sometimes the winds became fresher, less sticky, but on the whole, it remained hot, and I became increasingly uncomfortable as my belly swelled with the new life inside.

Randall remained in contact with Tim and even started casting about Georgetown for a satellite office for the Temple, but it would not be until January of seventy-five that I next saw Timothy Stoen.

The market was alive with its usual bustle. Vendors called out and the smell of fresh fruit and vegetables hung in the hot still air. Despite being only a week or so away from being due, and advised to stay off my feet, I found myself at my most comfortable when I was up and about.

I heard Randall's name called out, and we both turned to see Tim with two other Temple members. I recognised them both, and they smiled warmly, shaking our hands and enquiring about the baby. But Tim looked haggard, and he had dropped a few pounds. Still, he put a brave face on, and we swapped stories of our respective Christmas celebrations. Tim began to talk business with Randall, about the office, and drifted away from me for a few minutes, whilst I picked out vegetables for the evening supper.

Later, as I was preparing dinner, I mentioned to Randall that Tim had not looked well. He agreed but said that Tim had taken too much on with the Jonestown construction. It had taken its toll and he had been laid up with the flu for most of the festive period in San Francisco. He also mentioned that Tim was having some marital difficulties, and these had been exacerbated when a friend of his wife had left the Temple, claiming that her daughter had been beaten by members of Dad's 'Red Brigade'.

It turned out that the persecution of the Temple had followed them from Indiana, with members occasionally being attacked in the street, and more than once the Church had been broken into and vandalised. In response, Dad had armed some of the members and made them into a rapid response unit, so that if anyone was in trouble this 'Red Brigade' could be called and they would help.

This sounded inflammatory to me, and I reminded Randall that America was already involved in one seemingly endless arms race, and everyone would do well to remember that if everyone was a given a gun to shoot then pretty soon there would be no-one left. Randall agreed but told me that if he was in the same position he would do likewise.

From what Tim had told my husband, it seemed that the beatings endured by members of the congregation were not random crimes of hate but specifically targeted. Tim had hinted at CIA involvement, and that Dad had taken the claims so seriously that, in addition to setting up the Red Brigade in San Francisco, he had also done the same in Jonestown, where armed guards now patrolled the perimeter.

I scoffed at him. "Now you tell me, Randall Pitman," I said, "why would the CIA want to go poking their nose into a little church like Jim Jones'?"

Randall shrugged. "Probably the same reason they shot Dr King. There will always be those who want to maintain the status-quo, and if they can see someone who either is or is capable of challenging that... well, they don't take kindly to it."

"Oh really? And what is Jim Jones doing that the CIA don't take kindly to?"

Randall frowned. "Are you serious?"

"Yes I am, and I'll thank you not to address me in that tone."

"Baby, look at what Jonestown is. Black living with white. Nobody steals nothing because nobody has nothing, and everyone is just as happy as they could be. A man just gets up with his brother, does a day's work and gets a fair meal. Nobody cares about what sneakers you've got, or how much your Rolex cost, or what kitchen they should get fitted."

"I don't care about those things."

"Neither do I, but Baby, there are people out there who do care whether you think about those things. You see Jim as starting an arms race with the local hoods, but I see it that he's trying to check out of the consumption race. He doesn't want his Church to care what car their neighbours have. But if people aren't buying new cars, then what is going to happen to all the car manufacturers? And then the economy? Do you see? It's the same with televisions, and apartments, and everything. They just want to keep feeding you stuff you don't need so they can keep taking your money..."

"Yeah..." I interrupted, and leaned against the side of the counter, a peeler in one hand. "That's awful nice Randall, and I'm sure you tried extra hard to learn that little speech." I had found Temple pamphlets next to his bed saying much the same. "But right now we got bigger problems."

Randall looked confused. "What's that Hun?"

"My waters just broke."

*

During the previous few months, many people told me that the second one is always easier than the first. Many people were wrong. It took two days to get Paulo out, and I'm afraid I may have cussed. Randall was as dutiful as ever, waiting patiently outside whilst the nurses did what they do. But you should have seen his face when he held his new son that first time. He and his two boys. Right then, I don't think there was a prouder man on the whole planet.

After that, our life fell back into the familiar routine of feeding and changing that I knew so well from when Miguel was a baby. Randall went back to church work soon enough, but I could see he was itching to bring up the subject of Jonestown. I give him his due, he knew me well enough not to mention it until Paulo was a little stronger, and we were both distracted enough by what was going on back in Washington to really talk about it. Rumours were flying every which way, and we did not know what to believe.

*

It was April, and Georgetown was a riot of gossip. The US was quitting Vietnam. I knew that Randall had served over there, but he never said much about it, although I suspected it played it a part in his coming out of the Air Force. The whole Mission sat around the small wireless on the twenty-third, listening in disbelief as Ford announced the end of The War and the withdrawal of all US aid. No-one said anything. How could we have lost?

"Well that's that," Randall muttered, getting up, and went back to work.

It was July before we saw Tim again. The man looked a shadow, positively haunted. Randall told me he thought the man's marriage was over, and there would be a custody dispute over his son. But it seemed that things had settled down for the Temple in San Francisco. Moscone had been elected as mayor, and the rumour was that Dad had played a major part in his victory. As a result, the Temple was being treated more fairly, and everyone felt they had some breathing space.

It was September seventy-five when Tim came around again, and he and Randall renewed their conversations about a Temple satellite office. I took the boys into the other room to play, leaving the menfolk to their business. Later, Randall told me that Tim had offered us a weekend away in Jonestown. I was hesitant. Paulo was only six months old and had just begun weaning. But Tim had thought of that, and had offered the services of two ladies, who acted as wet-nurses for some of the other mothers at Jonestown, and who would come and babysit for the weekend.

MARTIN ADIL-SMITH

I knew how much Randall wanted to see Jonestown again... to see if the progress was really as Tim had described. We had spent very little time as husband and wife since Paulo had arrived, and when I heard that Dad would likely be there the same weekend... well I couldn't really say no, and so arrangements were made.

*

It was the first weekend in October, and the ride in the little airplane was just as bumpy as I remembered it to be, if not more so. I held my belly all the way, not through feeling sick this time, even though I did, but because I was already missing my boys. It was like a hole had opened up inside me. But I could see from the look on my husband's face, who was deep in conversation with Tim and two other Temple members, that this was what he wanted.

It was nearly dusk when we landed at Kaituma, and Dad was there to greet us personally. He looked nothing like I imagined. Slightly thick-set with well-combed black hair, he was nothing if not charismatic. We talked on the drive to Jonestown, and he thanked both of us for supporting Tim during his difficulties. At that time I did not refer to him as "Dad", but had noticed various Temple members using the name. When I asked him about it, he laughed.

"What you need to believe in is what you can see," he said. "If you see me as your friend, I'll be your friend. If you see me as your father, I'll be your father. For those of you that don't have a father ... you can call me whatever you like."

My own father had died at Iwo Jima, and hearing Dad speak like this suddenly reminded of how much I missed him. I hadn't thought of him since Paulo was born, and suddenly I had an ache welling up, tearing through me like a plough across a field. Without even realising it, I was crying, and both Randall and Dad hugged me.

"I'm sorry," I spluttered between sobs and tears.

"It's ok," Dad said. "You... you got nothing to be sorry for."

What little remained of our journey was conducted in silence as I rested between Randall and Dad. I felt exhausted.

The light was fading fast when we reached Jonestown. It was hard to believe that it was little more than a year since we had last visited, and my... what a transformation!

Nearly fifty huts had been completed, and at least seventy acres of jungle cleared. There was a pavilion where people gathered for prayer, and the makeshift canteen was gone, replaced by a much grander cabin. The field where Randall had worked that day had not done quite so well, and wheat still had to be imported. But more fields had been sown, and the Temple hoped for a better harvest the following year.

As we approached, I saw that the main drive was lined with people, some of whom I recognised from the last time that we were there. All were smiling and waving and, as we got out of the battered old jeep, Dad was mobbed.

I guessed that there were around six- or seven-hundred people now, and Tim said that there would be a thousand by the end of the year, once the new huts were finished. Our dinner that night was rice and vegetables, and even though it was not much, I knew the community were sharing what they had.

Later, Dad was persuaded to lead Mass at the pavilion, and under a clear sky and a hunter's moon we all gathered. It surprised me that Dad did not begin with a Bible reading, and I asked Tim about this. He smiled at me like I was a child.

"We don't need no paper idol," he whispered. "God's kingdom is coming here. That's why we got to make this Heaven. Right here."

These words both inspired and terrified me. All my life I had grown up with the Bible. I knew I had questions. Not everything made sense. But I had always been told to put them away - just accept it the way it is and be a good Christian. And now... now I could go beyond the word of God? To what? The Spirit?

I wanted so much to hang on to the Bible. It was my rock. It had always been there. But like a rock, it was dragging me down. All that rigidity... but it was the way I had been taught, like my mother had been, and her mother before her. All I had to do was let it go... all that dogmatism... and I could float free, back to the surface. Back to God.

When the Eucharist came I drank deeply and watched the others file past me. Then Dad began to talk, but I did not understand what he said.

"Oh my," Tim whispered. "He's taking us there. He's showing us God's Kingdom. You need to take my hand. Close your eyes, and just concentrate on Dad's words. Really listen to his voice."

I took Tim's hand in my right, and Randall's in my left. I closed my eyes and let the strange words wash over me. I could hear a distant buzzing in my ear, and then, despite the jungle humidity, I felt a cold wave against me, and then a second. My eyes snapped open, feeling a third wave, and the hairs on my arm stood up. I was goosey all over.

"Don't fight it," Tim said. A smile played on his face, and it looked to me that his entire being was bathed in a soft light.

I turned to Randall and he too seemed to gently glow, as he rocked slowly back and forth on his heels, and I felt my ears pop. Through the loose thatch of the pavilion roof, I could just make out the full moon. It seemed to spin and shimmer lazily like it was just a reflection in the water. And then parts began to spin independently until I saw that it was three concentric circles. The silver arcs seemed to slip in and out of one another as if they were children playing. And then I realised that I was no longer in the pavilion.

I half turned. Randall and Tim were still both with me, their eyes now open. The rest of the congregation were there too. We were at the bottom of a gentle hill. It was dusk, but what little light there was played softly in the short grass around our feet, illuminating the hill in soft yellows and lilacs. Behind me I could hear the sound of the sea, lapping gently on a shore. But I did not turn around. I did not need to.

There, at the top of the hill, stood a tree. A great tree that touched Heaven itself. On each of its ten branches, I saw the radiance of a Holy Choir, and each one sung out the praises of our Lord more beautifully than the last.

And there, at the top, I saw, cloaked in the finest light I have ever seen... like a thousand suns, the Eye of God. His Mighty Providence gazed down, and He saw me, and I knew that I was less than a grain of sand in the universe, but my Lord saw me all the same. He knew my name. He knew me.

My being was filled. I was saved. I was forgiven.

I felt love wash over me, like a warming tide, carrying away all my sin and fear and shame. I was loved. God loved me. The universe loved me. Tears ran down my face as though a dam had broken. I could hear others joyfully weeping too.

Letting go of Randall and Tim, I raised my hands high above my head towards the Lord's Eye and felt that wave of love come again. I was sobbing uncontrollably and felt my legs begin to buckle. I was beginning to fall, and Randall caught me.

And then I was back in the pavilion. We all were. I was lying on Randall's lap as he stroked my hair. Tim stood above me, his gaunt face showing concern. Dad knelt next to me.

"Hey... hey there little lady. Are you alright?"

I nodded.

"It's ok," Dad continued. "Sometimes... it... you know... can be a bit much first time."

I nodded again. It was not that I could not speak, I just could not think of anything to say. What do you say after God has personally told you how much He loves you?

"Thank you," I whispered.

Dad smiled and looked to Randall. "She... she'll be just fine."

Sleep did not come to either of us that night, but we did not talk. We just lay in the hut we were sharing, looking out at the night sky.

We both got up as dawn was breaking, and fetched breakfast. More rice and vegetables. We sat across from each other, still not saying anything but grinning all the same. It was like the morning after we got married all over again. We felt like naughty school children, but proud and happy and alive. Randall would describe it best later, but it was like we had both been wired up to God's own electrical grid. We were buzzing and sparking and fizzing and we just loved it.

Randall spent the rest of the morning helping out in the fields, and I worked with some of the ladies on what was to be the new medical building. It was around ten o'clock when I went to the sanitation block to use the facilities, and there I found Dad, on his hands and knees cleaning the porcelain.

He laughed that gentle loving laugh when I asked him what he was doing.

"What does it look like?"

"It looks like you're cleaning the toilet."

"Then that's... that's what I'm doing."

"But..." after the events of the previous night, my mind was reeling. This man should be out preaching or healing or something... anything but this. "But..." I said again, "why?"

Dad smiled at me. "It's a job that needs doing." And with that, he went back to scrubbing.

*

It was lunchtime when I saw Randall again. He was in the canteen, seeking respite from the midday sun, and talking with some of other men. Seeing me, he broke off his conversation and crossed the floor to where I was, and gave me a hug and a kiss.

"Hey," he said smiling and still holding me close.

"Hey you."

"How are you feeling?"

"Fine. You?" I replied.

"Bit tired."

"Me too. You're never going to guess what I saw," I said as we got my food – more rice – and returned to the table where he had been talking to his new friends, and recounted what I had seen Dad doing.

The three men he was with laughed when I finished with Dad's response, and even Randall smiled.

"We all pitch in here," one of them said. "We do what needs doing. Everyone."

*

Later that evening, as the jungle was coming alive with crickets and the like, Randall and I were looking out across Jonestown when we noticed an airplane high above.

Randall frowned. "That's a big bird," he said, squinting.

I shrugged. "Probably just a jet or something."

"No. We're not on any flight paths here. Tim told me a while ago, and I checked it out. We shouldn't be seeing anyone flying over."

"Maybe someone changed the flight path," I replied, disinterested. Anything to do with airplanes instantly took Randall away from me.

He looked at me hard. "You don't just change a flight path. It's not done like that."

I said nothing, watching as Tim approached us from the main square.

"What do you make of that?" Randall said to him, pointing at the now prominent contrail.

"Uh-huh. That'll be the Spooks. Actually, that is what I came to tell you. There's been some trouble in 'Frisco. Dad is leaving to sort it out."

"What? Now?" I had hoped he would hold Mass again.

"Uh-huh. Something about the Temple being illegally wire-tapped. There's quite a storm. We're going to see him off if you want to come."

We did.

The throng was intense, but I like to think that Dad saw me waving and looked me straight in the eye and smiled before getting into the transporter that would take him back to Kaituma. From there he would fly the short hop to Georgetown before getting a scheduled flight back to the US.

*

The next morning, Tim joined us for breakfast.

"You really think the CIA is after Dad?" I asked him.

"Uh-huh," he said between mouthfuls of rice. "Dad's been getting it forever. The Man just doesn't like it being stuck to him."

"But if he's setting up Jonestown, then why won't they just let him leave and get on?"

Tim put his spoon down and looked me right in the eye. "What if we succeed? Tell me that. What if we actually pull this off?"

I looked at Randall, and then back to Tim. "What do you mean?"

"Think about it, Izzy. What if we having a thriving community here? And there are no Cadillacs? There are no labels or brands or any of that fascist crap? And people are happy? I mean actually happy. Aren't people murdering each other for a few dollars? There're no hookers because all the love is free. And all the kids grow up educated and real polite. And what if the good old US of A says 'well hang on – those folks seem to be doing just fine. Do we need all our shit?' 'Scuse my language. Do you think the Man will let anyone think that way? No chance. No way José!"

Tim was leaning forward now, jabbing his finger into the table. "The Man wants us to fail. The Man wants to see us all to go back to 'Frisco with our tail between our legs and say 'we couldn't make it work'. And I tell you why it's so the Man can say to everyone else 'Look! Look at these saps! They tried to make it without... without a television. They tried to make it without... a toaster. Or a swimming pool. Or any other of that fascist crap that is poisoning our minds.

"But it isn't working. No. We've got more new members signing up every day. People have woken up to the Zionist lies. And I tell you what Izzy, that scares the crap out of them. It really does. Because who is going to buy their Cadillacs? No-one. So what do they do? What does the Man do? I'll tell you –

the Man says 'well if it's not going to fail on its own, well I'll just give it a little nudge.'

"And nudge becomes push. But we don't fall over. So the push becomes a punch and a kick. But we still don't go down. And then the knives come out. But they see we aren't scared of knives. We aren't scared, are we?"

Silence had fallen across the canteen as Tim's diatribe had steadily increased in volume.

"HELL NO!" the throng responded. Some began thumping the tables.

"No! No, we are not scared Izzy, so do you know what the Man does? He pulls out his guns. All of his guns. And the Man has got a lot of guns. Are we scared of guns?"

"HELL NO!"

"Hell no! And the Man says 'well, what are they scared of? What about the kids?' And there they have us. We are scared not of what they'll do to us - most of us saw what they are capable of in 'Nam. But what could they do to our children? Will we sit around and let them butcher our kids like they did in Binh Gia?"

"HELL NO!"

"That's right. Because this is our utopia. This is the heaven that Dad promised us. And they can come in here, and they can shoot us all up and they can torture our children. But then the whole world will see. They will see how scared the Man is of all the little consumers no longer buying His BS, and the scales will fall from the eyes of the world

"But the Man knows this. So what does he do? He sits. He watches. And he waits. And he tells us that is what he is doing, so the whole time we're having to look over our shoulders."

I sat in silence. One part of me was terrified. Tim had made wild leaps, but I could see his reasoning, and it made sense after a fashion. If it was all going too well and then suddenly everyone got themselves dead, well it could be put down to any number of the border skirmishes we often heard about. But the rational part of me said "come on – we're only a thousand people in the middle of nowhere just doing our thing. Who cares?"

But I knew. I knew that the good ol' US never leaves well enough alone. It never could.

"Tim?" I said eventually.

"Yeah?"

"If the Man is coming, how do we stay? How do we keep Jonestown?"

Tim smiled. "That's easy. We got a secret weapon."

I looked at him expectantly.

"We got God on our side! Can I get a 'hell yeah'!"

"HELL YEAH!" More banging on the tables.

"Can I get an 'amen'!"

"AMEN! AMEN! AMEN!"

This time, I joined in with them. Tim was no Jesse Jackson, but he could inspire us all the same.

I knew what I had seen. Randall had seen it too. God was on our side.

*

We barely discussed it on the airplane back. It was a foregone conclusion. We had met God at Jonestown, and all the love He had sent us... well it could only mean that he wanted us there.

Our Mission was not surprised. Disappointed but not surprised. We had done all the work we could do, and the Mission was in good shape to be handed over to the local lay-preachers. Randall finalised a lease for the Jonestown satellite office to begin in the December of seventy-five. Tim was grateful, but I could not help but be worried about his continued loss of weight. He was looking awful.

We began crating up what few possessions we had to be shipped to Jonestown. To be honest, most of it was the boys'. The winter once again brought no respite from the heat, and Randall and I had retreated into a cafe when we heard a commotion outside. Looking up we could see two Temple members being pushed around by a gang. It was getting ugly. I didn't even have time to say anything before Randall was on his feet and charging in to the melee. I kept the boys close to me and watched with the cafe owner through the window.

Randall pulled the two men out of the centre and faced up to the most vocal of the gang. When Randall got his military face on... well, you didn't want to be around. I'd seen it once or twice in Los Lunas when boys had gone beyond the usual insults to being physically threatening. They quickly wished they hadn't.

He had taught me a few moves, in case a patient ever got too much. Taking their weight. Using their strength. I asked him where he had learned it, and he told me that he had been stationed in Okinawa for a few years, and a local Nip had run some school that he had attended. It was a classical defence style but he was able to adapt it into his military training well enough. Those few times he had used it in Los Lunas... well, those boys had come to regret their actions.

It looked like these boys were going to regret theirs too.

Through the shouting, I could make out that the gang was claiming that the two Temple members had tried to fix the election of a local councillor. Randall told them they were mistaken, that he knew these men, and they wouldn't do something like that. But the gang insisted, claiming to have seen them stuffing the ballot boxes with pre-marked voting cards.

It didn't help that the candidate in question was well known for his support of Dad and Jonestown.

I don't know how he did it, but Randall talked the gang down and got the two Temple members back to the Mission. The three of them sat around the wireless as the election results were read out on the local broadcast. Their councillor won by a landslide, as did two others sympathetic to the Temple.

I had hoped to have left these kinds of politics behind. It was my turn to be disappointed.

*

The last of our crates were picked up, and we made our final flight to Kaituma in time for the Christmas celebrations, such as they were. More boiled rice. But we loved our new home despite the short-term hardships. This was where we belonged. These were our people. It felt that all the little steps along the paths of our lives had been leading us here. God had brought us to this place. Our joining the residents of Jonestown was inevitable as the sun rising, and we were thankful for it.

The boys settled in well, seeming to love the communal parenting approach. I know that I should feel guilty, but Randall and I enjoyed the extra time not being Daddy and Mommy, instead being husband and wife.

We were given a comprehensive induction, although we knew a lot of it already. However, it was our first time to be shown the radio operation. It was a basic shortwave connecting to San Francisco, although the size of the tower made it appear grander than it actually was. We were warned that the Federal Communication Commission was monitoring us, probably under orders from the CIA. If we broke any of the strict codes or laws, then we would have our licence revoked and that would mean losing our lifeline to San Francisco.

*

It was in the February of seventy-six that we next saw Dad. It was clear that the political goings on were beginning to affect him too, but he remained in good spirits. There had been some activity along the perimeter of the Jonestown estate, and it looked like someone had tried to cut through the fence before being disturbed. Dad had wanted to see for himself, and he led an impromptu sermon on how we had to be strong against the fascist agenda.

None of us were surprised that the Man was trying again. It had been quiet over Christmas, and in January some of the Temple workers had spotted strangers in Kaituma. At first, we thought that they were just new migrants working for the mining companies, but the Man always had a certain look about him that he could not hide. We knew.

It was the second night after his arrival that Dad led Mass. Jonestown had been alive that afternoon that he might and, as prayer was called, we all knew. A tingle was in the air. A spark.

It came as before. I drank of the Eucharist, and I heard Dad begin to chant. I was paying more attention this time, and it sounded like he was talking in tongues. Once again, I felt the world dissolve away, my ears popped, and I found myself standing at the foot of the hill gazing up at the giant tree.

The same feelings washed over me again and again and again, as I gazed with awe at the Majesty before me. Some Temple members knelt, others cried or laughed. I remember holding Randall's hand, and him squeezing me. How could we ever fail?

The next day a chemical tanker arrived, similar to the one I had seen before. Dad had obtained a jewellers licence for Jonestown. Whatever gold flakes we found we would pool together and smelt, and some of the men folk would then forge them into trinkets that we could trade with at Kaituma. It wasn't much. Maybe a few ounces. A pound at most. I know a lot of us felt that this was contradictory to the Temple's ethos. But for the time being the world was the way the world was, and we had to get along with it. And besides, the supplies we traded for were not luxuries, just basics like kerosene for the generators, and medicine for the children.

Dad left the following Monday, heading back to California. Stories were circulating that the San Francisco Chronicle had been compiling an article on the Temple. One of Dad's close friends had told him that the reporter had asked him very leading questions about Jonestown and whether people were being stopped from leaving.

Tim didn't seem fazed. "I wouldn't worry about it too much. It's just some gutter reporter who's taken money from the Man to write a hatchet-job on Dad. He's well enough connected to make sure the truth comes out. The editor is a member of the congregation."

*

By the time April rolled around, we had heard that the story had been pulled. But it was worrying. We'd seen more activity around Jonestown, and several times helicopters had made low sweeps. If there was one reporter who was willing to take money in exchange for publishing lies, then there would always be another.

It saddened me that my Motherland seemed to be increasingly obsessed with The Almighty Dollar. One of the nurses smiled and told me that the US was becoming so poor that people only had money. I would have smiled if it was not true. We were hearing more and more stories of pollution and industrial accidents as corners were cut all to save a few cents here or there. It made me wonder what people wanted to do with all that money, but Randall just shrugged.

"That's exactly the point," he said. "They just want more and more money, but don't know what to do with it. The more they get, they unhappier they become."

I couldn't disagree with him.

May and June were quieter, and we should have known that it was the calm before the storm.

*

July was bad. Really bad. It started in the first week. I saw Tim and he looked like death.

"Are you ok?" I asked him. It was mid-morning, and he was sitting on the steps of the radio hut. Randall and I were getting tea.

He looked up at me, he bottom lip trembling, but said nothing.

Astrid, his assistant, joined us a moment later.

"Grace... she's been taken," she said.

Grace was Tim's wife. Randall and I knew that there had been problems, but he never discussed it, and we didn't bring it up.

"What do you mean taken?"

"Smitty. He's CIA. He's got Grace."

Walter Jones, "Smitty" to us, had been a member of the Temple as long as I could remember. I'd met him maybe two or three times. Once when he had come to our Mission to speak to Randall, and the others in Jonestown. He seemed like a good sort. Quiet, but hard working. Randall, on the other hand, had never taken to him.

"I told you!" my husband said. "I told you there was something not right about him!"

"Tim, are you sure?" I asked. "What happened?"

Tim just looked up at me, and then back at the dirt.

"Apparently, there was some sort of argument last night," Astrid said. "He pulled a gun, and forced her into a car."

"Lord! Does anyone know where they are?"

Astrid nodded. "One of the members saw what was happening, and called Dad. He had someone in the Red Brigade follow them to Lake Tahoe. Smitty forced Grace to make a phone call to Dad, demanding that Tim returns home and that they are allowed to leave with John."

John was Tim and Grace's son and was about four. He and Grace lived at the Temple with Dad when Tim was in Jonestown with us.

"Did they give any sort of ultimatum?"

Astrid nodded. "If they don't do what Smitty says, he'll force Grace to file for divorce. There'll be a custody battle, and that'll give the DA a chance to smear the Temple in public."

"No!" I was shocked.

"There's something else, isn't there?" Randall said, looking hard at Astrid.

She nodded. "Joyce has disappeared too."

Joyce Houston was the treasurer of the Temple and kept all the financial matters right.

"How do you mean? Gone with Smitty?" Randall asked.

Astrid shook her head. "No. She was with Bob last night." Bob was her husband and the Company Secretary for the Temple. "She set off for work this morning as normal. But she never arrived. Bob is going out of his mind."

"Does Dad think the CIA has got her too?" Randall said.

"He thinks the CIA has killed her. There's been no phone call or nothing. Dad thinks she probably fought back too much, so they just killed her."

That sounded right. Joyce was always a fighter.

I looked up at Randall. The strain and worry was etched into his face. He put his arm around me, pulling me in closer to him. Suddenly I wanted the boys with me, to hold them too.

It was all over the commune soon enough, and we were all subdued. We could all feel the net beginning to tighten. That night, the radio operation was hooked up to the PA system in the pavilion, and Dad was able to address us directly from 'Frisco. He told us not to worry. They had no proof any harm had come to Joyce and they were doing all they could to find her.

As for Grace, well they had turned down Smitty's demands, and Dad was going to arrange a big fundraiser to raise awareness and hire the best lawyers he could find.

When it came, in September, it was huge. The fundraiser was attended by a glittering array of San Francisco's great and good. Harvey Milk, Mayor Moscone, Lieutenant Governor Dymally, District Attorney Freitas and Senator Marks to name but a few all spoke out in defence of Dad, commending the excellent work he was doing and his visionary leadership.

It was not enough.

*

Later in September, we were told that Joyce had made contact with Bob. She had clearly been drugged or brainwashed or something because she tried to convince Bob to leave the Temple. Dad had the conversation taped, and everyone agreed that Bob should set up a meeting with her so that the Red Brigade could rescue her.

It became apparent that the CIA still had undercover operatives in our midst, because in October, Bob's body was found next to the railroad. He had been going to meet Joyce when he'd disappeared. The autopsy claimed he was beaten to death, and we all knew that they were laying the ground to pin it on Dad.

Tim went back to San Francisco to help Dad get Grace back, and the atmosphere in Jonestown began to change. It was like the McCarthy era all over again. Everywhere we saw government agents, fascist capitalists, or traitors. Suspicion began to creep in, and we began to view each other with distrust. More than once a fight would break out amid accusations of spying.

It was November when I mentioned the possibility of leaving to Randall. This was no place for us to be bringing up the boys. They too had picked up on the change in atmosphere and had become withdrawn. Randall nodded and said if it wasn't better within twelve months then we would go. I think he still held on to the hope that it would get better. He believed in Dad's utopia. If only he would come back soon, things would settle down.

But things did not settle down.

Later that same month, proof came of Government spying. Unita Blackwell - a Mississippi Mayor - had given a speech at a pro-Temple rally. As was becoming increasingly common, a member of the Red Brigade drove her home. She invited him in for coffee, and just as she was about to serve it they heard a noise outside. Both saw two men running across the lawn, get in a car and drive off at high speed. The Red Brigade member was sufficiently quick-thinking to take the licence plate number, and DA Freitas had it traced. It was Air Force. They denied it, of course, saying that whilst the vehicle was theirs, the men who had signed it out had been on leave on the day in question and what they did in their own time was their business. That didn't wash with any of us, and we knew that we were now all being watched.

At the same time, it was becoming increasingly clear that Dad and Tim were not able to get Grace back, and there was a fear that she had been brainwashed like Joyce. As a precaution, Dad sent John to live with us all in Jonestown, in case the Man made a grab for him.

We barely noticed Christmas come and go, such was the atmosphere in Jonestown. It was January of seventy-seven, and for the first time, there was widespread talk of abandoning Jonestown. It wasn't that we didn't believe, but we knew we couldn't go on being watched the way that we were. It was driving us all insane. There was talk of going to Russia, and starting over there. Some even wanted to go out in a blaze of glory – take a gun and meet the Man head on. It didn't help that the harvests were failing, and we were living off just a little rice each day. Some said that the fields were being deliberately poisoned, and we had some of the Red Brigade set up a twenty-four-seven patrol.

*

It was late in the January seventy-seven that Dad organised another broadcast from 'Frisco. It raised our spirits just to hear his voice. He spoke of the disgusting things the government was trying to do, and how they were maligning and slandering the Temple through their journalistic stooges. But he also brought hope – he would soon be moving permanently to Jonestown, and we should prepare for his arrival. He also had some friends with him – Huey Newton, the founder of the Black Panthers, came on to say how inspired by us he was, and how we had to be strong against the Imperial Forces of Capitalism and that our fortitude of spirit would win the day.

We were buoyed, and for a short time, Jonestown was reinvigorated. Work commenced on the new huts, and the number of those moving out here increased. We could be strong. We could fight the Man. And we could win.

That might have been true if it was the Man we were fighting.

*

Tim returned in February and brought news that June would see another nine-hundred members move to Jonestown. And Dad would be coming with them, this time to stay. There were cheers but also dismay. We were barely keeping pace with the building of the new huts for the latest arrivals. An extra nine hundred souls would take the population over two-thousand, and we just didn't have the infrastructure to support that.

Tim started to draw up schedules, showing where we could build, how we could deploy the workforce. The fields would be a problem and if the harvest was as bad as the previous year, then we would have a serious food shortage. Tim acknowledged that this could be a problem, but said Dad was arranging to have additional supplies shipped into us.

The building work picked up again, and the pace was frenetic. There was a sense of renewed enthusiasm, and it reminded Randall and me of the Jonestown we had first known.

As June approached, we heard more bad news coming out of San Francisco. A low-life journalist, Marshall Kilduff, had taken the story that had been brewing at the Chronicle and sold it to New West Magazine. We shouldn't have been surprised. The magazine was owned by some Australian, Rupert Murdoch, who was renowned for publishing libellous tittle-tattle, and even though Dad co-ordinated all those who advertised in that rag to call and write in, they still published at the end of May.

It was nothing but a pack of lies, claiming fraud, assault, and kidnapping. Mayor Moscone had given Dad the tip that the vultures were gathering, and he flew out to us straight away. This time, his stay was permanent, even though Moscone himself went on to publicly denounce the article stating these were baseless allegations with absolutely no hard evidence that Dad had violated any laws, local, state or federal.

From the beginning of June, members began pouring into Jonestown, and we lined the driveway to Jonestown as Dad's transporter approached. There was a sense of jubilation in the air. Dad was coming. Dad was coming to be with us.

That sense was short lived. When his door open, he looked tired, haggard, and we could tell that he had been crying. He did not embrace anyone but directed that we should all immediately go to the pavilion.

What he had to say stunned us all.

Tim had defected.

There had been suspicions about him for some time, and when he had gone to Timehri to meet Dad off the plane, his hotel room had been searched by Temple members. They found several fake passports, one with a photo of John but with the name Michael, and a substantial amount of cash.

When he was confronted, he pulled a gun on Dad, demanding John be returned to him and that he was leaving. Of course, Dad tried to reason with him, but would not let him have John. The boy was a member of our community and this was where he belonged.

Tim had fled and had got on the first flight out of Guyana. We later found that it had been bound for Cairo. Dad had DA Freitas do a deep-dive on Tim, and what had come back a few hours later was not good. Tim's bank records showed that he had been in the pay of the CIA for years, maybe even a decade, but in the last few months he had also received payments from the United Kingdom. It came as no surprise to any of us when Freitas reported that Interpol had followed Tim's trail from Cairo, first to Istanbul, and then to London, England.

Worse was to follow. Tim was supposed to have ordered supplies of building materials and food, but when the ship had docked the cargo operator did not know anything about the order. Dad had spoken to the suppliers, and of course, the order had never been placed. Tim, if that was even his real name, had taken the money and run.

Dad ordered a full sweep of Jonestown. We were to look for listening devices and any sort of equipment that was out of place. With the aid of torches, we all searched deep into the night. We looked under every hut, through every wood pile, in every grain sack, even into the trees themselves. Nothing. But we knew. Tim and his cronies would be watching us.

The morning found Randall and me sitting on a bench in the canteen. A look of stunned weariness shared across our faces. We could not believe that Tim had done this to us. We knew he had, but we just could not believe it.

A shout went up from the opposite side of the square, and Raul, a Portuguese man with a funny lisp, came running from the tree line, making straight for Dad's hut. Dad came out and followed Raul back in the direction he had come from. Although tired, several of us followed them. Even before we got to the clearing where they had stopped, we had seen it. A rubber pipe had been partly buried and laid from the wheat fields, across a distance of about a kilometre, to where Dad and Raul now stood... surrounded by oil drums.

Randall walked past the two silent men and opened one of the drums.

Diesel.

Someone really had been poisoning the harvest, and it didn't need two guesses to know who was responsible. The fields would be useless for years to come, and we would need to start over, with a new area of the jungle to be chopped down and sown. But it also meant that this year's harvest would be poor if indeed we even had one.

Dad made the discoveries known to all the Temple members that evening.

The silence was absolute. No one knew what to say. Most of us felt sorry for John. That poor boy had to hear exactly what his no-good father had done, but we all still loved him no matter what. I brought my own two boys closer into me. They had a right to know what was going on, but at the same time, I didn't want them to be scared.

And then Dad showed us all why he was our Dad.

"We... we've had the gauntlet thrown down... thrown in our face. You all know what is going on... what is going on here. You know who has set their face against us. We don't mean no harm to no folk, but... I tell you, these Zionists... they offend the Lord himself. Now the next few months will be... well they'll be as tough as they can be. We got limited food, and not enough materials... building materials to make the new huts for all our brothers and sisters who are coming to join us.

"Now we can end it. We can go home right now. I wouldn't blame... I wouldn't blame none of you if you did. You didn't come here to be hungry. But let me tell you... those fascists. They're laughing at us. They think they've won. And if we all go home now, they... they will keep laughing at us for the rest of our lives.

"But they don't know... they don't know us. They don't know what we're capable of. They don't know we have the Lord on our side."

A smattering of applause and few "amen's" rippled across the pavilion.

"They don't know the strength the Lord gives... that he makes us strong."

Another ripple.

"So my children, I... I say to you all. We can go home. Or we can stay. And... it'll be hard, you know. On all of us. But what we can build, here... with the Lord's strength, is our Eden. And I say we will not be driven from our place by... by the lies of the vile serpents. I say I am here to do my Lord's work, and that I will fear no evil..."

Another ripple, louder now.

"I will not fear the Man and his money or the wolves he sends amongst our lambs. I will stand righteous. I will stand with my children, undivided, and my Lord will take my hand, and he will guide me against all those who envy what we have and seek to tear it down.

"Because I know the Lord... and you do too. You've seen Him here, with us. And so with His strength, we will... overcome. We will prevail. My children will prevail!"

The congregation burst, like a dam, into cheers and choruses of "hallelujah" and "amen", and our voices echoed out into the night.

We all knew it would be difficult. There would be hard times ahead. But we were resolved.

Of course, none of us knew how hard it would be.

*

What food we had was strictly rationed. San Francisco ordered us more container-loads of supplies, but it would take several months to reach us. The huts, although communal were designed for ten people, and now there was double that in each, sometimes more. We found ourselves sharing with a nice family from Bakersfield, and several of our neighbours were from Fresno. We all got along as best we could.

Despite the community spirit, there was no getting away from the fact that we were desperately short of essentials, such as blankets, and the tablets for the water treatment station.

The Fall of seventy-seven was hard. Another wave of members was due in February – up to a thousand, and Dad was trying to stall them until the new huts could be completed, which was difficult without any of the tools that were due on the next shipment.

In September we heard from San Francisco that Tim had returned to the US. He had reunited with Grace, and they had filed papers in Georgetown for John to be returned to them. The quality of their lawyer was more than they could have afforded on their own, and we knew that he was being bankrolled.

*

It was an evening in late October, and me and Randall were taking a walk around Jonestown with the boys. Despite everything, they were growing up so strong and happy, and we were both so proud of them. Miguel was six, coming up seven, and Paulo was nearly three. We both marvelled at how much the two boys loved each other. They were always playing, scampering between our legs, although Miguel was getting too big for that now. Randall had always worried about their relationship. Whilst things had settled down with his own brother, for several years there had been a tension between them as boys became men. Randall often told me how they would fight as children, and that was what had led him to leave home as soon as possible and join the Air Force.

But our boys… well, they were a product of us and their environment. They got on with everybody, and everybody got on with them. Miguel was the serious one, always deep in his books, or frowning in concentration as the principles of carpentry were explained to him. Paulo was the joker, laughing and giggling, pestering his brother away from his studies to come and play.

We loved them both dearly.

As we wandered around what was now a reasonably-sized village, we heard Dad shouting in the radio hut. As we approached, the door flew open, and he came storming out.

"Dad?" Randall said. "You ok?"

I brought the boys close to me, expecting more bad news from San Francisco. Things seemed to be as bad there as they were here, albeit in a different way.

"Ahhh… it's nothing."

"You sure?" Randall asked.

"Yeah. Just an old friend of mine from Indiana. Well, an ex-pat, he's Welsh. He's been trying to get hold of me for months. I told him… I'm right here."

"What did he say?" I asked.

Dad looked at me. "Hey says the Man is still at it. That we're all being poisoned. Or they're getting ready to poison us."

"How?"

"Something in the water. I... I told him it isn't possible. We got guards all over, but he still told me that we're being set up for... for something awful."

The Red Brigade numbers were increased, but it was still a bad Fall. The harvest was minimal, as we had suspected, and we heard that Tim had filed complaints with the FCC over the use of the radio. The worm was still trying to cut us off.

If seventy-seven had been unkind, seventy-eight showed every sign of being equally cruel.

Rumours surfaced in January that Tim was in Georgetown, trying to get John back. Several of the Temple members flew back to the capital, but I stayed, caring for the boys. We were later told that Tim had gone back to the US, but given what Dad had told us in October about the water supply being poisoned, I was not surprised when people started to fall in ill.

As a precaution, Dad suspended the relationship with the mining company which was using some of our facilities. Officially they were told it was because of the risk of infection, but there had been a growing shadow of suspicion as to who they really worked for.

As first it was just one or two who got sick, but then a dozen and then more. Diarrhoea, vomiting, and some sort of circulatory problem I hadn't seen before, but it looked like frostbite on the ends of their fingers and toes.

I suspected cholera, and soon we had over a hundred poor souls in the medical hut.

As the numbers increased, so the race was on to build one extension, and then a second and a third to the makeshift infirmary. All the sawing and banging was no good for those who were already ill, but we quickly got the extra beds that were so desperately needed.

And then we caught a break. The ship with our building and other supplies docked, and we were able to get the antibiotics that the patients urgently required.

Whatever kindness the Fates had afforded us was exhausted by the April of seventy-eight. Tim and Grace had returned to the US and had begun to orchestrate a political and media campaign against us, resulting in the distribution of an anti-Temple pack to anyone who would listen. And plenty of those phoneys did. We heard that it had gone to the editor of every major newspaper on the west coast, and even made it down to New York.

From May onwards, rumours started to circulate that Dad's health was deteriorating, and it was the end of that month that me and one of the doctors were called to his hut. He was in a dreadful state, having lost a lot of weight and judging by his babbling and his parched lips, he was probably dehydrated as well.

The doctor diagnosed a lung infection and administered more antibiotics.

That night, a number of the elders met, and it was agreed that Dad's wife, Marcy, would assume a number of his duties until he was better.

*

It was now October, and the harvest had failed completely. Dad was back on his feet, but only for limited periods. Marcy had been in the radio hut all day and did not seem surprised when a helicopter landed in the main square.

The rest of us were stunned and several members ran to get the Red Brigade. We really believed that this was it. The Man had finally come for us.

What we were not expecting, was the Soviets.

Dad came out to greet them and took them into the pavilion where they talked for several hours. It was dusk when they came out and addressed the throng that had gathered. Members had continued to come from San Francisco and by now there were over two thousand of us.

Dad began. "For many years, we... we have let our sympathies be quite publicly known, that the United States government was not our mother, but that the Soviet Union was our spiritual motherland. I'd like... I'd like you all to put your hands to... together for Comrade Timofeyev from the Soviet embassy."

Feodor Timofeyev, the Russian ambassador, raised his hand, asking the crowd to not to cheer or applaud. We did anyway.

"We, the people of the United Soviet States of Russia, would like to send to you all our deepest and the most sincere greetings to the people of this first socialist and communist community of the United States of America, in Guyana and in the world."

There were more cheers and applauding.

"I'd like to wish you, dear comrades, all the successes to your great... to your very big work you're doing here, but I fear that there are forces aligning against you. We have heard that within the next month a senator from your own US will come here, to your homes, on a so-called fact-finding mission. We cannot say for certain what he will report, but we believe he will seek the forced repatriation of each and every one of you."

The crowd was silent, taking this news in. Many of us had whispered about a day when the Man would come, and what we would do. But we had always thought that it would be to end us. To end our ideas. No-one had even thought that he would take us back to the US.

Feodor continued. "We would, therefore, like to offer you... all of you, the opportunity to relocate to the Soviet Union. I have discussed this with Reverend Jones today. No one will force you, and you may come and go as you please. You may take this offer up at any time."

That night, Randall and I lay awake.

"We're a long way from Kansas now Izzy," Randall said.

"I know hun... but think of the boys."

229

"I know. But God is here Izzy. God himself. We've both seen Him. You think God will let anything happen to His people? I tell you, we've been chosen. He has chosen us."

I didn't know it then, but there were similar conversations going all around Jonestown. This was our land. The land that God had brought us to, and where he had revealed Himself to us.

The next morning, the decision was unanimous. We were staying. Feodor accepted our decision but said that the offer remained open.

By the end of the month, we had heard that Congressman Leo Ryan was coming to Jonestown on the seventeenth of November on a fact-finding mission. There was much talk as to whether we should allow him in, but it was generally agreed that if we let him see everything then he could not claim that we were hiding anything. It later emerged that Congressman Ryan was friends with Bob Houston's father. Many of us suspected that he had been forced by the Man to make representations to Leo, no doubt pointing the finger at Dad over his son's death.

Despite the widely stated date of the November seventeen, none of us were too surprised to see a helicopter circling Jonestown on the sixteenth, before landing. It was just like the Man to try and catch us out. But we were ready. We had been ready for weeks.

Marcy greeted the two men who got out and took them to Dad's hut. One was in his early thirties, slender, but sinewy, with hair so black it looked like it had been dyed. The other man was older, maybe mid-fifties, and a good deal stouter. Later I would find out that the younger was simply known as Celus. His friend was George, although I only heard him speak a few times. The way that Marcy greeted Celus, with a hug, made me think that they were old friends. But she only greeted the other one with a handshake, so maybe he was new.

I didn't see them come out again from Dad's hut, but it was the next day that Congressman Ryan came. Most of us kept our distance. No-one wanted to say anything to him in case he tried to twist our words into something that they weren't. He spent most the day at Jonestown, before returning to the capital in the evening, promising that he would return the next morning to finish up.

I saw Celus emerge from Dad's hut, and turn to his friend. "See. Told you." Marcy was with them too. I've never seen a look on her face like the one she wore then. She was pale and gaunt. Like she was in shock.

Word quickly went around that there was to be a meeting in the pavilion. I saw Dad being half-carried. He looked so frail.

The congregation was restless. Everyone wanted to know how Congressman Ryan was going to report. Dad took to the stage, and I saw that Celus and his friend were sat up there, next to Marcy.

They must be honoured guests indeed…

From this distance, I appreciated how sick Dad looked. Really sick. I suspected that the lung infection had returned. Dad held up his hands, and the congregation quietened.

"You know..." His voice was painfully weak as he began. "I... I've never lied to you. I've always tried to tell you things the way they are. Sometimes I got things right. Other times... I... I wish I had made a different decision. But I always did it with the best intention. So... I... I'm going to tell you what I know... what's been told to me. And then... I turn myself over to you... and your... your mercy.

"Most of you can see that I got some friends with me tonight. From out of town. This here is Celus."

Celus raised his hand.

"Now I've known Celus all my life..."

I was amazed by this. Dad was nearly fifty, and this Celus... he was no more than thirty-five.

"I trust him," Dad continued. "He has taught me a lot. A lot about God. And His path. And now... my friend Celus has come to tell me about... what the Man has really been doing to us."

The silence was so absolute that I could hear my own heartbeat. I knew the Man had been up to something. I knew it. Instinctively I held Miguel and Paulo's hands tighter. Randall looked at me. The expression on his face said *Now we find out.*

"Some of... uh, some of you... most of you have... you have seen God with me... at our Masses. Well Celus here, and I trust him, has told me that these... visions are not what they seem. He has told me that the Man has been tracking us for years. Decades maybe... We know about Tim. And well... uh, the Man has been interfering with our Mass. He has been poisoning our supply of wine with a hallucino... hallucinogenic.

"Now he's not saying that what we... we're seeing isn't real. Because we all know it is. But he tells me that the Man knows... he *knows* about the war in Heaven. He knows about those vile usurpers who want to spoil... spoil all that God has made. And... well... the Man's hallucinogen... Celus claims that what we see and what we worship is actually Hell."

The congregation rippled. Some instantly denied it. Other gasped.

Dad pressed on. "Now... now... now I ain't saying it's true. But I have known Celus a long, long time. And he knows about these things. He tells me that what we see is just an illusion. That the Adversary is wearing a mask. He tells me that it has been this way all along and Tim... Tim was put here to make sure we never found out, but... they don't want us to find out. The Man wants... he wants us to keep worshipping this... this abomination.

"So this is what I am going to do. I... I'm going to lead Mass. And when we get to... wherever it is, Celus claims that he will lead us to a place where we can see for ourselves. Now there is something else. Cel... you all saw

Congressman Ryan today. And you all saw the little entourage with him. The reporters... and some of the others. Three... three of them were the Congressman's aides. The thin pale men, with that long, black, bobbed hair. Celus says... he says these men they ain't... they are creatures of the Adversary. And he says that we may see some more where we're going. And if we do, we need to holler because they are dangerous.

"Now if you don't want to be... to take part in tonight's Mass, it's ok, I... we understand. But I got... I need to know what is going on here. I need to know why we're all so ill. So anyone who... if you want to leave you can do. If you want to go back to 'Frisco you can do. We don't... I won't hold anyone here. If you want to stay... find the truth, then..."

His voice tailed off. No one in the congregation moved. It didn't make a lot of sense to me, but I could see the look on Randall's face.

"Hun, what is it?" I asked.

"I should have known," he said, turning to me.

"What?"

He sighed, looked around, and then shrugged. "When I was in the Air Force... the crews that flew over 'Nam... they didn't just spray Agent Orange."

"It's ok Hun, it's..."

"No. No Izzy, it's really not ok," his eyes were ablaze. "Some of the stuff we sprayed was... it was this stuff that made you see things. It was the CIA. We all knew it. They were experimenting with LSD and mind control and weird stuff. They were doing it all through the sixties."

"So?"

"So if what Dad and this Celus are saying is right, the Man knew that 'Nam was ending and that they wouldn't be allowed to experiment on Charlie... so they found the next best thing."

"Us?"

"Uh-huh. But this mystical stuff, I ain't so sure. Hell pretending to be Heaven?"

"Well it figures, doesn't it? The Man ain't God fearing. Maybe they've always... you know. Been for the other side."

Randall shrugged. "Maybe. But I gotta know Izzy. I gotta."

I nodded. "Me too."

Similar conversations seemed to be going on around the pavilion, but no one left.

Dad had sat down, obviously exhausted. Sensing that a consensus was forming he motioned to Marcy who began to prepare the Eucharist. As Dad stood to begin, we followed. We were all in this together.

When the time came, I drank deeply, and Dad began to intone whatever strange incantation it was that he had been taught. We all felt it. The cool wave of air, the popping of our ears... and then we were there. At the bottom of the hill, looking up. I half turned. Randall was there, gathering the boys to him. Everyone else seemed accounted for.

Dad was just a little way ahead, Celus and the other one with him. He had been awfully quiet the whole time.

"Come on," Celus said to us all. Marcy and Celus' friend were helping Dad down the hill. None of us dared look up at the tree.

Celus came past me, leading us down the gentle slope, and around the outer edge of some woods. Although I had always heard the sea in the background, this was the first time that I saw it, realising that we were actually on a low cliff. The ocean was dark, but below the surface I could see the silhouettes of immense creatures dancing in predatory union, bringing black swells to the surface. The waves seemed to lap and crash against the shoreline with a greasy slopping sound that I hadn't appreciated before.

The sky was a low violet, and heavy clouds skittered ominously overhead. I had never thought what else there might have been in that place where me and my God communed, but I'm sure that if I had, this is not what I would have imagined.

We followed Celus across the undulating terrain, and as we crested a rise he stopped, the people fanning out on either side of him. We gasped at what lay before us. A city of almost unimaginable proportions.

The entrance seemed to be through an old castle, the kind I had seen in medieval European history books when I was a child. But this quickly gave way to something far greater, as though it was a shadow of a shadow, being cast in the late evening. It was so long, like some invisible hand was pulling it taut.

The walls slipped around the perimeter at odd angles, and the city itself seemed to consist solely of bizarre towers. Each of these skyscrapers appeared to have been hewn from a single piece of rock, piercing upwards from the ground below, splitting and rupturing the rotten soil like the exit wound of some cosmic bullet. Some of the towers had what looked like metal cladding fitted as an afterthought, and even from this distance I could see some sort of engraving on them.

The breeze from the sea carried the smell of salt, but underneath it lay something else. Something pervasive and rotten, almost like bleach and vinegar had been mixed together and then forgotten about for many years. It caught in the back of my throat, and I gagged involuntarily as the smell came again, stronger this time. My eyes began to well up and, wiping the tears away, I noticed that I wasn't alone in my reaction.

Despite the breeze, it was hot and humid. I could feel the heavy atmosphere pushing up against me as if it was trying to find a way in through my pores. The air was thick with the grease of the ocean spray, and I could already see a thin grey film on my exposed arms. It was sticky to the touch and had the faint musty smell of an aged and crumbling relative.

Celus turned to look at us. He didn't have to say anything. No God of ours lived here. This was a place of the damned and the fallen. His friend remained silent, but his eyes were as wide as ours. I had the impression that this was his first time too.

Celus turned to him. "And Greine beheld the glory and wonder of the Heavens," he half whispered.

His friend simply nodded.

*

[Maiden Castle Stele 38]

Danu told Greine of a gathering force of Ghazal, marshalled by a forgotten Sky Lord, on the borders of Nod, and Greine gathered one-third of his army to meet them there.

So did Greine and Celus behold the multitude of sinners and usurpers, and fell upon them with righteous fury. The might of The Army of Danu drove the abominations back to the sea, and Greine, in his blood rage, followed them in.

The most powerful Ghazal took Greine, and dragged him down many fathoms, fighting and warring as only the Just and the Sinner can.

Fatally pierced, the Ghazal blew his last breath into the Champion's mouth, that the veil before his eyes may be lifted. And Greine beheld the glory and wonder of the Heavens in its true form.

Brave Celus saw Greine being pulled under the waves and dived into the sea. He returned his king to the land and sought his well being.

"Be at ease old friend," Greine smiled, "for I have seen the true nature of Heaven, and it is mighty for those that are of virtue in the eyes of our Goddess."

*

Celus turned to Dad. "Have you seen enough?"

Dad shook his head. "What... what's down there," he asked, pointing towards the citadel before us.

"Nothing good."

Dad looked at him hard but said nothing.

"What have we done, Jim?" I couldn't see her but it sounded like Marcy. Her voice was strained as if she were on the edge of tears.

Dad sighed. "There is always a cost. Always a price to pay. This is mine."

"You didn't know," Celus said. "There are plenty of others who have done far worse. Some pay with their lives. Some pay with their families." He shot his friend a look. "Others pay a far higher price."

Silence fell slowly over us again. Even the children were quiet.

Randall stepped forward. "What is it? What is this place?"

Celus shrugged. "Have you ever known someone who was just bad news? And it didn't matter how much you tried to change your ways and do the right thing, that someone always brought you back... always brought you down, until you were doing the things you promised you'd never do again."

Randall nodded, as did several others. We had all known someone like that at one time or another. Someone who turned us into someone we didn't want to be. Most of us had been lucky and severed the tie.

"That's what this place is," Celus continued. "You can only be one way here. And it isn't the way you want to be."

"Is it Hell? Are we in Hell?" It sounded like Marcy again.

Celus shrugged again. "Depends on your definition, but..."

"Does the Devil live here?"

Celus half chuckled. "You people and your labels. Yeah, I guess you could say that the Devil lives here."

"It is safe? For us I... I mean?" Dad asked.

Celus looked about him, and then down towards the obscene fortress before us. "Yeah. Looks like it. The Devil isn't home right now. You'd know if She was."

"I want to go inside." It was the first time I had heard his friend speak. He was British too, but his accent was clipped.

"I'm not sure that's such a..." Celus began.

"Why not?" Randall asked. "If the Devil is not here..."

"Because it doesn't work like that," Celus snapped. I had the sense that he was being pressed for answers he didn't want to give. But we had followed him and Dad this far, and we needed to know the truth.

"She... She has... you saw Congressman Ryan's aides? There are more of them. Thousands. Maybe even millions. And they all serve Her."

"Are they here?" Marcy again.

"They're always somewhere," Celus half-whispered and looked at his friend in a rather pointed way.

"So what was in the tree? What was it we all saw and felt?" Marcy asked.

"I won't tell you that I have all the answers," Celus said, "but what you see is what you need to see. You feel... what you need to feel. It tells you that you are tiny and insignificant, but you are important to It. Isn't that right Jim? You see what you need to see?"

Dad looked at him but said nothing. He didn't need to. We all knew those words.

George laughed sarcastically. "Vanity," he said to Celus. "Hers and yours."

We stood for some time on that rise, taking it all in. I could see that Dad was shaken. He had promised us Heaven on Earth. Our own Eden. There didn't need to be a vote to know that no-one wanted this - the abomination of desolation.

"Are there others?" Dad asked.

Celus looked to him. "How do you mean?"

"Are we the only dupes? Or have... have there been others?"

"You aren't the first. You won't be the last." Celus nodded.

"Did... did they know? Did they learn the truth?"

"Some did... not all..."

"And?" Dad asked

"And what?"

"Where are they now?"

Celus frowned. "Jim, I don't understand. What is that you're asking?"

"Are they down there? Are there lost souls... trapped down there?"

Celus looked about him again. "Maybe. I don't know. It's difficult to say. I don't think so. I'm guessing it's still early here."

I followed his gaze, not understanding what he meant. The sky was darkening. Night was falling. How could it be so late?

George spoke again. "Celus, he's saying that if there are people there, then we need to get them out."

Celus looked at his friend, and then back to Dad. "If there are people down there... they won't be in any state to be moved out. Whatever chance they've had has been and gone."

"I still want to go down there," George said. "I need to see what is on that metal cladding. It maybe the scripture of the Third Twine."

This made no sense to any of us.

"Care to explain that?" Randall asked.

George looked to Celus, and then to Randall, but said nothing.

Randall tried again. "What have you done that you need to be here with us?"

George remained silent. When he eventually spoke, his voice was strained. "I... I'm not sure. But I think I need to undo it."

"That's not an answer." I could hear Randall was getting angry, and I put my hand on his arm to calm him.

"It doesn't matter," Celus had stepped between the two of them. He turned to his friend. "You know this is a long shot?"

George just nodded.

Celus looked at Dad. "I can send you back. I can send you all back. This isn't your fight."

"The... the hell it isn't... I... got a wrong to right... to be here."

The crowd all seemed to mutter in agreement. Whatever we had all been tricked in to worshipping... we knew that we didn't yet have all the answers. And we really needed to know.

Celus looked uncomfortable. He had clearly never planned to bring this many people along, let alone take them all into whatever bastion of corruption lay before us.

"Let me at least send the kids back," Celus implored. Despite Dad's glowing character reference, he was looking increasingly out of his depth.

Dad nodded. "Uh-huh... ok".

The whisper rippled through the congregation and the children were brought forward. Some of the older congregation volunteered to go as well, to look after them back at Jonestown. In total, nearly four hundred came forward, but I could see that Celus was still looking nervously at the size of the remaining crowd. There were still too many for his liking.

The returnees were led back around the edge of the wood, out of sight. Our eyes followed them for as long they could, and we heard a soft *wumpf* followed by a bright glow. A wave of cool air rushed forward to meet us, giving a temporary respite from the sticky heat.

A few minutes later Celus returned.

"That was it?" Randall asked.

Celus nodded.

His friend looked at Celus and smiled. "You're looking worried Old Man." I wondered again at the relationship between these and the connection with Dad. It all seemed to be upside down.

Again, Celus said nothing, seeming to be contemplating his next course of action.

"You're sure you want to go in?" Celus said eventually, looking at Dad.

"I'm sure."

Celus looked nervously back towards the citadel. From the ridge, it looked empty, completely deserted. Not a light flickered and not a sound was heard.

"Ok," he said. "We should form up. Maybe some lines." He started to direct people. "That's it. Ten lines. No, make it eleven. Right, the rest of you fall in behind."

His voice had taken on a military tone that I recognised in Randall. Whoever this Celus was, he was clearly a man of many layers.

"Ok... can you all hear me?"

There was a murmur of assent across the crowd.

"Right... this place... it should be empty... but you never know. If you see anyone - I mean anyone at all - you need to let me know. Just send word up the line. But do it quietly. Ok. So, stay together, and stay quiet."

The lines began to advance towards the citadel.

"Did what he said make any sense to you?" Randall muttered. I could see that he was itching to get in and start exploring, but also relieved that the boys had been sent back. "You know the whole 'worry if you see anyone...'"

I looked up at him. "I think we're through the looking-glass. Anything could be down there."

He didn't smile.

The field sloped down towards what looked liked the castle gateway of the citadel, and we covered the ground in a matter of minutes. Stopping at the entrance, Celus looked about, making sure we were all together. We were.

The portcullis was up and for the briefest of moments I fancied that it was the gaping maw of some primitive beast, ready to slam shut at any moment.

We entered as silently as we could, crossing a muddy courtyard, and into the fortress proper.

From this vantage point, I could see that the towers looming high above us were not straight, but twisted like corrupted roots, and little tendrils jutted out madly, like some giant Virginia Creeper.

There seemed no organisation to the layout of the city. Paths zigzagged and snaked and in and out of each other. Wide avenues would narrow without warning until we could pass only by a single file, and trails would finish abruptly in dead ends. The whole maddening place had a sense of confusion and frustration about it and, whatever effect it was having, was not limited to me. I heard previously level-headed folk getting ratty with each other, snapping and using the kind of language I hadn't heard in a long while.

You can only be one way in a place like this...

Progress was slow, and the shadows continued to lengthen. I heard Celus whisper to his friend that they had done enough, that it was time to go. The reply he got was short and curt.

Despite the sense of abandonment, there was no rubbish or any impression that the inhabitants had left in a hurry. Some of the towers seemed to wear a coat of an ivy-like plant, but there were no signs of weeds or any other growth on the ground. We made our way deeper into the city, towards a cluster of towers with the metal cladding. The glowing embers of the dying sun reflected off them, and for a while, the city was better illuminated.

The paths all appeared to be formed of the same dusty compacted mud, and they reminded me of the Kaituma airstrip, dry and cracked, but solid. Had the paths been straight, we could have been able to cross the city in under an hour. But with the myriad of forks, blind alleys, and the constant twisting, it took us more than two hours to get close to the towers Celus' friend wanted to see. There was a constant need to stop and make sure that we had everyone with us, and as we entered one of the many squares, I saw the sun beginning to slip below the horizon.

"Hmm..."

I turned to Randall. "Hun?"

He wasn't listening to me.

"Celus," he shouted his whisper, beckoning the man over. "Have you been here before?"

Celus looked awkward. "It's a long story," he said. "Yes and no. But mainly no."

Randall was a man used to direct and clear answers, and I could see by the look on his face that he was not in the mood to play games. "What is this place?" He asked again.

"Everyone has a different name for it..."

"Cut the crap..." Randall snapped, far too loudly. Everyone was had stopped talking and was looking at us. "Where are we? Are we still on Earth?"

"You're asking questions with very complex answers."

"Try me."

"Yes. No... It's not your Earth."

"Uh-huh. Then why are the stars the same?"

"What?"

"You're telling us we're in some parallel universe or Hell or something. But look at the constellations. They're the same. We're still on Earth," Randall pointed to the darkening sky, where tiny pinpricks of light could be clearly made out of the clouds. "Orion. The Plough. Taurus. Cancer. Gemini. They're all there. This is our Earth. Where have you brought us?"

I could hear people start to mutter, and point to the sky. There were others who knew the stars as well as Randall, and they had begun to point out the familiar constellations.

Celus, sensing the balance of power was in danger of swinging away from him, sighed. "Guyana. November. Right? What is it - about seven in the evening? If this was your Earth, the moon should be right there," he pointed to an empty patch of sky. "Where is it?"

We all stopped, and immediately began scouring the heavens.

Celus turned, not waiting for the answer he already knew.

Randall stopped playing the game. "Just wait. What is going here?"

Celus stopped and turned back to face him. "I don't have all the answers. There is a place, back home, similar to this. Not the city, but the castle entrance, except it's in ruins. But it has writing, carved into its walls. And it tells of this place. And a war. But the scripts are incomplete – they've been damaged. That's why we need to see what's on this cladding. George is trying to find a way... to stop it. Stop it reaching us."

Randall stopped. "Then what is it that we've been seeing here? What is it that we've been worshipping?"

Celus was silent, and for a moment I thought that he was not going to answer. "The thing you've seen... The Eye. It tries to recruit people. Promising power and glory and... well, you know the rest... But there is more to The Eye than just that tree..."

"You're trying to beat it, aren't you?" Randall said. "You're trying to destroy the Devil."

Celus shook his head. "I don't think we can. We've tried. You have no idea how hard we've tried. But maybe stop Her coming through. Stop Her sucking us in. But destroy it? Do you have any idea how insignificant we are? How small and meaningless our world really is. We might as well throw rocks at the sun. Ours is not even one hundredth of one drop in the ocean of the stars." He looked skywards as the pinpricks of light continued to come out.

"If we are so unimportant, why is the Devil here? Why bother with us?" asked Randall.

"Because She bothers with all of creation. Everything everywhere."

Randall thought for a moment. "You mean aliens, don't you?"

"I don't know. I've never met one. But there are stories of what happens if she doesn't get her own way. And I do know that you can't read the stars as well as you think you can."

"What's that supposed to mean?" Randall was becoming aggressive again.

Celus made no reply but rolled his eyes skyward. I could hear mutterings from the crowd. They had already begun to notice other anomalies in the night sky. Randall was looking around frantically, playing a celestial spot-the-difference game. He wasn't winning.

"It's Venus," someone said. "Where's Venus?"

"Shouldn't we be able to see Mars too?"

"I'm telling you... I swear Alpha Centauri should be right there."

"That shouldn't be there... what's that spiral? Celus? What's that constellation?"

Celus looked at the ground instead of the sky. His friend stood next to him, gazing at the sky. "That's the one, isn't it?" he said. "That's the constellation you cannot see."

Celus harrumphed, and then nodded. Despite the oppressive heat, I shivered. People were still chattering, spotting a myriad of stars that weren't there and others in the wrong place. Celus said nothing but let realisation slowly break against our bewildered minds.

"Like I said," he eventually continued, "this isn't your Earth."

"Then whose is it?" I asked.

Celus made no reply, and instead looked at Dad, who had propped himself up against the wall of a tower. He was looking old and exhausted. The lines around his eyes seemed to have deepened since we had been here, and he had moved from being worried through to a state of fearful trepidation. I think Dad knew that he was going to have to pay, and as his friend had said, there were worse things to pay with than with your life.

"Why won't you say?" I pressed Celus again.

"Because," he snapped, "words have power. That's what worship and prayer are. It feeds Her."

Randall took a step forward, not liking the way Celus was speaking to me.

Celus looked to him, and then back to me. "Sorry. I... this place makes me nervous."

I could tell that he wasn't the only one.

"It's ok," I said, accepting the apology. I understood what he meant. This place was doing something to all of us. We could feel it, as though it was slowly stripping a thin veneer of restraint and civilisation from us, revealing the savage within us all.

"When we came here," I continued, "you said it was early. What did you mean?"

Celus looked to his friend.

"Time... it's not a straight line. Not like we think it is," George answered on his friend's behalf. "I can't explain it. We think of causality. You are born, then you live then you die. A chain of events... but... it's not always like that. Sometimes the future comes first. And it affects the past..."

"That sounds like some hippy talk to me," muttered Randall. His mood was not improving.

Dad chuckled. "I'm sure it does Randall. I thought the same at first. But think about it. You've probably experienced it yourself. Déjà vu. A dream so vivid it could be real. I swear, when I was growing up, my daddy used to tell me about this oriental actor who was a big noise in China and how people were out to get him because he was teaching the secrets of kung fu and then he died in mysterious circumstances. It was only after the fact I realised he was talking about Bruce Lee, and when I mentioned it to my mom she denied those conversations ever happened. It's like... a false memory. But it's real as well."

I knew what Dad meant. Sort of. I had a false memory. My great-grandfather feeding me a spoon of something as a baby. Except he had died years before I was born. But I could still see it. I recognised him from one of those old sepia style photos.

"So why is it early?" I continued.

"There are... some people claim to have been here. Sometimes the city is full of people. Sometimes it is empty like now. Other times there are weeds everywhere. Some just see the castle at the front, as if the city hasn't been built yet. But all the accounts are jumbled like they are out of order."

"So because there are no people here, you think it is early?"

"CELUS!" someone shouted. "CELUS!"

Celus snapped his head around and then made his way through the crowd "Keep your voice down! What is it? Did you see something? Someone?"

Someone was pointing towards the horizon. Several more people realised what they were seeing, and began to point too. A hush descended over us all.

The land continued round to the west, in a long arcing curve so that the headland seemed to meet the sea and the sky all at the same point.

We all saw it. A single solitary silver line, ascending into the night sky. A few moments later it was joined by a second, and then a third. Within a minute that little patch of sky was filled more than a dozen streaking white trails. And then a score.

Dad and George were frowning, trying to understand what they were seeing. Celus had gone deathly pale.

Dad turned to him. "What is it? Missiles? Nuclear holocaust?"

241

Celus looked through him, to his friend. "No. It's the exodus of the Sky Lords." Tears were brimming in his eyes. We all wanted to ask more questions but were so transfixed by the display before us that we held our tongues.

"... when the Iyrians left," George whispered. "The Ghazals of Nod."

More than a hundred contrails now filled that distant patch of sky. All on a slightly different trajectory. I guessed that the headland must continue for another four of five miles. I had seen a rocket launch from Kennedy once. Not the moon shot, but one of the low orbiters – a satellite. We were a few miles out that time too. That had been similar, although the smoke and steam they left behind seemed little more than a pencil line from my distant vantage point. But these... these were as wide my thumb. I realised that whatever was going up had to be huge. And there were now so many.

We saw it before we heard it. One of the silver plumes stopped dead and then began to fall back to the ground in a spray of smoke and debris. The sound of a crack rolled out to us, as though a rolling pin had been smashed against a worktop. The impact threw up an ominous pillar of flame, and an all too familiar mushroom cloud began to form.

"What just happened? Who are they?" I whispered to Celus. We all knew instinctively that people had had just perished. A lot of people.

Tears rolled down Celus' face. When it came, his voice was strained. "The ruined castle... back home. The story... it tells of a race before Man, who were expelled so that Man could be brought to this land. The Sky Lords. No-one... no-one really knows who they were or what they were or even if they were real. Some thought they were as the Greeks or Romans appeared to their primitive tribal neighbours – this advanced civilisation. Others have thought it was a race before ours. The Sky Lords... not all of them escaped. Not all of their Cloud Ships sailed well..." his voice trailed off.

If it was an exodus, there would have been women and children on each and every one of those arks – like the story from the bible. Whole families. Maybe even several generations.

I felt a strange pang of grief for the passing of people I had never known.

By now the only remnant of the sun was a glow beneath the horizon. Celus eventually looked to his friend, his face strained. "We should go."

"I still need to get into those towers."

"Another time. It's been enough for one day. We know how to get through together now."

"We're nearly there," George protested. "I can just take some rubbings." He produced a few sheaves of plain paper from his rucksack.

Someone gasped. And then a shriek. Our heads collectively snapped around to locate the source.

"What is it?" Celus asked, craning his neck to see.

"There's someone here!" A voice called back. "I saw them. Moving between the buildings."

I shivered as fear flashed through my veins. Randall stepped protectively in front of me.

Celus looked to his friend. "We need to go right now!"

For a second the air seemed to thrum, as though with the distant sound of helicopter blades. Someone screamed, and the crowd scattered.

Raul lay on the ground. A stave stuck out of his chest at a sickening angle. His eyes wide open in death.

"Don't run! For..." Celus bellowed.

It was too late.

People were scattering, streaming everywhere, desperately searching for some cover. The air thrummed again, and this time, in the half-light, I saw the shape of something flying through the air. It glanced off a huddled woman, taking a chunk of flesh from her arm... nearly severing it. Her scream rang out high against the noise of the congregation. People were suddenly by her side, trying to get her to stand, to take her to safety.

"Stay down! Stay..."

The air was filled with that noise again, and we all instinctively ducked. Three more staves flew through the air, embedding themselves deeply into the cluster of people trying to help the first woman. They fell with little more than a wheeze.

More people started screaming.

"This is going to be a massacre!" Dad hissed. "Celus! Get us out of here!"

"I... we're not close enough together." Celus had a look of panic descending on him, like being caught in a net.

And then we saw them. Dark silhouettes moving between the buildings. Lean. Agile. They were all carrying the staves we had seen being thrown through the air. A few at first. And then more. Hundreds of them. Circling us like wolves. More staves came flying. More people fell. Beneath the shrieks and cries, I could hear sobbing.

And then something else. Like a chanting.

George looked to Celus. "We've got to run for it!"

"We won't all make it!"

"Then we *all* die!"

"What is it?" Dad asked.

In the gloom, I could see the two men look at each other.

"They're calling Her," Celus said.

I could see more and more dark silhouettes pouring down the hillside and into the city. The chanting around us began to swell, becoming rapturous.

"Celus!" George barked. "We're out of time!"

"I can't leave them here!"

"Take back whoever you can!"

243

Celus was defiant. "NO! We all go!"

The clouds above our heads began to swirl, thickening like the coils of a mighty serpent. The wind picked up, ramming the sea against the city walls and sending a fine spray over all of us.

Dad's voice was pleading. "Celus!"

"I said no!"

George grabbed his friend's arm. "We're sitting ducks out here!"

The chanting was reaching a fever pitch, and still more of the shadowy assassins were pouring down the hill, like a swarm of black death. Celus looked around. It had grown darker, the cloud obscuring the starlight.

"Through that door." Celus pointed to a tower. Its entrance faced into the square, and although we knew that we were surrounded, our would-be killers had not actually breached the line of the city-block.

The tower seemed to be one of the bigger ones, and Celus was clearly hoping that there would be room for all of us in there. The entrance was maybe two hundred yards from where we were.

The air thrummed again.

"DOWN!" Randall roared.

Almost as one, we dived into the dirt, as a volley of staves passed overhead. Somewhere we heard more screaming that ended in a gurgling choke and was then silenced forever.

"We're going to have to run for it," Celus said.

"Across... the... square?" Dad was labouring. His face was purpling as if he was having difficulty breathing.

Celus looked up. The gathering clouds were boiling. "Yup," he said.

Word was quickly passed around, and we got ready to sprint.

"THREE!" Celus set off, and the rest of us surged forward into the middle of the square.

Time seemed to slow. I saw Randall next to me. Other friends were on either side of us. And then, high above... I don't know if I heard it, or I felt it, but the cloud base darkened and began to descend. I felt a sound... like a bass note... pass through me. Some of us stopped, looking skyward. Others kept going.

And then It snapped open, and I was again looking into the Eye of Providence. Except this was not the Eye of my God. It covered the sky and was filled with rage and bitterness and pure malice. I don't know if it was in my head or not, but I heard such a howl of such hatred and vengeance that it filled my whole being, and I sank to the ground. Others followed me down or were already there.

It came again, this time echoing and reverberating, and from the ground, I rolled onto my back, as another wave of loathing and disgust swept over me. What I thought were clouds began to unfurl into vast tentacles, miles across.

Things began falling. I could see them. Plummeting from clouds and the Eye and the tentacles.

I saw one smash onto the roof of a building and then slide down the back, out of sight. Another came down. And another. Raining all over the city. One crashed into the ground not far from me and began thrashing on the ground. I turned back onto my stomach and tried to crawl.

The scream of hatred came again and this time, I felt the citadel physically shake. I got up onto all fours and managed to raise my head, looking to the side as another thing landed, this time right on top of a small huddle of Temple members. It thrashed, and I realised it was some sort of giant worm or maggot. It was at least six foot high and longer than I could guess. I saw what I thought was a mouth, filled with razor-like teeth, against the fat folds of the gray fetid flesh.

The thrashing continued and I could see its open maw buried into the small of a huddle of people as they pressed up against the building walls trying to escape the blur of teeth. Gore spurted up the wall, like a spray of paint. From the edge of my vision, I saw the silhouettes that had surrounded the square advancing. The staves were clenched by their sides and they seemed unaffected by the screaming from the sky.

I felt two hands underneath my armpits and suddenly I was scooped up. "C'mon Izzy!" It was Randall. I had lost him when that thing... when The Eye had opened.

He almost carried me under his arm and made for an open doorway. All around me I could hear chanting and screaming above the ever increasing wind. There was no door, just a twisting staircase that went up and down. Randall didn't even break his stride and started his descent.

"It's ok," I panted. "Randall... you can put me down."

He gently brought my feet to the floor but did not let me go. "Are you alright?"

"Uh-huh."

"Are you hurt?"

"I... don't think so." I realised that despite the dark of the building I could see in the gloom. The walls seemed to give off a low iridescence, and I could just make out Randall's features.

"Come on." Randall took my hand and led me down the winding staircase.

"Where are we going?"

Randall said nothing.

"Hun?"

"We're just going... we'll find somewhere to hole up. And then... we'll figure something out."

Figure something out. Part of me wanted to laugh or scream or pass out, but my feet kept walking.

Figure something out. We had been worshipping... something, and now we were trapped in an alien city, even as our comrades were being butchered by an army of men with their staves and their pet worm monsters, whilst The Eye of Hate raged down at us. And we had no way of getting home.

Figure something out.

The stairs ended and we found ourselves in a small room, probably no more than three or four meters square. From the look of it, I guessed it was a basement store, and there were what looked like old wooden crates against one wall.

"You have a sit down... just there." Randall directed me to the far wall, and I sat without hesitation. I felt exhausted.

A rumble came from above and I felt the building shake. I had been in Kern County in fifty-two when that earthquake had struck. Although only a child, I remembered how the buildings shook. Instinctively I covered my head.

What I did not see was the floor.

"IZZY!" Randall crossed the room and picked me up, and quickly moved back to the stairs.

"Wha...?" I turned to look over his shoulder.

The wooden crates had begun to sink into the mud floor. My eyes must have been wide as plates as I saw them begin to slip beneath the once solid surface. The building stopped shaking, and after a minute or so my husband released me. I looked at Randall, and then to the floor. It looked solid. I gingerly put a foot on it. It felt solid.

"It's called liquefaction," Randall said. "I saw it happen in Niigata in sixty-four. Whole buildings had slipped."

I looked at him, mouth open, still not comprehending what he was saying.

"It's because we're on the coast," he continued. "The ground is saturated with water. Give it a shake, and it acts like quicksand."

"The world is ending and you're giving me a lecture in geology?"

Randall looked at me, and even through the gloom, I could tell he was ticked off at me. "I'm doing the best I can Izzy. You don't get trained for this."

A smart remark rose to the surface of my mind, but I held it in check. Like he said, he was doing the best he could. Randall stepped back into the basement store and began searching through one of the now sunken crates.

"Is there anything in there we can use?" I asked.

"I don't think so. They're empty, but..."

The building trembled again. Not as hard this time, but Randall still quickly crossed to the stone stairs, where I still stood, for safety. From high above us, we heard more screams. I knew that both of us wanted to return to the ground level, to do what we could. But what would be the point? We had no weapons, or escape plan, and we didn't even know what it was we were fighting. A distant part of me began to panic.

The trembling subsided, and Randall went back to the crates. "... maybe we can use these to block the stairs up. If those... *things* come looking for us they might think this whole area is filled with crates." Randall continued as if the interruption was little more than someone coughing excessively, and not the very real likelihood of our friends being slaughtered.

It seemed like as good a plan as any and I joined him trying to heave the crates up.

"And then what?" I asked him, as we pulled one crate free.

Randall began walking it over to the staircase. "Wait it out for a day. Maybe two. We've got no water. I wouldn't want to go much longer than that. Then scout about, see if it is clear. Try and get out of the city. Try and get help."

I didn't mean for my voice to come out as shrill as it did. "Help? Where are we going to get help from?" Randall looked at me, demanding a better idea.

"I don't know Izzy, but I'm working on it," he replied through gritted teeth. The last thing he needed was a hysterical woman. Hell, the last thing *I* needed was to be a hysterical woman.

Silence settled between us as we moved the remainder of the crates. There were just enough to make three stacks under the staircase spiral, blocking the view of our little room completely. Anyone coming down the stairs would assume that it just ended at the wooden boxes.

"What about those Sky Lords?" I asked as we sat back down on the earthen floor.

"You saw them as well as I did Hun. They were hightailing it out of here."

Randall was right. The Sky Lords had been defeated as well. My mind began to reach for other options, but each was more ridiculous and improbable than the last. Despite the adrenaline in my system, a wave of weariness washed over me, and I felt my eyes begin to droop.

"It's ok Hun. You sleep. I'll take the first watch."

I don't know how long I slept for. It may have been a few minutes or a few hours, but it was deep, like I had been pulled down to the bottom of a dark ocean. I stirred once, feeling a tremor run through the building, but Randall told me it was ok and I went back to sleep again.

When I did wake, my bladder was bursting. "Baby, I gotta pee," I told him. Randall looked at me and nodded. I could see that he had been thinking about this. A day or two without water is one thing, but what is in still has to come out.

"We'll dig a little hole and ... well, we'll just go in that."

Randall went to the far corner of the room and began to dig with his hands. I joined him. The ground was loose and felt a little warm and sticky, like watered clay. The smell was none too good, but we had got used the stench of the city. We each brought up clumps of earth with our bare hands, until after a few minutes...

"What the..." Randall stood up quickly, and stepped back, trying to examine something in the poor light.

"What is it?"

"I don't know. A bone I think?"

"Let me see." I stood and joined him, picking through the dirt in hands. I could feel a solid object in there and began to sweep away the filth with my fingers.

"Oh my," I said, realising what he held.

"What is it?"

"Baby put it down. Please"

"What is it?"

"It's a forearm." I could clearly make out the all too familiar shape of a radius and ulna bone that I recognised from my days in Accident and Emergency.

"What? But it's tiny."

"It's a baby's. Randall, please put it down." He laid it gently on the dirt floor, and I realised that I didn't need to pee anymore.

Randall went back to the hole and began tearing up more earth.

"God. There is more down here. Izzy, come and take a look..."

"I'd really rather not." I was feeling sick. I could see Randall pulling more bones out of the small hole. Ribs. Part of a skull. A thigh. Another part of a skull. A jaw. More arm pieces.

"Randall, please stop, please..." the sobs had begun and I knew I couldn't stop.

"Hey, hey there," Randall came across the small room and took me in his arms. And that was when my dam broke. Whatever reserves I had to hold back the fear and the panic of our situation were exhausted, and I began to shriek. Hysteria finally wrapped around me like a cloak.

Randall put his hand over my mouth, in case anyone above heard us. "Sshh, Izzy. Sshh. It'll be ok."

He tried to rock me a little, but I just kept screaming and crying through his hand. Those babies. All those tiny little babies. I didn't need to see any more. I knew the whole damned city would have been built on the corpses of a million babies. It was like Tim had said. That was how they get to you. Through the children.

God knows what had been done to them. Strangled or stabbed or just plain neglected. In my mind, I could see every single one of them. Every mewling face. Every tiny little arm reaching out for a mommy who wasn't there. I heard every single cry that rose and then fell unanswered. I saw the distended stomachs, the rheumy eyes, and the skin as thin as paper.

My mind began to fold in on itself. Maybe Randall was pressing too hard. I don't know. But I passed out.

When I came to, it felt as though days had passed. I was propped up, seated in a corner, my head against the wall. Randall was crouching by the crates and looked at me raising one finger to his lips.

Sshh

I held my breath and heard a movement above us. I realised that it was on the stairs. I had a vision of the black clad men, armed with those cruel staves. They had found us. They had found us, and we were trapped, and they would hurt us and they would make us watch before sacrificing us to whatever hellbeast it was that had reigned over us from the sky.

Hysteria crept back in like a returning rapist, leering over me, readying itself for the next assault. I put my hand to my quivering mouth, but too late a whimper escaped.

"Hello?" A voice filtered down to us, echoing off the stony walls. I'd recognise that accent anywhere. It was Celus.

Randall realised it too. "Hey! Celus?"

"Who's that? Where are you?"

"It's Randall. I got Izzy here with me too. Is it safe to come out?"

"As safe as it's going to get. I can't see you."

"We're behind the crates. Hang on..."

Randall began to move the crates and I joined him, helping to send them tumbling into the room behind. We quickly had the stairs cleared and Celus came down. I heard another set of footsteps behind him, clanking like metal on the stone stairs. I looked to Randall. Surely Celus would not have led them to us...

Celus appeared, smeared in dirt and blood. Behind him was another figure, clad in armour. I instantly stepped back, afraid of more strangers.

"It's ok," Celus said, raising a hand. "He's with us."

The figure stepped from the darkness of the stairwell into the gloom of the store room. Clad in some oriental battle-dress, two swords hung by his side, and all I could see of him were two glittering eyes through the black battle helmet.

"Nipponai?" Randall asked. The word meant nothing to me.

The stranger stopped, turned to face him and stared. "Your accent is terrible. But yes, I am Japanese."

Celus stepped forward. "This is Jion. Randall. Izzy." He gestured to each of us as he said our names.

I realised that, like Celus, Jion's armour was similarly covered in filth and blood.

"Are you hurt?" I asked, stepping forward. "I... I'm a nurse."

"Thank you. No." Jion bowed his head a little.

Celus looked to Randall. "We're here to take you home."

249

"How many others..." his voice trailed off.

Celus looked at him. "Not many. We've spent the last day crawling around the buildings looking for... Most of the Temple were caught in the square when..." His voice tailed off. "Jion... he held them off for as long..."

Randall looked to Jion and bowed his head. "Domo. Aragato..."

"It really is better if you stick to your English," the voice behind the helmet said.

"We need to get you home," Celus said. "Others are waiting for you..."

"What about you?" I asked.

"We will stay," Celus looked to Jion, "for another day?"

The armoured figure nodded and grunted an affirmation.

"Then we'll come back to Jonestown." Celus continued. "We need to get up to the square. This room is too small... Come with us."

There were of course so many questions, but we were both too tired to ask. My arms ached, and I had knots in my back and shoulders from sleeping on the floor. Jion led the way, then Randall, myself, and Celus brought up the rear. If it had been another time and place, I would have marvelled at the intricacy of Jion's attire, and the way he held his swords close and moved with barely a sound. But I was hungry and thirsty and still terrified that the things from the previous night would pounce on us at any moment, like lions on an unsuspecting antelope.

As we exited through the doorway we had come hurriedly through the night before, I squinted in the glare of the sunlight. The scene that greeted us was like something we had read about the Nazi concentration camps.

Bodies were strewn everywhere and their essential fluids had pooled creating the effect of nightmarish bog or swamp. I could pick out the still forms of temple members, and there were a lot, but I quickly realised that these were far outnumbered by the corpses of those who had come for us the night before.

The bodies of the black-clad devils were strewn all over the square. Sometimes just lying side by side, but more often in piles of a dozen or more. Next to them lay the impossible carcasses of the giant maggot-things I had witnessed before, now seeming to steam and slowly deflate before our very eyes.

"How did you...?" I asked, looking to Celus.

He shook his head and nodded to Jion. "You can thank him."

I turned to Jion. I could not comprehend how a single man could be responsible for all of this. How he alone could have saved us from... everything this place had thrown at us.

Randall seemed as overwhelmed as I was. Several times during our marriage he had let slip the destruction he had seen in Vietnam. It was something he seldom ever brought up, but I could see from the look on his face that this vision of savagery was another order of magnitude from anything he had seen before.

The sound of the sea slopping against the city walls brought us back to the reality around us. Just off from the centre of the square, I could see a small depression in the mud, clear of any bodies, and I sensed that this is where we were being led to.

It was then that we heard a sound. Like a chittering clattering clacking coming from behind us. In hindsight, we should have just run for that small clearing. But we didn't. We turned, and there, swarming down the side of the tower was a blanket of our black-clad adversaries.

Jion had already turned and was running towards them, although I don't know how he intended to scale the sheer sides of the tower. Celus shouted something, and I saw a volley of the staves coming at us. Jion had drawn his longer sword, and I realised that it was an ornate katana blade, and batted them all away. Another volley, and this time we heard another sound, similar to the first, as more assailants entered the square from the opposite end.

Jion half-turned, and in that instant, his sword missed one of the staves, and I knew it would slam into us. I felt Celus push both of us towards the clearing... and then Randall slammed forward. I knew it. I knew it. I didn't have to look, but I did. I watched him fall in front of me. A stave had pierced his back and exited through his chest. I was screaming. I knew it was me screaming, but it sounded so distant like it was someone else.

I tried to grab my husband, but Celus had hold of me and bundled me into the clearing. I was kicking and screaming, and as he put me down I spun around to try to go back for Randall.

Over Celus' shoulder, I could see that Jion had been almost completely enveloped by the first horde, and the second wave was nearly on top of Randall. My husband looked at straight at me, life fading fast, and smiled.

It is difficult to explain what happened next. I felt Celus grab both my shoulders, and I am certain that he said something. I felt a cool wave, and my ears popped. And then I was back in the pavilion, the shriek of battle still in my ears.

*

All around me were my muddied and blood streaked friends. Most were sitting on the floor, a look of stunned resignation on their face. The older members, who had come back earlier with the children, were tending the wounded as best they could. Some were weeping. Others just held themselves or each other.

I could see Dad sitting at the far end of the pavilion, his head in his hands. Marcy was to his left, with a cruel cut to her temple. To his right sat Celus' friend, staring into the distance as though he continued to see the horror I had just left.

Several people came over to me, although I'm not sure who. I think I may still have been screaming or crying. I can't be sure. Someone put an arm around my shoulders and steered me towards a chair. Someone else put a cup of hot black tea in my shaking hands. I know I should have been scalded, but I don't even remember feeling it. I was too numb.

All around my were the worn and weary faces of the congregation, streaked with blood and mud and who knew what else. Each member seemed to be in their own world, reeling from what they had all just gone through, like a platoon of defeated soldiers. And yet it was more than the loss of our comrades that brought such a silence. We were broken. That part of us that held our faith so dear had been shattered into a million pieces and the truth of our object of worship had been revealed... revealed as something hellish and beyond our comprehension. Whatever the eye was, it was not the god I wanted, and with the breaking of that tenet so was the hope of a better tomorrow utterly extinguished. I could see that all those around me just didn't want to go on.

For my own part... I felt hollow, as though I had been physically gutted like some fattened calf, and yet I still lived. Whatever hopes and dreams I had for the future had been torn away from me with the loss of Randall. When I tried to consider what my next move should be, all that greeted me was an inky blackness and I could see no way forward from our present position.

I just wanted to lay down... for the ground to swallow me.

One of the girls from the medical tent came over. Chris, I think. She wiped down my face, and I realised that it too was streaked with blood and earth. She checked me over, but outside of a few bruises and grazes I was in remarkably good shape. Far better than I had any right to be.

Over the next few hours, a few more survivors materialised around us. I had given up asking questions by now. There were probably no answers, and if there were, we wouldn't understand them. Randall was gone, and at some point, I would have to tell the boys. I felt a cold weight, like a cannonball, in my stomach. I had seen people being given bad news before. I had even had to do it myself a few times. The look on their faces. Some would go into shock. Others would crumple immediately.

Later, I found myself with Dad, both of us feeling as though we had been gutted and were now nothing but walking husks. He had asked about Randall, but I did not answer him.

"Did the Olds hold Congressman Ryan off?" someone said eventually.

Dad half-laughed. "We were just gone a few hours. It's only the eighteenth."

I looked up with an expression of incredulity that said, *"But we were gone at least a day."*

Dawn's light was beginning to creep over the horizon when Celus finally reappeared. There was no sign of Jion. Various Temple members made their way over to him, asking about those still missing. He just shook his head. Some just sat down. Others began crying. Still more berated him, haranguing him to go back. To do more.

The look on his face told me he had done everything he could.

Of some nineteen-hundred of us who had gone into that citadel, I guessed that less than five hundred had come back. Just thinking about that makes it seem even less real. It is not possible to lose that many people in one go. It can't be. But it was. I had seen some of their bodies. Bloody and battered and torn. People will tell you that war is horror. It is pain and suffering. But it isn't. It is worse than that. War is numbness. Numbness for things you must do, like leaving loved ones behind. Numbness for having to carry on as if it doesn't matter. Numbness towards the things that you have seen.

And if you aren't numbed... well then you have to feel. And that is a whole lot worse.

Celus and his friend sat with Dad.

"This isn't over yet," Celus said.

Dad just looked at him.

"Ryan will be back today. And he'll have his aides with him. They'll know what's happened. We have to protect these people."

Dad continued to stare, his eyes vacant.

"What can we do?" It was the voice of Larry.

Larry Layton was an evangelical hothead. A real firebrand. Randall and I had always given him a wide berth.

Celus shrugged. "Do you... this is a war. I'm sorry that you people have got involved in the way you have, but..." his voice trailed off.

"Well, then we fight!" Larry replied loudly, stamping his feet and standing up. "They've taken from us... our homes. This place ain't no home for us no more. It's... a... a... a war memorial now."

There was a general muttering of agreement, but I could see these people were in no mood to fight. The pavilion felt big and empty without the full congregation. It was as if we had collectively been winded.

"Larry," Celus said, "Man, I respect you. You know that right. Hell, I saw you pull one of those staves and try to have a go back. What happened?"

"They... they wouldn't go down."

Celus nodded. "Wouldn't go down. You all hear that. Larry tried to cave in the skull of one of those men last night, and it just bounced off him. Like it was made of rubber."

"How do we kill them?" someone from the back said.

"What about that samurai guy?" another voice asked.

"Whoa guys. One at a time. The samurai guy... we have a difficult relationship. He ain't exactly on our side, and if we get in his way, he will roll straight over us. But he is set against... the thing we have been fighting. Now as for killing those things..."

Celus pulled out a pendant from underneath his shirt. A small round metal amulet hung from a leather string and those of us near enough collectively leaned forward to look at it. From my position, I could not make out the design on it.

Dad looked up at him. "The Gates of Namlu?"

Celus nodded and then continued addressing what remained of the congregation. "The things we fought... that killed your friends. They're not human. It's a bit difficult to describe. Imagine the wind is trapped in a cave by an avalanche. You can release it by clearing the rubble away, but you've gotta be quick before more rocks fall."

Even through my fatigue, this made no sense to me. I could see that I was not alone.

"Bullets. Knives... just about anything you can imagine. It won't work. These things will just get back up. You need to keep their wound open long enough for their wind to escape."

There was silence for a moment.

"You're saying that they're trapped souls, aren'tcha?" Larry said. "Like golems or somethin'."

Celus looked uncomfortable with the analogy. "Something like that."

"That thing," Larry pointed to Celus' pendant, "That set 'em free?"

"Yes."

"How many have you got?"

"Just this one. They're not the sort of thing you can buy from Wal-Mart."

"Well, then we just hold 'em down and do 'em one at a time! Get some payback! There's only three of 'em with the congressman."

"Larry," Dad spoke, his voice tinny and strained, "You want to kill the Congressman's aides and then tell him they were something unholy? How many hours will it be before the Man has a whole Special Ops team in here shooting the place up? One? Two?"

Larry thought about this. "Then we kill him too. Hell, he's probably on their side anyway."

A collective groan could be heard around the pavilion.

Dad spoke again. "Larry... I love your energy... but what'll we do when they send someone to look for him? They'll be in radio contact, the whole time. C'mon."

"What about if it looks like an accident? No wait..." more groans had gone up, and Larry was being heckled to shut the hell up. "Ok. Ok, try this, and then I swear I'll be quiet. They wanna shut us down, right? So we let 'em in. I tell Ryan I want to go home – that I've had enough. We all get on the plane, and that's when I get 'em. All of them. The plane goes down. You tell the Russians, and they get you out of here before the Man comes back."

For a moment there was silence.

Celus looked to Dad. "Could work. Gets you some place safe."

"Larry," Dad said. "What about you?"

"He," Larry nodded at Celus, "couldn't save Emily. I ain't blamin' him. Nor his little friend neither. But she's gone. I gotta be honest with you Dad, I've gone with her. You know what I mean? We've been doin' somethin' we shouldn't be doin'. I gotta fix that."

There was a collective murmur around the pavilion. We all felt like that. Like our arms had been torn off. Another man stood. Jim McElvane. He had only recently arrived but had been active in the Temple for years, running security in San Francisco. He had lost his eldest daughter the night before, and his wife had been dead for years.

"You can't do it on your own. There'll be too many of them. I'll go with you," Jim said.

There seemed to be something of a consensus growing, and three others stepped forward.

"Ok," Celus said. "That's enough. Too many and they'll get suspicious. You just hole up in one of the huts. When the Congressman comes past, you make your case. You'll need this," Celus took his pendant and gave it to Larry.

"What about you?" Dad asked.

Celus looked at his friend. "We should get out of here. We can't let the Congressman's aides see us, and the Cossacks and I... we've got history. Best not to shake things up with them. Can we use your radio to call our helo in?"

"The FCC will be monitoring it. They'll tell Ryan."

Celus turned to his friend. "Walk to the airstrip?"

The older man nodded.

"You'd best go through the jungle," Dad said. "You wouldn't want to meet Ryan on the road."

It didn't take long for a rucksack of provisions to be put together, and the two of them made their way to the edge of the estate before being swallowed by the jungle.

It was maybe an hour or so later that the familiar Jeeps of the Congressman's convoy were spotted on the road. Few people were interested in engaging with the delegation and those that were no longer in the pavilion spread themselves about, pretending to look busy. Marcy showed Ryan and his entourage around, telling them that most of the townsfolk were in the jungle harvesting fruits.

It was around noon that I saw the delegation nearing the hut which housed Larry and Jim and the others. Marcy waited outside whilst they went in, and it was not long before they came back out again, this time with all five of the would-be deserters. Ryan had some sort of conversation with Marcy and I saw her step back from the group, putting up her hands as if to say "Fine!"

They made their way back to the Jeeps, and I heard the engines gun hard as they exited the compound, no doubt thinking they had scored a major victory. Marcy gave it a few minutes and headed to the pavilion.

I jogged across the square to join her. "Well?"

"It'll be twenty minutes back to Kaituma and another ten for them to get in the air. Then we'll radio the Russians. Send the word out and tell everyone to gather in the pavilion. They're not to bring anything with them. Just the clothes that they're wearing."

Chris, the woman who had tended to me earlier, helped spread the message, and it was not long before there was a steady stream of the nine-hundred or so remaining Temple members into the pavilion.

Marcy had been in the radio hut, and sensing the growing impatience of the crowd, Dad went in after her. Twenty minutes passed. Then thirty. It was a full hour before they came out. Dad was ashen, and Marcy had been crying. They both went into the pavilion and we followed them, desperately seeking news of our rescue.

"I... I've always tried my best to give you a good life," Dad began, addressing the crowd. "In spite... in spite of it... of all of my trying.... a handful of damned souls, with their lies, have made our lives impossible. There's no way to detach ourselves from what's happened today.

"The... uh... The Russian's aren't coming. The Man knows about what we... something went wrong with Larry. They uh... They didn't get up in the air. There was a gun fight or something at Kaituma. It's all over the wires. The... uh, the Congressman got killed. But the aides... his creatures... they escaped. They... they've sent for... they radioed for their support. There's a team on their way now. Maybe a few hours out. Maybe more. Maybe less.

"The Russians... they were listening-in to the wire. They won't get dragged in now that... this whole thing has gone public. We're all wanted for murder."

The silence was absolute.

"I don't have any easy answers for you," Dad continued. "Uh... we can sit here and wait for the catastrophe that's going to happen... it'll be a catastrophe. They'll come for us... just parachute in here. You know that. I know that. They'll want the children... but you can't steal people's children. You can't take off with people's children without expecting a violent reaction. They never let us live in peace. Now they won't let us die in peace.

"I'm going to be just as plain as I know how to tell you. I've never lied to you. I never... never lied to any of you. I know that's what's gonna happen. That's what the Man intends to do, and he will do it. So we can run. We can go into the jungle. I... I don't know how long we'll last out there. I don't know if the Man will catch up with us or not. He's good at that kind of thing. Learned it in 'Nam.

"Or we can stay here. We... we could fight, we've got enough guns. It won't be much of a fight. There'll be plenty more of them than us. You'll have to see... see them shoot the children. You'll have to feel the pain of being shot. I... I don't know.

"But Marcy... me and Marcy have got to talking. We don't much like the jungle anymore. It ain't been as kind to us as we'd hoped. And you know what I think about meeting the Man. So... so my... our opinion is that we'll do ourselves a kindness. We got a potion like they used... in ancient Rome or Greece.

"I know what you're thinking. It's a sin. But... no, it's not. Because it's not suicide. It's not, because we're already dead. We just don't know it yet. It'll be a revolutionary act. That's all I got to say. I won't force nobody. You can go your own way. But Marcy and me, we need to lie down... we just cannot continue like this anymore... being treated like animals."

No-one said anything.

Ujara, an old hand at Jonestown, spoke up. "Ah... Dad? You know I followed you from Indiana, to 'Frisco and now to here... I guess... I guess I'm saying I ain't done following you yet..."

People started to applaud. I knew I should be appalled by what I was hearing, but after the revelations of the past twenty-four hours, it seemed like the best solution. The Man was coming. I wasn't going to let Him take me or my boys. As for the jungle... well it was like Dad had said – it hadn't been kind to us so far. And there was no god here that I wanted to worship.

Ujara continued. "So... what I guess I'm saying is... have you got enough of your potion for me too?"

Dad smiled, and I realised that it had been a long time since I had seen him smile... really smile. "We got enough for everyone if that's what you want. We... we got some cyanide in gold-cleaning stock. You shouldn't feel a thing."

And that's how we decided it. I've been recording for hours now. I don't suppose there is much time left. But we are resolved. We are all united. A quick and painless exit in defiance of the Man's violence. I've told my boys they'll be seeing Daddy again real soon. I hope we do.

So you see. We are responsible. But we are not to blame.

*

"She killed her own sons?" Danielle asked incredulously.

"She did. All nine hundred of them committed suicide."

Danielle sat in stunned silence, trying to take it all in. "Ok," she said eventually, leaning forward. "Just how much of that can you really verify? I mean, on the one hand, it sounds convincing, but on the other... well they could be taken for a bunch of cultists."

"Oh they were, and still are by the history books. But a lot of her testimony stacks up. Broadly the timelines are as Izzy described, with the exceptions of Tim Stoen. A number of times she claimed to have seen him in Guyana, whereas official history says he was elsewhere.

"There was a formal investigation, and Stoen, in particular, was singled out for aggravating the situation, probably at the behest of the CIA. But the description of Congressman Ryan, the failure of the harvests, the rallies, the newspaper articles, and the outbreak of diarrhoea and vomiting. Even the murders. All independently documented facts."

Danielle took it all in. "What about Celus and George?"

"You remember the first account? George's disciplinary hearing? Sam Cotrahens said that he saw Celus with George just after they got back from holiday in November seventy-eight. He couldn't remember exactly where they had gone but thought it Guinea or..."

"Guyana," Danielle nearly whispered. "It really was them? Not just a coincidence of names?"

"Almost certainly. Izzy's testament is the only one to refer to Celus and George by name, but there are several others that describe Celus and his strange friend, and the descriptions match."

"But the visions... how could that have really happened?"

"Do you remember that Jonestown briefly shared some of its facilities with the gold prospecting company? Have a guess which company that was?"

Danielle shook her head.

"A subsidiary of Corvus."

Danielle raised an eyebrow. "Kethron's company?"

"Uh-huh. The same subsidiary that had the contract in the fifties for supplying the CIA with LSD, and other mind-control chemicals, for their experiments."

"What? What were they doing prospecting for gold?"

"According to the company reports from the time, they weren't. They were testing a variant of LSD on primates. Instead of having to build a whole new compound, they had their experiment site a few kilometres into the jungle but rented welfare facilities in Jonestown. But, the project was a failure and was shut down."

Danielle was confused. "Why?"

"A large percentage of the primates got ill and died. Vomiting, diarrhoea, and vasoconstriction of the extremities – presents itself as something similar to frostbite."

"That's almost exactly what Isabelle described as affecting Jonestown. Do you think that whatever chemicals they were using got into the water system?"

"Officially no. There were no industrial accidents. No clean-up required. A clean safety report."

Danielle thought for a moment. "How did Celus know what was going on?"

"There is someone that matches his description in Indiana in fifty-two and fifty-three, right about the time that Jim Jones was radicalised. That's probably not the right word to use. Jim Jones was a lot more political than he was religious. But you get my drift.

"There are religions – the Gnostics, the Bogomils, the Cathars – that have subscribed to asceticism, an intense frugality if you will... well that was Jim Jones all over. I think he probably got that from Celus. What happened later...? I'm not sure. I suspect that someone corrupted his message. Probably in the sixties."

"Who?" Danielle was already drawing up a mental list of names.

"I can't be certain. I have some ideas, but I can't prove it. But one minute Jim Jones is preaching to a minority congregation about giving up worldly possessions, and the next everyone is seeing God? That was probably the giveaway. Celus got wind - albeit too late - that his one-time protégé was seeing The Creator and then with the media reports of the sickness he put two and two together."

"You've lost me. You're saying that Corvus corrupted Jim Jones?"

"Almost certainly yes. Or one of their subsidiaries. I think that Corvus has been involved with this whole thing for a very, very long time indeed. But, like I said, I can't prove it. What I can prove is that Celus knew exactly what sort of poison was being used on Jonestown because he had run the same experiment himself, nearly thirty years before."

Danielle was incredulous. If Celus was experimenting in the same way as Corvus, how was he any better? "What? Where?" she asked.

"France, fifty-one."

The story concludes in "The Beggar of Beliefs" – out March 2014

ACKNOWLEDGEMENTS

There are so many people who have had an input into this story, from editing to recommendations and on to possible routes to publication, that it will be difficult to thank all of you.

Firstly to my wife and daughter, Jennifer and Jasmine, who have put up with seeing considerably less of me than they deserve, and my keeping of the most unsocial of hours. I love you both more than words can ever say.

To my most trusted instructor, Soke Kevin Pell of Ishin Ryu Ju-Jitsu, who has stood by, inspired, and supported me ever since the first day I met him. A true father to us all.

To Graham and Judith McMillan-Cox for all their hard work and support.

To Jonathan Weiss and his wife Anna for their support without which this book would simply not have been finished.

To Marius Ronge, David Ross and Simon McCarroll for their technical expertise. If a scientific or technical aspect is right, then all credit is due to them. If it is not, then it is down to me.

To my good friends Matthew Hartnell, Nikki Slack, Emma Merrygold and Katy Wallis who have given generously of their time by making recommendations on the various drafts.

And finally to those teachers who spotted a spark in me, nurtured and encouraged it: Cath Fox, Nikki Stone, and Steve Imisson of Vyners Secondary School.

Sincerely, thank you all.

Martin

Made in the USA
Middletown, DE
21 October 2020